To Venice With Love

Jane Beck

AuthorHouse™ UK Ltd.
500 Avebury Boulevard
Central Milton Keynes, MK9 2BE
www.authorhouse.co.uk
Phone: 08001974150

This book is a work of fiction. People, places, events, and situations are the product of the author's imagination. Any resemblance to actual persons, living or dead, is purely coincidental.

First published by AuthorHouse 12/7/2007

ISBN: 978-1-4343-3705-4 (sc)

Library of Congress Control Number: 2007907505

Printed in the United States of America
Bloomington, Indiana

This book is printed on acid-free paper.

Artwork for Jacket Design - Anthony B Gilman
Author photograph - Madeleine Beck

For my late husband Max
who never saw Venice.

Bibliography

Venice for Pleasure - J. G. Links

Venice - Jan Morris

Venice - Francesco Da Mosto

Paradise of Cities: Venice and its Nineteenth Century Visitors - John Julius Norwich

Ruskin's Venice The Stones Revisited - Sarah Quill

Charlie Waite's Venice

John Ruskin - James S Dearden

You in Venice - Amadeo Storti

The Age of Baroque: Landmarks of the World's Art - Michael Kitson

Italy: A Grand Tour for the Modern Traveller - Charles Fitzroy

Insight Guides: Italy - APA Publications

All Rome and the Vatican - Eugenio Pucci

All of the above books have provided valuable historic, artistic and architectural background. I'm particularly grateful to J G Links. His prose is peerless, his knowledge prolific and his love of Venice leaps from every page of his book. His guided walks around Venice show the traveller many things he didn't know he wanted to see!

I took information on Tuscany from the Times and on Tuscan properties from the brochure supplied by Rainbow International Ltd.

Acknowledgements

I am grateful to the following people who have helped me with either literary or technical advice to take this book on its journey from an original idea to a finished publication.

Barbara Carr - Tutor of Creative Writing, Writer's News: Leone Ross - Writer and p/t tutor, City Literary Institute: Alex Elam - PFD Literary Agents: Lindsay Jones RIBA: Kevin McCarron LLB.(Hons), Dip.L.P.,N.P. Jane Stork: Anthony Gilman: Sally Beck: Max Beck: Members of Broxbourne U3A Creative Writing Group: All support staff at Authorhouse who took the book on its final journey.

I would also like to thank all the friends and family who have inadvertently given me lines of dialogue which I have shamelessly pinched! They will know who they are!

Chapter One

"You're not going to believe this but I'm phoning you from a brothel!" Isobel smiled into her mobile knowing that, for the next few minutes anyway, she had the full and undivided attention of her youngest son.

"Oh my God!" Steve laughed. "And after all my warnings to look out for Casanova!"

"Well you'll be relieved to hear that I'm alone, nor am I waiting for the knock on the door. I've discovered that my hotel is a converted brothel."

"Well there's a turn-up! How did you find that out ?"

"Oh just a fellow traveller who knows Venice very well." Isobel wasn't going to tell him any more. If he'd been a daughter she might have felt differently and they'd have had a gossip and a good giggle but she'd listened to enough teasing about Casanova and dark alleys from Steve and his elder brother Ian before she left home and wasn't going to give him any more ammunition.

"Maybe you'll let Ian know I've arrived. Save me making another call. I'll leave you to get on with things. Is that Tom I can hear in the background? It must be nearly teatime. Give my love to Joy." She terminated the call quickly before Steve could ask any more questions and hoped she hadn't sounded like a burbly old grannie.

She crossed the room, opened the shutters and leaning out of the window looked down at the canal, mentally consigning everything marked "home" into its depths. This holiday was the fulfilment of a long-held dream to visit Venice alone and for the next two weeks she resolved to surrender herself completely to its charms. The air was still and warm and the afternoon quiet as only a place without traffic can be. It was, she thought, absolutely perfect.

She looked around the room at the delicate white and gold furniture, blue brocade upholstery and old Venetian mirrors; James would have hated it just as he'd hated Italy. Irrationally.

They'd spent their honeymoon in Florence, his first and only visit. She'd been reading "A Room With A View" and wanted him to share her enthusiasm for both Forster and Florence. She was wasting her time. At the end of a blistering day, when they'd visited Santa Croce in the morning and the Uffizi in the afternoon, he'd emerged blinking into the sunlight. "Quite honestly Isobel," he complained, dragging her to the nearest bar, "it will be a long time before I can face another bleeding Christ." It was only then that she realised she'd married a philistine. The knowledge niggled at the back of her mind and she wondered time and again in future years how a man as intelligent as James could remain so impervious to art. It was the only time she ever had her own way over their holiday destination.

As she unpacked she thought about the previous occupants of her room. All those women who'd sold themselves for sex and the men who'd been happy to pay. How did it feel to be a courtesan, never knowing who would walk in through the door? Did one smile a welcome, pretend enjoyment, hope for gentle treatment? She remembered all the orgasms she'd faked with James and realised that she had no idea if he'd ever paid for sex. She pushed the thoughts aside as she realised they came under the heading of "home" and carried on unpacking. So far it had been a fabulous day and if the remaining fourteen matched up it was going to be one hell of a holiday!

She'd been in the Club lounge at Heathrow. Steve had just dropped her off. She'd bought herself a glass of mineral water and was turning away from the bar looking for a seat. Half her mind was already visualising Venice the other half hoped that Steve wasn't driving too fast on his way home to Berkhamsted. At any rate she wasn't concentrating and bumped into a fellow traveller. She managed to hold on to her glass but most of the water spilt and in the confusion her guidebook fell to the floor. The other half of the collision bent to retrieve it for her and when he straightened up Isobel saw a large patch of damp across the front of what looked to be an expensive shirt. The light pink checks grew darker the longer she stared. Eventually her eyes flicked up into the face of the owner. "Oh God! I'm sorry! I wasn't looking. Are you *very* wet?" She had, she realised, accepted responsibility for the accident without thinking and wondered if her mother's voice would ever go away.

"Don't worry about it. I was just as much to blame. I should have given you more room." His dark brown eyes looked more tolerant than angry. Perhaps *his* mother had accepted clumsiness with more grace than her own. He held out his hand for her glass. "Fizzy or still?"

"I'm sorry?" Her mind seemed to have seized up.

"I'll get you another glass. Would you prefer fizzy or still water?"

She realised with relief that he wasn't going to make a fuss.

"Oh fizzy I think. Thank you." She watched him as he bought coffee for himself and more water for her and then carried both to a small table. He managed to hold his briefcase firmly under his arm without spilling a drop of either drink. She scrabbled in her bag for a tissue for him to dry his shirt front but before she'd found it he'd pulled out a handkerchief. A pristine, white square it had been lovingly ironed by someone she noticed as he dabbed at the wet patch before replacing it in the pocket of his trousers. She was certain the skin underneath that shirt was freshly showered.

He picked up his coffee, Espresso, and drained it Italian style in one go. Was he Italian or just another traveller like herself? Isobel was intrigued.

"I see you're off to Venice," he said looking at her guidebook. "Do you know it well?"

"This is my first trip but I've used every spare minute to study this." She waved the guidebook at him, "I've prepared a list of things I want to see, places I intend to visit."

"Oh you'll love it! There's a Canaletto or a Turner round every corner!"

As he spoke she spotted a fine line of gold where a front tooth had been expertly filled. His hair was thick, flecked with grey, whoever cut it had smoothed out the curl. He had a small scar, no more than two centimetres long, slanting across his left eyebrow, a legacy from some childhood accident perhaps.

"You obviously know it well," Isobel said, keen to know more but, in view of her earlier clumsiness, deciding on the indirect approach.

He told her that he was flying out to supervise work on a building project in Chioggia. He was an architect and his Italian partner needed him urgently. Fortunately his current English build was safely in the hands of his assistant. He paused as their flight was called and got to his feet with the ease of the seasoned traveller.

There were few passengers in their section of the plane and Isobel felt unaccountably pleased when he settled himself in the seat next to hers. "I'm Rupert Northcote by the way," he said as they fastened their seat belts.

"Isobel Campbell," she volunteered, delighted that he'd put her out of her misery. She'd been trying, unsuccessfully, to guess his name for the last ten minutes.

"You sound remarkably English for someone with a Scots surname," Rupert continued. Had he noticed that she wore no wedding ring?

"James, my husband was born in Scotland." She was always meaning to change back to her maiden name but somehow never got around to it.

"Is he waiting for you in Venice?"

"No," she hesitated, "I'm afraid we're divorced." There she was apologising again but she had to admit that every time she told someone it hurt. She felt as if she were on the cut price goods shelf at Tesco or a remaindered book reduced for a quick sale. A reject at any rate.

"I'm sorry." He sounded genuinely sympathetic.

"It happened five years ago so in theory I've had plenty of time to adjust." She lifted her shoulders slightly, shrugging off thirty years of marriage in a split second.

"Adjusting's the easy part, forgetting is another matter and forgiving is perhaps hardest of all." His voice was so full of regret that Isobel said quickly; "Not you too?"

"My wife died only a couple of years ago. I still miss her although the pain does get easier as time passes." He twisted the wedding ring which he still wore. His earlier smoothness had now completely disappeared.

It was Isobel's turn to sympathise. "I'm really sorry. It must be devastating to lose someone you care for deeply."

"The price one pays for love perhaps? I'm slowly learning to value the time we had rather than what we haven't, but it isn't easy. Liz died just six months after her illness was diagnosed not much time for adjusting is it?" The pain in his voice surprised Isobel and she realised that like many ex-wives she'd fallen into the trap of thinking that all men were heartless bastards. Now here was someone telling her indirectly that men could feel pain every bit as much as women.

They stopped talking as the plane started to taxi towards the runway and the stewardess went through the safety routine. Although she couldn't see him without deliberately turning her head she was acutely aware of his presence. She could feel the warmth of his shoulder close to her own and caught a drift of some masculine fragrance she didn't recognise. She stole a quick look at his profile. Definitely a cut above.

Once they were airborne it was Rupert who restarted their conversation. She'd put her guidebook on her lap in case he didn't feel like talking. Pointing to the picture of San Giorgio Maggiore on the front he said, "I never get tired of looking at that wonderful church. When I'm having problems with a build I go and stare across the lagoon and know that what I'm seeing is a masterpiece. I love the simplicity. And the stark elegance and beautiful proportions of that building always help to ease away the stress.

Isobel followed the direction of his gaze and saw the white marble columns supporting the triangular pediment with its single circular inset at the entrance to the church. The photographer must have waited for the sun to highlight the whiteness of the marble which glittered in its reflected rays. The surface of the lagoon sparkled like mackerel skin where the sun streamed across the water.

"Inside the space has been used to maximum effect" Rupert sketched an imaginary arc in the air with his hands. "Or to put it another way the separate parts are all perfectly brought together; although the interior was once described as being like a large assembly room but that's Ruskin for you."

"I've wanted to see it for ages." Isobel cut in when he paused for breath. It looks as if it's been there forever. Amazing how such a solid building appears to float on the water."

"You'll gather Ruskin didn't like it; dismissed it as 'barbarous, childish and contemptible.' But then Ruskin hated Renaissance architecture."

Isobel took a deep breath. This could be the end of a promising conversation she reckoned. "I can't say I have a lot of time for Ruskin."

"How's that?" She heard a flicker of real interest in his voice and hoped she wasn't about to dispel it. It was impossible to read about Venice without coming across quotations by Ruskin. She didn't always agree with his opinions and admitted this to Rupert.

The stewardess appeared with a drinks trolley. "Have some wine," Rupert invited. "It will help to wash down the airline lunch."

Isobel chose white, knowing that drinking red wine at lunchtime would give her a headache. He filled her glass and raised his own. "Here's to *La Serenissima*! I hope you enjoy your stay." He touched his glass to the rim of hers.

She realised she'd met someone who was passionate about his profession and thought perhaps that Ruskin had been shelved as a topic of conversation. She was casting around in her mind for what she hoped might be an intelligent question when he went on. "Don't you think you're being a bit hard on poor old Ruskin? Remember his vision, to say nothing of his philanthropy, when you judge him as an art critic. After all disagreeing with his views is surely not a good reason to dismiss him?"

Well she'd asked for that she supposed but at the same time her interest was kindled. It wasn't everyday she met someone astute enough to see how she formed her opinions. Even so she wasn't going to change them. She took a sip of wine and pressed on. "Admit it now, his wife had a really tough time. Think about all the soul searching she must have done. I mean to be married to someone for six years and then to be forced to admit that the marriage was never consummated. Imagine all the sleepless nights she must have endured! I'm glad she made a bid for freedom and ran away with Millais."

He smiled as the stewardess returned with their lunch; handed the tray across to her. "Let's hope the two of them found happiness together. I think Ruskin's mother was a touch over-protective and that could have had a big influence on his attitude to women."

Isobel's mind was whirling as she unpacked her lunch. She'd never had this kind of conversation with James. He'd been a final year law student at London University when she'd gone up to read English.

An ex-public schoolboy soon to join an established élite he'd epitomised everything she craved for in a potential husband. Naïvely she'd expected middle-class life to be peppered with stimulating conversation, a far cry from the doings of the neighbours about which her mother talked non-stop. She couldn't have been more wrong. At the first party they went to as a married couple the men stood at one end of the room, the women at the other. The women talked about babies, breast feeding, nappy rash. She never discovered what the men discussed. When she'd asked James he was noncommittal, "Oh this and that, you know, nothing very interesting." Now, in 1997, dinner party chat was all about mortgages, the possibility of another recession, share prices, overdrafts and school fees. But in the last half hour a perfect stranger had given her a taste of what it could be like and she felt as excited as a child included for the first time in a grown up conversation.

Rupert's voice cut across her thoughts. "We should be landing in about half an hour. Is anyone meeting you?"

"No, not this trip. I made up my mind some time ago that I was going to do this on my own."

"You must let me drop you off. Giovanni, my business partner is picking me up and we're going across to Chioggia. As this is your first trip to Venice it will take you some time to find your way around. Where are you staying by the way?"

"The Hotel San Antonio. Do you know it?"

He laughed. "I should say so. Do you know it used to be a brothel?"

It was Isobel's turn to laugh. "Oh! That's wonderful! My first time inside a brothel! I hope it's been converted!"

"That's the reason I know it so well. Giovanni and I did the conversion. One of our more interesting assignments I'd say! It stood empty for years until the family who owned it finally decided to sell and the present owners moved in. Considering the number of courtesans there used to be in Venice there must be many more brothels in the city, converted or otherwise. In medieval times Venice even had its own red light district." Rupert was still smiling as the voice came over the Tannoy asking them to fasten their seatbelts in preparation for landing.

Isobel looked out of the window eager to catch a glimpse of the city she'd waited a lifetime to visit. A lump came into her throat as a gap opened up in the clouds and she saw, spread out below her, the faded beauty of the city she would soon be exploring. All her years of repressed longing for Italy welled up inside her and the sight of ancient stone criss-crossed with water was, to her eyes, magical. She was looking down at the miraculous fusion of nature and engineering which combined to make this a unique city. She fished in her bag for her dark glasses in case the tears which came into her eyes should run over and streak her mascara.

"If you want to get away from the madding crowd go to Canareggio." Rupert's voice created a welcome diversion. "There's an exquisite church, Santa Maria dell'Orto which most tourists never see. The floods in 1966 severely damaged it and it was the first church to be restored with what is now the Venice in Peril Fund. The damage was horrendous, a lot of the lower part of the church has been rebuilt and the final repairs were only completed last year. There are some important paintings by Tintoretto. Ruskin's wife didn't like them, ran out of the church when he took her to see them, I suspect she was terrified by The Last Judgement. Ruskin later described the corpses with clay clinging to their clotted hair. Great alliteration but not much consideration for his wife's sensitivity."

He grinned disarmingly and Isobel knew instantly that she had to see it. She opened her guidebook and handed him a sheet of paper, one of several dotted with page references and places she intended to visit. "Will you write it down for me?" she asked. He scribbled instructions and handed the paper back. Do buy a good map if you don't have one already," he advised, "it's so easy to get lost otherwise." His writing, she noticed, was scrawling and untidy.

As they left the plane and walked through the airport terminal Isobel lengthened her steps to keep up with him. Just before they reached the exit he turned to her and said, "I'm afraid I'm tied up for the next two days but I'm free on Tuesday and I could show you round if you like." Isobel thought she would like - very much - but felt that perhaps she should make a token protest. She heard her mother's voice again, advising her as a teenager to 'save herself' until the right man came along, although she'd been a bit vague about how to recognise him when Isobel had pressed for more details. "Wouldn't that be a bit boring for you," she asked, "as you know Venice so well?" He waved a hand dismissively. "Venice is God's gift to architects and I always enjoy showing people around so if you accept you'll be doing me a great favour." His voice sounded so sincere that Isobel wanted to believe him although she couldn't help wondering about 'the people he'd shown around'. Could this perhaps be one of the undesirable characters her sons had warned her about before she left home? Well Casanova would certainly be an improvement on all those boring golfing cronies of James who'd been an inevitable part of all their holidays together. "In that case I accept," she said, "and I'm sure you'll make it come alive for me."

"That's settled then. I'll pick you up at nine thirty. Ah, there's Giovanni with the launch." He put a hand under her elbow and steered her towards the quay and a smart looking motor cruiser. "*Ciao* Giovanni!" he called out, as his partner waved a greeting and then, "Signora Campbell," he added by way of introduction as he hefted their luggage on board.

Giovanni was completely unlike his launch. Rotund, smiling. Isobel felt that 'unstructured' was the best way to describe him. An ample girth overflowed crumpled trousers which appeared, against all the odds, to be self-supporting. *"Caio Signora!"* he said, grasping Isobel's hand tightly in both his own. *"Benvenuto a Venezia*!"

What was it about the way Italian men looked at you? Isobel wondered as his eyes met her own. There was a directness about the gaze which was unapologetic, speculative, sizing you up. Whatever. It made you feel as if you were standing there absolutely stark naked. She looked away hastily.

Rupert began a conversation with Giovanni in fluent Italian. The two of them spoke quickly and Isobel couldn't follow what they were saying. She cursed herself silently for not persevering with her Italian language tapes but caught the words San Antonio and guessed Rupert was explaining to Giovanni that they would be dropping her off. The next minute the engine fired and their voices were completely drowned. The boat skimmed across the lagoon towards Venice and Isobel's spirits soared as she felt the wind blow through her hair.

Rupert came to stand beside her. "It's an amazing façade, don't you think?" He pointed towards the Piazza San Marco and the Doge's Palace. From this distance its double row of arches looked as delicate as old lace. The campanile soared skywards to the left and Isobel filed it away as a future landmark. "It's absolutely wonderful," she agreed. "everything I expected and more." She grabbed the rail of the launch to steady herself as they hit the wash of a passing boat and bounced briefly over the churned up water. She felt ice-cold droplets spatter her face.

"If you turn around now," Rupert added, "you'll be able to see San Giorgio Maggiore in all her splendour." Isobel turned obediently and looked towards Palladio's church. The perfect symmetry made her catch her breath and for a moment she couldn't speak. Finally she turned towards Rupert, feeling him waiting for her opinion. "All I can say is Ruskin was so, so wrong," she said. At that precise moment she would have backed her own opinion against Ruskin's to anyone.

Giovanni steered the launch into the mouth of the Grand Canal and slowed down expertly before turning into a much smaller waterway. They were closer now to the buildings and Isobel was able to look upwards to where old rose bricks showed beneath faded, peeling stucco. An occasional window box spilled scarlet geraniums like a defiant slash of lipstick on an ageing face. She sighed with a deep contentment she hadn't felt in ages.

There was a gentle thump as the launch stopped and bumped against the wall. Rupert jumped out, deftly hitched a rope around a convenient stanchion and held his hand out to help her ashore. "This is the back of the San Antonio," he explained before jumping back on board and handing up her luggage. "Do you think you can manage that on your own or would you like some help?" He nodded towards her case. "I'll be fine," she said, sensing that he was keen to get away and do whatever it was that he and Giovanni were planning in Chioggia. She held out her hand. "Until Tuesday then and thank you for delivering me." He shook her hand firmly and then waved as Giovanni turned the launch. She stood watching for a few seconds until they rounded a corner and there was only a ruffle of white on the surface of the canal to show where they had been. The warmth of Rupert's smile had reached all the way to his eyes she remembered as she picked up her case and walked towards the entrance to the hotel.

The marble-floored reception area was blissfully cool. The receptionist greeted her warmly and, after she'd checked in, insisted on carrying Isobel's case up to her room. She was the owner's daughter and all the family worked in the hotel, she explained as they walked up the marble stairs. Isobel looked at the smooth, smiling face, admired the light olive skin innocent of make-up, the shining dark hair tied in a pony-tail and wished she had a daughter. Perhaps they might have shared this holiday together?

Finally she was alone, the only sound the clattering of heels on the bare floor as the girl went back to reception.

Once she'd finished unpacking she showered and applied a new face. As she blotted her lips with a tissue the memory came back to her of the moment she'd discovered James' hanky, lipstick-smeared in the laundry basket. She was then a stay-at-home wife, struggling on a limited income as James built up his legal practice, coping with three year old Ian and his eighteen month old brother Steven. "You're no fun any more," James flung at her when she confronted him, waving the hanky in his face as evidence. "Well you bloody well try staying at home!" she screamed back. "I've got an English degree for God's sake and if I use a word with more than two syllables during the day it's a big event, believe me!"

She'd started to look for a job the next day, realising it was the only way she could get back any vestige of self-esteem and, at the same time, achieve some financial independence, however small.

It took three months of combing situations vacant columns before she found a suitable job. All her interviews went well until, sooner or later, the inevitable question about the children came up. She got used to the look of surprise she was given when she admitted that both her children were under five. In the end she invented, and later employed, an efficient nanny and managed to land a job working for the chairman of a major multi-national. She discovered she had organisational skills as well as a facility with the English language. The two of them worked well together and she ran his office like clockwork until a corporate merger made both of them redundant.

"Why don't you give up working?" James said when she broke the news. By this time things were easier in his firm and she knew he felt that to have a working wife reflected on his ability to provide. Apart from that, juggling home and work meant that Isobel didn't have as much time to devote to his own needs and there were times when she knew he felt decidedly neglected. "With your redundancy money we could buy a place in France," he went on and Isobel could see him making a mental note to choose somewhere near to a reputable golf course.

But he'd reckoned without her. By then she'd lost all her illusions about his fidelity. From time-to-time she went through the laundry basket like a super sleuth, looking at his collars for smears of face powder; smelling his shirts to see if she could catch a hint of perfume. Every time her suspicions were confirmed her stomach would screw up into a tight knot as she realised that he'd found yet another woman. She was damned if she was going to fund a place in France. If he wanted a *pied à terre* for his latest pick-up let him buy it himself.

She invested her redundancy money in her own business and eighteen months later had a secretarial agency with a reputation for efficiency and quality. It was much harder than when she'd been a mere employee and she lost count of the times she stayed late at her office to finish a job. On those occasions she would arrive home, her eyes watering from the effort of concentrating on the screen, and feel a profound relief if James was out.

Even so when he asked for a divorce she was surprised. After all he'd played around for thirty years and always came back. She'd reassured herself that whatever he found so attractive in his other women there was something special about her which he appreciated. But he was impervious to argument. "I want a wife who doesn't work, I'm fed up of taking second place to your business." He looked straight through her as he spoke, his eyes twin flints, his body rigid as steel. In a bleak moment she realised that he didn't love her any more. She felt bereft. Had she been so wrong to try to remain a person in her own right? Was she useless in bed? If so how come they'd never discussed it? Come to think of it emotions, like Italy, were off limits. James had ideas about many things and tried to get her to accept them in the way that a bulldozer flattens a building. He never accepted that it was OK for them to have different points of view. It seemed to her pointless to prolong their misery. Shortly after their divorce he'd married Zelda, thirty years his junior, and she was now happily staying at home to look after two year old Samantha - the precocious manifestation of their brief marriage.

It was a good deal harder to consign "home" to the canal than Isobel realised and she brushed aside these latest memories and replaced them with more recent recollections of Rupert. Although he'd put his own point of view, at the same time he'd accepted that she might think differently, although he *had* tried to persuade her to look at the better side of Ruskin. But he'd quoted Hardy correctly and *that* was definitely a bonus.

Instinctively she knew that she'd been right to strike out and take this holiday on her own. For years she'd tried to please James, investing emotional ballast in him and the two boys in an effort to build a successful marriage. After her divorce she'd taken her summer holidays with Ian or Steve and their families. On the evenings when they took themselves off; ("Sure you'll be alright Mum? Thanks. You're a star!") she'd spent her evenings straining her ears for the sound of a crying child or gazing dreamily at the Mediterranean thinking about the kind of holiday she might be having. Now, at last, it was her turn and she really mustn't keep on drifting back "home".

Chapter Two

Ian's face relaxed and he smiled into the mouthpiece as Susan's voice came over the wire. He could always rely on her to give his ego a good massage even when, as now, she had a problem which would keep her at the office until late, coincidentally, the night their *au pair* would be going to college to try to improve her English. Public relations was an unpredictable kind of business and she frequently worked unsocial hours. Sometimes he joined her, smiling his way through some bash or other. He wasn't complaining though as Susan's income more than compensated for any hours spent pressing the flesh. He flicked through his diary and confirmed to Susan that his last appointment was at four thirty.

"So do you think you could persuade your esteemed father that this is one night you have to leave on time?" Susan asked.

"Consider it done." There was no way he was going to admit that he was in thrall to James even though there were occasions when he felt like it.

He heard Susan's sigh of relief from the other end of the phone. "Don't forget the children are reading Winnie the Pooh will you? Oh, and remember to do all the voices."

"Bugger the voices, it's time those two horrors learned to read themselves to sleep."

"I don't think you'll actually find the word bugger in the AA Milne text!" Susan laughed before adding, "Roaring like Tigger might be a far cry from your usual high-powered dialogue but we all have to make sacrifices. You know they love it when you pretend to be fierce!"

"There'll be no pretending if they aren't on their best behaviour. I'll see you when I see you," he said and hung up.

How the hell had his father managed to get out of such domestic duties all those years? Was it his mother's super efficiency or James' low cunning? As far as he could remember he'd usually been tucked up in bed by the time his father arrived home. The crafty old sod still managed to avoid being a hands-on parent judging by the time he left the office each evening. Still, under his rather brusque exterior he could be amazingly generous. He'd given them a hefty down payment on their first house, dismissing it as part bonus part wedding present. Sue's father, not to be outdone, had matched it and now, thanks to both of them, Ian and Sue were able to choose where to live rather than compromising on a place they could afford.

Of course James had screwed around a bit if what his mother said was true. In fact if he were to be honest he sort of envied him. In a few years he would be forty and so far he'd stayed faithful to Susan. Chance would be a fine thing. What with the extra study he'd taken on to drag this stuffy old practice into the twentieth century, supporting Susan in her career - as well as deputising for her when necessary - to say nothing of the copious amounts of work he faced each day, he never had the time to look twice at a likely prospect.

How would Susan react if he found the time for a bit on the side? Would she stoically soldier on like his mother or find consolation elsewhere? Perhaps it would be better to get on with some work instead of wasting time speculating on a hypothetical situation. He buzzed his secretary and asked her to get him a sandwich before going in search of his father hoping he wasn't closeted with a client. He'd butter him up a bit, ask his advice about a case. That approach always put him in a good mood. Then he'd mention casually that he'd be leaving early. After all his father could scarcely complain after the nights he'd spent away from home when working on a case in France. He was due to go over again soon and it wouldn't do any harm to remind James about that either.

He was back in his office phoning a client when Gail came in with his lunch. She stretched in front of him and plonked a sandwich and a cup of coffee on the only free space on his desk. The twin peaks of her breasts narrowly missed grazing his ear and pointed enticingly instead towards his coffee. He mouthed his thanks and watched her pert backside wiggle its way towards the door as he brought his attention back with difficulty to his client. He hung up at last and reached for a sandwich. The coffee was slopped in the saucer - again. What a pity Gail's practical skills didn't match her sex appeal. He reached for a tissue to soak up the dark brown pool from under his cup wondering if she even noticed her carelessness and if so why the hell didn't she do something about it? He should call her back and ask for a fresh cup, he knew that was the way to bring an employee up to your standard. But how would she react? Sulk, flounce out of his office, burst into tears or embark on a go-slow for the rest of the afternoon? She might even walk out and leave him high and dry and then he'd be left to the mercy of some disinterested temp. Well he'd just have to keep an eye out in future and deal with the problem when it occurred. He brushed the crumbs from his client's file, unscrewed the cap from his fountain pen and got down to it.

In spite of his good intentions it was six thirty when he arrived home to find a dark blue Jaguar parked askew, straddling his own and his neighbour's parking space. "That's all I need," he muttered and leaving the engine running climbed out to investigate. At least the owner was still in the front seat so it could be worse. Some old buffer reading a newspaper by the look of things. What did the silly sod think he was playing at? Ian was by now in a confrontational mood. He thumped on the roof of the car several times and then jumped back smartly as the driver's door flew open. The two men glared silently at each other for a couple of seconds. Ian was just about to tell the driver what he thought of him when he released he was facing none other than his father-in-law. "You're the last person I expected to see," he said. "I'm sorry if I scared you but do you realise you're parked in my slot?" The visitor's car park is over there. He pointed to the clearly visible VISITORS ONLY sign.

He wasn't to know that Bruce had been sitting in his car for the last half hour. He'd already tried to gain entry to their apartment but couldn't for the life of him understand what the *au pair* was trying to tell him over the intercom. He'd simply returned to his car to wait for a member of the family to arrive home and wondered why his daughter couldn't have a straightforward door bell like everybody else. He was now cold, stiff and he needed a drink. "You scared me half to death," he accused. "This damn place always confuses me. Park it for me will you?" He handed the keys to Ian.

"Please," Ian said under his breath as he trod hard on the accelerator and reversed out, making the tyres squeal and narrowly missing a concrete pillar. He parked the car fast, locked it, retraced his steps, handed the keys to Bruce and parked his own car plumb in the middle of his numbered space. "Right then, you'd better come up." He faced his father-in-law once again.

"Did you bring my grip?" Bruce asked, making no effort to disguise his dislike.

"I'm sorry?" Ian looked straight into the washed out watery eyes, noticed with some satisfaction the slightly receding hairline.

"My grip, as in holdall." Bruce articulated each word with infinite care as if speaking English to a foreigner. "It's on the back seat of the car." He handed the car keys to Ian once again.

It dawned on Ian as he returned to the Jaguar that his father-in-law must be here to stay. Had Susan mentioned it? He could swear she hadn't. And why was she working late, knowing that her father was expected? She must have forgotten. Perhaps Bruce had simply taken it into his head to descend on them? Oh well, he'd sort it out with her later. Until then he had the dubious pleasure of entertaining his father-in-law to occupy him.

Susan swallowed an extra strong pain killer before she left the office hoping to dull the headache before it got any worse. Thankfully the journey from her office in Docklands to their loft in Wapping was a short one which spared her a long crawl home through London traffic. She mustn't forget to tell Ian later that her father was coming to stay. It was tomorrow wasn't it? He'd rung just yesterday to say that his housekeeper was going into hospital and was it alright to come to them for a couple of weeks. It was typical of him to give her such short notice and then expect a four star service once he arrived.

He'd been much easier to entertain when her mother was alive and he'd still been working. In the two years since her death he'd become introverted and waspish, difficult to amuse. From time-to-time she felt guilty because she saw so little of him but life was so frantic with work and the children. Her brother had taken himself off to Zimbabwe after her mother died so was never available in a crisis. It wouldn't be quite so bad if her father and Ian saw eye-to-eye but there was always a coolness between them which made it hard for her to welcome Bruce with open arms.

The painkiller had started to work by the time she pulled into the car park. She managed to switch off the office at the same time as the engine and was relieved to be shot of both. The car park was eerily quiet and she scrabbled in her handbag for her keys as she walked towards the exit, needing to divert her attention. "Oh shit!" she said as, in her haste to get to the flat, she caught her shin on a car bumper. "Who the hell left that sticking out?" Her words addressed no one in particular. She bent down to rub her shin glancing at the number plate at the same time. Oh my God it couldn't be. It was. Her father's car. She could have sworn he'd said tomorrow. She broke into a run. What must Ian be thinking?

The silence told her all she didn't want to know when she went into the sitting room. The television was switched off, the image of the two disgruntled men was reflected in the blank screen. "I'm sorry Dad." She planted an uneasy kiss on his rigid cheek.

"You're out of Jack Daniels." Bruce accused by way of a greeting.

"Sorry twice," Susan said. "I honestly didn't expect you until tomorrow."

Ian got to his feet and kissed Susan on the mouth, making it last to annoy Bruce a bit more. "Now you're home I'll nip down to the off-license and grab a bottle of Jack Daniels. I would have gone earlier but Denise left for college shortly after we arrived. I ordered a takeaway from that new Indian place so I'll pick that up at the same time." He watched Bruce top up his glass from Ian's best Malt and shot him a triumphant glance. I'm in control here it said, what's more I'm married to your daughter and I'm keeping her.

It was seven thirty when James arrived home. He heaved himself out of his car but felt too tired to put it away and so left it on the drive. He hoped Zelda had no last minute plans to visit friends, eat out or, worst of all, drag him off to some ghastly West End entertainment. Time at home together was a rarity and therefore precious. He let himself in, put his briefcase under the hall table, picked up the mail and went in search of his wife. Finding the drawing room empty he made his way to the kitchen.

"Ah, there you are," he sniffed appreciatively. "Mmm can I smell something Mediterranean?"

Zelda put down the wooden spoon with which she'd been stirring a *passata,* crossed the kitchen floor and wound her arms around his neck. "Something special just for you."

She was so good at making even the smallest task sound like a great achievement requiring hours of concentrated effort. Mostly James believed her. He liked to think she devoted lots of time to pleasing him and, as he frequently reminded himself, he paid her very well to do just that.

He knew it hadn't been easy for her to learn to cook but he hated convenience food and encouraged her to persevere. He pretended ignorance of her initial failures which she'd thrown in the bin so that he shouldn't witness her humiliation at being unable to master the instructions in even the most basic cookery book.

James kissed her lightly on the cheek taking care not to disarrange her carefully groomed hair. She always looked immaculate even when, as now, she was performing some pedestrian household task. He appreciated the trouble she took to make herself 'presentable' as she called it. After years of being married to a working wife it was a luxury to find Zelda at home at the end of each day.

"I thought we'd stay in this evening, just the two of us." Zelda flashed her freshly cleaned teeth at him as if bestowing some great favour.

"Good, it's been a swine of a day and I'm not really feeling very sociable." He hoped there might be something worth watching on TV for a change or failing that a video that they hadn't seen. But Zelda had other ideas. "I thought we could talk about our plans to re-landscape the garden." she said.

James was only half listening as he sat at the kitchen table sorting the post. Anything which looked like junk mail he chucked straight in the bin without bothering to open it. Out of the corner of his eye he could see Zelda watching him carefully as he made his way through the pile and thought he knew why when he opened the bill from Harvey Nicks. Jesus Christ would she never stop spending! If she knew the sweat he put in every day . . . He looked up frowning. "This bill from Harvey Nicholls, a bit steep isn't it?"

"I haven't seen it darling." Zelda was now back at the stove stirring the sauce with all the concentration of an alchemist working on a new elixir.

He stretched out an arm waving the paper in her direction. Her sigh was barely audible as she put down the wooden spoon for the second time and crossed the kitchen to take it from him. The total was pretty staggering and would have disposed of most of her after tax salary for a month in the days when she'd worked as James' secretary.

"Is there some mistake?" James asked, trying, and failing, to make his voice sound severe. Zelda slipped an arm around his neck and pointed to an item for £750. "Aren't you forgetting the dress I bought for your legal dinner? You did say at the time that it was OK to buy a new one."

James remembered only too well. That night he'd basked in the envy of many of his colleagues. Zelda not only looked sensational but had gone out of her way to be charming to his friends. The dress, a slither of black silk, the *décolleté* showing her cleavage to advantage but stopping short of vulgarity. At the time he'd been really proud of her but even so he felt that £750 was a high price to pay for the privilege of watching his fellow lawyers ogle his wife.

He was appalled at the speed with which the money flowed out of their joint account. It remained a mystery to him how one small family could spend so much on food when they ate out so often. The clothes bills for Zelda and Samantha beggared belief and on top of that were wages for the *au pair*, a cleaning lady and a gardener/handyman who came one day a week to deal with the more routine gardening tasks.

Oh God dammit he needed a drink, he'd worry about money tomorrow. "Did I hear you say something about the garden earlier?" he asked, crossing to the wine rack and selecting a bottle.

"Oh, I thought we'd talk about our plans to re-design the garden, but if you're too tired we can leave it until another time." He didn't miss the emphasis on the word our. Had they really discussed improvements to the garden? Damned if he could remember. And if she thought he was going to foot the bill for some fancy designer she'd discovered via one of her many girl friends she could think again. Perhaps now wasn't the best time to tell her however. He'd leave it until after they'd eaten. He opened a bottle and poured two glasses, putting more in Zelda's than his own. He'd lunched with a client, his head was only just beginning to clear and, in view of the forthcoming negotiations, he was keen for it to stay that way.

They ate tender veal escallopes (obligingly prepared by a small and exclusive butcher that Zelda had been cultivating) with the *passata*, *sa*utê potatoes and a mixed salad. They had puddings only when they ate out and this evening finished their meal with a few late raspberries on which Zelda had sprinkled a generous measure of kirsch. By the time they'd finished and moved across to the drawing room James' mood had improved considerably and he sipped his coffee contentedly.

Zelda flicked the lobe of his ear with her tongue and refilled his coffee cup before curling up next to him on the sofa. "Now let me talk to you about the garden," she began, producing one of his legal pads on which she'd written copious notes and attached pictures cut from several glossy magazines. James was relieved that she hadn't commissioned a landscape architect and forced himself to stay awake long enough to listen to her ideas which, as it turned out, weren't nearly as grandiose as he'd expected.

"How did he feel," she asked, "about creating a small play area for Samantha, perhaps with a swing and a sandpit? Then perhaps they could extend the patio, make it more of a terrace and maybe put in a purpose built barbecue?"

When she'd finished, the relief he felt made it easy for him to smile and agree with her suggestions. He promised he'd have a word with Fred, their gardener, get him to do as much of the donkey work as possible.

"I don't see too much of a problem," he told her. "In fact I think that this is something that Fred and I could easily tackle between us." He sounded considerably more optimistic than he felt.

He enjoyed pottering about the garden providing the work wasn't too onerous. He even kept a pair of corduroy trousers and an old and much loved sweater specifically for the purpose. Zelda frequently teased him about his gardening clothes and was always threatening to give them to the church jumble sale as he wore them so rarely.

"Do you mind if I watch the news?" he asked when she'd slipped the pad back into the top drawer of the desk.

"Of course not my darling." She spoke with the generosity of someone who knows she has just got her own way. "But I think I'll go straight to bed if you don't mind."

"Fine, I'll try not to be too long."

He sighed deeply once she'd left the room and hoped she'd be asleep by the time he joined her. He doubted whether he could even get an erection at the moment leave alone maintain it for long enough to satisfy Zelda. All his life women had given him comfort when he needed it; his mother, house master's wives or school matrons, even Isobel when she wasn't tied up with work. Not contented with the many demands she made on his money and his time Zelda also made, to his mind anyway, excessive demands in bed. But in his younger days he'd never been satisfied with just one woman so surely he was being unreasonable to complain now? In fact if he were honest it wasn't a bad problem to have. His friends were always clapping him on the back and telling him what a lucky sod he was.

Just at the moment he was finding it difficult to keep up with her. They were working flat out on a government investigation at the office. The monthly retainer was a godsend but the work required painstaking attention to detail and he'd spent several nights already checking and re-checking their findings. He didn't want a return to the late eighties when the property market went into decline and they couldn't even rely on the bread and butter conveyancing. He'd only proposed to Zelda once the business started to rally and he knew that if there was another downturn she'd be off in a flash. However far he stretched his imagination he couldn't visualise Zelda adjusting to a life where she had to tighten the purse strings.

Ian had been a godsend to the business, even learning French and qualifying in the complexities of French property law to capitalise on the current trend for the Brits to buy second homes in France. He'd told James that the average British punter fell in love with a broken down wreck or more particularly the view from it, usually miles from anywhere, and that was that. They said goodbye to their brains as soon as they drove off the ferry at Calais.

The news bulletin came to an end. He switched off the set, poured himself a brandy from the decanter on a side table and settled back again into the corner of the sofa. This room was a good place to relax on the rare occasions when he was alone . Their decorator had created an uncluttered space taking a large golden Afghan rug as his inspiration for the colour scheme. It glowed now in front of the modern fireplace. There was a total absence of clutter, the latest trend in interior design which would, no doubt, be *passé* by the end of the decade. During daylight hours there was an unrestricted view of the garden through the large picture window that slid back to allow access to what was now the patio but which would soon become a terrace.

He'd been so lucky to find this place. When they'd talked about where they might live Zelda refused to go anywhere that didn't have a decent London postmark and, after he'd sold his old home and paid cash for Isobel's cottage, he was afraid they might have to compromise on a flat somewhere. A colleague had given him the tip that this place was about to come on the market because the former owner, a Lloyd's name in an unsuccessful syndicate, needed the cash in a hurry to pay off his losses. He'd accepted James' offer with alacrity even though it was well below market value. James congratulated himself on his ability to recognise a desperate man when he saw one and he, in his turn, did the man a big favour by pushing through the sale quickly and waiving the legal fee to give the man a break.

Zelda smiled to herself as she sat in front of her dressing table mirror brushing her hair. James really was a pussy cat under all that surface bluster. She put down the brush, stroked cleanser onto her face with burgundy-tipped fingers, and remembered how she'd seduced him. She'd played him with all the skill of a fisherman attempting to lure the monarch of the river, offering her favours in turn like flamboyant flies only to flick them away before he had time to bite. She'd been happy to undo the top two buttons of her shirt but stopped short of allowing him into her bra'. Over several months she'd slowly reeled him in until finally he lay gasping and submissive but, crucially, believing he'd been the one to do the catching.

She'd made up her mind to pursue him when, working as his secretary, she'd taken tea into his office and overheard him talking to a female client about her divorce settlement. "The three most important things for a woman," he began, "are her hair, her clothes and her holidays so we must think carefully about building in sufficient funds to meet those requirements when we come to court."

She couldn't believe that a man of James' age thought like that and she knew she might have to look long and hard before she found another who could be so accommodating over such important expenses. On the whole she hadn't been disappointed, although there were occasions, like this evening for instance, when there was quite a gap between theory and practise. She'd have to draw her horns in for a couple of months. It would be annoying if he closed her accounts and she had to stop flashing her credit cards whenever it suited her. On the whole she managed him very well deferring to him over major items of expenditure like the gardening project for instance. She'd even modified her ideas a bit after he'd been so picky about the bill from Harvey Nicks.

At eleven thirty James switched off the lights and walked slowly and quietly up the stairs. He opened the bedroom door and cautiously put his head round, pausing just long enough to hear the sounds of regular breathing coming from their bed. He eased his pyjamas from under the pillow and tiptoed down the landing to use the other bathroom, knowing that the sound of running water would wake Zelda up. He'd hoped the brandy would have settled his indigestion but he still felt a niggling pain in his chest. He found a bottle of Alka Seltzer, took a couple of tablets and just before midnight climbed thankfully into bed and tried to sleep.

Chapter Three

Rupert walked briskly towards the Rialto Bridge looking forward to a day off for the first time in months. Since Liz died he'd buried himself in work to try to shut out the memories that insisted on flooding into his head when he stopped. It would be easier to live with himself if he didn't feel so guilty all the time but, try as he might, he couldn't forgive himself for not spotting her illness sooner. If they'd seen the consultant earlier her life might have been saved and they would have had the pleasure of growing old together.

When she died he'd felt a raw, searing pain which was like nothing he'd experienced before. He'd paced up and down her studio night after night. The place looked as if she had just left it; paints, brushes, plans. He willed her ghost to come back and talk to him, laugh with him just one more time. Nothing. Nothing. Nothing. Not the smallest hint that she might be watching him. *That* had been the hardest thing to accept, that she could just go and leave him to deal with the dreadful emptiness. It was so completely out of character for her to hurt anyone and for a time he'd actually hated her for ignoring the symptoms which had finally been diagnosed as colon cancer. Although he wasn't angry any more he still felt an underlying sadness and a permanent need to occupy his time.

He couldn't imagine feeling the same way about anyone ever again. He measured every woman he met against Liz and none of them could hold a candle to her. He'd never thought of himself as hard to please and surprised himself by finding so many things about women that he didn't like. A particular voice or a laugh would grate; they didn't smell the way Liz smelled; their clothes were either too flashy or staid for his taste.

He'd been so lucky to find Liz who'd been absolutely right for him. He remembered the night they met at the engagement party of a friend. She stood there, a mass of dark hair, huge blue eyes, a soft grey cloud of a dress. He'd been completely besotted. She was always such a happy woman; uncomplicated; rarely moody although very quick to tune in to his own. She would look at him at a party and know if he were ready to leave, take the initiative when she sensed he wanted her. Once she'd dragged him into the summer house when they'd been spending the weekend with her parents. Before he knew what was happening she'd unzipped his trousers and they were making love on the floor on a cobwebby travelling rug. He'd loved that and her, more and more as the years went by.

She'd just left horticultural college when they met and shortly afterwards began to design gardens. After they married he suggested that they could build up a working relationship; become the new Jekyll and Lutyens. She'd waved away his suggestion. "I'd drive you crazy in a week," she said. "You're far too tidy and precise. Gardening is all about curves, drifts, great swathes of colour and my studio would irritate you it's such a mess." She hadn't exaggerated.

Whenever he put his head round the door he had to search for her in the clutter and he frequently teased her that the place looked as if she'd stirred it with a spoon. She laughed and told him that disorder fuelled her creative juices. He'd hoped that she might ask him to design a building to go with one of her gardens or, better still, create a garden for one of his houses. It would have been a comfort to look back on a happy and successful working partnership and, in spite of her reservations, he still believed they would have made a good team.

The breeze from the Grand Canal ruffled his hair as he turned right and crossed over the Rialto Bridge. He loved this part of the city, particularly early in the morning. There was always plenty going on. He wished he had the vision to design such a bridge, decorate it with saints and madonnas and then have the effrontery to top it off with rows of shops! He could smell the fish market and the noise of trading was all around him. Boats arrived and disgorged their contents, stall holders shouted to each other and everywhere were piles of fruit and vegetables looking fresh enough to leap off the stalls.

His long, loping stride covered the distance rapidly and within twenty minutes he arrived at the small reception area of the San Antonio. Signor Gallini, the owner, was on duty behind the desk, brow furrowed as he checked accounts, gold framed spectacles on the end of his nose, slicked hair smelling of Parma violets. He greeted Rupert like a long lost friend.

"*Bon giorno Signor* Northcote!" He leaned across the desk and seized Rupert by the hand. "I 'ope you don't come to tell me there is something wrong with my building." He waved a podgy hand to embrace the modest reception area.

"No need to worry on that score," Rupert replied. "Your foundations are as sound as ever. That's what comes of employing a reliable architect, despite the cost!" He shot what he judged to be an old fashioned look at the owner. He couldn't resist teasing the man who'd constantly worried about money throughout the conversion. *Signor* Gallini laughed. "I'm glad to 'ear it. So what brings you to San Antonio?"

"Ah." Rupert paused for a fraction of a second. "I'm here to collect an old friend of mine *Signora* Campbell."

"She is outside I think, 'aving breakfast. Please to go through." His expression, Rupert noted, was impassive.

He spotted Isobel as soon as he entered the courtyard. She was deep in conversation with a couple at the next table, so absorbed she failed to notice him. She was wearing cream linen slacks, a shirt of terracotta silk. The blonde streaks in her hair shone in the early morning sun. He felt an unexpected stab of pleasure as he walked towards her.

"Buon giorno!" he said, repeating his greeting to the couple. Isobel looked up at him, her smile showed him how pleased she was that he was punctual.

"Would you like me to order some fresh coffee for you?" she asked.

"No thanks, I had some at home and my apartment is only twenty minutes away."

"In that case shall we go?" She picked up her shoulder bag and a camera.

"I hope you're wearing something comfortable on your feet, one does a lot of walking in Venice."

She held out a sandaled foot for his inspection and wriggled her toes. Pretty toes too; slim, brown, nails like pink shells.

"So what have you been up to?" he asked as they left the hotel.

"Well I spent Sunday trying to find my way around. I took your advice and bought a good map. The standard hotel handout isn't really up to the job is it? Yesterday I took your advice again and went to explore Canareggio and your beautiful church."

"Oh!" Rupert was surprised she'd taken the trouble. "What did you think of it?"

"Well I'm not really a Gothic fan but I loved the window traceries and the absolute peace of the cloister and of course I was bowled over by the Tintoretto's. I didn't react in quite the same way as Ruskin's wife but afterwards I sat for a long time in the square enjoying the emptiness and the silence. I was the only person there but I reckoned with St Christopher looking down at me from the entrance I'd be quite safe!"

"The church was originally dedicated to St Christopher but then they found this miraculous statue of the Virgin in a nearby orchard and moved it into the church. She was said to be miraculous because various people reported seeing a light over her head and concluded that she was obviously too good to be wasted in an orchard."

Rupert remembered all the times he'd sat in that square. Not only had Isobel flattered him by taking his advice but she'd also appreciated the charm and peace of it. Coincidence or what?

"So where are we going today?" Isobel's voice cut across his thoughts.

"Well I thought we might take the *vaporetto* across the Grand Canal and I can show you Santa Maria della Salute to begin with. After that we'll see how it goes."

When they reached the end of the Mercerie and walked into St Mark's Square he paused to show her the clock tower. Surmounted by one of the lions of St Mark silhouetted against a vivid blue background sprinkled with gold stars it was a stunning example of early Renaissance architecture. Rupert checked the time against his watch and, seeing that it was almost ten o'clock, suggested they wait for the two mechanical Moors to come out and strike the bell. "It should be possible to get to the top," he said, "but at the moment it's closed for restoration. There's an old Venetian legend which says that anyone who can get close enough to stroke the Moor's backsides is guaranteed sexual potency for the following year!"

Isobel listened keenly, soaking up information like blotting paper. Her face lit up with pleasure when the Moors appeared, hammers raised ready to strike the bell. Time had coated their bronze skin with a grey-green patina. "I completely missed them when I walked through on Sunday," she confessed. The ghost of a smile still lingered after his story. "The square is so stunning I'm afraid I looked at it as a whole and overlooked the individual features."

As they walked across the piazza towards the *vaporetto* stop he paused again and pointed towards St Mark's basilica. "It looks a bit of a hotch potch, don't you think? The original was built, mainly of wood, in the ninth century as a chapel for the doges. Hardly surprising, it burned down and the present building replaced it. The mosaics inside are thirteenth century and absolutely stunning. Try to see it if you can but be sure to go early in the morning. There are still masses of tourists around and the place gets impossibly crowded even though we're coming to the end of the season. Most of the contents have been looted I'm afraid. The four horses you see up there came from the top of Trajan's arch in Rome, or the originals did. They've now been taken inside to avoid pollution damage. Those are copies. They look as if they're about to fly into space, don't you think?"

They moved on towards the Doge's Palace and he showed her where Byzantine architecture ended, Renaissance began and where both merged into Gothic. He couldn't resist the opportunity to get in another plug for Ruskin. "Of course, as you can imagine, Ruskin was wild about the Gothic." His mouth twitched. "He wrote seventy pages in The Stones of Venice describing the columns facing the lagoon. Let me show you just one."

He put a hand under her elbow and walked briskly towards the front of the *piazzetta* and pointed to a column which was thicker than the rest. "If you look carefully you'll see a young lover spotting his mistress at a window. Then he courts her, brings her presents. You can see their first kiss, their wedding, the birth and childhood of their son and finally the child's death."

"I suppose that story could be a fair summary of life for most of us," Isobel began. "What I mean is that when we're young we believe everything's possible until sooner or later some set back or deep sorrow comes along and jolts our complacency. To put it in a nutshell; aspiration, reality, inevitability."

"Are you telling me that sorrow is inevitable?" Rupert asked, wondering if the pain he heard in her voice had all been inflicted by James or if there were other sources of unhappiness in her life that he might discover in the future.

"I didn't mean that every situation must end in tears but simply that we're very lucky if we're spared from deep sadness, regret or disappointment. We see something, want it, get it or achieve it and then discover that, whatever, isn't all it's cracked up to be."

"But repair and recovery are possible." Rupert said, believing it for the first time since Liz's death. "Let me show you what I mean." He turned away from the Doge's Palace and walked back into the *piazzetta*, pausing when they reached the *campanile*. He pointed upwards. "That little lot fell down in 1902 and totally destroyed that beautiful marble *loggetta* you see at the bottom which Sansovino designed in 1540. It was completely rebuilt. The pieces of stone were fished out of the rubble and Sansovino's masterpiece was recreated like a huge jigsaw puzzle.

Isobel looked up at the exquisitely carved angels which fitted so perfectly into the spandrels on either side of the arched doorway; at the bronze statues and their attendant *putti* sitting proudly on top of the gates.

"Sansovino was responsible for the sculpture as well," said Rupert, following the direction of her gaze. "I'm sure you'll agree the repair was worth the effort." He watched as she pointed her camera and thought; take your own advice Rupe. Your tragedy might have hurt like hell at the time but it didn't smash you into thousands of pieces, so where's your problem?

"Thank you for bringing it all to life for me." Isobel said, putting away her camera. She'd taken off her dark glasses. He could see that her eyes were moist and was touched that she'd been moved, either by the story or by what she'd seen.

As they crossed the Grand Canal in the *vaporetto* he pointed to the vast dome of Santa Maria della Salute. "I want to show you one of the greatest churches in Venice. You probably read up on it before you arrived? It was built to thank the Virgin for the return of health after the plague in 1630 when almost a third of the population was wiped out. You can see how it guards the entrance to the Grand

Canal and dominates the view from whichever direction you look. The architect placed it to take advantage of what must be one of the most magnificent sites in the entire city. It looks really magical at night when it's floodlit."

They left the *vaporetto* and walked slowly up the long, imposing flight of steps which led from the entrance of the church to the edge of the Grand Canal. They took time to admire the impressive façade, the huge dome at the front surmounted by a statue of the Virgin. Rupert explained that the sculptor had chosen to depict her as Ruler of the Sea. Immediately under the dome was a balustraded walkway decorated here and there with carved angels. Once inside Isobel walked across the inlaid marble floor and stood at the centre of the vast octagonal space which was flooded with light from the dome which, by a miracle had survived overhead fire from two world wars. Corinthian columns supported an arched cloister surrounding the octagon. Rupert stood watching her for several minutes before moving closer and whispering in her ear. "There are some beautiful pictures in the sacristy, I'd hate you to miss them while you're here," and with a guiding hand under her elbow, led her towards the entrance.

The collection, though small, was impressive and included several Titian's and a Tintoretto. They walked slowly around the sacristy admiring each painting in turn. When Isobel reached the last painting she immediately retraced her steps to an early Titian; St Mark enthroned and surrounded by saints. "This is the picture for me," she said turning towards Rupert. "Titian really knew about sensuality didn't he? It makes you want to dip your finger in and lick it!" Her eyes stayed on the young St Sebastian standing defiantly in the forefront both his stance and his expression giving no indication of the pain he must be suffering from the arrow piercing his chest. The model must have been about twenty; dark, lithe and with beautiful legs and feet. "I wonder who posed for that?" she said. "Isn't he handsome? Who do you think he was? How and where did he live? Who did he love?"

Rupert smiled but made no reference to her romantic curiosity. Instead he wondered why he'd never before thought of dipping his finger into a painting and licking it! He turned the thought around in his mind and realised with a shock that it was the kind of remark Liz might have made; but before he had the opportunity to mull it over Isobel's voice cut across his thoughts. "Thank you for taking the trouble to show me such a wonderful church."

"Oh it's been pure self-indulgence," he replied as they started to walk away. "Thank *you* for being such a patient listener. Now," he continued briskly as they reached the foot of the steps, "Would you like some lunch?" It crossed his mind that if they bought some food and took it across to St Georgio Maggiore they would almost certainly be able to picnic alone. The church closed at twelve thirty and all the tourists would leave. On the other hand it might be a bit early in their relationship to have a solitary picnic, even in broad daylight. After her divorce she was probably a bit wary, possibly disillusioned at the way some men behaved. "Can you face a short walk?" he asked. "If so there's a very good place I think you might like where we can eat in the open air." Isobel shielded her eyes against the sun before taking her sunglasses out of her handbag. "It sounds ideal for a day like today," she replied.

He slowed his pace to match hers and once again paused from time-to-time to point out some item of interest. It took them a good half hour to reach the restaurant which was in a stunning garden shaded by huge pergolas and, judging by the number of people already seated, Rupert wasn't the only one to appreciate its charm. "I should have booked" he said, looking around for an empty table. "I'd forgotten just how popular this place is." He caught the eye of the proprietor who told them that the only table he had available was for four people and, although empty at the moment, he might have to ask them to share before the end of lunch. Rupert looked at Isobel and asked, "Will you risk it? Only this place will be closed this evening and tomorrow so we might not have an opportunity to try it again."

"It looks so welcoming and I love gardens. Shall we take a chance? And it would be wonderful to sit down if only for half an hour or so."

"I'm sorry, I've kept you on your feet all morning, carried away by my own enthusiasm for Venetian architecture." He nodded to the proprietor and Isobel sank gratefully onto a chair,

They were half way through their second course when a waiter brought another couple over to their table. Rupert saw Isobel look up briefly, glanced quickly across at the newcomers and took in a large expanse of brilliant floral dress before turning back to Isobel. One look at her told him that the newcomers were less than welcome. The smile had gone from her face and she'd stopped eating but her fork remained suspended halfway to her mouth.

"My God Isobel! What on earth are *you* doing here?" The woman had no need of a microphone and several heads turned in their direction.

"Rupert," said Isobel, her voice sounding flat and expressionless, "this is Barbara and Henry Whitehouse. Barbara, Henry this is an -erm old friend of mine Rupert Northcote. Barbara is James' sister," she added lamely by way of explanation.

Barbara sank down heavily next to Rupert, picked up the menu and fanned herself vigorously. "Get me a drink for God's sake!" The remark was meant for her husband but Rupert immediately offered her their own carafe of white wine. Barbara held out her glass and scarcely had Rupert filled it when she drank half of it in one gulp and then immediately held it out again.

"God! I needed that! What a morning! Henry insisted on dragging me round the Accademia. I don't want to see another bloody painting for a long, long time."

Isobel felt her brain cringe and her spirits sink to the soles of her feet. Barbara had never liked her. James had explained years ago that Barbara envied her degree, her two sons, her looks and above all her place in his own affections. Isobel, who never thought of herself as anything special, found this hard to believe. In the early days of her marriage she'd tried to make a friend of her new sister-in-law but gave up one day after fielding a particularly vicious verbal attack. Steve had mentioned when he drove her to the airport that his aunt would be in Venice around this time but she'd been so excited by the thoughts of her own trip that she put the information to the back of her mind, thinking it unlikely that they would run into each other.

Barbara was three years older than James and never tired of reminding the family how she'd protected him at their preparatory school; fighting and winning their childish battles and doing her best to shield him from the school bullies. Isobel could never quite imagine James being bullied by anyone but was in no position to contradict the story so let it ride. Barbara had always disapproved of Isobel's career saying over and over again how essential it was for young children to have their mothers at home.

Isobel looked desperately across the table at Rupert trying to signal her disappointment whilst Barbara and Henry studied the menu. She continued eating her lunch mechanically but her *fettuccine* was cold and she poked about with her fork, retrieved a tiny shrimp or two, speared them and transferred them almost reluctantly to her mouth. Ten minutes ago they were absolutely delicious, now they tasted of nothing at all.

Henry was attempting to order. Barbara persistently interrupted him asking irrelevant questions. "Is it fresh? Is it well cooked do you think?" Finally she reminded Henry to be sure to order another carafe of wine. When their order was complete she turned to Isobel and asked, "So how long have you been over here?"

"This is my fourth day," Isobel said. "I flew in on Saturday."

"And how about you?" She turned her attention to Rupert who replied in a voice of studied calm. "Oh, the same, I'm here partly on business."

"And where are you staying?" Again the question was fired at Rupert.

"I have an apartment, fairly modest but it serves me for business trips and the occasional holiday."

"We're at the Gritti Palace," Barbara went on, "place costs an absolute fortune of course but it's worth it for the comfort."

Dear God, thought Isobel, will she never stop? She saw the look of blatant curiosity on Barbara's face and realised she'd probably jumped to the conclusion that she and Rupert were sharing his apartment.

"I'm staying at a very small hotel, quiet and tucked away, *much* more me." she said in a rush, looking Barbara directly in the eye. She could see that Barbara didn't believe her. Well that was her hard luck. It was five years now since her divorce and it was her own business what she did with her spare time. In an attempt to change the subject she said, "How's James these days? I haven't seen him since Tom's christening, it must be nearly two years now?"

"Well we saw him a couple of weeks ago and thought he looked *very* tired. He gave a party for Zelda's thirtieth birthday, just a few *close* friends and *family.* Zelda is James' new wife," she elaborated turning again towards Rupert.

Rupert studied Barbara and Henry thinking what an unlikely couple they were. Although Barbara had a fine complexion, whatever make-up she used hadn't disguised the high colour in her cheeks. She looked like the sort of woman who would feel hot even on a cold day. He could smell a faint odour of perspiration which added to his feeling of distaste. Had she been taller he would have described her as Junoesque but on such a short woman the spare flesh made her look dumpy. Every so often he felt a fat thigh brush against his own as she shifted her position. He moved his chair slightly away from her.

Henry, on the other hand, looked a bit too smooth for Rupert's taste. Although he took very little part in the conversation, hardly surprising with a wife like Barbara, he addressed the occasional remark to Isobel, placing his hand over hers in a proprietary way which irritated Rupert. He told himself that he was being unreasonable. The poor man was probably harmless enough but it was clear he'd fancied Isobel at some stage.

"So how long have you two known each other?" boomed Barbara, tearing into a veal chop. Isobel glanced at Rupert before replying. "Oh, absolutely ages! But we're just good friends Barbara and you can quote me on that."

"No need to be so prickly," Barbara replied with her mouth full. "I'm only showing an interest." Rupert caught Isobel's eye and looked pointedly at his watch. Isobel was quick to pick up the signal. She pushed her chair back from the table slightly. "I'm sorry," she said, "but Rupert and I have to go. We're meeting some friends and they'll worry if we're late. Maybe we'll run into you again before you leave?" she added as an after thought.

"Highly unlikely," Barbara replied. "We're leaving for Florence in the morning." Thank God for that. Isobel thought, sighing with relief and rising to her feet as Rupert paid the bill.

As soon as they were out of earshot Barbara turned to Henry . "Well! Isobel's manners have taken a turn for the worse since she left James. And what about Rupert Northcote then?"

Henry shrugged. "What about him?"

"Well it's obvious they're having some sort of a fling together."

"You don't know for certain." Henry replied, not bothering to keep the exasperation out of his voice. "After all Isobel said they were just good friends. Anyway what Isobel does with her life has nothing to do with us."

Barbara snorted loudly as she demolished the last of her veal chop and scooped the few fried potatoes remaining in the vegetable dish onto her plate. "I've just got to tell James," she said with considerable relish. "Now, how about some pudding?" As she looked at the menu she was already planning her telephone call to her brother. She would ring him when they went back to the hotel for a siesta; give it to him hot off the press before she forgot all the details.

As soon as they were clear of the restaurant Isobel turned towards Rupert. "Oh! I'm sorry. What an awful end to a lovely morning." The expression on her face was tragic and there was a catch in her voice. "Look," Rupert said easily, "there's really no need to apologise. Let's walk down to the Zattere, get ourselves some coffee, have a good old bitch and get our own back!" Isobel couldn't help laughing in spite of the way she was feeling. "Of all the restaurants in the world, of all the countries that awful Barbara could have chosen to take a holiday, she had to pick Venice."

As they walked along her emotions were mixed. She felt so ashamed to be related, even indirectly, to that rude insufferable woman. What must Rupert think? Did it matter what he thought? Yes it did. The realisation hit her. What if he'd made his excuses and just walked away? He could have walked away quite easily but crucially he hadn't. He could still walk away. That's what Casanova did, not once but hundreds of times. Isobel what is happening to you? You've spent two half days in his company and already . . .

"Here we are." Rupert pointed to a small wooden platform facing the Giudecca Canal. He ordered their coffee and sat back waiting for her to recover. Suddenly Isobel clapped her hand to her mouth and felt her cheeks grow warm. "I'm afraid I owe you another apology," she said.

"How's that?" He raised his right eyebrow, the left stayed put.

"I introduced you to Barbara and Henry as an old friend. I'm really sorry, I didn't mean to compromise you in any way."

"Perish the thought!" He leaned forward and took both her hands in his and, looking her straight in the eyes he volunteered, "I have a similar confession. When I came to collect you this morning I told Signor Gallini that I'd come to collect an old friend. You see I didn't want to compromise *you*."

Isobel's mouth curved upwards in a huge smile of gratitude. "Here we are almost at the end of the century. We were swinging in the sixties for goodness sake and now we're behaving like a couple of prim Victorians! Henry James would be proud of us!" They laughed together with relief that their honesty had paid off. When they'd calmed down Rupert released her hands and was serious again.

"I'd half intended to show you the Accademia this afternoon and work this evening but somehow or another I don't think we should enjoy it, do you?"

"Too many bloody paintings!" she said in perfect imitation of Barbara and they both burst out laughing again.

"Let's be serious for a minute," he said at last. "If I take myself off now I could work for the rest of the afternoon and then we could meet for dinner this evening. That's if you could bear it of course."

Could she bear it! Oh thank you God! Thank you all the Santa Marias in Venice! Rupert wasn't going to behave like Casanova after all! She tried to keep her voice neutral as she replied. "That would be really lovely. But may I set a condition? *Please* don't let's eat anywhere near the Gritti Palace!" They both exploded into fresh peals of laughter.

Chapter Four

"If I were you I'd think twice about making that phone call." Henry said as they reached the air-conditioned comfort of their room at the Gritti Palace and Barbara made a beeline for the telephone.

"But you're *not* me Henry, as I've reminded you more than once, and I think James has a perfect right to know what his ex-wife gets up to." Barbara deliberately turned her back on him as she picked up the receiver.

Her body hung over the delicate chair on both sides like a partly inflated air cushion. Henry sighed heavily, stretched himself on the bed, reached for his book and wondered what satisfaction Barbara gained from making mischief. Couldn't she see that her actions were doing nobody any favours, least of all herself? He was afraid that one of these days, if she continued to spread malicious gossip, she might end up in serious trouble. As it was she was turning into an embittered, disagreeable old woman. He wished he could persuade her to channel her formidable energy into something worthwhile, do some good to someone for a change maybe work for a charity, then perhaps she might put her unfortunate childhood memories behind her.

He closed his eyes as Barbara put down the phone, knowing that any minute now she would take off her dress and climb into bed. Thank the Lord they had a twin bedded room so if he feigned sleep she'd get the message and leave him alone. The last thing he wanted to see was Barbara stripped down to her underwear. He squeezed his eyelids together trying to blot out the picture of rolls of fat escaping from her bra' and pants, the bulging belly that would never again be flat.

He'd had enough disturbance for one day. Seeing Isobel again leaning across the table her face lovely in its animation, her eyes fixed firmly on Rupert Northcote, lucky swine. Henry didn't for one moment believe her story that they had to meet friends. Were they now back in Rupert's apartment having their own version of an Italian siesta? He tried to picture Isobel without her clothes, felt a familiar frisson, groaned inwardly, turned his face to the wall and tried to sleep.

James swivelled his chair away from the office window to face his desk again and slammed down the phone. His hands were shaking, his heart knocking against his ribs. "The bitch! The bloody duplicitous bitch! How could she!" He was so angry he hadn't realised that he'd spoken aloud until his secretary put her head around the door, an anxious expression on her face. "Did you call Mr Campbell?" she enquired and then, as he glared at her, "are you alright? Can I get you anything?"

James fought to control both his voice and his temper, failed on both counts and demanded tea. He felt in his pocket for his indigestion pills swallowed two and then took a packet of cigarettes from the top drawer of the desk. Zelda wouldn't allow him to smoke at home and his doctor never stopped telling him that he shouldn't smoke ever. He lit one, in the mood to defy anybody.

His secretary returned with the tea tray, poured a cup for him and withdrew hastily when he failed to thank her. James was left alone with his thoughts which did nothing to cool his temper. He was remembering the expression of surprise and pain on Isobel's face when he'd told her about Zelda. How those big blue eyes of hers brimmed when he said he wanted to leave!

He realised with sudden clarity how quickly she'd changed from the wronged wife into a predatory avenger. She'd fought him for every last penny, retaining a smart arse feminist lawyer with a grudge against every man in Christendom. As a result he'd ended up buying her a cottage and letting her have the pick of their joint furniture, seeking at the time to ease his guilt, when all along she'd been having her own affair with a bloody dago architect; with a love-nest in Venice to cap it all!

He'd spent the best part of his life out-smarting lecherous husbands and getting the best possible deal for their wives but was an innocent when he came to handle his own case. He'd be the laughing stock of the legal fraternity if ever this leaked out. Suddenly James wanted to hit something. He walked instead into the adjoining office.

"Do I have any more appointments today?" he asked his secretary.

"A Mrs Sinclair-Lewis at four thirty."

"Put her off until tomorrow will you? Tell her I'm detained elsewhere on a difficult case and then let Ian know I've left." He neither waited for her reply or collected his briefcase, simply walked out to his car. He was the bloody senior partner and he'd take the afternoon off if he chose.

Zelda was in the drawing room reading a story to Samantha when he walked into the house slamming the front door behind him. He saw her head jerk up in surprise as he appeared in the doorway. Alright for some, he thought, sitting down and reading all afternoon while I slave to keep them in luxury.

"Hello darling!" she said. James saw to his satisfaction that her welcoming smile looked a trifle uncertain. "You're home nice and early," she went on, "we're not expected at the Simpsons until seven thirty."

"Bugger the Simpsons, I'm going to the golf club." He turned on his heel before Zelda could reply.

Ten minutes later Zelda heard the front door slam for a second time and the unmistakable sound of tyres skidding on gravel as James' car sped away. What on earth was eating him she wondered? Thank God her own conscience was clear. She hadn't been near Harvey Nicks since the last bill arrived neither had she raised the question of the garden improvements. Well if he wasn't back in time she would jolly well go to the Simpsons on her own. In fact it might be more fun. If James was in a mood and insisted on coming along with her the whole evening could be ruined. She put an arm round Samantha and carried on reading.

James got a bucket of a hundred balls and carried them over to the golf range. He pulled out his driver and brought it down with a violent swish onto the first ball. Travelling fast it curved high into the air and landed just beyond the hundred and fifty yard marker. He placed the second ball. "This one's for you, bloody Rupert Northcote," he muttered to himself and brought the club down a second time. The ball travelled two hundred yards. James' temper began to cool.

Zelda was in the bath when he arrived home for the second time. Normally he would have used the shower or the second bathroom but today was different. Today he had to prove to himself that he was more than a match for any Casanova architect. "Mind if I join you?" His voice was deliberately casual as he pulled off his sweater and tossed it towards the chair. The trousers and underpants followed. All three missed their intended target.

If Zelda minded she certainly didn't show it. She smiled a slow bewitching smile and sat up to make room for him. "Be my guest darling," she said. Then as an afterthought, "whatever was wrong when you came home earlier come here and let me make it all better."

Later he heard her pick up the bedside phone, call the Simpsons and make their excuses. Seconds later he felt her fingertips tracing a spiral down his spine as she spoke. Her body pressed against his back and her hand slid between his thighs. He groaned softly and resigned himself to an exhausting evening.

Susan looked at her watch. Seven o'clock, half an hour to go before the first guests arrived. She was promoting a range of ready-mixed cocktails which, the manufacturing company hoped, would soon be in every major supermarket in the UK. Susan hoped right along with them otherwise her job as account manager would be on the line. She walked into the room check list in hand to see that everything was in place. It would have been easier to hire a function room in an hotel but her client insisted that they wanted potential buyers to see their head office hoping to impress them with what they described as their flagship. They didn't appreciate the mammoth organisation required to turn an office canteen into a venue for a party. The room had been in use until four o'clock which meant shipping in flowers, caterers, press releases, promotional literature, product samples and what seemed to Susan like a million and one other things, all in the space of three hours.

Earlier in the day she'd had to re-locate the poncey prima donna she'd booked to kick off the event when he threatened to pull out if he weren't allocated a more suitable (by which he meant more expensive) hotel in which to rest his over-priced bones for the night. Honestly two minutes on television and they expected the world to kowtow. If what she heard on the grapevine was true they'd have to try and limit the number of ready mixed he imbibed otherwise he'd be carried out half way through the evening.

Ten past seven. Sue grabbed her briefcase and legged it to the cloakroom to change. Her mobile rang as she ran. Oh now what! Probably Gervase the prima donna throwing another wobbly. She was tempted not to answer but if he wasn't going to show she'd have to think up a pretty good story in the next twenty minutes. "Susan Campbell speaking," she panted into the mouthpiece hoping she sounded calmer than she felt.

"Sue, thank God I managed to catch you." Ian sounded agitated. "Look I'm stuck in traffic in Shaftsbury Avenue, perhaps there's a first night or something? I'm afraid I left the office later than I intended. Had to see a client for Dad and she went rabbiting on forever."

"That's OK darling, get here as soon as you can." Susan was by now trying to wriggle out of her trousers in a lavatory cubicle. "Anyway what are you doing dealing with your father's clients? Don't tell me he left early for once."

"Got it in one!" His secretary passed on a message simply saying he'd left, about half past two if you please and I'd no alternative but to see her. He'd tried to put her off but she couldn't manage any other day this week so I really didn't have a choice. All I can say is it's totally unlike Dad to behave like that."

"Did you ring him at home?" Sue shook out the dress that she'd carefully rolled up and put in her briefcase earlier.

"Sure. According to Zelda he arrived home in a furious temper, changed and went to the golf club. I called again before I left the office and got their answer phone."

"Well perhaps Zelda arranged something. You know what a frantic social life they lead. Sometimes I wonder if your father's really up to it any more."

"You and me both. Anyway I'll sort it out with him tomorrow. That's if he decides to show up of course."

"Your father may be many things but stupid he certainly isn't. I'm sure he'll be at the office with a perfectly satisfactory explanation." Susan was trying to do up her zip with one hand. "Look we'll talk about it when we meet. Right now I've got to dash. I'll see you later."

Susan switched off her mobile, finished zipping up her frock, crammed her suit into her briefcase and emerged with relief from the lavatory cubicle. Whilst she applied fresh lipstick she remembered her own father. She'd meant to ring him earlier but had gone from one job to another all day and simply run out of time. As she walked towards reception she thought back to last night. It hadn't been an unqualified success if she was really honest. At least her father liked curry so full marks to Ian for choosing it but half way through the meal he'd made the most alarming suggestion.

He'd led up to it in a devious way, pretending concern for the children growing up in London when they could be in the country. Then he'd gone on about the size of his house and how he had far too much space. Then suddenly he'd dropped his bombshell and asked them how they would feel about moving in with him. He'd talked about converting part of the house into a self-contained flat for himself and letting them have the rest. He'd painted a rosy picture for them saying that they would be able to release some of their capital and invest it elsewhere and done his damndest to make them think he was doing them a favour. Susan suspected that he was desperately lonely and she could foresee a life where he would be dropping in on them at all hours of the day and night.

They'd done their best to wriggle out of the offer, explaining about the problems of commuting to London every day from Esher and pointing out the importance of the children's education and not disrupting it unnecessarily. Bruce had listened to both of them but didn't really take on board anything they were saying and finally went to bed in a sulk. When she'd left the house this morning he hadn't put in an appearance and she guessed he was still in a mood. Oh well she'd just have to try and make it up to him sometime soon. Perhaps when Ian was away in France? Meanwhile she had some ready-mixed cocktails to launch. She spotted a bright pink jacket and a shop window full of bling and guessed that Gervase was about to make his entrance. She signalled to the photographer, pasted a smile on her face and went forward to make the necessary introductions.

An hour later she was trapped in a corner with the chairman of Yorkshire foods. He'd planted his enormous bulk in front of her and she knew it was going to be hard to escape. He helped himself to a fresh cocktail from a passing waiter. "These should go down a treat north of Watford." He lifted his glass slightly as he spoke but his eyes strayed towards Susan's cleavage. She raised her left arm and twiddled the earring in her right ear but then let her arm stay put. Her feet were killing her, she was hungry and the last thing she needed was some perv from 'oop north' trying to get into her knickers after a few free cocktails. "Glad you're enjoying them," she said. "Let me introduce you to the head of marketing. I'm sure he'll be willing to negotiate a discount on your first order."

"Done that already!" He flashed her what was meant to be a winning smile. His large teeth looked expensively capped. He'd also just closed the only escape route she could think of. She was casting around in her mind for someone else she could introduce him to when he said, "I only came along this evening because I met your father-in-law at the golf club. He happened to mention you were promoting this stuff." He waved his glass around.

"You know James?" Susan allowed herself to smile and dropped her left arm.

"Oh we go back a long way, he's sorted out many a legal tangle for me. Bright lawyer is our James. I could be out at do's like this every night if I wanted. There's always somebody trying to sell me something but James twisted my arm."

Well bully for James! Susan made a mental note to give James a call tomorrow and thank him. She had no idea that he was interested in what she did, certainly not enough to press-gang his pals into action. Which reminded her she hadn't yet seen Ian. Her eyes flicked quickly round the room until finally she spotted him standing near to the entrance, glass in hand, laughing down at a wraith-like blonde who looked about twenty and a size eight. She saw them both laugh and wondered what they found so funny. Perhaps the cocktails were responsible? If so she'd better get hold of some promotional samples and try them out on her father. She turned back to Mr Northern Foods, as she'd christened him in her mind, and flashed him a dazzling smile. If nothing else he might carry a good report back to James.

A few minutes later Ian made his way over, slipped an arm round Susan's waist and bent to kiss her cheek. Was it his imagination or did that cheek feel just a tad frigid? "Sorry to be so late darling. The traffic was unbelievable. I only got here about half an hour ago."

Susan chose not to acknowledge his apology. "Meet Arnold Thompson," she invited. "He's the chairman of Northern Foods and a dear old friend of your father."

"We play golf together. Pleased to meet you." Arnold Thompson took Ian's outstretched hand and shook it and Ian's arm up and down vigorously. For all the world as if he were pumping water, Ian thought.

"Well I'll leave you to mull over old times." Susan said brightly. "I've just spotted someone I must speak to before the evening's over. So nice to meet you," she said to Arnold Thompson. Then standing on tiptoe she kissed him warmly on the cheek. "I'm really pleased you came."

Ian tried to concentrate on Arnold Thompson but his mind was elsewhere. It was unlike Sue to be mad at him, particularly when she was in PR mode and he'd bothered to come along and support her. Perhaps she'd had a particularly hard day? Maybe she was more worried about her father than she'd let on last night? Christ almighty, his own day had been bad enough and he'd made a supreme effort to be here when he'd much rather be back at home with his feet up and a beer in his hand instead of this disgusting cocktail.

Arnold Thompson ran out of conversation at last and, as the room began to empty, Ian wandered across the floor leaving his half drunk cocktail on a convenient table. Sue was near the exit shaking hands, occasionally kissing, the guests as they left. He waited until she was alone before joining her. "Looks like another success." He smiled cautiously. Susan shrugged. "Hard to say at this stage. We've taken lots of orders but ultimately its down to the punters. Right now I'm starving. I've been promoting those bloody cocktails all evening and never managed to get near to the food."

Ian seized the opportunity. "Why don't we grab a quick bite on the way home and you can tell me all about it."

"Have you forgotten Father? I haven't seen him all day. We really should get back." She looked defeated, worried, not at all like someone at the end of a successful evening.

"Your father's going to be mad at us whatever we do. Personally I can face up to him better if my stomach isn't rumbling. I haven't eaten either. Most of the food disappeared before I arrived." It wouldn't do any harm to let her know she wasn't the only one who was hungry.

"OK but we'll have to make it snappy. Who was your friend by the way?"

"You mean Arnold? He's more a friend of Dad. *I* don't have time to play golf."

"I wasn't thinking about Arnold but the blonde nymphette I saw you talking to earlier."

Ian assumed a puzzled expression. "Blonde? Nymphette? Not many of those around this evening."

"Bright red dress, mouth to match."

Realisation dawned. He'd better play it cool. "Oh, just some minor journo., from the Grocer or some such. Don't remember her name." His fingers closed over the card in his pocket which Sonia had given him earlier. He put his arm around Susan's shoulders and steered her towards the door, stroking her bare arm as they walked. "I really talked up your old cocktails you know. I'll be surprised if there isn't at least a full page spread in the Grocer next week.

"Well thanks." Susan's voice still had an edge to it, he'd have to try a bit harder. They'd almost reached the car park when he pulled her into a doorway, slid his hands around her bottom and gave her the benefit of his years of experience as James' son. He felt her body relax at last against him and knew he was on his way.

"'Fraid I'm still hungry," she said at last.

"Then let's go eat." Ian took her hand and they ran towards the car. He opened the door for her and closed it carefully before walking round to his own side. Before he got into the driving seat he screwed up Sonia's card and dropped it into the car park, wondering as he did so how his father had managed his many infidelities for all those years.

Chapter Five

The owner of the shop was charming; offering to package the glasses and send them to England, relieving Isobel of the responsibility for finding space in her luggage and worrying about the possibility of breakages on the flight home. His charm certainly didn't come cheaply Isobel thought as she signed her credit card slip, slightly uneasy at the number of noughts after the lire sign. Ian had telephoned just before she left home asking if by any chance she should find herself in Murano could she pick up some claret glasses to match the champagne flutes that he and Sue had bought on a previous trip. He'd supplied a reference number for the glasses and the name and address of the shop but was vague about the location. It was typical of Ian to be precise about his own needs, vague about anyone else's and she wandered for some time along the narrow *fondamenta* gazing into window after window in search of the shop. She was about to give up when she finally found it and, with considerable relief, carried out her commission.

Now, sitting in the open air, she sipped cool white wine, lifted her face to the sun and thought of Rupert as she waited for her lunch to arrive. At the moment he seemed to take over her thoughts whenever she was alone and unoccupied. So far he'd transformed what promised to be a pleasant holiday into something very special. His physical attraction helped she had to admit but he had other qualities like courtesy and good manners which lifted him higher in her esteem.

Last night he'd taken her to dinner in a small *trattoria* tucked away in a quiet street close to the Accademia Bridge. The entrance was so unprepossessing that a casual passer-by wouldn't have recognised it as a restaurant but, walking through a dimly lit lobby, they entered a charming marble-floored dining room with about a dozen tables. The glass roof was shaded by an ancient vine which filtered the light, turning it to a cool green. The candlelit tables were covered in sparkling white damask and the whole place exuded an air of understated elegance.

"I don't think the dreaded Barbara will know about this place." Rupert said with the faintest of smiles as they sat down.

"I sincerely hope not!" Isobel replied with feeling.

As the evening progressed she persuaded Rupert to talk about himself and discovered that his mother was Italian. That would explain his fluency in the language. His elder brother Miles, an art historian, was also married to an Italian, Gianna and they lived in Rome. When she asked Rupert whether or not he had children his face clouded over. He was silent for a moment then replied with a deep sigh. "Oh yes, I have a daughter Tory - her abbreviation of Victoria - last heard of in Paris about six months ago."

Isobel was afraid that she'd inadvertently strayed into forbidden territory and continued in a rush. "Tell me to shut up and mind my own business if you'd rather not talk about her."

"What an admission for a father to make." Rupert's voice was rueful and he stroked the scar on his left eyebrow with a finger tip as he spoke. "I find it painful to talk about her because, like many parents, I had great ambitions for her and sadly they haven't been realised."

"Don't we have to forget what our ambitions are and allow our children to develop and build their own lives?" Isobel queried, hoping that he wasn't about to reveal himself as a tyrannical father with hopelessly high expectations for his daughter.

"I couldn't agree more. But for some reason Tory seems to go out of her way to shock, to do anything unconventional. If it were simply a matter of teenage rebellion I could accept it but she's thirty now and I think it's time she grew up."

Isobel listened, her head inclined sympathetically, as Rupert skated over the story. "Expelled from school in the sixth form for smoking pot; refusing to study for 'A' levels therefore forfeiting a university place; leaving home to live in a squat with a group of middle class junkies whose motto was 'screw the Establishment'; a series of short-lived jobs." Rupert left it there saying, "I take it you get the picture?"

Isobel, watching his face darken as he spoke, was aware that she'd stirred up unwelcome memories and thought how fragile were the relationships between parents and children. She remembered vividly the day her father came back from the war. She was two years old when he left and, although he'd been home on leave from time-to-time, for an eight year old girl it was still like having a stranger in the house. He'd worked really hard to get to know her again and then it hadn't been the easiest of relationships. After living in almost exclusively male company for six years it had been difficult for him to settle down again to civilian life with only his wife and small daughter for company in the evenings. There was no post-traumatic stress counselling in those days. The situation wasn't helped by her mother's anger at having to quit her job to make room for the men coming back from the war and needing employment. She'd found it hard to give up her independence and to be financially reliant on her husband. Isobel cowered under the bedclothes night after night, her hands pressed tightly over her ears, unable to sleep as her parents shouted at each other; trying to live together again after their long, enforced separation.

She could only begin to guess at the kind of scenes that might have taken place between Tory and her parents and felt it might be tactful to try and change the subject. They moved on to other topics and discovered a mutual interest in classical music. Rupert explained that he must work during today but offered to take her to a concert this evening at the Scuola di San Rocco. "I can promise you a visual treat as well as an aural one," he said.

Unlike concerts in England this one started at nine o'clock in the evening which would leave time for an early dinner. Isobel hadn't been to a concert in years. It was hard to book weeks in advance when you never knew what time your working day would end and she was really looking forward to this evening. Every moment she spent with Rupert she found stimulating and exciting, better even than the early days of her relationship with James. Although Rupert didn't always agree with her he never tried to bulldoze her into changing her opinions and she appreciated that. He always listened carefully to what she had to say and, when he'd taken her hands yesterday, her pulse had speeded up alarmingly and she'd realised suddenly how long it had been since anyone had touched her intimately.

Rupert mentioned that he would be short of time and asked if she would mind a short journey to San Tomà, promising to wait for her at the *vaporetto* stop. Arriving back at the hotel at the end of the afternoon she sank gratefully into a hot bath and agonised about what to wear. She was desperate to look as stunning as possible, She'd heard Steven talk about 'Eye Candy' on several occasions although normally with reference to much younger women. If only she were thirty five again, or forty five would do at a pinch. But to be sixty and trying to tart up like a teenager on a first date. Well . . .

Even so she took great care and chose a brilliant emerald green dress which went well with her blonde highlights. On an impulse in Murano she'd bought a long bead necklace of lapis lazuli blue and she hung it around her neck, together with an antique gold chain which had previously belonged to her grandmother. Her excitement grew as she got ready and she almost ran towards the *vaporetto* stop in her eagerness to see Rupert again.

She caught sight of him waiting for her as they approached San Tomà and the butterflies which had been fluttering wildly in her stomach began to fly in a more orderly formation and were completely quiet once she and Rupert were seated at a table under a tree in a small square.

"So how was your day?" Rupert asked, handing her the menu.

"Oh wonderful! I went first to Murano and spent a lot of money and then on to Torcello where I spent nothing at all."

"I'm glad to have missed Murano although I do occasionally go across to a particular factory if a client wants a chandelier."

"I hate to think of the cost. The glasses I bought were expensive enough." She leaned towards him eagerly as she continued.

"I really missed your encyclopaedic knowledge today. The interior of the cathedral in Torcello was wonderful. I loved the mosaics and that amazing statue of Christ on the cross high above the altar looked stunning against the gilded dome of the ceiling. What really intrigued me was a relief of a mother and daughter that I saw on the wall just as I got off the boat."

"Oh you're going to love this!" Rupert's eyes twinkled even more than usual. "It was your old friend Ruskin who first referred to Venice and Torcello as mother and daughter. Surprisingly Torcello was the mother and the island was inhabited long before Venice. Twenty thousand people lived there originally and now there are only about a hundred. When the canals in Torcello began to silt up there was an outbreak of malaria and gradually people left."

"I knew you'd fill in the details for me." Isobel smiled her gratitude. "Now tell me about the mosaics."

"Well," Rupert tried hard not to look flattered by her belief in his erudition. "Expert opinion says they're the best in Italy outside Ravenna. They're Byzantine, about twelfth century, like the cathedral, but I expect you found that out already? The subject matter's rather grisly don't you think? All those sinners being despatched to hell. But the black-robed Madonna compensates, she really dominates her space. Do you agree?"

It was easy for Isobel to go along with his opinions and it was an added bonus that they coincided with her own. "Now tell me about the concert," she said. "Last night you promised a visual as well as an aural treat. Will you give me a clue as to what it might be? I promise you I didn't have time to look it up."

"I'd rather keep it as a surprise if you don't mind but I will whet your appetite. I'm sure you'll be glad to hear that Ruskin reckoned the paintings in San Rocco helped to make it one of the three most precious buildings in the world on a par with the Sistine Chapel and the Campo Santa of Pisa. You see how determined I am to convert you to Ruskin?" he added. His smile made her heart flip over.

When they'd finished eating she persuaded him to let her pay for dinner for a change and they walked the short distance to San Rocco. On the way Rupert explained that they were going to hear a young chamber orchestra who were giving a series of concerts in the city until the end of the year. Several historic violins had been lent for the series, by a variety of musical museums, for the soloists at each performance to use. She would hear Italian music played on wonderful instruments in one of the most beautiful buildings in Venice.

Isobel couldn't believe that so many wonderful experiences were being handed to her and, although not religious, sent a short, silent prayer of gratitude to anyone who might be listening. But as she entered the building, she was totally unprepared for the sight that met her eyes. The unbelievable grandeur of the room, the soaring columns and a series of huge Tintoretto canvasses ranged round the room depicting the days before the birth of Christ. The figures made more potent by the flashes of dazzling light which almost eclipsed them. She gasped with the sheer surprise of it all and clutched Rupert's arm in her enthusiasm as she tried to take it all in.

The physical contact with her was like an electric shock and Rupert, wanting to prolong it, tucked her arm more firmly under his own. They had ten minutes to spare before the concert began. He walked her briefly round the hall so that she could see all the paintings pointing out Tintoretto's love of violent movement and his use of artificial light and unreal colours to enhance the spiritual content of his work.

"I never expected to agree so wholeheartedly with Ruskin," Isobel said as they took their seats, "but the paintings are so beautifully lit they seem to glow. You certainly succeeded in surprising me." Rupert silently congratulated himself and handed her the programme watching her as she scanned it. "Oh look!" she said, pointing to the final work, "A piece by Allessandro Marcello, his Concerto in D minor for oboe. It's one of my favourite pieces. The second movement is one of the most moving pieces of music I've ever heard."

"I don't think I know it," Rupert replied, beginning to clap as the conductor appeared. It seemed appropriate somehow to be hearing a new piece of music at the beginning of a relationship. Life was rarely so accommodating.

The orchestra played for an hour and then went off for a short break. Rupert leaned towards Isobel and whispered, "Come and see the second part of my surprise." He led the way to a wide, sweeping staircase half way down the room. Many members of the audience were already in front of them. As they reached the upper hall Isobel stood quite still and stared in astonishment. Both the magnificently gilded ceiling and the walls were covered in still more paintings by Tintoretto and the effect was even more dramatic than the downstairs room. Rupert picked up a hand mirror and gave it to her so that she could look at the ceiling without getting a crick in her neck and watched her closely as she moved the mirror to and fro.

"These paintings had a profound effect on Ruskin and helped him to make up his mind to study Venetian history." Rupert said.

"It took twenty three years to paint those sixty canvasses. They've recently been restored which explains why they look so stunning. Whenever I look at them I feel I'm not looking at mere painting but at the work of a man who poured his soul onto canvas."

"They're overpowering, absolutely stupendous." Isobel said, her eyes shining with excitement.

They returned to their seats and as the first scintillating notes of the oboe floated into the air, Rupert closed his eyes so that he could concentrate completely. As the second movement began his mind went back to his old home in England on the evening Liz died. He heard again Tory's voice, using unbelievable language, shouting at him for not telling her sooner that her mother was ill. By the time Tory reached her mother's bedside Liz was barely conscious. He'd taken the coward's way out telling her he'd expected Liz to recover, unable to admit that he'd tried to spare Liz from any encounter with Tory's volatile temper at a time when she needed all her energy to fight her illness. When, after listening to her outburst and wincing at the language, he'd asked Tory to forgive him she'd well and truly lost it. She picked up a heavy crystal vase and threw it at him. Fortunately for him her aim was as wild as her temper and the vase shattered in the fireplace. The force of the impact sent shards of glass flying in all directions. Luckily the splinter caught his eyebrow, a few centimetres lower . . .

He opened his eyes as the second movement ended and glanced down at Isobel just in time to see her wiping away a tear. He took her hand and held it tightly until the last notes of the concerto climaxed in a display of virtuosic brilliance. She'd opened a door for him. If she hadn't drawn attention to the piece he probably wouldn't have listened to it quite so carefully.

"That was a truly wonderful evening." Isobel said when the applause finally died away and they turned to leave. Her eyes were shining and her face radiated pleasure.

Rupert tried unsuccessfully to speak, cleared his throat and tried again, this time with more success. Glancing quickly at his watch he said, "I'm really glad you enjoyed it; it's always good to hear talented, young musicians. I see it's eleven o'clock already but we should be able to find a cup of coffee and then I'll walk you back."

It should have been the most natural thing in the world to invite him into the hotel on the pretext of offering him a nightcap. In a larger, more impersonal establishment they would simply merge with the crowd. In a tiny place like the San Antonio it was impossible to go either in or out without meeting a member of the family on duty behind the reception desk and Isobel just couldn't do it. She kissed Rupert briefly on the cheek as they parted, thanked him again for a perfect evening and went up to her room.

She couldn't sleep. Her mind was whirling and every one of her senses was in a high state of arousal. She felt again the smoothness of Rupert's cheek, the faint scent of his aftershave as she'd kissed him. How had she found the courage? He hadn't kissed her back, even though he'd taken her hand earlier and before that tucked her arm through his own. Isobel had fended off a few marauding males since her divorce and Rupert's restraint made him infinitely more desirable. The briefest contact with him acted in the same way as an *apéritif* and she realised with a sudden shock that she badly wanted the rest of the meal!

He'd told her over coffee that he would be working again to morrow. He and Giovanni were going to check on their development in Chioggia and he expected to be tied up for most of the day. And then, out of the blue, he'd invited her to his apartment for supper.

Arriving back in her room she'd first hugged herself with joy and then started to panic at the thought of being alone with him. Would she be able to deal with it? She reasoned that he wouldn't have invited her if he didn't want her company and he would have to handle the situation as well. Then she became angry. Told herself to grow up and act her age and then, almost immediately said, "No! No! No! I don't want to behave like a sixty year old. I'm a pensioner for God's sake and old age pensioners don't get themselves invited to supper by men they scarcely know! They putter down to the supermarket with their shopping trolleys and sit down in the afternoon to watch 'Countdown'!"

She tossed and turned and read several pages of her book without taking in any of the text. Finally she admitted to herself that she wanted this man. Now; tomorrow; forever. She'd spent fewer than three whole days in his company but that was enough. What would her children say? "Don't go down that road Isobel." she said aloud, her mind still ringing with their warnings to 'Look out for Casanova when you're exploring all those mysterious alleys!' She picked up her guidebook and took out the piece of paper on which he'd scribbled directions, was it really only five days ago? She stared hard at his scrawling instructions, wanting the writing to speak to her then impulsively she tucked it under her pillow and finally she slept.

Rupert walked back to his apartment deep in thought. When he reached his front door he realised that he was whistling the second movement of the Marcello concerto and felt an unaccustomed peace as he let himself in.

In spite of her restless night Isobel woke early and decided to go to St Mark's Basilica. After that she would visit the Doge's Palace, find somewhere for lunch, perhaps do some shopping. She had twelve hours to fill before she met Rupert again and she was determined to spend them constructively not just mooning about looking at her watch every half hour. She'd been so busy since she arrived she hadn't sent a single postcard so perhaps she'd try to do that as well. At least she could write 'Having a wonderful time' and really mean it.

By four o'clock, she'd finished her sightseeing and looked around for a suitable place to buy tea and sit and write her postcards. The window of a hairdressing salon caught her eye and, without hesitating, she went inside wanting desperately to look her best for this evening. An hour and a half later she still hadn't written a single card but, thanks to a personable young man called Paulo, her hair had been transformed. She felt light-headed, happy with life and in the mood to spend money. She walked across St Mark's Square to Florian's and ordered an ice cream. She sat outside enjoying the late afternoon sun and, at last, began to write her cards telling everyone that she was eating ice cream in what had once been a favourite haunt of Casanova. She made a point of underlining Casanova on her cards to Ian and Steve.

In the end she was short of time and had to rush back to her hotel to change before the short walk to Rupert's apartment. Her heart was thudding as she followed the signs to the Rialto Bridge. On the way she passed a small, exclusive florist and bought an armful of lilies. It was ten minutes past eight when she finally rang the bell and, as she waited for him to answer, she pushed her nose into the bouquet, breathing deeply and trying to slow her heartbeat. She'd been expecting to hear his voice over the intercom and was surprised when the door opened and another scent drifted out onto the evening air, Rupert's scent. She looked up in surprise but managed a smile as she offered him the lilies and apologised for being late.

Rupert was touched. No one had given him flowers before, not even Liz. He bent to kiss her cheek, the merest graze, completely unaware of the effect this had on Isobel. She had pollen on the end of her nose but he felt that to mention it might embarrass her. "Welcome," he said, leading the way, and then, "Let me get you a drink." He poured wine from a bottle on a side table and handed her a slender glass flute. "I hope you like this. I pinched the recipe from Harry's Bar. It's a mixture of peach juice and fizzy white wine, although some people insist on using champagne. Now may I leave you for a minute? I must go and put these lovely flowers in water."

Isobel sank gratefully onto a large squashy sofa and took advantage of Rupert's absence to look around. He'd described the apartment as modest but the room was about forty feet long with floor to ceiling windows on two sides. It was furnished sparely but with choice pieces. The colours were muted: cream, beige, russet, the only exception a large Kelim rug which covered the mellow parquet floor between the two sofas. Although it was still daylight the room was bathed in a soft glow from several lamps. There was no Venetian glass chandelier so, although he chose them for some of his clients, he preferred not to make them part of his own décor.

"What a lovely room!" she exclaimed as Rupert returned carrying her flowers. He'd put them in a plain, tall, rectangular vase made from what looked like very expensive glass. He placed them carefully on a polished, mahogany chest by one of the windows. The lilies were reflected in its surface and their perfume drifted into the room.

"I'm glad you like it. This used to be a *palazzo* but the whole place has now been converted into apartments. They're normally let to tourists but Giovanni did the conversion and pulled a lot of complicated strings to allow me to buy one. Italian property laws can be very involved. If, as in this case, the place is jointly owned by several members of one family, everyone has to agree before the sale can go ahead. Giovanni convinced them that the capital I put up for the purchase would pay for converting the rest of the property. After that, as you can imagine, it was plain sailing." He refilled her glass and handed her a dish of olives before sitting down beside her.

Isobel wasn't ready for his closeness and scrabbled about in her mind for a diversion. "It's a great treat for me to have someone prepare dinner. Is there anything I can do to help?" she asked. "After all you've been working all day, I've simply been enjoying myself." The words came out in a rush.

"Well to be honest we're having a few problems with these houses in Chioggia and I arrived home later than I expected so perhaps we'll go into the kitchen in a moment and see what still has to be done." He'd been rushing around for most of the day and was in no hurry to move.

But he'd given Isobel the lead she needed and she jumped to her feet immediately. "I'm used to drinking and preparing food at the same time, just lead the way!" she said. Rupert rose to his feet reluctantly.

His kitchen was spacious, austere, tidy. An old oak refectory table provided the only mellow touch. The rest was all pristine work surfaces with a very modern cooker. A man's workshop rather than the usual domestic space. There was an appetising smell in the air. Isobel wrinkled her nose appreciatively.

"Supper smells good."

"*Ossobuco,* hope you like it."

"It's ages since I had it. I know I'll enjoy it."

"Could you make a salad?" He pointed to an outsize chopping board, a collection of leaves and salad vegetables and a large teak bowl before passing her a striped butcher's apron. To Isobel's relief he didn't offer to tie it on for her.

He filled her glass for a third time and when she protested he said, "It's little more than fruit juice and anyway you don't have to drive home." Isobel laughed a trifle nervously, wondering if she'd be able to stay sober for the rest of the evening and then almost immediately thought that sobriety was the last thing she wanted. She began to make the salad.

"It's still warm enough to eat outside I think. Is that OK by you?" he asked.

"Fine. You have a garden?"

"Well it's little more than a patio although this is supposed to be the garden flat. Of course I'm lucky to have that in a city like Venice where garden space is at a premium. It does overlook the Grand Canal so the view is memorable." He stirred the *Ossobuco.* "This will look after itself while we have our first course. Shall we go?"

He led the way back through the sitting room and opened a window. They stepped onto a square, balustraded terrace, where a table was laid. Although there was an outside light Rupert lit two glass-shaded candles and pulled out a chair for her before placing a large dish of prawns, a bowl of mayonnaise and some slices of *focaccia* bread in front of her. "I'm afraid this is a do-it-yourself starter," he apologised. "I bought the prawns in Chioggia, so I know they're fresh but I cheated and got the mayonnaise ready made."

"You make it all sound so easy."

"It is if you want it to be. My mother was a superb cook and taught me how to look after myself. Nowadays, like so many other busy people, I make the most of convenience foods. Mama would have made that mayonnaise herself. She used to persuade me to dribble in the oil in the days before food processors."

Is there no end to his talents? Isobel wondered as she broke off the head of a prawn, peeled off the shell, dunked the flesh in mayonnaise, pressed it between her tongue and the roof of her mouth. Aloud she said, "My grandchildren would describe this as yummy! I'll never buy frozen prawns again. I'll swear I can taste the sea." She heard her mother's voice briefly and wished she could stop herself from gushing.

The *Ossobuco* was memorable. She could taste lemon zest, the slight saltiness of anchovies, a faint hint of garlic. When they'd finished she sat back and sighed contentedly. "Your mother must have been an inspired cook if she taught you to prepare food like this." Rupert shrugged modestly whilst smiling his pleasure at the compliment. He went off to make coffee, refusing her offer of help.

Isobel walked across to the balustrade and looked out over the Grand Canal. Streaks of red from the setting sun bled into the sky before falling into the water. There were a couple of gondolas, an isolated motor launch, the ever present *vaporetto*. She closed her eyes and sniffed the air which smelt of saline and the green weed which clung to the base of the wall. She could hear the gentle lap of water against the landing stage below as she waited for Rupert to bring their coffee.

Chapter Six

James went into his office as usual on Wednesday but after talking to clients throughout the day he was certain it was the last place he wanted to be. His sister's phone call had unsettled him and whenever he tried to get his mind round a legal problem visions of Isobel swam into his head interfering with his judgement and keeping him from an objective appraisal. He felt like beating up any man who'd ever strayed outside marriage, conveniently forgetting his own colourful track record. In the past he'd always been sympathetic towards any woman who asked his advice before petitioning for divorce. Now he viewed them in a different light and wondered what they might have done to precipitate the breakdown in the relationship.

Acting uncharacteristically on impulse he decided to take a few days off and start the work to turn his patio into a terrace. He wanted it all finished before the weather turned colder and aimed to have it completed by the end of October at the latest. Hard physical exercise was exactly what he needed to take his mind off Isobel and a short period away from the office and other people's marital crises would, he was sure, help to restore his judgement to its previous impartiality. He'd offered Fred, his gardener, some overtime as an inducement to come in and help and together they'd spent Thursday morning preparing the foundations.

James worked frenziedly, visualising bits of Rupert Northcote that he would like to chop off every time his spade hit the soil. He wondered as he worked what the bloody man was currently doing to Isobel. When he'd walked out of his marriage he'd never thought ahead to the day when someone else might take his place. In fact for the past five years he'd scarcely given her a second thought. But now that someone else was interested it was a different matter and it irked him to think what he might be missing.

He took only half an hour for lunch, just long enough to have a bowl of soup and a sandwich. He told Zelda that he and Fred would carry on working until the light faded and asked her to bring them out some tea at around three o'clock. He found it supremely satisfying after all his efforts to sit in the autumn sunshine drinking his tea and looking over their progress and thought that in many ways manual work was so much more satisfying than spending the day behind a desk listening sympathetically to the problems of his clients.

He tried to imagine what the terrace would look like once it was finished and wondered whether or not to make a hollow wall, fill it with soil and perhaps plant geraniums. Bright red would cheer things up in the summer. But quite suddenly he realised how tired he felt and there was a rather worrying pain in his back, just below his right shoulder blade. He told himself that it would probably go away once he got under the shower after they finished work for the day at the same time acknowledging that it would be hard to continue at his present pace if the pain continued.

The pain grew worse as the afternoon wore on. James did his very best to ignore it but by five o'clock it had moved to the middle of his chest. Suddenly he was frightened. "I think I'm going to knock off for a while," he said to Fred and went in search of Zelda. He stopped at the back door to take off his boots and just couldn't summon enough strength. He sat down heavily on the doorstep telling himself he would feel better in a few minutes. Fifteen minutes later he was still sitting there when Samantha ran up to him calling, "Daddy! Daddy! Pretty flowers!" She was carrying a small basket in her hand which was filled with an assortment of flower heads picked at random from the herbaceous border.

James pulled himself up with difficulty and opened the back door. "Do you think you can be a very grown up girl and fetch Mummy for me?" he asked. Samantha looked at him steadily for a few seconds then nodded her head solemnly several times before running indoors. James resumed his seat on the step. The minutes ticked slowly by. His backside was growing numb from sitting on the cold stone. Just when he was beginning to think that Samantha had forgotten her errand, or failed in some way to make Zelda understand, the pair of them appeared, Samantha dragging Zelda by the hand.

He looked up and did his best to smile. How he hated dependency! "Sorry to be a nuisance," he said, "but do you think you could help me off with my boots?"

Zelda knelt in front of him and saw the fear in his eyes as he clutched his chest with both hands. She pulled at his boots, took them off and kicked them to one side before putting one of his arms around her neck and doing her best to lift him to his feet. All of James' thirteen stone rested on her shoulder and she had to brace every muscle to get both of them into a standing position. She'd never in her wildest dreams anticipated that her weekly workouts at the gym would ever be of use to James. "Don't hurry," she said, "just take it gently, we'll soon make you comfortable." She managed to get them both to the drawing room and helped James into an easy chair. "Don't even think about moving," she warned him. "I'm going to ring the doctor and then I'll make you a nice hot cup of tea." James, for once in his life, didn't argue.

An hour later he was admitted to the Royal Brompton Hospital and placed in intensive care. Doctor Carstairs, whose advice James had been ignoring for several months, explained very patiently to Zelda that James should look at his heart attack as a warning and take life more easily in future.

She was scarcely conscious of his words. Her world had been turned upside down in the space of an afternoon. Later she remembered snatches of sentences from her conversation with him. ". . . man of his age; too much good living . . .; . . . Not a good idea to burn the candle in the middle as well as both ends; . . .stress of running a business nowadays."

The only thing that gave her any hope at all was the indisputable fact that James was still alive. She couldn't bear to think what her own life would become without him. Her marriage gave her status, financial security and regular, if not always satisfactory, sex. She had no idea what her future would be like if, dear God it didn't bear thinking about, if the worst should happen. A fleeting image of her parents modest three bedroom semi in Harlow flashed into her mind. At the same time she remembered her mother telling her what a risk she was taking marrying a man 'old enough to be her father'. She closed her eyes tightly and willed the memories to go away. Please God, she prayed, as she walked out of the hospital and pulled out her mobile phone to call Ian. Please God let him survive.

When Rupert returned with the coffee Isobel was still leaning on the balustrade.

"You're so lucky," she called across to him. "This view is unbelievable."

"Glad you approve." He placed the tray on the table, crossed the terrace and stood behind her, waiting. At last she straightened slowly as if reluctant to move away. Rupert put his arms around her shoulders, holding her against him. Neither of them spoke but stood quietly for several seconds until Isobel turned towards him still in the circle of his arms. He kissed her slowly, gently, needing time to gauge her response, knowing instinctively that a wrong move at this stage would frighten her away. They stayed there for several minutes in the dying light of a perfect evening before moving towards the table, his arm still around her shoulders.

"Come and have some coffee, before it gets cold," he said, swallowing the lump in his throat. "Would you like to go in or shall we stay out here?" Isobel chose to stay put and settled herself in her chair in the fading light.

She poured coffee for them and then took him completely by surprise. Leaning towards him she held his hand and said, "Are you going to ask me to stay?"

"Isobel, are you absolutely sure that's what you want?" He tried to keep his voice steady. "I wouldn't like you to do anything this evening that you might regret tomorrow."

"I've never been more certain about anything."

"Then I'll go and phone your hotel before you change your mind." His pulse raced as he walked towards the telephone, spoke briefly into the instrument and returned to the terrace.

"That's settled then." He smiled across at her as he sat down and poured more coffee. "I must admit you've really surprised me."

"Not nearly as much as I've surprised myself. You may find it hard to believe but, after I left you last night, I tried to talk myself out of coming this evening."

"I'm glad you didn't succeed. What changed your mind?"

"My mind didn't really need changing. What I had to do was forget about the conventions which ruled when women like me were brought up."

"You mean nice girls don't even if they want to?"

"Precisely." She laughed. "Inevitably there comes a time when there's an argument between convention and intuition."

"And last night intuition won?"

"Exactly."

"Well I must say I'm delighted it did."

It was easier for both of them to talk now that the tension had been broken. Isobel confided that the last few days had been some of the happiest she'd spent, ever. Rupert told her that sharing bits of Venice with her had been a pleasure. He was only sorry his work had taken up so much of his time. They were both delaying, looking forward. Finally Rupert said, "Do you realise the first part of you that I saw properly was your foot when I bent down to pick up your guidebook?"

"Oh dear! Not the most auspicious beginning was it?" Isobel laughed.

"I disagree. You have a beautiful foot." He bent down, took off her sandal and kissed her toes, one at a time. As he looked up she took his face in both her hands. "What a lovely man you are."

"I've been called many things but 'lovely' isn't an adjective that is normally used when referring to me. Thank you." He rose to his feet, pulled her towards him and kissed her again, much less gently than before; then picked up one of the candles from the table and led the way through the sitting room and across the wide entrance hall. He opened a door on the opposite side. "I always said it was a modest apartment," he said. "There's only one bedroom so I can't offer you a choice." He placed the candle carefully on the small bedside table.

"Somehow," said Isobel, and he heard the smile in her voice, "somehow, I don't think the location is going to be all that important."

Rupert took his time, wanting to help her forget whatever James had done to her that had resulted in their divorce. The whole night lay ahead of them. He knew instinctively it would be special. Although he felt relaxed and in control he was trembling below the surface realising suddenly that it had been many years since his last 'first night'. He hoped to God he wouldn't fall victim to first night nerves! Isobel's skin felt like silk under his fingers and the close proximity of a woman to whom he was attracted made him feel slightly dizzy after two years of total abstinence.

The intensity of her response surprised him. Although physically attractive he wouldn't have described her as sexy, although she had warmth and enthusiasm which he'd seen repeatedly during the short time they'd spent together. He was totally unprepared for the passion she unleashed which, although flattering to him, was, at a deeper level disturbing. For a few moments he'd imagined he was making love to Liz and the sudden realisation completely shook his equilibrium.

Isobel was the first to speak. "Thank you is an understatement but, thanks to you, I feel like a woman again."

"It's been a long time for me Isobel." Rupert replied.

"For me too, I promise. Not since James in fact."

"Believe me I'm very honoured." He kissed the corner of her mouth.

Isobel's emotions were mixed as she lay in the circle of Rupert's arms. It had never, ever, been like this with James. Rupert had taken such care to please her, talked to her, shown her exquisite tenderness and yet she was unsure of the degree of his involvement. It was difficult to gauge his response. One thing she did know, she hadn't imagined the trembling. So what did that mean? Surely he wasn't nervous? Perhaps he was simply taking advantage of the fact that she'd offered herself? Did that matter? She heard her mother's voice again in her head warning her not to make herself cheap and dismissed the thought quickly before it could take hold and ruin what had, after all, been a beautiful evening. Of one thing she was quite certain that in her present state of arousal she wouldn't be able to sleep. "What I'd really like now is a hot shower," she said getting out of bed and shivering slightly as she felt the cool air on her skin.

"You'll find the bathroom just behind that door in the corner," Rupert said lazily, switching on the bedside light and blowing out the candle. "Use my bathrobe and help yourself to anything you need."

Isobel went into the bathroom and found the robe which smelt satisfyingly of Rupert. She snuggled gratefully into it as she put it around her shoulders inhaling his scent at the same time. Other people's bathrooms had always intrigued her. Was it that they contained the most intimate of the owner's possessions or simply that their state of cleanliness and tidiness gave a true indication of the owner's personality?

Rupert's bathroom gleamed. The spotless terrazzo floor was cold against her bare feet. A large glass walled shower cabinet invited her from the far corner. A marble shelf held an assortment of deep blue glass bottles, from Murano she guessed. The same blue was echoed in the tiles which made a border round the room. The only softness was provided by a thick cotton rug by the side of the bath. A bottle of after-shave stood in the deep window recess behind the washbasin. Isobel sniffed it. 'CK' by Calvin Klein. Ah so that was it! That was one fragrance that she would always remember.

The night air was chilly and she took off the robe reluctantly, placed it carefully over a chair, stepped into the shower, adjusted the temperature control and tried to turn on the water. She struggled for several seconds and finally admitted defeat. Feeling unusually feeble she put the bathrobe on again and went in search of Rupert who was in the kitchen making more coffee.

He was wearing a short, blue silk dressing gown. Isobel paused long enough to admire his legs which were slim, brown and muscular. His feet she noticed were bare, highly arched and he was standing on the outside edges to minimise contact with the cold floor. She felt her cheeks grow warm as she recalled how he had kissed her toes, then brought herself back with difficulty to immediate practicalities.

"Sorry Rupert but my strength seems to have deserted me. I'm afraid I can't turn the shower on."

"Ah. It does have a tendency to stick. Let's see if I can sort it out."

He led the way back to the bathroom, took off his dressing gown, went into the shower cabinet and, after a brief struggle with the tap, succeeded in turning on the water. Isobel, her gaze averted from the unaccustomed sight of a naked male body, stood waiting for him to come out. Instead he opened the door. "Why don't you come and join me?" he invited, "Much more fun than showering on your own."

She hesitated for a brief moment before taking off his bathrobe for the second time and stepping into his outstretched arms. The water had warmed up by this time and the cabinet was hot and steamy. Rupert unhooked the shower head and sprayed her gently, gave her a bottle of bath essence, held out a large, natural sponge.

"Sorry, only two hands, will you help me?" His right eyebrow was lifted, his head tilted slightly to the left. Now it was Isobel's turn to tremble as she closed her eyes and clung to him. Finally she took the sponge from him.

"My turn now." she said.

When he finally turned off the shower she said, "Believe me Rupert, that was a first."

He kissed her shoulder. "That husband of yours will never know what he missed. Hang on, I'll get a towel." He stepped out of the shower, grabbed a large, thick bath towel, put it round her shoulders, held her against him, kissed the top of her head. She drew her instep over his ankle, his calf, the back of his knee. He held her slightly away from him, lifted her chin, raised his right eyebrow.

"Yes?"

"Oh definitely."

The rug on the bathroom floor was so thick that neither of them felt the hardness of the terrazzo floor.

By the time she got up the next morning Rupert had already been out to buy fresh rolls. She found him in the kitchen again making coffee.

"Ah! *Buon giorno*!" he said as she appeared.

"Buon giorno! Are you always this cheerful so early in the morning?"

"Only after the more *memorable* evenings! Coffee, or would you prefer tea?"

"Coffee's fine. Thank you. Do you have to go to Chioggia today?"

"'Fraid so. We have a problem with the government planning officer who keeps on changing his mind about what's acceptable and what isn't."

"Can he do that?" Isobel asked.

"Oh yes! We shall have to offer him a bribe of course which is what it's really all about. I hate the system as much as anybody but if these apartments aren't ready on time we have a penalty clause in our contract which will halve our profit. There really isn't an alternative."

Isobel buttered a piece of roll and wondered why she never bothered to go out and buy them freshly baked in England. She tried as she ate to equate this brisk and businesslike architect with the man with whom she'd just spent the night and wondered about what other facets there were to his character. It seemed to her that all his mental energy was already focussed on business. She watched him as he unplugged his mobile phone, stuffed it into his briefcase and scribbled a note, explaining; "This is for my daily help. Without her my life would be so much more complicated. As you can see she keeps the place immaculately clean."

"Heavens!" said Isobel, "What time does she arrive?"

"Don't worry you've got masses of time." Rupert covered her hand briefly with his own, reassuring her slightly. "Maria won't be here until ten o'clock. She takes her children to school before coming to me." Isobel looked at her watch and was relieved to see that it was only seven forty five. Thank goodness she had time to get her act together.

Even so she felt she should get dressed. It was obvious that Rupert was preparing to leave. Before she could ask the question he said, "Giovanni usually collects me just before eight o'clock. If you feel up to it I could get him to drop me off at San Giorgio Maggiore at about two o'clock and I can show you Palladio's masterpiece when it opens at three."

"Mmm, I'd like that. Shall I bring a picnic?" she asked, guessing that he might not have time for lunch.

"Perfect. Now I must dash. Are you happy to let yourself out?"

He crossed to where she still sat at the kitchen table and kissed her lightly on the cheek, started to walk towards the door, stopped before he reached it and said, "I nearly forgot. I left a toothbrush in the bathroom for you. Help yourself to toothpaste and anything else you need."

Isobel sat motionless at the kitchen table, cradling her mug of coffee in both hands. She heard him cross the hall, listened as the door closed behind him. Touched by his thoughtfulness she felt the tears sting the back of her eyes. Now that he'd gone she felt bereft. The apartment was empty, alien, silent and suddenly she wanted to leave.

Chapter Seven

James had never felt more impotent. Lying flat on his back, a position in which he'd never been comfortable, in intensive care, he was afraid to move in case he inadvertently disturbed one of the pieces of equipment to which he was still attached. He'd been here for less than twenty four hours but it seemed like a lifetime. He was used to time passing far too quickly, now the minutes crawled by. Even though he drifted in and out of sleep he felt that this must surely be the longest day of his life. Zelda had looked in briefly this morning but she'd seemed harassed and he felt she had absolutely no idea either what to say to him or of what he must be feeling at the moment. He'd been relieved when she left after half an hour, pleading that she had a million things to do.

He wished he had a complicated legal case to occupy his thoughts. The conversation with his sister was going round and round in his head and a diversion at this stage would be so welcome. She'd given him such a graphic description of her lunch with Isobel; told him how displeased Isobel appeared when she and Henry joined her and Rupert. The two of them were holding hands across the table and gazing longingly into each others eyes according to Barbara. She'd gone on to paint a picture of Rupert; a cross between Cary Grant and Rossano Brazzi by all accounts. What was that supposed to mean for God's sake? Anyway Barbara stressed he was very handsome. Isobel had gone to great lengths to explain that she was staying in a modest, small hotel but Barbara hadn't believed that story for a single moment. After all she stressed ' Would you pay for a hotel in Venice if your *friend*,' and here her voice became positively vitriolic, 'if your friend had his own apartment?'

Barbara had always been out to get him of course. Ever since their father had refused to allow her to go to university she'd done her best to try to mar his pleasure whenever possible. It wasn't his fault for Christ's sake that his father had been against further education for women but Barbara either couldn't or wouldn't accept that he, James, hadn't tried to influence the decision. If only she knew how hard he'd tried to persuade their father to change his mind.

He must stop thinking about it. The feelings which these memories evoked were doing nothing for his stress level and the therapist, or whatever she called herself, specifically asked him to try and relax. He wondered if she would be able to relax if her ex-husband was playing around with some half Italian bimbette. That bastard Northcote was most likely pawing Isobel at this very minute and no doubt the two of them would have a bloody good laugh when they heard what had happened to him.

James, feeling lonely, unloved and abandoned, pressed the button on his morphine drip, closed his eyes and prayed for oblivion.

Isobel sat on the wall on the island of San Giorgio Maggiore soothed by the sound of the waves plashing gently against the worn stone. She'd spent a good bit of the morning shopping for lunch and now had some time to collect her thoughts as she waited for Rupert. Had she really been brazen enough to invite herself into his bed? Of course she'd drunk quite a bit but surely not enough to make her lose all her inhibitions? Not only that but after his patience and the care he'd taken to satisfy her she'd abandoned herself totally to the wilder moments on the bathroom rug. She couldn't remember a time when she'd felt such an intense physical desire. After five years without sex her appetite was well and truly whetted and now, waiting for him, she felt again a keen, almost insatiable hunger.

In spite of the new intimacy of their relationship there was still a part of him which she felt she couldn't reach. She guessed that perhaps he found it difficult to talk about his deeper feelings. Whenever he spoke about either his wife or his daughter his eyes, usually so lively, became veiled as if he were closing off a part of his mind, perhaps to make living with the truth more bearable? There were no photographs in his flat; no evidence of previously happy times, nothing at all to give her a clue about his past life with Liz.

The other question which she could neither ask or answer was how did he really feel about her, if indeed he felt anything at all? Was she just a passing diversion as James' many women friends had been over the years? It was all most intriguing. Astonishing that this was her first affair, not once throughout her thirty year marriage had she been tempted to get her own back on James. She smiled to herself. Who knows what she might have missed?

Her thoughts were interrupted by the sound of a motor boat engine and she looked across the lagoon just in time to see Rupert raise his hand in a brief salute. She waved eagerly back as the boat stopped at the foot of the steps which led up from the lagoon, smiled and called "*Buon giorno*!" to Giovanni who returned her greeting before decanting his passenger and heading back towards the Grand Canal.

Rupert bounded up the steps three at a time and kissed Isobel on the mouth. "You look very lively for someone who had such an exhausting night!" he said, laughing down at her, his eyes echoing his good humour. She smiled back but she could feel her cheeks growing warm and she spoke quickly to hide her renewed desire for him.

"Well I've had the morning to recover whilst you've been wheeling and dealing with corrupt planning officials. How did it go?"

"We bought him off, but please don't hold it against me. As I explained earlier it's the way things work over here. I take it we have the island to ourselves?" He looked around quickly for confirmation.

"Yes as far as I can see. The only people here are having lunch on a yacht moored around the corner where I've left our food in the shade."

"Good, I'm starving, all that tedious negotiating has given me an appetite." He followed her round to the side of the church and picked up two plastic carrier bags which were leaning against the wall.

"Not the most elegant picnic hampers are they?" Isobel said. "But I guarantee the contents, although it was quite a challenge shopping in a city which I really don't know all that well."

They sat on the steps in front of the church and Isobel unpacked green olives, ciabatta bread, Prosciutto di San Daniele, some enormous tomatoes, tiny savoury pastries filled with an assortment of seafood and a large bunch of grapes. Finally she produced a bottle of white wine. "I persuaded the charming man who sold me this to take the cork out for me," she explained. "I couldn't make up my mind whether you were the kind of man who would have a Swiss Army knife so I decided not to take any chances. I'm afraid the choice of drinking utensils is limited to either a plastic mug or the wine bottle."

"Nothing can persuade me that Venetian wine will taste less good from a plastic mug than it does from a glass," Rupert replied helping himself to an olive. He picked up the bottle and poured for both of them, raised his mug. "What shall we drink to?"

"I think it should be Palladio, don't you agree? After all if it weren't for him we shouldn't be here."

"Palladio it is then, a constant inspiration to architects."

"I hope he isn't turning in his grave." Isobel said as they began to eat. "I shouldn't think he had picnics in mind when he designed this beautiful church."

"I'm sure he wouldn't mind. Even Ruskin indulged in picnics from time-to-time. I read an account somewhere, written by his wife, of a picnic they had on Torcello. This is absolutely delicious," he continued. "I'm so glad you didn't buy pizza. It's been so adulterated by the fast food concerns that one rarely finds any that is worth eating even in Venice."

"I'm relieved you approve the menu," Isobel smiled. "Your delicious meal last night was a hard act to follow."

They continued to eat in silence for a while, looking across the lagoon towards San Marco, enjoying the temporary solitude. After a few moments Rupert leaned forward and took her hand.

"How would you like to come to Rome for the weekend?" he said. "I promised my brother I'd try and look in and as you'll be flying home in just over a week if we leave it until next weekend it will make your last days rather hectic. What do you say?"

A moment ago Isobel had bitten into a tomato, thinking how good it tasted, her mind centred on the pure pleasure of eating in the open air. His suggestion surprised her so much she swallowed too quickly, choking on the half chewed fragments. Rupert thumped her back, wiped the tears from her eyes - handkerchief pristine as usual. Then, waiting for her to recover, he broke off a piece of ciabatta bread and carefully laid a slice of ham on it, selected a tomato, took a large bite and chewed carefully. Then, his right eyebrow lifted. "Please say you'll come," he said.

Isobel's mind felt like a piece of tangled knitting. Oh boy! You had to run fast to keep up with this man! The thought of Venice without him seemed like a pretty bleak prospect. After all since Tuesday they'd spent part of every day together. But going to meet his family so soon, wasn't that moving their relationship forward just a little too quickly? Finally she looked at him and said. "How will you explain me to your brother? Hi Miles! Meet Isobel, someone I met a week ago!"

"Oh dear!" said Rupert, an expression of mock disapproval on his face. "I thought we'd agreed not to be prudish? Why don't we just continue the old friends story? It seems to have worked quite well so far."

"Are you sure they won't mind? After all it will be quite a surprise for them. Once you ask them, what's the betting they'll both be racking their brains trying to remember if you've mentioned me before!"

Rupert laughed, "That's their problem!" But then his voice took on a more serious note. "Please say yes. I'm sure you'll like my brother." He paused for a moment and then continued, "And to be absolutely honest, after last night, I really don't look forward to spending two or three days in Rome without you."

Isobel was flattered but at the same time couldn't resist teasing him. "Does your brother have a thick rug on his bathroom floor?" she asked, smiling broadly and looking at a point just over Rupert's left shoulder.

He threw back his head and roared with laughter. "I'm just beginning to realise what a shameless woman you are! But you've just reminded me why I'd like to get to know you better. All morning I've been telling myself that you'll be going home in just over a week and I'm anxious to make the most of the next few days."

This is what life should be like and so rarely is, Isobel thought, basking in the unusual luxury of being with someone whose company she enjoyed, in a place she'd longed to see and hearing words that made her feel treasured. Even so a small worry surfaced at the back of her mind and, looking steadily into his eyes she said, "One thing we really must do if I'm to spend the weekend with your brother is to be quite clear about when and where we met so that if they ask we shall both come up with a similar story."

"Agreed, that's settled then? There's a plane leaving just before seven this evening and I must confess, in anticipation that you might say yes, I've already bought you a ticket! We should be in Rome in time for a late dinner. We'll have a quick look round the church and that'll give you time to pack a few things." He helped himself calmly to grapes and, looking out across the lagoon, spotted the first *vaporetto* of the afternoon on its way across to the island.

"I'm afraid we won't be alone for much longer." he said. "Thank you for the delicious lunch, you've no idea how much I appreciate it."

Isobel began to pack away the remnants of the picnic trying to remember the last time James had either thanked her for providing a meal or complemented her on its content. Instead she remembered a series of complaints: 'The wine wasn't cool enough. He could taste the Thermos flask through the coffee. He didn't like picnics anyway.' She brushed them firmly from her mind, reminding herself of her pledge not to think about home or him.

They joined the small group disembarking from the *vaporetto* and walked into the welcome coolness of the church. Isobel was surprised by the amount of light flooding in through the dome, which appeared almost to float above the cross axis of the nave and transepts. Rupert pointed out the characteristics which he so admired in Palladio; his strict symmetry, sharp angles, undecorated corners. Isobel could see that some of these qualities were echoed in Rupert's own apartment which had similar clean lines and the minimum of decoration.

She closed her eyes trying to commit it all to memory, smelling the faint aroma of myrrh, wondering about the countless feet that had walked across the chequered floor in the four hundred year life of the church. Rupert waited until she opened them and then said, "I have to take you to the top of the *campanile* the view from there is spectacular. There is a lift so you won't have to climb the stairs."

She turned and looked back over her shoulder as they left the church, wondered if she would ever return and prayed silently that she might retain some of the peace of the place before following Rupert to the lift.

A single monk stood in the corner as they rose slowly to the top of the *campanile*. Next to him was a tall stool, initially designed for sitting, but now bearing a few jars of honey. He was almost a caricature of a monk, smiling at them from behind spectacles with thick, pebble-like lenses, his hands folded and concealed in the sleeves of his habit. Knowing he had a captive market he extolled the virtues of his honey which, he explained, was pittosporum and, like the flowers of that shrub, particularly fragrant. Rupert produced a 5000 lire note and handed it over in exchange for a pot of the honey which he presented to Isobel. "A small memory of Venice for you," he said, as they stepped out of the lift. Isobel thanked him and then caught her breath as she looked out yet again across the lagoon and then into the cloistered courtyard to the left of the church.

"It's so beautiful," she said. "I'm sure if I lived here I should never get tired of looking at all this."

"Wasn't it Turner who described Venice as a city of rose and white, rising out of an emerald sea against a sky of sapphire blue?" Rupert asked. "An over-simplification perhaps but you can see what he meant."

"Oh absolutely and I'm sure England is going to look dirty, grey and unwelcoming when I get back. Tell me what's that place over there?" Rupert followed the direction of her gaze. "Ah. The perfect place for the seriously wealthy, the Cipriani. You can only reach it by boat. The hotel has its own of course, you may have noticed a landing stage marked Cipriani separate from the other *vaporetto* stops?"

Isobel admitted she hadn't then, suddenly remembering that they were catching a plane in a few hours, she opened her camera taking shots from every conceivable angle including one of Rupert leaning over the railing which surrounded the platform. Thinking back over her life she could scarcely remember an afternoon when she'd been so happy and she wanted to capture it forever.

Without turning round he pointed across to a small church to the right of the Doge's Palace. "That's the church of the Pietà where Vivaldi taught music to the orphans of the Conservatorio of the Pietà. It has some remarkable Tiepolo frescoes. I'll try and show them to you next week if you like."

The lift took them back to ground level and they waited for a few minutes for the *vaporetto* back to the mainland. "I've seen that church in so many photographs of Venice," Isobel said, "and now I've actually been inside. I can scarcely believe it. I'm only sorry it took me so long to get here."

"The important thing is that you came at all," Rupert replied.

"James and I spent our honeymoon in Florence." Isobel went on. "He didn't much care for it and I haven't been back to Italy since. I'm so excited at the thought of visiting Rome for the first time."

"It tends to be crowded and noisy in the tourist season and although we're nearly at the end of September it could still be quite hot so don't raise your hopes too high." Rupert warned her.

But, now that she'd found someone who shared her enthusiasm for Italy, Isobel didn't give a damn about heat, noise or crowds.

Ian was trying to reorganise the office in his father's absence. He wished with all his heart that there was a verbal form of shorthand so that at least he could reduce the time he had to spend explaining things to people to the absolute minimum. He made a point of telling all James' clients that his father's heart attack had been very slight and that he would be back in the office before they knew it, hoping to God he was right. The last thing he needed at this stage was for valued clients to start jumping overboard like so many lemmings and hot footing to another legal practice. It had taken long enough to turn it round after the last recession and he didn't fancy having to do that again in a hurry. For the moment he decided he would take on the most urgent cases himself. After all if he worked late he wouldn't have to spend more evenings at home wondering what to say to his father-in-law so *that* would be a plus.

When he rang the hospital this morning they'd told him that there was always a possibility that his father could have another heart attack and that the weekend would be critical. Zelda was the only visitor allowed for the moment so he couldn't ask James' advice on any of his cases. He'd done the next best thing and briefed his father's secretary to read the files and fill him in on key points so that he could get a grip on the problem before he had to face an anxious litigant across the desk.

Long term plans were quite another matter and he may have to take on a locum if his father was going to be away for some time. It was virtually impossible to get any sense out of Zelda, who'd been distraught when she'd phoned him last night and no more coherent this morning. What a pity his mother was out of the country she'd have been just the person to come and take over the office organisation. She'd always been brilliant in a crisis and her secretarial skills would have been useful as well. In fact now he came to think of it if she hadn't taken it into her head to go gadding off to Venice none of this would have happened. He didn't want to think about that now. Worry about the things you can change old son he said to himself as he picked up the phone to make yet another call.

Chapter Eight

Rupert sighed with relief as Miles covered the last few kilometres from the airport and drove across the Tiber into Trastevere. He hated road traffic after the tranquillity of Venice and was, at the best of times, a nervous passenger. The reckless driving in Rome terrified him and he frequently described it as being like dodgem cars driving round a formula one racing circuit.

Once they were over the bridge both he and Miles were so keen to point out the artistic merits of the area that they both began speaking at once. "You've had your turn in Venice." Miles laughed and placed a restraining hand on Rupert's arm. "Time to defer to your elder brother for once."

"Just trying to take my mind away from your driving!" Rupert replied. "I've bored the pants off Isobel for the past week and I'm sure she'll be only too pleased to hear your artistic rather than my architectural point of view."

"This is one of the oldest areas of Rome." Miles explained. "The earliest church dedicated to the Virgin is Santa Maria in

Trastevere. The oldest part dates back to the fourth century and there are some wonderful twelfth century mosaics which glorify the Virgin, but the statues on the external balustrade are comparatively new and were added in the seventeenth century. In the church of San Francesco there's a fine Bernini sculpture, the Ecstasy of Beata Ludovica. When she died her family wanted her to be sanctified. She didn't quite make it but at least her tomb is decorated by one of the world's greatest sculptors." Miles lectured on art history at the University of Rome and was in his element. "Normally I take guests to see it," he continued, "but I suspect my brother has dragged you into every church in Venice so rest assured I sha'n't burden you with a tour."

"When I look at old Beata Ludovica I always think the expression on her face is more orgasmic than saintly!" Rupert volunteered. "So perhaps whoever made the final decision about her saintliness or lack of it knew something that we don't!"

Isobel smiled at their easy banter contrasting it with the kind of verbal sparring that occurred whenever James and his sister were in the same room. She looked out of the car window and noticed that the roads were becoming quieter and the area more residential. "This is Monteverde Vecchio," Miles explained. "We're almost home."

After a few minutes he turned into a short drive and stopped outside an elegant villa. In the fading light Isobel could just make out the green shutters that were folded back against pale ochre walls. A short flight of steps led up to a massive front door which looked as if it had been built to withstand a siege. Miles, after opening the boot of the car, left Rupert to take out their few pieces of luggage, walked over to the entrance and rang the bell. Seconds later the door opened and there stood Gianna.

"Rupee darling!" She kissed Rupert on both cheeks and then, turning immediately towards Isobel, she repeated the embrace and cried, "Welcome!" before Rupert had time to introduce them.

My God she doesn't look a day over forty! Isobel thought as she followed her into the villa, noting the smart black linen slacks, black and white silk shirt, high heeled sandals, short elegantly styled hair, the wide vivid red mouth and matching finger nails. She seemed to Isobel to be the epitome of Italian chic but a wave of warmth and vivacity reached out and wrapped itself around her visitors and she knew it would be impossible to dislike her - in spite of that, "Rupee darling!"

Once inside Gianna led the way up a short flight of stairs and along a corridor towards a solid oak door. "We 'ave a small guest wing." she explained to Isobel as she opened the door. "So you can be quite private." The 'guest wing' was simply two bedrooms and a bathroom which Gianna insisted on showing them, the heels of her sandals tap-tapping on the old tiled floor as she flung open doors and indicated the rooms behind them. There was no rug, thick or otherwise, on the marble floor of the bathroom Isobel noticed as she glanced inside and tried not to smile.

"I'll leave you in peace, please join us when you are ready." Gianna said before leaving them, taking care to close the large oak door before tapping down the stairs.

Rupert glanced across at Isobel as the sound of Gianna's heels died away. "Are you wishing you'd stayed in Venice?" he asked, imagining a subdued expression on her face. "I'm afraid my sister-in-law has a tendency to effervesce."

"Not a bit!" Isobel reassured him. "But I must admit I hadn't expected Gianna to be quite so young. Is she Miles' second wife?"

"No, just a well preserved first! She must be in her late fifties. As a young woman she was absolutely stunning. She refuses to drive a car, says the traffic in Rome terrifies her and I can't say I blame her. Instead she walks quite a lot and that obviously helps to keep her in trim. Now, to more practical matters, by which I mean sleeping arrangements. Shall we observe the proprieties and use both bedrooms or throw caution to the winds and share one?"

Isobel suddenly felt gauche and completely out of her depth. "This isn't a decision I've had to take before," she admitted. It was one thing to invite herself into Rupert's bed at the end of a *récherché* dinner, quite another to be staying with his brother as Rupert's - what? Mistress; partner; or God forbid, the title she seemed to be stuck with, old friend. She shrugged helplessly and looked appealingly across at him willing him to make the decision for her.

"Well why don't we try to have the best of all possible worlds? We can use both rooms, that will make the 'good friends' story more convincing and you can leave at the end of the weekend with your reputation intact."

"You make me sound like some Victorian heroine." Isobel smiled at the thought.

"Heroine yes, Victorian never. I don't think even the most liberated Victorian woman would abandon herself quite so wildly on the bathroom rug and I'm pretty sure that you won't lock your door after dinner!"

Isobel felt herself blush. She seemed to have blushed more in the past few days than in the preceding several years. The children would describe her as definitely uncool but then they were in no position to appreciate all the other things she'd been up to since the beginning of her holiday! She thought for a moment before replying.

"It's as I said before. We were brought up to behave in a certain way and suddenly our instincts tell us that maybe the alternatives are not only more enjoyable but much nearer to our true character."

"And is your true character closer to the woman to whom I made love on the bathroom rug or the woman your mother no doubt tried to turn you into?"

"I'll leave that to you to decide. Now let *me* move to practicalities. May I have ten minutes to unpack and tidy up?"

Rupert inclined his head. "Take as long as you need. You're a guest of the family after all."

Isobel tried her best to feel at home as Rupert picked up her overnight bag and carried it into one of the bedrooms before disappearing into the other; but as she unpacked she was aware of being an outsider in what appeared on the surface to be a close knit family. There was an easy intimacy which she envied and found inhibiting at the same time. As an only child herself she was a stranger to the close relationships that many of her friends shared with their siblings and, although she always enjoyed this kind of affinity within other families she was always pained by the lack of it in her own.

The gulf between herself and her parents had widened as her education progressed, first at grammar school, later at university. None of them wanted it to happen but gradually the common ground between them shrank. Her parents found it impossible to like the music she began listening to on Radio 3 and when they tuned in to 'Grand Hotel' or a similar light music programme she would make some excuse and go to her own room. In her early teens she'd devoured her mothers' copies of 'Woman's Own'. As she grew older she saved up for 'Vogue' and read the articles as well as studying the fashion. "You've got champagne tastes and beer money," her mother reminded her every time she found Isobel curled up on their less-than-fashionable sofa. Isobel ignored her, knowing that the time would come when she would have enough money with which to indulge her developing tastes.

There was a wood fire burning in the drawing room when she joined the others which reminded her that autumn was approaching. Soon the temperature would begin to fall and the nights become longer. The thought deepened her, already sombre, mood. Autumn always spoke to her of endings and she was much more excited by beginnings. She thought of returning to England and her solitary existence, of leaving Rupert behind in Venice and she wanted to cry. Would the physical distance put an end to the relationship? She shivered at the thought and moved instinctively towards the fire, holding out her hands towards its warmth, expressing pleasure.

"The walls of this 'ouse are so thick," Gianna explained. "Even on warm days we feel cold." She patted the space on the sofa beside her, inviting Isobel to sit down. Miles poured white wine for all of them.

"Benvenuto a Roma!" Gianna said, raising her glass and flashing a smile at Isobel. "Now we must get to know each other."

Help! Thought Isobel, any minute now she's going to ask where we met, how long we've known each other. She cast around for a diversion and her eyes fell on a collection of magazines which were lying on top of an old, carved oak chest standing in front of the sofa, doing duty as a coffee table. Every single one had a picture of the late Princess Diana on its front cover.

"I see you've been reading about our tragic princess," Isobel commented. "I've noticed every time I look at a news stand that she's being featured in magazines all around the world."

"Such a dreadful calamity!" Gianna's face took on a tragic expression. "It is so sad that she died at the 'eight of her beauty."

The two men exchanged glances. "Well at least she won't have to grow old like the rest of us," Miles said. "How many people would like to think of themselves going to their graves without wrinkles, sagging flesh and all the other maladies that afflict us as we grow older?"

Gianna fluttered her fingers at him. "Speak for yourself darling! I 'ave no intention of letting my flesh sag!"

The men looked at each other again, this time in wry amusement. Rupert's right eyebrow lifted a fraction. "Gianna I'm sure you'll be as beautiful in old age as you are now." He raised his glass and saluted her. "Here's wishing you an extremely long life - with or without sagging flesh." The scarlet mouth curved upwards as Gianna beamed her thanks and the fingers fluttered again, this time in Rupert's direction.

"Rupee, you're an old flatterer and I love you! If I were not married to Miles you would be my first choice!" Rupert inclined his head and smiled but before he could reply Miles interrupted.

"Why don't we go and eat. We can continue the mutual admiration over dinner. Suddenly I feel enormously hungry."

"I suppose you don't eat lunch again?" Gianna said. "If you will shut yourself away in some stuffy old library all day you should take time for a little snack. He does this all the time," she added, turning towards Isobel who assumed a sympathetic expression as she drained her glass. Then, feeling that she should make an attempt to become part of the conversation she said; "Time doesn't really have any meaning when you're doing something you feel really passionate about does it?" She looked across at Miles.

"At last! A woman who understands. You're a lucky man Rupe." Miles clapped his brother on the back as they began to move towards the dining room.

You simply *mustn't* blush, Isobel told herself as she followed the two men, grateful for the slight diversion that avoided, yet again, any discussion about the true nature of their relationship.

The dining room walls were covered in dark green damask. The furniture was heavy mahogany and large, in keeping with the size of the room. The table could seat ten quite comfortably but Gianna had chosen to place them all at one end. A pyramid of assorted fruit had been arranged on an enormous pewter platter and placed on a credenza which took up almost all the space on one wall.

Gianna disappeared towards the kitchen. Miles poured wine. Rupert lit candles. It was all so beautifully orchestrated! They'd obviously dined together many times before. It was impossible not to envy their empathy.

They ate fettucini with artichoke hearts and a creamy sauce with a hint of Gorgonzola; a chicken roasted with lemon. Their mood grew mellower as the evening progressed.

"Is there anything you'd like to do or see whilst you're here?" Miles asked Isobel. The question caught her unawares. Getting here had been such a whirl. Rupert had calmly carried on showing her the church while she tried to think about what to bring and at the same time attempted to listen to what he was saying. In the end she'd done her packing in half an hour flat and they'd jumped into a *motoscafo* and whizzed across to the airport.

Conscious that the others were waiting for her reply, she tried to pull ideas from nowhere. Finally she had a moment of inspiration. "It would be really wonderful to see the Sistine Chapel now that the ceiling has been restored and then, if we have time, I could pay my respects to Keats and visit his house near the Spanish Steps."

"*Ah benissimo!*" Gianna clapped her hands. "You and I can go together in the morning. And after we visit the Keats 'ouse we can perhaps do a little shopping in the Via Condotti." Then turning her attention to the men she said. "I'm sure you two boys can amuse yourselves for the morning and then perhaps you join us for lunch?"

Rupert looked across at Miles whose face bore the resigned expression of one who waits for others to do the organising. "It seems our morning has been planned for us. Is that OK by you Rupe or would you rather go with Isobel?"

"If shopping is part of the itinerary I think I'll spend the morning with you," Rupert said easily. "If the worse comes to the worst I can always drag you off to San Francesco and say hello to Beata Ludovica. It's some time now since I saw her and as I get older I'm learning to seize the moment."

Ah, thought Isobel, is that why we've been seeing so much of each other since we first met?

"Let me buy you a drink and then we can sit down somewhere and wait for the men in comfort." Isobel, after a morning spent sight-seeing and shopping, was longing to take the weight off her feet, besides which her throat was parched. Gianna was absolutely tireless; walking them briskly from one place to another, pausing only when absolutely necessary.

They'd left the villa at seven thirty, leaving the men to linger over their breakfast and the newspapers. Gianna insisted that they arrive at the Sistine Chapel early so that they could see the ceiling in comfort before the crowds became too dense. After that they took a bus to the Via del Corso and stopped briefly for a cappuccino in the Via Condotti before walking up the Spanish Steps to the Keats - Shelley Memorial Museum, based in the small house where Keats lived during the last few months of his life.

They took their coffee Italian style, standing up at the bar, Gianna insisting that it was much cheaper than sitting at a table. Finally they toured the shops and Isobel threw caution to the winds splurging on a pale, caramel coloured suede jacket. The skin felt like silk as she slipped into it and Gianna assured her that she looked "*bellissima!*"

At the moment Isobel didn't care how much it cost to sit down and drink she only knew that she needed time to recover. When they'd ordered she turned to Gianna; "Such a tiny, modest little house for a great poet isn't it?"

Gianna shrugged and spread her hands. "But he's immortal, he doesn't need a grand 'ouse!"

"Well no, not any more, but he must have found it a little . . .," she paused searching for the right word, "confining is perhaps the best way to describe it. Even so there's a very strong atmosphere. I can really imagine poor Keats spending his last months wasting away in that tiny bedroom before finally losing the battle to stay alive. I'm glad his friend Joseph Severn stayed with him until the end, I think I'm right in saying that he died in Severn's arms. It's amazing that he managed to pack so much into his twenty six years, after all most of us are only just beginning to live at that age."

Gianna sighed; "So romantic! To die in the arms of a friend! 'ow many of us will be so lucky?" She sipped Campari and soda, looking at Isobel over the rim of her glass. "Did you know that Liz died in Rupert's arms?" she asked.

Isobel's heart lurched towards her ribs. Her mind was still with Keats and Severn and Gianna's question caught her off guard. "I didn't know but then Rupert's not the type to talk about such intimate details is he?" She tried to make her voice sound casual, unemotional, remembering that as far as Gianna was concerned she and Rupert were old friends. She stared into her glass as she spoke and then to drive the point home she added, "Rupert doesn't talk about Liz very often. I think the memories of her are still very painful for him and I feel I should respect his privacy." She hoped this last remark would deflect any further questions or snippets of information from Gianna. If she heard this kind of confidence from anyone she would prefer to hear it from Rupert.

She looked around her pretending interest in an Italian family at the next table. A young over-weight mother was indulging herself and her two offspring. The three of them were tucking into huge ice creams, scooping up vanilla ice, bits of fruit and whipped cream as if they hadn't eaten for a week. The mother's satin blouse stretched tightly across the over-large breasts and Isobel wondered how long it would be before one or more of the buttons would give way under the strain.

Gianna however was in the mood for a *tête à tête* and wasn't going to be discouraged so easily. "Poor Rupee, after Liz's death he was nearly, 'ow you say - destroyed? He blame himself over and over. We tell him he could 'ave done nothing to save her, but he so adored her I think he didn't hear us. At one time we think he might lose his mind. And then there was the nasty business with Tory."

Ah Tory! Now here was a subject that Isobel was keen to discuss. "You mean the drugs, the unsuitable friends?" she queried, hoping to prompt Gianna into telling her more. The ploy worked and Gianna pausing just long enough to order more drinks continued. "Liz was close to death when Rupert asked Tory to come home. He was afraid Tory might upset her and with all those drugs around . . . well that was another problem. Rupert and Tory had a terrible row. Afterwards Rupert was so angry it was terrifying, his eyebrow was cut, the doctor had to stitch it and Tory said she'd never speak to him again."

Isobel hoped she'd never see Rupert in a rage. Visions of him and his daughter resorting to physical violence flickered across her mind. She looked again at the Italian family in an attempt to blot out the pictures. The mother was now wiping creamy moustaches from the upper lips of both children and putting a renewed strain on the blouse as she moved towards them. Isobel turned reluctantly back to Gianna. "Perhaps Tory made the best decision under the circumstances?" she said.

"Oh no!" Gianna said quickly. "Poor Tory always idolised Rupert. For her 'e was the perfect father. They had always been so, so close when she was a child and she was devastated when 'e turned against her."

At last Isobel began to understand why Rupert was so reluctant to talk about his family and thought she could appreciate his unwillingness to commit to close relationships. The wounds inflicted by Liz's death and the rift with Tory must have been particularly deep, the scars perhaps still healing? This would explain the lack of photographs in his flat, the veiled look in his eyes when he spoke about either of them. She was so deep in thought she didn't hear Gianna's next question, was unaware even that she had spoken until Gianna paused.

"I'm sorry," she said, looking at Gianna again. "Did you say something? I'm afraid I was miles away."

"I was only asking if you and Rupert 'ave any plans for the future?" Gianna repeated with a searching glance at Isobel who wished she'd simply gone on ignoring Gianna's chatter. She took a long pull at her spritzer, playing for time, wanting to give an answer that would sound credible and, at the same time, to deflect any other questions that Gianna might put. Finally she responded, speaking slowly to give herself time to put her thoughts into words. "We both bear the scars of previous relationships, although for different reasons. I am divorced. My ex-husband's behaviour hurt me deeply just as Tory must have hurt Rupert. I think for the moment we're content to take each day as it comes and to be grateful. After all happiness, true happiness, can be a fairly elusive emotion don't you agree?"

She looked at Gianna trying to assess whether Gianna's interest in her future with Rupert was simply that of a concerned relative or if perhaps she had other reasons. What was it she'd said to Rupert last night? "If I weren't married to Miles you would be my first choice." But Gianna *was* married to Miles and, on the surface anyway, it was a happy marriage. Or was it?

She told herself it was none of her business and to begin looking for complications where perhaps none existed was no way in which to begin a new relationship. Take your own advice Isobel, she warned, take each day as it comes and be grateful.

She looked at her watch. "Where are we meeting the men, isn't it time we were making a move?" she said. She stopped a passing waiter, asked him for the bill, counted out notes, waved aside Gianna's proferred lire.

"Isobel, you worry too much." Gianna stilled her fingers long enough to squeeze Isobel's hand. "The restaurant is only two streets away. And if the men 'ave to wait . ." She fluttered her fingers again and left the sentence unfinished.

Two bright spots of colour burned on Renate's cheeks as she stood in front of Zelda. "But Mrs Campbell I've made arrangements to meet friends this evening."

"Well you'll just have to un-arrange them won't you? I have to go to the hospital and I can't very well take Samantha with me can I?" Zelda's dark eyes flashed dangerously. God almighty wasn't it bad enough that her husband had nearly died this week without having to bandy words with the *au pair* about time off?

Renate was used to Zelda's outbursts of temper when things weren't going her way and was determined to stand her ground. "I've arranged to meet my friends in a restaurant. Where they are now I don't know. I have no way of getting in touch with them to let them know I can't make it."

"Well that's just *too* bad." Zelda's voice was heavily sarcastic. "I expect someone who's treated like one of the family to help out in a crisis instead of which you only think of yourself at a time when I'm out of my mind with worry."

Renate felt waves of homesickness break over her and her blue eyes filled with tears at the mention of the word family. She'd soon discovered that she was treated as a member of the family only when Mr Campbell was around. The rest of the time Zelda treated her like a particularly stupid servant. "I'm sorry Mrs Campbell but tonight is special. My friend's birthday, I simply can't let him down."

The moment the words were out Renate realised her mistake. She watched Zelda's mouth tighten, the eyes narrow, and braced herself for whatever was coming next.

"I thought I'd made myself perfectly clear," Zelda said, speaking slowly as she did when Samantha had been naughty. "You cannot go out this evening, or any other evening until Mr Campbell is well again. Now is that clear enough for you?"

Renate burst into tears, ran from the room and raced up the stairs. She flung her possessions into a suitcase, called a taxi and left the house forever.

Chapter Nine

When Isobel woke up on Sunday morning every bone in her body ached. She turned towards the centre of the bed, put out an exploratory hand and encountered nothing. The room was silent. Pale light filtered through the closed curtains. She struggled to brush away the cobwebs of sleep and tried hard to kick-start her brain into something resembling action. Where was she? Surely in Rome? Rupert and Rome, the two were synonymous in her mind. So where was Rupert?

She re-wound the tape in her head back to Saturday. After lunch they'd been to the Villa Medici. There, when Rupert told the others that Isobel loved gardens, Miles had shown her the best surviving Renaissance garden in Rome, just behind the Medici villa. She was grateful to Rupert for remembering and thankful for the opportunity to make the most of the slight breeze which stirred the hot air of the afternoon. They'd strolled along tree-lined avenues punctuated by statues and fountains, the latter adding to the coolness and tranquillity of the seventeen acre site. They completed their tour by walking through the wood to the south of the villa and up a crumbling stairway leading to a belvedere from where they had a panoramic view over the city. Miles told her that Henry James had once described it as the most enchanting place in Rome. Isobel couldn't disagree - as her scant knowledge of Rome precluded an informed opinion - but the sylvan peace provided a welcome contrast to the frenzied Roman traffic.

After that the memory became more fuzzy. They'd come home, changed, had drinks with some friends of Gianna and Miles before going off to a restaurant. It had been quite an evening., lots of laughter, sparkling conversation, excellent food. It was well after midnight when they finally left the friends. What happened then? She dimly remembered saying goodnight and walking up the stairs to the oak door, Rupert's arm around her waist. Mmm nice memory that one! And what then? Oh my God! She sat up in bed, wide awake at last and covered her eyes to try and blot out the memory. "Isobel," she said aloud. "How could you?"

"How indeed?" Rupert's voice cut across her thoughts as he appeared in the bedroom doorway, apparently freshly showered. Isobel caught the usual drift of "CK" as he approached the bed. She held out her hand which Rupert took, kissing her fingers gently.

"Did I really fall asleep?" she asked, cursing herself silently when there had been so much to stay awake for.

"Yup." He looked at her with mock gravity.

"Am I forgiven?"

"Nothing to forgive. You were obviously completely exhausted. If you think about it the last few days have been action-packed to say the least! Roman pavements are less kind than Venetian *fondamenta* and we drank quite a lot, ate well. The combination of all this manic activity and my frenetic family obviously took its toll."

"Even so."

"Three Hail Mary's and one Our Father should square things with the Almighty!"

She couldn't see the tragic expression in her eyes and was relieved when he laughed, sat on the edge of the bed and pulled her into his arms. His mouth tasted of peppermint, his chin felt smooth, freshly shaved. He was naked under his bathrobe.

His fingers soothed her aching muscles. She untied his bathrobe, held him close, kissed the hollow just above his collar bone. She welcomed the feel of his flesh against her own and did her best to compensate for falling asleep the previous evening.

Afterwards she was reluctant to move thinking how lovely it would be to stay in bed for the rest of the morning and indulge her appetite for Rupert! I've just made love before breakfast, she thought, with a kind of wonder at her own temerity. Even on holiday James had been eager to have an early breakfast - always the full English - ignoring her warnings about cholesterol, and he'd always wolfed it down as quickly as possible. His goal; to be on the first tee by eight thirty sharp. It was "home" a world to which she never wanted to return.

They heard, through the open window, the sound of footsteps scrunching on gravel and were forcibly reminded that there was a world outside.

"It sounds as if Gianna's returning from early mass." Rupert's voice sounded drowsy. "I suppose I should make an effort and try to get myself down to breakfast."

Isobel kissed him slowly, wanting him all over again but, since he'd said that he should move, she unwound herself reluctantly and moved away from him. "I'll follow you down presently," she said. "Just give me time to take a shower and dress."

"It's Sunday and there's no great hurry." Rupert replied. "There was some talk yesterday of driving out to Tivoli and meeting my niece, her husband and their daughter, but if you're too tired we can have a quiet morning here."

"I'll be ready for anything after a shower." Isobel said and headed for the bathroom.

Half an hour later she closed the oak door behind her and went in search of the others. As she reached the bottom of the staircase she heard the murmur of voices coming from the direction of the kitchen. She turned and walked along the passageway towards the open door, stopping briefly to admire a watercolour which hung halfway along on the right hand wall. The picture showed a bridge over the Tiber, a cluster of buildings to the left, an overhanging tree to the right. She searched for the signature and found it; Miles Northcote. She was just about to turn away when the drift of conversation coming from the kitchen caught up with her.

"I warn you Gianna it won't be easy." Isobel's heart quickened as she recognised Rupert's voice.

"But don't you see Rupee darling that's exactly why I need your 'elp." Gianna's voice sounded pleading.

"Well I'd intended to fly back to England with Isobel but I guess I could stay over a few more days. You say Miles is going off to a conference in Prague on Monday week?"

"Yes, he's giving a paper on Donatello. He think he stays for ten days."

"If things run true to form we shall need all of that time. I promise you I'll do my very best Gianna." Rupert's voice sounded as smooth as silk.

"I knew I could rely on you Rupee, now, 'ave some more coffee."

The front door opened and Miles appeared carrying newspapers. "Old habits die hard." His voice was apologetic as he spotted Isobel. "I've just been admiring your lovely painting." She smiled at him. "Is that one of the Tiber bridges?" She needed time to calm down before joining the others. Her mind was spinning after what she'd just heard. Endless questions were forming. What? Why? Where? She already knew when and with whom.

She brought her mind back to Miles with difficulty. He was explaining his picture.

". . . the oldest bridge in Rome constructed by the Consul L Fabricio in 62 BC. It's in an excellent state of preservation, not bad when you think it's over 2000 years old." Isobel heard him out and then asked. "Have you had breakfast or am I the only one who still hasn't eaten?" "I always enjoy breakfast more if I've had a walk first." Miles reassured her. "Shall we go and join the others?" He led the way to the kitchen.

"Ah! There you both are!" Gianna and Rupert spoke in unison. Rupert pulled out a chair next to his own and Isobel sank onto it not daring to look at him in case he could read the agitation in her eyes; particularly not wanting to see the feelings reflected in his own. Afraid she might see what? Triumph, smugness, self-satisfaction?

Fortunately for her the conversation moved swiftly into generalities; newspapers were passed around; coffee circulated and drunk. Isobel forced herself to concentrate on a day old copy of the Times. The news seemed unimportant, Britain was miles away; for her, Rome was the stage where all the drama was being enacted. What the hell was happening? The phrase ran round and round in her mind like a hamster on a treadmill.

Rupert's voice jerked her sharply back to reality. She looked up from the newspaper to find three pairs of eyes looking in her direction. She stared back uncomprehendingly.

"Hello!" Rupert waved a hand at her, a half smile on his face.

"I'm sorry," Isobel apologised. I wasn't really listening, just catching up on the news. She waved the paper in an effort to convince them.

"We're wondering if you'd like to visit the Villa d'Este or is there somewhere else you'd prefer? It gets quite crowded on Sundays so if we're going we should leave fairly soon." Rupert said.

How easily he switches his mind, Isobel thought. One minute he's planning goodness knows what with his sister-in-law, the next he's talking calmly about trips to Tivoli. She'd noticed before how swiftly he changed; one minute the passionate lover the next the assured architect apparently ready and eager for work. She'd also learned from Gianna that he could be a ruthless father. For the first time since they met Isobel began to wonder seriously if she really wanted to get to know this man better, afraid she might discover other sides to his personality that she would dislike.

"I'd really love to see the Villa d'Este." She made her reply sound enthusiastic. She was after all a perfect stranger and they really were trying hard to make her weekend as enjoyable as possible. "I believe there are lots of amazing fountains in the garden? Or would it be more accurate to describe them as water features?" she added.

At that moment the telephone rang and Gianna jumped up to answer it. She returned after only a few moments. "That was Caterina." She spoke to the room at large. "They meet us outside the villa in an hour. Can we all be ready in fifteen minutes?"

They parked the car in the piazza in Tivoli and walked the short distance to the Villa d'Este. Isobel, feeling a slight nip in the early morning air and badly needing to boost her spirits, was wearing her new suede jacket. As they approached the villa a small child ran towards them, arms outstretched, face wreathed in smiles, dark curls gleaming where the sun touched them. Gianna stopped, held out her arms, bent down and scooped up her granddaughter. The pair hugged each other with obvious joy. Isobel glanced quickly at Rupert. His mouth smiled a greeting at his great-niece but the smile failed to reach his eyes which were completely without expression.

"Meet your namesake Isabella," he said to Isobel, gesturing towards the child before turning to greet his niece and her husband.

Caterina was a younger version of Gianna, olive skinned, her hair longer but with the same undeniable chic. Both she and her husband Gino embraced Isobel warmly. She was touched by their immediate and unconditional acceptance of her.

A few moments later, they stood in front of the villa looking out over a terraced garden which sloped away from them. The hillside was covered with plants and shrubs. They glimpsed the view through the spray of huge fountains which caught flecks of sunlight before releasing them again in sparkling drops. The water added the most exciting dimension to the garden which, Miles explained, had in some places been carved out of the solid rock of the hillside. Long, rectangular pools, flanked by rows of ancient cypresses added length and increased the perspective. The sound of water was everywhere, spouting from obelisks or gushing from the mouths of mythological creatures and here and there was a small cascade. To say that the architect had succeeded in using water imaginatively was an understatement. Isobel's spirits began to lift at last as she and Rupert began to walk further into the garden.

"What a stunning place," she said turning towards him.

"If I could design something as gloriously over-the-top as this I could probably retire tomorrow, although Liz was the garden designer in our partnership and she would no doubt have made a much better job of it."

Isobel's heart lurched uncomfortably for the second time that morning. Since their initial meeting Rupert hadn't mentioned Liz at all. "Were you in partnership together as a business?" she asked.

"Unfortunately not. I tried to persuade her to design a garden for one of my properties on more than one occasion. I'm sorry to say she refused, insisted that I'd find it impossible to work with her." He shrugged his shoulders. "I couldn't force her could I?"

His face bore such a look of resigned sadness that Isobel felt compelled to change the subject. She back-tracked to his earlier remark. "Would you be really happy if you retired?" she asked.

"Probably not, although I suppose in time one learns to retire as one learns to work. I have to admit that I still get tremendous satisfaction from seeing an idea develop from a drawing into a finished building."

"Your contribution to posterity?" She smiled at him, relieved to see the veil lift from his eyes.

He laughed. "It's a nice thought. I'm not sure I'd describe the stuff I design in quite such glowing terms."

"I'm sure you're being unduly modest. This weekend has shown me that you're a vital part of a talented and beautiful family."

He looked pleased by the compliment. "It's kind of you to say so. I find it difficult sometimes to slip back into family mode. Living alone one tends to become self-indulgent. Take this morning for instance. I'd've found it very easy to stay in bed although normally I'm up and around quite early."

Isobel suddenly felt absurdly happy in the same way she'd felt as a teenager when the telephone rang and, running to answer it before her mother could get to the receiver, she'd heard the voice of the current boyfriend and knew she wouldn't have to spend the evening at home.

Suddenly Miles' voice interrupted their conversation, reminding them that they were still very much *en famille*.

"We thought lunch in about half an hour if that's OK by you?"

They smiled their assent, turned and walked slowly towards the exit, stopping every now and again to examine a fountain or a plant, prolonging their pleasure in the garden and each other before re-joining the family. Rupert had a sudden, irrational desire to return to Venice, wanting Isobel to himself for what was, after all, only another week. He considered the possibility of catching a late plane but, remembering Isobel's tiredness the previous evening, decided to revert to his original plan and leave early on Monday.

They lunched in an old inn next to the Temple of the Sibyl in a spectacular setting overlooking the ancient falls of Tivoli. The restaurant was full of Italian families and, for the first time since her arrival in Rome, Isobel began to feel at home.

A long wooden table carried an amazing display of antipasti. A vast array of cold meats; glistening olives; assorted fish; vegetables; salads of mixed beans. Isobel couldn't take her eyes away from it and her mouth began to water.

"You could select a complete meal from that table alone." Rupert had followed the direction of her gaze, noticed the tip of her tongue appear for an instant and couldn't resist adding; "Looks yummy doesn't it?" Isobel laughed, pleased that he'd not only remembered, but used, the childish adjective.

"No need to ask me what I'd like to start with is there? I assure you I'm not always quite so predictable."

"Predictable is the last word that springs to mind when I'm thinking about you."

"May I ask what words do spring?" She hadn't imagined him thinking about her but supposed he must, as indeed she thought of him.

"I'd describe you as completely unpredictable. I've noticed several changes of mood this weekend for instance."

She looked at him in surprise feeling uneasy that he'd noticed. "I hope unpredictable isn't a euphemism for moody?"

"Perish the thought! I realise that it must be quite difficult to find yourself suddenly pitched into the midst of a family you've never met before. I'd like you to know that I appreciate the effort you've made."

"As I said before, they're a fascinating and interesting family but there's such an empathy between you it's difficult not to feel an outsider at times."

He covered her hand with his own and squeezed it lightly. She felt a frisson, desire rekindled and supposed he could see that as well.

"Let's go and help ourselves from that delicious table shall we?" His voice was low, husky, as intimate as it had been earlier when they were alone. He made the choosing of food seem like an erotic experience.

As they ate she looked around the table, wanting to fix them all in her memory. She was struck by the difference between Rupert and his brother. Miles was quiet, introspective, eloquent when describing an old building or a work of art but otherwise speaking only when strictly necessary. Rupert was more outgoing and much readier to enter into general conversation but with a veneer of reserve in spite of the twinkling eyes. But the thing that made him so exciting, Isobel realised, was a covert sexuality which made her long to explore him further. Gianna was a complete contrast to all of them; animated, vivacious, the restless fingers constantly fluttering and with enough small talk for everybody. Gino was laid back, relaxed and easy but obviously completely besotted by his beautiful wife and daughter. They fitted together like a constantly changing montage forming a colourful and absorbing picture. Isobel couldn't help but compare the harmony of this lunch with the embarrassing and difficult meal they'd shared with Barbara and Henry in Venice. *Then* she couldn't wait to get away *now* she wanted to stay forever.

She had the warm feeling that she was accepted unconditionally and felt comfortable, wrapped in the warmth of Rupert's family. If only she could be sure about the depth of Rupert's true feelings for her. There were moments when she felt she had always known him, others when he seemed far away and there were parts of his life which appeared to be secret. What on earth had he been planning with Gianna this morning? Why was Miles excluded? The scene before her gave no indication of secrecy. The more she looked at them all the more she felt there must be some simple explanation and that if she were patient her fears would prove groundless. She had a whole week of Rupert ahead of her. Perhaps by the end she would know more?

"Honestly Jude I feel like the meat in the middle of the sandwich!" Susan said, taking a long pull from her glass of Pinot Grigio and looking across the table at her oldest friend. They were treating themselves to what they laughingly described as a business lunch, a monthly event when they were supposed to share information about the latest moves in the world of public relations but which invariably turned into an exchange of gossip and shared angst about their respective families.

"What's up now then?" Judy asked, waving at a business acquaintance who was seated on the opposite side of the restaurant. "I wonder if *his* wife knows that he's taking rather more than a passing interest in that new trainee of his? Sorry, you were saying?"

Susan glanced across at the couple who were gazing into each other's eyes and trying at the same time to eat their respective lunches which were cooling rapidly. "OK for some," she commented. "If I were to take a lover right now I think it would really drive me over the edge."

"Bad as that huh?"

"I don't think it *could* get any worse. One, I've had Father staying for a week now. He's got this crazy idea that we should up sticks and move in with him and, as if that weren't enough, Ian's father had a heart attack last Thursday and poor Ian doesn't know whether he's coming or going. It's just nothing but pressure at the moment."

Judy made sympathetic noises before enquiring. "So how's old Grizzle Guts responding to the crisis?" When the family discovered that Zelda had really been christened Grizelda they'd adopted the silly nickname which a few of their close friends shared.

"Just as you would expect," Susan replied. "Behaving like a tragedy queen already and telling us all that we're not giving her the support she needs. Honestly she's got bloody staff coming out of her ears and last night she had the cheek to ring up and have a go at Ian for not calling in to see her since James was taken ill. Would you believe it?"

"Of Zelda I'd believe anything. She always did have more front than Brighton! So what's the prognosis on James?"

"He has to stay in hospital until the doctors are satisfied it's safe for him to come home. Obviously he has to rest as much as possible but they make him get out of bed every day to go walkabout. They started him off with five minutes and they double up as he progresses. The final check is walking upstairs. When and if he's able to do that without having a second attack or dropping down dead he'll be allowed home."

"To the peace, quiet and restorative mercies of Grizzle?"

"Yes. I can honestly say that I really pity poor old James. I know he can be full of himself at times but he has a generous side for which we don't always give him credit. Do you know he actually sent one of his well-heeled buddies to one of my promotions the other evening he gave us a really big order."

"Personally," Judy said, picking an anchovy out of her Salade Niçoise and examining it minutely before putting it in her mouth.

"Personally I've always thought James rather attractive. All that grey wavy hair makes him look *distingué*. Not my taste exactly but definitely above average."

"Hmm, I can see what you mean, but honestly Jude since he married Grizzle there are times when he struts about like the proverbial peacock. You should have seen him at Grizzle's birthday party. There were times when you couldn't slide a piece of paper between them!"

"No wonder he had a heart attack! I should think Grizzle's a bit of a goer between the sheets!"

Susan held up both hands in mock horror. "Say no more! The prospect of James and Zelda making love is one I'd rather not think about if you don't mind. In any case I imagine that sex will definitely be off the agenda when James gets out of hospital so Grizzle will just have to cool it."

"Well you'd better lock your father up in case she takes a fancy to him and you have another heart attack victim on your hands," said Judy.

"You have to be joking. My father hasn't pulled anything more exciting than a weed from his garden in years! Anyway he's seventy, far too old to be thinking about sex. Well maybe he thinks about it but I shouldn't think for a moment that he can actually do it any more."

"Don't be too sure," Judy said, wagging her finger. "I have this friend whose grandfather is ninety. He has a sixty year old housekeeper, the grandfather I mean, not the friend. Well one day my friend dropped in unexpectedly, as you do, and what do you think he found?"

"Go on surprise me," said Susan.

"Well, and I promise you this is absolutely true, he found the two of them in the sitting room and my dear they were at it! Going like the proverbial clappers! So don't be too complacent about your father, he's a youngster by comparison."

"All I can say," said Susan, "is that any woman prepared to take him on will be more than welcome. My father would make a saint commit a sin! I've never in all my life met anyone so infuriatingly inept about the simplest things. He's great in the brain department but ask him to make a cup of tea and if he can find the kettle he won't know how to switch it on. If he does manage to boil the water he can't find the tea. All those years as a management consultant have turned him into someone who's great at delegating."

"Well your mother seemed to manage OK."

"Yes but you forget Dad was out of the country a lot. I guess that made it bearable."

"Shall we treat ourselves to a pudding?" Judy asked when the waiter came to clear their table.

"No thanks, not for me." Susan replied. "I shall have to provide a proper dinner when I get home this evening or Father will go back and tell his housekeeper that I starved him to death. You go ahead and order something really wicked and I'll watch while you pile on the kilos. Anyway I've got some absolutely riveting news to pass on and I won't have time to tell you if I'm eating pudding at the same time."

"Don't keep me in suspense then," said Judy. "Tell me who has done what and with whom."

"Well obviously Ian's been to see James a couple of times since he went into hospital and has been trying to discover if his father had any warning before his attack; asked him if work was getting him down and so on. A few days before he was taken ill he left the office unexpectedly early without a word to Ian and naturally Ian was keen to know why. Thought James might have been overdoing things. Anyway James finally admitted that he'd received what he described as a very upsetting phone call from his sister and, you'll never guess what?"

Judy stopped eating, her fork poised over the remains of a piece of Death by Chocolate. "It seems," Susan paused briefly for effect and then went on. "It seems that my aunt Barbara ran into Ian's mother in Venice of all places, having lunch in a very tucked away little restaurant."

"So?"

"Well she wasn't eating on her own but, according to my aunt she was having a very intimate lunch with some sleek Italian stallion, a rather glamorous architect by all accounts. Not only that but she told Barbara they'd known each other for years and years."

"So why was James so het up then? He's been getting his leg over regularly if what you've told me in the past is true."

"Well what really bugged James was that Isobel insisted at the time of their divorce that she was the innocent party. Completely convinced someone who describes himself as an expert in divorce and then promptly took him to the cleaners. Ian thinks it may have been the phone call that helped to trigger his heart attack, although of course James will never admit it."

"Isn't that a bit unfair? After all James was the one who asked for the divorce wasn't he?"

"Sure. But James always plays to win. I suppose that's his legal training coming out?"

"It sounds a bit more like double standards to me. Typical behaviour from men of that generation. They screw around for all they're worth and think it's an acceptable way to behave. But just let their wives, or ex-wives for that matter, try it and suddenly it becomes totally unacceptable. What does Ian think?"

"Well it's difficult to say. He's so busy at work that we don't really have too much time to talk, particularly with Father around all the time. Ian always blamed his mother for the break-up; said if she hadn't insisted on working James wouldn't have played the field."

"Ian might like to think that but he can't be absolutely certain, can he? After all your mother-in-law didn't tell James to go out and find another wife did she? Ian and Steven were both grown up by the time their parents separated so he can hardly say that Isobel abandoned him at a crucial stage of his life can he?"

"I think it's more to do with Ian supporting his father in everything he does. He's always stood up for James against all comers. It makes sense if you think about it. He followed his father's footsteps by studying law. Then he joined the practice, became a partner and, if everything goes according to plan, he'll take over when James retires. Although he's worked hard he's had the benefit of building up an established firm whereas some of his old buddies from law school had to start absolutely from scratch which is much harder."

"Who knows?" said Judy. "He could be the senior partner sooner than he expected."

"I don't think James will give up that easily. After all if he stopped working he'd have to spend all day and every day at Grizzle's beck and call. Which option would you choose?"

"No contest," said Judy laughing and then, looking at her watch, "My God! Look at the time! I've got a meeting with a client at four. I'm going to have to run I'm afraid." She fished in her bag, found her notecase, pulled out a couple of twenty pound notes and held them out towards Susan.

"Here's my share of the lunch. Can you be a dear and pay the bill, otherwise I'm going to be seriously late? Be sure to keep me in touch with developments."

"Sure; remember me to Mark. If and when we ever get any free time we must all meet up again, perhaps have dinner somewhere?"

"That would be lovely. Give the tinies a big kiss from their favourite aunty," Judy said and paused just long enough to kiss the air next to Susan's ear before she left.

Susan waited to pay the bill thinking what a treat it was to be able to talk candidly to a friend. She felt much more cheerful now than before lunch and Jude had given her a lot of food for thought. How would life go in the future for Ian and her? Would he follow in his father's footsteps in every respect? Would he want to leave her when their children were grown up or, God forbid, even earlier? After all one in every three marriages currently ended in divorce perhaps she should start looking around for a replacement? Is that what Isobel had done all those years ago? Seeing Ian the other evening laughing down at that blonde she'd realised suddenly how much she loved him, depended on him. Without him life would be insupportable. She'd miss his presence at PR promotions, his help with the children, his support, his opinions, to say nothing of the great sex. It would be terrible if she had to hand over the children on alternate Friday evenings to allow them to spend the mandatory weekends with their father.

Now Sue, you're really getting depressed, she told herself. There's only one problem at the moment and that's your father. And Jude had planted one very constructive idea. Perhaps if she succeeded in persuading Bruce to get married again that problem would be very neatly solved.

Chapter Ten

Steve stood in the porch of his father's house in Wandsworth listening to the sound of screaming coming from inside and rang the bell a second time. He was returning from a meeting with a client and on the spur of the moment decided to pay his father a visit and, as he was passing through Wandsworth, to offer Zelda a lift. He was just beginning to wonder if anyone was ever going to answer when the door opened and Zelda stood in front of him holding a tearful Samantha.

"Hi!" Steve said looking carefully at Zelda. The woman who stood in front of him was not the immaculately groomed step-mother that he was used to seeing at family parties. Her hair needed washing and, although it was two o'clock in the afternoon, she wasn't wearing make-up. Her tee shirt was crumpled and not overly clean and her jeans were bagging out at the knees.

"Aren't you going to invite me in?" he said at length as she continued to stand and look at him.

"Sorry Steve but things are a bit hectic at the moment. Come and have some tea or coffee or something." And then, "Shut up Samantha!" she snapped, as a fresh outburst of sobbing made it impossible to talk in a normal voice. Samantha paused long enough to shriek, "Naughty mummy!" and then started to drum her heels into Zelda's back.

"Here, let me take her for a minute." Steve reached out and grabbed Samantha. "Having an attack of the Terrible Two's are we?" His remark was addressed to no one in particular but to his surprise Zelda said, "Oh Steve! It's all terrible at the moment!" and burst into tears.

"Hey now take it easy." Steve followed Zelda into the kitchen, deposited Samantha on the nearest chair and put his arms round her mother in an attempt to comfort her. "I know Dad's illness has been a shock for you as it has for the whole family but he'll soon be home again and then you'll be able to take up where you left off." He hoped his words might reassure her, cheer her up even, but Zelda continued to sob and after a few minutes he persuaded her to sit down while he made them both some tea.

"At the moment I can't see how anything will ever be the same again," Zelda said. "I seem to have made an absolute mess of everything since James went into hospital."

Things must be really bad if Zelda was taking responsibility for her mistakes, Steven thought. Aloud and trying to make his voice sound soothing he said, "Don't be too hard on yourself. After all things are bound to be a bit disorganised at the moment, what with having to fit in visits to the hospital and everything." He put tea bags into mugs and poured boiling water onto them.

Zelda pulled a crumpled tissue from her pocket and blew her nose. "If only that was all." Her voice had become almost a whine. "The *au pair* walked out on Sunday. The phone never stops ringing because people want to know how James is progressing. I've told the same story so many times I'm reciting it in my sleep and, as if that weren't enough, Samantha has taken it into her head to be really naughty because I don't have the time for all the things we normally do together." The tears flowed more freely as the story came out and Zelda abandoned the sodden tissue and replaced it with a piece of kitchen paper which she ripped savagely from the roll hanging on the wall. "I daren't think what things will be like when James comes home. He can be so demanding and to have him here all day, as well as coping with visitors, well honestly Steve I just don't know how I'm going to manage." She gave him the full benefit of her large, flooded, brown eyes and Steve cast about desperately for some kind of solution.

"Will your mother come up for a few days to help out?" he asked.

"Ma and Pa are off to Tenerife for a month, it's cheaper in October and I don't think it's fair to ask them to cancel their holiday. Anyway I'm not sure James will want people around when he gets home. How I'm going to keep Samantha out of his hair I can't imagine. She absolutely adores him and never leaves his side when he's at home. James doesn't find my parents' company very stimulating at the best of times. Mother tends to chatter on about nothing and James usually finds some excuse to escape, either to the golf club or the garden when they're here. If he can't get away because he's house-bound, well . . ." She let the sentence tail away and left the outcome to Steve's imagination.

"Well perhaps *we* can help out somehow." Steven said, pouring milk into their tea and handing a mug to Zelda. "Tell you what, I'll give Joy a ring and ask her if we can have Samantha for a day or two until you get yourself sorted. We dovetail our schedules so that one of us works from home if the other has to be out for any reason. What do you think?"

It didn't take Zelda long to realise that the prospect of freedom was being waved in front of her and she stopped crying as easily as turning off a tap. "I'm sure Samantha wouldn't be any trouble," she said, dabbing her eyes one last time, "and of course she'd be good company for Tom wouldn't she? He must be quite lonely as you're both working."

Any minute from now she'll convince me that she's doing me the favour Steve thought but aloud said, "I'll just give Joy a ring then." He pulled out his mobile and went through the back door into the garden on the pretext of being able to get a better signal.

"You've done what?" Joy exclaimed into the telephone when Steven had put her in the picture.

"Just for a few days." Steven smiled into his phone knowing in his heart that Joy wouldn't let him down.

"Well just make sure that you set a time limit and thank your lucky stars I'm crazy about you or I wouldn't be such a pushover. Did I ever tell you what a big softie you are?"

"Frequently. And you're the best wife a man ever had. I'll go and break the glad news to Zelda. We're off to see Dad fairly soon so you've got two or three hours to get used to the idea. Thanks a million. 'Bye."

He pocketed his mobile and went back to the kitchen. "So how long will it take you to pack a bag for Samantha?" he asked Zelda.

"Oh Steve! You're an absolute angel!" Relief flooded her face as she jumped to her feet and much to Steve's embarrassment flung her arms around his neck. "It won't take me a minute to throw a few things into a bag and then I'll change quickly and we can go and see James!"

While he was waiting for Zelda Steve thought about the crises his mother had dealt with, particularly her divorce. He remembered clearly her calm command of various situations as they presented themselves and her firm resolve to carry on at all costs. Perhaps part of the attraction between his father and Zelda was that, patently, she needed him more than he her whereas there were times when his mother appeared as the more competent partner in their relationship, remaining calm when James raged, finding things that James lost, remembering when his father forgot.

Thank God Joy never lost her cool. On the contrary she was so laid back he sometimes wished that she'd just occasionally blow her top. It was marvellous the way she met any event without turning a hair. Occasionally he worried in case there was a tight knot of emotion building up inside which might one day erupt in the frightening way that an apparently dormant volcano could suddenly break out and devastate the surrounding area. He glanced at his watch and saw that half an hour had passed since Zelda had told him that it wouldn't take her a minute to have everything ready, including herself. At least for once he was in no hurry to be anywhere except home again. He'd call Ian later and they'd try to make plans for when their father came out of hospital. That wasn't going to be an easy problem to solve but it sure as hell wouldn't go away so the sooner they all put their heads together the better.

Barbara stood in her kitchen beating eggs much too savagely for an omelette and wondering why she didn't feel happier. James' current setback was long overdue she argued. After all he'd succeeded in getting his own way for most of his life and, by comparison with all the success he'd had, his current illness was a mere flea-bite.

She cast her mind back to Zelda's birthday party when she'd caught sight of James sliding his hand over Zelda's silk-clad rump - apparently not caring who saw him. It was disgusting that a man of his age was behaving like some sex-obsessed teenager. No doubt when everybody had left he'd spent most of the night trying to prove his manhood. She chopped parsley viciously, flung it into the egg mixture and reached for the omelette pan.

She remembered James going off to university without a backward glance when he could so easily have persuaded their father that she too would have made an excellent law student. She'd always fought for privileges for both of them. The right to join the church youth club for instance which had opened doors to other social events in the village. Selfish, self-centred and over-sexed would just about sum him up and now he was paying. She poured the omelette mixture onto sizzling butter, stirred vigorously and tried once again to forget the moment in Venice when she'd picked up the telephone.

Isobel's final week flew by as quickly as the ubiquitous pigeons ducking and diving around St Mark's Square. Rupert did his best to free himself from his work which was reaching the stage where he could safely leave it to the builders. On Wednesday he took the day off and drove them to Ravenna and showed Isobel the marvellous mosaics. Friday afternoon found them in Padua looking at Giotto's faded frescoes in the Scrovegni Chapel. On the journey back to Venice, Rupert, with his usual penchant for planning, asked Isobel how she would like to spend Saturday, her last full day, promising to do whatever she wanted. He was surprised when she asked him to take her to Chioggia to see his project. She further astonished him by turning down his offer of dinner at the Cipriani in favour of a second meal in his apartment. Although he was pleased by her choice it also puzzled him. When they'd returned from Rome he'd asked if she would like to move out of her hotel and into his flat but she'd turned him down. He'd thought that perhaps the apartment wasn't to her taste or that for some reason she wanted to be independent, perhaps needing her own space. Now here she was asking to spend her last evening there.

"Are you sure that's what you'd really like to do?"

"Absolutely. You look surprised," she said, as he turned towards her with a puzzled expression.

"I thought perhaps you didn't like the place."

"I don't like it when it's empty. After all I've only spent one evening there and after you left it all felt rather strange, almost as if I were trespassing. And I'd love to see some of your work. We've looked at so much of the old architecture since I arrived I'd like an opportunity to see some of the new. Chioggia will also be quite new to me so whatever I see will be different and exciting."

Everything I do with Rupert is a new and special experience, she thought and wondered again how on earth she was going to adjust back into the life she'd left behind. She thought of being at the end of a telephone every time one of the family rang to ask a favour. Hadn't Rupert said something about finding it difficult to slip back into family mode when they were at the Villa d'Este? She understood exactly what he meant.

She'd imagined Chioggia as a small fishing village without really knowing why but as the launch drew nearer Isobel was surprised to see a large semi-circular bay crowded with every conceivable kind of boat and the many buildings climbing the hillside away from the quay indicated that Chioggia was more of a thriving port. Although fishing was in evidence there were also restaurants, shops, the usual tourist attractions. Rupert's development was, he explained, a small collection of two story apartments which he'd designed with the prevailing landscape in mind. The last thing he wanted was something that stuck out like a sore thumb as 'new'.

"Prince Charles would love you!" Isobel teased him.

"I can promise you there are no monstrous carbuncles here but then I hope we've managed something a little less bland than that awful Dorset village, what's it called, Poundbury or some such?"

Isobel was afraid she'd touched a nerve and moved the conversation quickly on. "So tell me about your apartments," she urged.

"Space is a real problem in an area like this which is made up of so many small islands and where residential accommodation is in short supply. Many young families are forced to live with the parents of one or the other. In places like this, dedicated to the tourist, a lot of the new development is geared to visitors. But what about the residents? These apartments are an experiment for this neck of the woods. I've borrowed the idea from the UK and have built family apartments with some self-contained accommodation for an elderly parent. It can't be easy for families to find privacy when the in-laws are around."

They'd been walking away from the quayside and up the hill as they talked and Rupert pointed to a small two-story development built round three sides of a courtyard. "We've used traditional materials as you can see." Rupert waved an arm towards the building. The roofs were finished with terra cotta tiles in contrast to the cream washed walls so that they blended in with traditional architecture. They picked their way across bits of masonry and assorted builders rubbish before going inside.

The rooms felt shaded and cool after the glare of the sun and as Rupert explained various features to her Isobel could see that he'd thought very carefully about the overall design. He'd made the most of the available space by building in cupboards and kitchen equipment, providing wheel chair access and, he confided, he had plans to develop the courtyard into a play area for children; his aim, to help three generations of the same family to co-exist together in harmony.

Every so often he paused to have a word with one of the builders. He spoke easily, in Italian, answering a question, making a suggestion, asking after their families, laughing with them. She'd never seen him working before and she added these other facets of his character to the picture she was building in her mind, gradually creating a portrait in the way an artist might. Every time they met she discovered something new about him and she realised suddenly that life with him would never be predictable or boring.

"Well there you have it, a Rupert Northcote development," he said, when at last they'd finished looking round. "I hope you feel the trip was worth it?" He looked at her quizzically and Isobel sensed that he was waiting for her approval. She searched around in her mind for appropriate words.

"I'm really glad I came. It's a charming development. It would be interesting to hear in a few years time how the families respond to it. You're almost orchestrating a lifestyle aren't you if this kind of place is so unusual in Italy?"

"Hmm, I hadn't thought of it quite like that. Makes me sound like a modern Machiavelli and I must admit there were various stages in the planning when I felt like him, the end justifies the means and all that nonsense."

They began to retrace their steps turning back towards the lagoon. "It's at times like this I really miss our English pubs," Rupert said. "I thought I'd make us a real Venetian risotto this evening. I'll buy a lobster and some prawns later before we leave. We could have a traditional Italian lunch but it will probably ruin our appetites for dinner. Shall we try to find some *crostini* and perhaps a cold beer?"

Isobel didn't reply. Our last lunch; final dinner; she was thinking. Her throat was suddenly tight with unshed tears. Her fists were tightly clenched and both hands were thrust into the pocket of her slacks. Her head was bent and she was looking at her toes as if she'd never really seen them before. They were dusty from the building site, her varnished toe nails misted in fine powder.

Waiting for her reply Rupert glanced sideways at her as they continued walking. She was wearing dark glasses making it impossible for him to see the expression in her eyes. But he read the body language thinking that she looked like a child at the end of a special treat, all hunched and wondering how long before the next. He put an arm around her shoulders, pulling her close to him. She inhaled his familiar smell and smiled in spite of her gloomy introspection.

"Sorry Rupert but I hate endings." She suddenly felt churlish. He was taking such care to make her last day everything she'd wanted and his consideration touched her deeply but also made her feel guilty for the times that she'd doubted his integrity, suspected his motives.

"Who said anything about endings?" His voice was light hearted, amused.

"Parting then if you prefer, but that's almost as bad. Promise me that you'll drop me off at the airport tomorrow and turn the boat straight around again and head back to your apartment as fast as possible. I hate protracted farewells."

"Of course, if that's what you want. I'd originally hoped that we could fly home together but Gianna asked me to do her a favour so I shall go to Rome on Monday."

He paused as they reached a small bistro. A canopied terrace overlooked the lagoon, They were still some way up the hillside and there was a welcoming breeze. I have to know more about this trip to Rome, Isobel thought as they took their seats but waited until their food arrived before asking, "Does Gianna have a problem."

Rupert took a long pull at his beer and demolished a *crostino* before replying. "My sister-in-law, as you've probably gathered, is wildly romantic. An elderly aunt of hers died about six months ago and left Gianna a tidy legacy. She wants to buy an old farmhouse or something like it in Tuscany and asked me if I'd go along to help. The whole scheme is planned as a surprise for Miles' sixtieth birthday next year so it has to be a secret from him. He's leaving for a conference on Monday which gives us an opportunity to set the wheels in motion."

Relief washed all her doubts away. She knew, hoped, that there'd be a simple explanation, now here it was. Her appetite returned. She nibbled a *crostino* thinking how good it tasted. "Has Gianna actually found a place or is she still searching?" she asked.

"She has her eye on a pair of broken down, empty cottages in Bagni di Lucca. Bagni used to be a thriving spa town. It's scarcely changed for a hundred and fifty years and is very picturesque. There are several small villages around and some lovely landscapes in the vicinity. Gianna thinks it will be an ideal place for Miles to work in peace and quiet and hopes the surrounding countryside will inspire him to paint more. Long term she'd like them to sell up in Rome and move permanently to more rural surroundings after Miles retires."

"Do you think Miles will go along with her plan?"

"If it's presented as a *fait accompli* Miles will accept, rather than going to the trouble of reversing the procedure. My guess is they'll probably end up compromising; possibly dividing their time between the two places. After all it's one thing to be in the countryside when the sun's shining and the roads passable but once winter sets in the whole landscape changes as you can imagine. I can't say I blame Gianna for wanting to get out of Rome in the summer. It can be absolute hell on a hot day. Think Dante's 'Inferno' and you won't be far wrong."

"How long do you think you'll be away?" Isobel asked.

"We only have ten days before Miles returns from Prague. I'm going along to make sure Gianna doesn't commit to a property which has no water supply or electricity. She's such an air-head she wouldn't even think about the expense of bringing major utilities along two or three miles of rough terrain, to say nothing of the delay, the bureaucracy and all the other tedious bits of officialdom we have to cope with in Italy. The lawyer will have to make sure that there are no outstanding taxes due on the property and, if it's jointly owned by several members of the same family, all the parties will have to agree before the sale can go ahead. We could be lucky and find somewhere quickly. I'll do the conversion plans when I get home. I haven't really answered your question have I?" He paused and thought for a few moments before adding; "At the most optimistic I would say five days to a week but we might need all ten days before Gianna is satisfied. When I get back to Venice I'll come over here to take a quick look and then come back to the UK for a while. I've another project waiting for me and I'm keen to get on with it as you can imagine."

"Oh! His life's all planned out so carefully, Isobel thought and was just beginning to feel bleak again when Rupert reached across the table and took her hand.

"I meant what I said earlier you know."

"You mean about tomorrow just being the beginning of a brief parting?"

"Exactly. We've come a long way in two weeks when you think about it." His eyes were twinkling again but then his face suddenly became serious.

"I think both of us need some time and space don't you? I certainly feel I'd like to experience life without you for a while in order to appreciate what it was like when we were together. Does that make sense or do I sound mixed up?"

The thought of Rupert being mixed up wasn't a possibility as far as Isobel was concerned. What if . . .? No she wouldn't think about that. The fear that, once she'd left Venice, he would resume his old life and forget her. But then he'd introduced her to his family, spent a lot of time with her and she felt she knew him well enough to know that he wouldn't waste his time on lost causes. The thought cheered her up and she managed to smile at him.

"By the time you come home you'll be wondering how you can possibly live the rest of your life without me or . . ." and here she paused, daring herself to finish the sentence; "you'll look back at the last two weeks and feel you made a dreadful mistake." She watched him carefully from behind her sunglasses. His eyes were veiled again. He shrugged. "As I said before Isobel, I need time."

Isobel realised that the conversation was at an end and that she would have to be satisfied. "You mentioned buying lobster earlier," she said. "Would you like to get moving?"

"The boats come in about four o'clock so we've time for some coffee." He signalled to the waiter.

It was whilst they were waiting that a particular sentence of Rupert's came back into her mind. Gianna was planning to buy a property as a surprise for Miles' sixtieth birthday next year. Rupert had earlier referred to Miles as his elder brother which meant that Rupert was not yet sixty, that made him younger than her. By how many years and did it matter? She could scarcely describe him as a toy boy but had he realised that she was older than he and would that worry him? The thought preoccupied her until their coffee arrived and then she put it firmly to the back of her mind. She would cross that particular bridge if and when . . .

Later she watched him haggle good naturedly with a fisherman before selecting a lobster and a kilo of prawns. As they made their way back to the launch, tubular sardine nets were being hung up to dry. There was a fresh aroma of fish carried on the breeze and the quay was busy as catches were unloaded. She continued watching as he cast off and turned towards Venice thinking how handsome he looked. He was wearing cream cotton trousers, a navy cotton sweater, espadrilles and presented a picture of casual elegance which she'd found so attractive when they first met. Now he was concentrating on steering the boat as they cruised past Pellestrina towards the Lido and she fixed yet another image of him in her mind.

They prepared supper together, drinking prosecco and dividing the tasks. They were relaxed as two friends, no tension. They talked of films they'd seen, books they'd read and tasted each other's cooking as the preparation progressed. For her it was a new experience, for him a return to previous occasions with Liz.

They ate in the kitchen, congratulating each other on their teamwork. The conversation continued to flow easily. When they'd finished they carried their coffee into Rupert's immaculate sitting room. Isobel felt light-headed with the combination of wine and happiness. Rupert put down the tray, crossed to the mahogany chest, opened the top drawer and pulled out a slim rectangular package.

"Here's a small memory of Venice for you." He was smiling as he handed her the parcel.

"A present for me? Rupert what a lovely surprise!" She kissed him lightly on the cheek. "May I open it now?"

"Please do." Now it was his turn to watch *her* as she opened the wrapping and he saw the expression on her face change from curiosity through puzzlement to pleased surprise.

"Oh! It's a painting of your garden!" She was looking at a delicate watercolour which had obviously been painted from his sitting room window. It included part of the terrace, a section of balustrade and the palazzo opposite. Rupert's initials were in the bottom right hand corner.

"You painted it yourself." It was a statement rather than a question.

"Like many architects I daub a bit although sadly I lack the talent of Michelangelo or Bernini."

"It's absolutely lovely, I shall treasure it. Thank you."

She blinked back her tears as he bent and kissed her mouth. His lips were warm and tasted of wine. She reached up for him, twining her arms about his neck, wanting to keep him there, absorbing the feel of him, drinking in his scent.

The sound of the telephone shattered the moment. Rupert cursed, muttered something about having switched off the answer phone when they came home. He pulled away from her abruptly and strode purposefully across the room towards the hall. The strident sound of the telephone continued, intrusive, insistent. The door of the sitting room slammed shut behind him and Isobel was left to herself.

"*Pronto.*" Rupert barked into the instrument.

"Hi Pa! It's Tory."

"Tory!" Rupert's voice was incredulous.

"Listen Pa, I think my battery's low, so I'll have to talk fast. I'm on a train from Paris, should hit Venice in about half an hour. Can I come and doss down at your place for a couple of days?"

Rupert winced at the expression. "I'm not exactly running a doss house Tory."

"Thanks for the welcome Pa. May I sleep on your sofa then for a couple of nights?" She'd changed her voice, adopting a genteel accent. "I have some business in Venice," she continued, "didn't have time to sort out an hotel."

Rupert, for once in his life, had no idea what to say. "It's a bit short notice," he said, aware that he sounded feeble, but saying the first words that came into his head.

"I left a message on your machine earlier. Didn't you pick it up?"

"I've been out all day, haven't cleared the answer phone." Rupert cursed himself silently. He'd seen the flashing light when he returned with Isobel but switched it off, making a mental note to clear his messages later.

"Do you have much luggage? I'm not sure if I can get to the station in time to meet your train," he said, moving swiftly into practicalities.

"That's OK. I'll hop on a *vaporetto*."

"Take the number eighty two and I'll meet you at the Rialto Bridge."

"'Bye Pa. See you." The line went dead.

Rupert stood by the phone, trying to regain his composure. "Ten out of ten for timing Tory," he said softly to himself before squaring his shoulders and returning to Isobel. The smile on her face faded swiftly as she caught his expression.

"Trouble?" The question seemed superfluous; the set of his mouth was so forbidding.

"With a capital T for Tory. Arriving in Venice in half an hour if you please and wants to stay here for a couple of nights. I haven't heard a word from her in six months and now she expects to use me as a hotel . . ." His voice tailed away, he shrugged and held out his hands helplessly towards her.

Isobel jumped to her feet, walked towards him and took his outstretched hands. "I think it's time for me to leave, don't you? Suddenly I feel quite tired. It's been a perfect day Rupert, I've loved every minute."

He put an arm round her shoulders and pulled her close, laid his cheek against her hair. "Isobel I'm so sorry. Believe me I didn't intend your last day to end quite like this."

She managed a tentative smile in spite of her disappointment. "I'm sure you didn't. As you said in Rome, it's sometimes difficult to slip back into family mode."

"Right this minute that seems like a gross understatement but at least I have time to walk you back to your hotel." Isobel started to protest but he laid his index finger across her mouth. "Please Isobel, no arguments." His voice sounded weary and she noticed for the first time that there were sharp lines etched around his mouth. The scar on his eyebrow stood out, white against his tanned face. She smoothed the eyebrow gently trying to hide the scar and felt him wince slightly. She was relieved she'd decided not to move out of her hotel so that at least she had somewhere to sleep which wouldn't be charged with tension and who knows what else? Her intuition told her that the forthcoming encounter between Rupert and Tory was one she'd rather not see.

Susan, attempting to kill two birds with one stone, was driving her father to the hospital to visit James. The poor old thing had been left to his own devices for so much of his stay and with any luck they would have time to spare after the visit and she could take him out for tea. At least they'd be spending time together and she reckoned she owed him that at least.

"I hate hospitals." Bruce grumbled as they walked into the entrance.

"Well thank your lucky stars you're a visitor and not a patient." Susan said, attempting to placate him. "I'm sure James has been starved of intelligent male company and he'll enjoy seeing you again." She prayed silently that Bruce would at least make an effort to be pleasant.

James was sitting by his bed when they arrived. He looked pale and tired and seemed to have shrunk since Susan last saw him. "Hi Dad!" she said brightly, bending to plant a kiss on his cheek which felt flabby under her mouth.

"Susan. How nice!" James attempted a smile before extending a hand towards Bruce.

Bruce shook the proffered hand without enthusiasm. "Hope you're feeling better," he said, settling himself in the only chair.

"Oh! The days seem to crawl by," James replied. "I guess that's a sign that I'm over the worst. I miss using this I'm afraid." He tapped his forehead with a shaky finger.

"The rest will do you good." Susan put in, wishing there was a good visitors guide to help on occasions like this when she was lost for words. "Ian seems to be keeping things ticking over so no need to think about rushing back." She ignored the derisory grunt that came from Bruce as she mentioned Ian.

"Right now I'm much more worried about the effect that my illness is having on Zelda." James said. "The poor little thing is rushed off her feet with one thing and another."

"Well Steve and Joy have taken Samantha off her hands for a few days." Susan felt impelled to leap towards the family's defence. It's too bad the *au pair* left but I guess Zelda will sort herself out given time.

James had a doubtful expression on his face but even so Susan was completely unprepared for his next remark. "You know it's at times like this that I miss Isobel. *She* would have coped - somehow." His voice sounded wistful. His eyes told them his thoughts were elsewhere.

"Well Isobel will be back from Venice soon. Maybe she'll come and see you when she's back home. We haven't told her yet about your heart attack. We didn't want to cast a cloud over the last few days of her holiday." Susan prattled on wanting to lift his mood and quite suddenly feeling sorry for him.

"I don't think that news of my illness is likely to spoil Isobel's holiday." James said. His voice now had a bitter edge to it. Susan heard him sigh deeply and wondered if he might just be regretting his past treatment of his first wife. She was casting around desperately for something, anything she could say that might offer a crumb of comfort when the door of his room opened and Zelda appeared.

"Darling! Oh darling! I'm sorry I'm so late! So many things to do! So much to think about!" She bent to kiss him. "I brought these from the garden. I thought they might cheer you up." She placed a small bunch of late roses on his bedside locker.

Bruce struggled to his feet and offered Zelda his chair. "Hello Zelda." Susan said wondering if she'd become invisible or if Zelda really was so keen to see James she'd failed to notice her. "Oh hello!" Zelda said absently. "James is looking so much better don't you think?"

"He looks good to me." Susan lied before turning to Bruce. "I think it's time we were going Dad." she said. "I'm sure James and Zelda have lots to talk about." As they said their goodbyes and left she hoped, for James' sake, that she was right.

Chapter Eleven

Later that same evening Steve, Ian and their wives were at last able to get together for their family conference. Susan and Ian drove down to Berkhamsted and, after demolishing a couple of Pizza's delivered by the local takeaway they finally got around to discussing James and what should or shouldn't happen to him when he came out of hospital.

Steve told them about his visit to Zelda, embellishing the details a bit to try and persuade the others of the need for some positive action and hands-on help. He'd been prepared for both Sue and Ian to dismiss his suggestion but, to his surprise, Sue backed him up.

She described her own earlier encounter with Zelda at the hospital. "To be honest James didn't look all that thrilled when Zelda walked in." She told the others. "Of course our stepmother was late and full of excuses as you'd expect from her. You'd think with no job and no children to look after she might have made just the tiniest effort to be on time, particularly when James has had such a life-threatening experience."

Ian tried hard to suppress a yawn. "Sorry everybody but I'm knackered. I've been putting in a twelve hour day since the start of Father's illness and, as if that weren't enough, my father-in-law is at home waiting to be entertained every evening. Not an easy task at the best of times, well nigh impossible if he's in a sulk. He seems incapable of grasping the fact that Sue and I have to earn a living even though he spent so much of his own life working away from home."

Joy, who was herself struggling to juggle work, home and the care of two children under three, smiled sympathetically at Ian. "I think James will find it pretty intolerable to have a frisky two year old, to say nothing of her mother, making demands on his time when he finally gets home. What he really needs is peace and quiet and I can't see him getting that in Wandsworth. Like it or not I think we have to try to give Zelda the opportunity to replace the *au pair* before burdening her with the care of a sick husband."

"We've had nearly forty trouble free years so we can't really complain." Steven was trying to look on the bright side and to force a ray of sunshine into what was fast becoming a gloomy Saturday evening. "Let's face it old James has been good to all of us at different times. We can't turn our backs on him the minute he runs into trouble." The others agreed reluctantly.

Sue looked at her watch, conscious that time was ticking by and that her father was home alone with the *au pair* and the children for the second evening that week. They really must reach a decision soon so that she and Ian could get home in time to spend an hour with Bruce before bedtime. "What about a convalescent home for a while?" she asked, trying to find a creative solution to the problem without involving any of them in additional work.

"Can you really see James in a nursing home?" Joy said. "Even if we could find a place that was half way possible James would deliberately behave so badly that they'd throw him out before he'd been there a week and then we should be back where we started. Remember too that James will have to visit the hospital for periodic check-ups so our choice is limited."

"And he won't be allowed to drive for at least a month so someone will have to take him." Steve topped up their glasses and looked around again for fresh inspiration.

"Why don't we spell out the problem before we start thinking solutions." Susan said. "Let's make a list of all the things that James will need and then decide how we can best give them to him."

Steve produced paper and a pen. "Right then, fire away, I'll take notes. Joy's already pointed out that he'll need peace and quiet and chauffeured trips to the hospital, anybody else got any bright ideas?" He looked around hopefully at the others. It had been a hard week for all of them but they did their best and within a short time had a list which included: freedom from worry - either business or financial, gentle daily exercise, a carefully controlled diet, no strenuous activity - "including sex!" they all chorused at once amid the first real laughter of the evening. Absolutely no smoking and limited alcohol were the last two requirements, after which their ideas dried up.

Ian kicked off the discussion. "Obviously I'm the only one who can deal with the business side. Maybe I can take on a locum to do the routine stuff until James is ready to return. It stands to reason I shall have to talk to Dad from time-to-time over the finer details of his work with his own clients but I'll try to keep that to the minimum. In the meantime we shall continue to pay his salary so he won't have any money worries."

"We must persuade Zelda to replace her *au pair* as quickly as possible so that Samantha's routine can get back to normal," Joy added. Samantha and Tom were partners in crime already and each day were in competition to see who could become the dirtiest, noisiest or most disobedient. It was hardly surprising that Joy was keen for Samantha to return home sooner rather than later.

This left the day-to-day supervision of James to be decided. They all agreed that small children and peace and quiet were not exactly synonymous and looked at each other for further inspiration.

"I'm just beginning to realise how much stability Mum provided for Dad when they were still together," Steve put in.

"Do you know Steve you've hit the nail right on the head!" Susan jumped in with both feet. "In fact only this afternoon James was telling me how much he missed her and how good she was at coping in a crisis." Ian looked at her sharply. "Are you sure you heard correctly?" he said. "It's just that I was under the impression that she wasn't exactly his favourite person at the moment." "I'm absolutely sure," Sue replied, "and I know this is a very long shot, but do you think we could persuade Isobel to have him to stay, perhaps just for a couple of weeks until Zelda gets herself sorted out and James is on the mend."

"You mean ask *our* mother to take back her ex-husband because his new, young wife can't cope with a sick man." Steve's voice was incredulous at Susan's suggestion. "The very mention of Mother in James' hearing might even trigger another heart attack."

"Well if we suggest to Isobel that it was news of her romance that actually helped to put James into hospital . . ." She let the sentence tail off and Ian, who'd been waiting desperately for a straw to clutch, exclaimed; "Susan my darling that's a brilliant idea! We'll simply appeal to her better nature!"

"She may even decide that she prefers your father to this Rupert character and lure him back into her life." Having come up with the idea in the first place Susan decided to embellish it. "If we could see old Grizzle off at the same time it would really be worth the effort."

"Oh puh-leeze!" Steve's exasperation boiled over. "Just listen to yourselves folks. We can't go around playing God with our parents or even step-parents."

"I suppose it could work." Joy was as keen as anybody to find a solution. "But we shall have to use supreme tact with both James and Isobel if we're to get them to agree."

"Think of it logically," Sue went on, "Isobel can certainly offer peace and quiet. She has few commitments compared with the rest of us. She can drive James to hospital, supervise his exercise and diet and," she paused before adding triumphantly, "if this Rupert is as dishy as Barbara says, Isobel will be so brimful of energy and feeling so on top of the world that she'll be ready to agree to anything!"

Steven looked round the table and saw three pairs of eyes fixed on him. It didn't need genius to see that they were waiting for his approval. He knew he was on a hiding to nothing but, knowing instinctively that he would be the one selected to break the news to his mother, he felt he should try at least one alternative suggestion. "Perhaps Father would prefer to stay with Aunt Barbara?" He braced himself for their scorn.

"She'd kill him in a week!" Ian put in. "We all know you have to be really fit to cope with Barbara at the best of times!" He looked at each of them in turn daring them to contradict.

Steven could see that from now on it would just be a question of selling the idea as sensitively as possible, but he couldn't help feeling uneasy at the possible outcome. "What if Ma and Pa simply refuse?" He appealed to them all again but knew in his heart of hearts that none of them were prepared to consider the possibility that their plan might fail.

Ian rose swiftly to his feet and slapped his brother on the back. "With you and me in the driving seat we can't lose! Think solutions not problems! I'll deal with Dad and Zelda and I'll leave you to break the news to Mum." He kissed Joy, pulled Susan to her feet and was out of the house before Steven could protest.

"Did I ever tell you how brilliant you are?" he said to Susan as they drove away. "And if you can persuade that father of yours to go to bed before midnight I'll be delighted to show you just how grateful I am."

Rupert felt his mood darken for the first time in two weeks as he turned the boat away from Marco Polo Airport and headed for the Grand Canal. He glanced down at the parcel which Isobel had given him shortly after he tied up at the airport, asking him not to open it until he arrived home. "I bought it in Rome," she'd explained with a brief smile. "Gianna was good enough to help me track it down. Without her help I doubt if I should have found it."

"How intriguing!" He'd exclaimed as she handed it over.

"I hope you enjoy it."

"I rarely receive presents, particularly not from beautiful women, I'm sure I'll love it, thank you." He bent and kissed her, lingering, not really wanting to leave. "Are you sure you wouldn't like me to come in with you?" he asked, nodding towards the airport building and thinking that perhaps they might have a last coffee together.

She replied briskly and without the slightest hesitation. “I’m quite sure, thanks all the same. As I said before I hate protracted farewells.” After that he had no option but to climb back on board and head for home. If he had turned back he would have seen Isobel wipe her eyes before putting on her dark glasses and taking a last, longing look across the lagoon at the city she’d grown to love in just two short weeks.

Rupert braced himself for what he guessed might be a sticky encounter with Tory. Last night she’d told him about her new job with a holiday property company. She was in Venice to look at some apartments which they might consider promoting next year. He’d given her coffee and clean sheets and then left her to her own devices deciding that it wouldn’t be tactful to tell her about the evening with Isobel that she’d just interrupted.

When he’d left to collect Isobel, at eleven thirty this morning, the door to the sitting room was firmly closed and he assumed that Tory was still asleep. He’d picked up the damp towel which she’d flung over the side of the bath and replaced it with a clean one which he’d put, neatly folded, on the towel rail. He clicked his tongue in annoyance at the sight of assorted cosmetics spilling out of her wash bag which was open on the deep window ledge and at the crumpled, grubby face flannel and squidged up tube of toothpaste which lay, minus its top, on the edge of the wash basin.

Now as he walked into the apartment he saw, through the open door of the sitting room, a jumble of bed linen spilling from one of the sofas onto the floor and assumed that Tory was now up and about. He slipped quietly into his study, carefully unwrapped Isobel's parcel and took out a second hand abridged version of the first volume of The Stones of Venice, with illustrations by Ruskin himself. Inside was a note.

Dear Rupert,

I can't thank you enough for introducing me to the magic of Venice. The past two weeks have been really wonderful and I'm taking home so many happy memories which I'll continue to treasure. I still haven't overcome all my prejudices as far as Ruskin is concerned but, thanks entirely to you I now think more kindly of him!

I hope that you don't already have a copy of what seems to me to be a prolific work of scholarship.

With love,

Isobel

The penultimate sentence made Rupert smile as he folded the note and slipped it inside the book. He was touched that she'd taken such care in choosing a gift for him and surprised that someone so anti-Ruskin knew of the publication. Not even Liz . . .

Astonished by the admission, which would have been unthinkable just a couple of weeks ago, he stroked the worn leather binding, smelt the faint mustiness of the paper and flicked through the volume renewing his appreciation of Ruskin's drawings. His throat constricted, she'd written with love. Could she really mean that or was that simply her way of signing off? Was Isobel giving him more than he was capable of giving her? Was he being fair to her? Would it have been kinder to end the relationship at the end of the holiday? Why the hell was he dithering when normally he was decisive?

The sudden blast of pop music shattered his thoughts. He placed the book carefully on his desk, crossed his study floor in two long strides and walked towards the kitchen, slamming the study door behind him. The loud echo hung like a reproach in the air. He raised his voice so that he could be heard above the music. "For God's sake Tory, can you turn that bloody racket down a decibel or two?"

"Cool it Pa. I was only trying to amuse myself until you came home." She was sitting at the kitchen table, the remains of a hastily assembled breakfast littered around her. She tilted her chair so that it balanced precariously on its two back legs, stretched out an arm and turned off the radio on top of the work top.

To Rupert's relief she was dressed, and smartly too, he noticed. The frizzed up, claret-coloured hair that she'd been sporting on her previous visit had been replaced by a smooth bob and she'd gone back to her normal dark chestnut. She did however look stick thin which was worrying. He hoped she wasn't suffering from anorexia on top of everything else. He began mechanically to clear away the remnants of her breakfast. Tory watched him in silence for a minute, making no offer to help, and then; "Do you know you get more like a mother hen every time we meet Pa?" she said, holding firmly onto a half drunk mug of coffee to stop him removing it along with the rest.

He eyed the coffee mug warily and his mind flew back to that terrible evening when Liz died. Would he never be able to wipe it from his memory? Tory had been uncontrollable once she'd seen that the vase had missed him and, before he could stop her, she'd picked up an empty coffee mug and smashed it into his mouth. He winced, feeling his tooth crack all over again. He must never allow anything like that to happen again, ever.

It was such a pity she hadn't inherited his love of tidiness. He found it impossible to live or work in a mess, clutter irritated him and he needed order to enable him to function with any kind of efficiency. "Perhaps," he said coldly, "perhaps you'll be good enough to tidy your sheets away instead of sitting there making fatuous remarks about my housekeeping." He was about to suggest that they might go out for lunch once the chores were done when, to his horror, she burst into tears and fled, knocking over her chair in her haste.

Rupert picked up the chair, sighed heavily and followed her into the sitting room where she was trying, unsuccessfully, to fold sheets using the corner of one of them as a handkerchief at the same time.

"I'm sorry Tory, I didn't mean to make you cry." He put an arm awkwardly around her shoulder and offered her his own handkerchief with his spare hand. "only you do try my patience sometimes." Tory blew her nose loudly and looked helplessly at the crumpled sheet. Rupert saw his opportunity to mend the damage and took the sheet from her. "Here, let's do it together," he said, taking one end and giving her the other. As they folded sheets and collected pillows and stowed them away in the hall cupboard he offered to take her out for lunch, telling her of a place he'd discovered near to the Rialto Bridge which she might like to try.

Tory had eaten only half a roll for breakfast and was already starving. She felt her stomach give a joyful leap at the prospect of food. She dabbed her eyes one last time, sniffed loudly and handed

Rupert back his handkerchief which now looked like a grubby, melting snowball. "Give me a few minutes to repair the damage will you?" she said grudgingly before disappearing into the bathroom.

Well at least the prospect of a good lunch seemed to have cheered her up. He'd half expected, feared even, a prolonged outburst. Perhaps at last she was beginning to mature?

They were well into their meal before, in a further effort at appeasement, he told her how well she was looking and expressed the hope that she was now feeling better. He'd seen her become more relaxed under the dual influence of food and wine and was relieved to see her eating as if she were enjoying her lunch. She drank deeply from her glass before replying. "Sorry to turn on the waterworks earlier Pa, but you're always so bloody perfect. Has it ever occurred to you that we lesser mortals might find it just a tad difficult to live up to your exacting standards?" He watched as she twirled spaghetti expertly round her fork, saw the stubborn set of her mouth and realised he wasn't going to win her over with a casual compliment. "Tory, I'm speechless." He refilled both their glasses, needing time to compose a suitable reply. "Is that really how you see me? I'm just a human being with faults like anyone else."

"Well you could have fooled me." Tory shot back at him. "I've spent all my life trying to live up to your excellence. Do you realise for instance that I've never once known you to be late for an appointment, never heard you raise your voice to Mum, can't remember you ever forgetting a birthday. Those standards are really hard to live up to. Would you like me to go on?" She picked up her fork again and stabbed savagely at her spaghetti.

Rupert played for time again. He'd always thought of himself as an exemplary husband, a caring parent, a good provider. Now here was his daughter telling him that he'd managed somehow to get it all horribly wrong. It was a bit rich that she'd been happy to take all the benefits of a secure home life for as long as it suited her and the moment she'd begun to take responsibility for herself and things had started to go wrong she rounded on her family and blamed them for all her failures. How on earth was he to get it across to her that part of being an adult was to take responsibility for mistakes as well as the credit for successes?

"Believe me Tory I'm deeply sorry," he began. "As far as punctuality is concerned I have every respect for other people's time and I feel I owe it to whoever I'm meeting not to keep them waiting. You know I worshipped your mother and there was never an occasion when I felt it necessary to 'raise my voice' as you put it. As for birthdays . . ." He paused, shrugged and smiled whilst holding up one hand and spreading his fingers before continuing. "I could count on one hand the people to whom I send birthday cards or presents; hardly an exhaustive list is it?"

"Well you know what I mean." Tory was warming to her subject. "It all seemed too good to be true when I was growing up. You and Mum that is. If I look for a million years I can never hope to find a man who'll love me enough never to raise his voice at me." She didn't need to tell him of the litter of broken romances going back over the last fourteen years.

Now Rupert was really worried. The last thing he wanted was for Tory to measure all her past and future relationships against his own marriage to Liz. He made the most of the fact that the waiter was clearing away their plates and preparing to bring the next course before replying, wondering how best to get across to her that 'ideal' partnerships were the product of hard work, rather than a starting point for living 'happily ever after.' He poured more wine, saw her twisting the stem of her glass between her thumb and finger and guessed that she was a good deal more nervous than he'd originally thought. He made up his mind to be as gentle as possible.

"When two people love each other as much as your mother and I, there's a desire on both sides to please. I'm not talking about self-sacrifice but a mutual accommodation of needs. It's not a question of one or other partner consistently getting their own way but rather of conceding to the other on occasions. We all of us have desires which change with circumstances and we really do have to be unselfish sometimes if we're aiming for the sort of harmony which your mother and I achieved. Believe me," and here he paused and looked at her very directly across the table. If she forgot everything else he wanted her to remember his next point. "Believe me Tory both your mother and I worked incredibly hard at our marriage. I thought the benefits worth the effort until a few minutes ago when you made me realise the effect we had on you. I'd hoped to smooth your path. I seem to have given you a rough ride. I'm sorry."

Tory had no answer. She chewed a piece of veal carefully, thinking back to last weekend when she'd unceremoniously bundled Pierre's possessions into a plastic bin liner and thrown them and him out of her flat. Not surprisingly she hadn't heard from him since. "Well thanks for the good advice Pa," she said grudgingly. "I'll remember your words of wisdom when the next desirable hunk crosses my path. In the meantime what about us?"

The question caught him off guard. What did she mean? More to the point, what did she want? Was the unexpected visit a prelude to an even longer, perhaps permanent association? He felt his front tooth with the tip of his tongue, playing for time, trying to decide on the best way forward. "I'll always be your father Tory," he began. "I love you and I'll help you in any way I can whenever you need it. But I have to say this. I have a life to lead and it requires very careful planning. I shall be pleased to see you at any time but in future I'd like a little more than a few minutes notice if it's all the same with you."

"I'll bear it in mind," Tory replied flicking back her hair as if she didn't care one way or the other.

When they got back to his apartment Rupert told her that she was welcome to use the flat for as long as she wanted but that he would be leaving early in the morning for Tuscany and expected to be away for at least a week. He realised as he spoke that it didn't sound like the warmest of welcomes but his mind was already on tomorrow and his long drive to Rome and he was anxious to get on with the preparations for the trip.

He excused himself as best he could, told Tory to help herself to anything she needed and took himself off to pack.

When he'd finished he returned the boat to Giovanni and stayed briefly for a drink. At nine o'clock he reckoned that Isobel should have reached home and dialled her number from the phone in his study. He was surprised when he heard her recorded message; either she wasn't back yet or hadn't got around to clearing her answer phone. He worried a little, hoping she was alright and left a brief message. Finally he said 'goodnight' to Tory and went to bed early. He needed all his energy for tomorrow.

Chapter Twelve

Steven lifted his hand to a point just above his head to try and attract his mother's attention as she walked into the arrivals hall at Heathrow. Whatever she'd been doing seemed to have agreed with her, she looked positively glowing as she walked towards him. "Good trip?" he asked as they met, kissing her on the cheek and taking over her luggage trolley.

"Wonderful! I can't remember when I enjoyed myself more. I'm longing to tell you all about it." Her words spilled out as they walked towards the car park and Steven couldn't help wondering how much he'd get to know. Would she come clean about this Rupert bloke or limit her account to the sights she'd seen?

"How are things back home, is everyone OK?" she asked.

"Mostly we're fine. However there has been one unexpected development. I'll fill in the details later. Nice jacket by the way." He didn't want to spoil her home-coming too quickly and he was keen to put off asking her to have James to stay for as long as possible.

"I'm glad you like the jacket, I bought it in Rome." The words slipped out before she could stop them.

Steven glanced sideways and saw that she was blushing under her tan. "A bit far for a day trip isn't it?"

"Well actually I was there for a weekend. I'll tell you about it on the way home."

So she *was* going to tell him. Joy had warned him earlier to pretend to be pleased for her if she volunteered the information, although if he were really honest he had mixed feelings about his mother gallivanting around Italy and having an affair with a strange man. He wanted her to be happy of course but it was so untypical of her, or of the mothers of any of his friends as far as he knew.

"So how come you went to Rome then?" he asked as he cleared the airport and drove towards the M25.

"Oh, I bumped into a friend and we went to Rome for the weekend and I managed to go shopping in the Via Condotti, hence the jacket."

Steven waited for her to elaborate and, as the silence between them lengthened, realised that she'd given him all the information she intended, for the moment anyway. He decided to try and wheedle it out of her. "And this friend," he paused for a second, "anyone I know?" He looked sideways at her again, saw the blush reappear and thought, my God this is serious.

"Do keep your eyes on the road darling. Remember I've been travelling mainly on water for the last two weeks. All this traffic makes me nervous suddenly." She gestured towards the crowded motorway.

She isn't going to tell me, Steven thought, I'll have to help her. He pulled out and accelerated to overtake a Fiesta doing a steady sixty miles an hour in the centre lane. "So this friend," he persisted, "is his name Rupert Northcote by any chance?"

Isobel turned her head sharply, her eyes wide with astonishment, her mouth slightly open in surprise. "How on earth did you know?"

"Radio Barbara. You might have known she'd broadcast a full bulletin."

Isobel paled under her tan. "I simply don't believe it." Her voice sounded exasperated. In the excitement of the past week she'd put all thoughts of Barbara to the back of her mind. Now the realisation that Barbara had been gossiping about her stripped all the magic from her lovely holiday in the space of a few seconds. "Well I suppose I'd better know the worst," she said, looking straight ahead but not really seeing the traffic any more. "Tell me exactly what she said."

"Only that she'd run into the two of you in Venice. That you were having what she described as a very intimate lunch together. You didn't look particularly pleased to see either her or Henry and that you and Rupert were very old friends."

"Intimate lunch my foot!" It was a long time since he'd heard his mother sound so angry. "If you must know I met Rupert on my way out to Venice," she went on. "In the Club Lounge to be precise. We'd spent less than twenty four hours together when we had the misfortune to bump into Barbara and Henry. Imagine the fun she'd've had putting that around the family. I hoped the 'old friends' angle might put an end to her curiosity. I should have known better."

Steven took his left hand from the steering wheel and touched her fingers lightly. This was probably just a holiday romance after all. She's said goodbye to him and there's an end to it, he thought, at the same time wondering how he was going to tell her about James. It hadn't been such a great home-coming after all. Perhaps he shouldn't have pursued his enquiries about Rupert? In the meantime he was eating up the miles between Heathrow and Berkhamsted and he'd promised Joy he'd explain about James before they arrived home. He was just about to begin when Isobel said, "You mentioned some unexpected development back at the airport, are you going to tell me what it is? Nothing serious I hope?"

"Ah well." Steven searched for words, wanting to break the news as gently as possible. "I'm afraid that Barbara phoned James shortly after she'd met you in Venice."

"Bloody interfering woman! How did he take it?"

"Well, you know Dad," Steven hedged.

"Oh, for God's sake Steven spit it out." Isobel said irritably, thinking, Rupert where are you? I need you. If you'd been able to fly back with me I might have had a different home-coming.

"I'm afraid Dad had a heart attack." Steven reached for her hand again. "He is recovering," he added quickly seeing the colour ebb from her face again. "He's still in hospital but they're hoping to discharge him any day now."

"Oh, my God!" Isobel said slowly, beginning to wish she'd never come home. "I didn't know James had a heart condition."

"Neither did anyone else, least of all Zelda, who should know better than any of us. Apparently he was helping Fred with some building work in the garden when he was taken ill. That could have been the trigger."

"How is Zelda taking it?"

"Completely gone to pieces. Had a major row with the *au pair*, who promptly upped sticks and left and expects the whole family to rally round to help until she can get herself sorted out. Right now Joy's looking after Samantha so that Zelda's free to visit the hospital, look for another *au pair* and do all the other things so necessary in her life. One way and another things are a bit hectic as you can imagine. Ian's swamped with work, trying to handle his own and Father's cases. Sue's father's staying with them at the moment because his housekeeper's in hospital. Fun and games all round as you can see."

Steven stopped talking, hoping against hope that she might ask if there was anything she could do. They would be home soon and he'd looked forward to telling Joy that everything was sorted. His mother however stayed silent completely lost in thought.

Isobel was remembering James' possessiveness in the past and was trying hard to imagine his reaction when Barbara told him about Rupert. In the days before he'd married Zelda and was having one of his affairs it hadn't stopped his annoyance if she'd flirted with one of their male friends at a Law Society dinner or other social occasion. She could just imagine Barbara's nasty mind making as much capital as possible from their encounter in Venice and suddenly her holiday, so beautiful twenty four hours ago, became smeared and shabby. What if James thought she'd been lying to him for years? It really wasn't fair. She'd put up with God knows what in the past and the first time she stepped out of line there was a family furore.

"You will come home and have a meal with us before I drop you off at your place? Joy was making what she described as a typical English dinner when I left." Steven said.

Isobel was longing to get home to peace and quiet where she could be alone with her thoughts. She started to make excuses but Steven cut her short. "Joy will be really disappointed if you say no. I'm sure there's no fresh food at the cottage and you can't survive for the rest of the day on an airline lunch."

Isobel wasn't hungry enough to think about food. Since leaving Venice Rupert had dominated her thoughts. What was he doing? How was he getting on with Tory? Did he like his present? Would she ever see him again? Was he finding it as difficult to be part of a family again as she was? She realised suddenly that Steven was turning the car into his own drive and resigned herself to a family dinner, resolving to get away as soon as she decently could and promptly feeling guilty for wanting to be on her own.

Samantha and Tom were having tea when Steven and Isobel walked into the kitchen. Samantha was eating a poached egg by dipping her index finger into the yolk and sucking hard and slowly. It looked to Isobel as if tea was going to take quite a while. She went across the kitchen to kiss Joy and her grandson.

"Hello Ganny!" Tom waved his spoon at her. Isobel wanted to cry when she heard the childish pronunciation which she seemed to be stuck with, even though Tom was getting better all the time at pronouncing the letter 'r'. She ruffled his hair affectionately and turned back to Joy.

"Not a very cheerful return for you is it?" Joy asked.

"It could have been better. You appear to have your hands full. Are you managing to cope with two children and the business?" Joy had taken over Isobel's secretarial agency when Isobel retired and was paying for it in annual instalments providing Isobel with a regular income as opposed to a capital. sum. Isobel thought how tired she looked and remembered only too well the days when she too juggled family and career without the support of a husband like Steven and was deeply thankful that she no longer had to. "Is there anything I can do?" she asked, looking around the kitchen.

"No thanks, everything's organised. I bathed these two horrors before I gave them their tea, although looking at Samantha, I'm not so sure that was a good idea. We can eat as soon as they're finished and tucked up. Let Steven take you through to the sitting room and give you a drink." Joy smiled her thanks and reaching for a face flannel began to remove traces of egg from around Tom's mouth.

Isobel followed Steven and accepted a gin and tonic gratefully. "You will let me know if I can help in any way won't you?" she said as he handed her the glass, not realising that she'd given Steven exactly the opening he needed. He plunged straight in, outlining the problem as far as James and the rest of the family were concerned. "We've had a really long talk and I promise you we've explored all the possibilities and we wondered if you could sort of take James in for a few days until Zelda manages to reorganise herself. I had a word with her before I left to pick you up and she tells me that the agency are sending three *au pairs* for her to interview tomorrow. Once she's found a replacement I should think she'll be able to pick up the threads again fairly quickly and Dad can go back home. At the moment it's organised chaos every time I visit and I don't think that would be very good for Dad, do you?" He opened a bottle of beer and took a long pull, thankful that at long last he'd managed to ask the question. He sat back and waited.

Isobel put down her glass on the coffee table and looked steadily across at him. She couldn't believe what she'd just heard.

"Are you seriously suggesting that *I* should have James to stay?" Not for the first time in the last two hours she began to wish she'd stayed in Venice.

"It would help all of us so much."

"And what does James think?"

"Well," Steven hesitated, "we haven't actually approached him yet. It seemed more appropriate to ask you first."

"Well thank you for that at least. I'm certain the last person James wants to spend any time with at the moment is me."

"You might be surprised to hear that James mentioned to Sue when she went to visit him that you'd always been good in a crisis.

"Hmm. I can't say I remember him showing much appreciation for my crisis management skills in the past. Zelda's had a pretty easy ride until now, let *her* sort it out."

"Zelda's not one of the world's leading problem solvers at the best of times. Remember she's had a severe shock and so has James. I think the least we can do is try to pull together to help them over the crisis."

That did it. If it were a friend or any other member of the family but James, Isobel thought, I'd do everything possible to help. So what was the difference here? It seemed that everybody else was mucking in and here she was making excuses and trying her best not to become involved. After all if James did agree to stay with her it would give her the opportunity to tell him the truth about Rupert and if she were to be really honest wasn't it simply hurt pride that was getting in the way? That wasn't a good enough reason to be selfish. Suddenly her mind was made up. "OK Steve I'll do it. There are however two conditions. First, James has to agree, I don't want him in my house under sufferance and second, Zelda must take him back in two weeks, sooner if possible."

Steven crossed the room and gave her a bear hug. "Thanks Ma," he said. "You've just taken a great weight from all our shoulders."

It was after nine o'clock when Isobel finally arrived home. Steven carried her luggage up to her bedroom and then went home to Joy. Isobel absorbed the peace of the place and immediately felt soothed. She went into the kitchen and switched on the light. Digby, her ginger tom, blinked in the sudden glare, yawned, uncurled himself from sleep and came over to rub himself against her legs. She bent to scratch the top of his head. "I'm glad to see you're still fighting fit," she said and was rewarded by a muted purr. Her daily help had cut a few late flowers from the garden and left them on the kitchen table in a pottery jug. You couldn't really call it a flower arrangement but at least it looked welcoming. Assorted mail was stacked on the dresser. It could wait until tomorrow Isobel decided and pausing only to switch off the light she went upstairs to run a bath. As she looked for clean pyjamas her thoughts bumped clumsily into each other.

She could understand Barbara trying to make trouble but James' reaction was more puzzling. Surely he couldn't expect her to live a celibate life now that they were divorced? Her thoughts moved over to Zelda. She'd want James back again as soon as possible wouldn't she? Perhaps she'd raise some last minute objection to prevent him coming to stay? It was all too much to sort out at the moment. Her brain felt like a piece of worn out elastic. She'd try and get a good nights sleep and deal with everything tomorrow.

At precisely seven am on Monday morning Rupert let himself out of his apartment and walked towards the *vaporetto* stop. The number two would take him to the Piazzale Romà where the company car was garaged. He took with him only a light grip and his briefcase, not wanting to carry heavy luggage, even for the short journey to the Rialto Bridge. He'd thought about phoning Isobel before he left but decided against it, realising that it would be six o'clock in the morning in the UK, an indecently early hour to call, particularly as she was probably feeling tired after the flight home.

The prospect of driving the best part of 500 miles by the end of the day was daunting but, having promised in a weak moment to help Gianna, he was resigned to the journey and in preparation put several CD's in his briefcase before leaving. The smell of diesel and the noise of the traffic in the Piazzale Romà did nothing to lift his spirits. One of the things he enjoyed about living in Venice was the complete absence of motor traffic and he always disliked this first encounter with it every time he left the city.

Arriving at the garage he stowed his grip, together with his briefcase, in the boot, leaving his mobile switched on but deciding not to take it into the car. Negotiating Italian traffic was bad enough without the distraction of phone calls *en route*. He stowed the CD's after first putting on Schubert's C major string quintet, knowing it would soothe him and as the first notes drifted out he settled back in his seat and turned the car towards Padua.

At the back of his mind there was still a slight worry about whether Isobel had arrived home safely with no unexpected delays to mar her flight. It was a long time since he'd felt real concern for anybody which made him think he might be growing selfish in his old age. The last two weeks had reminded him that selfishness came at a price. He'd begun to enjoy himself again. Saturday, for instance, had been a wonderful day until Tory turned up out of the blue. He was grateful that Isobel had been so tactful. Not every woman would have been so understanding.

Isobel didn't clear her answer phone until ten o'clock on Monday morning. She'd woken early, filled the washing machine, made a separate pile for the dry cleaner, caught up with the news from Marilyn, her cleaning lady. Finally she collected the mail and took it into her study. The winking light on the machine reminded her that she had messages to collect. She pressed the play button and tried to scribble them down as she listened. There was a message from the bookshop in Berkhamsted telling her that a biography she'd ordered was waiting collection; a friend wanted to know if she could help out at a charity sale; her best friend Joanna was longing to hear all about her trip and asked if they could meet for lunch later this week.

Then, miraculously, there was Rupert's voice; thanking her for his beautiful present, hoping she had a good journey home, asking her not to worry about phoning back that he'd catch her sometime tomorrow. She played the message three times, her eyes closed, enjoying the sound of his voice, trying to visualise him in her mind. It was a small compensation for the lack of him but it would have to do. The day stretched ahead. She knew she would fill it somehow but realised that the excitement of the last two weeks had now given way to emptiness; the possibility of sharing part of her day with Rupert was replaced by solitude and the anticipation of his closeness to anguish for lack of him. Suddenly life felt about as exciting as flat tonic water.

She looked at her watch, ten fifteen, a quarter past eleven in Italy. He would have left by now for Rome, perhaps she could contact him on his mobile? She went upstairs to look for her handbag and found his card which she'd slipped inside her notecase before leaving Venice. Her hands were shaking as she dialled the number. His voice told her, first in Italian and then English, that Rupert Northcote was either in a meeting or out of range and that if she left a message he would get back to her as soon as possible. She left a message. When she'd replaced the receiver she wondered if he'd taken his mobile with him or left it in the apartment. Surely he would try to keep in touch with business clients and his partner? What if he'd forgotten to pack it? Did Rupert forget? The thoughts tumbled on and on until suddenly she remembered that Tory was still at the apartment. Perhaps if Rupert had forgotten his mobile he would phone later to see if anyone had called? She dialled the apartment and left a second message. Satisfied that she could do no more she replaced the receiver and began to open her mail.

Tory let herself into Rupert's apartment late on Monday afternoon and faced the bleak prospect of spending an evening on her own. Whoever said that travelling for a living was exciting had probably never done it. Staying alone in a town where you knew nobody had nothing to recommend it and trying to fill in time by shopping was no fun at all if you were short of cash. Although her company paid her expenses when she went to inspect properties, the salary wasn't over-generous and she was always struggling to make ends meet.

The apartment was so quiet it was positively unnerving. She switched on the radio and made herself a cup of tea wondering how she was going to fill the next few hours. She walked aimlessly round the flat stopping occasionally to open a cupboard or drawer. God it was boring, not a thing out of place.

It was a mixture of boredom and curiosity that made her open the door to her father's study. She walked over to his desk, picked up a book, flipped the pages and then bent down to pick up the piece of paper which fluttered to the floor. She read Isobel's letter and felt her stomach contract. No wonder the old rat bag had asked for 'a little more than a few minutes notice' if she were to come and stay with him again. After all the crap he'd talked on Sunday about his perfect marriage and all the time he was screwing around. The father whom she'd always thought of as perfect was no better than any of the other men she'd met.

She folded Isobel's letter and replaced it in the book before retracing her steps, glancing idly at the answering machine on the hall table as she passed. The red light was on, funny she hadn't noticed before. She put down her cup and saucer, pressed the play button and heard Isobel's voice. "Sorry to miss you last night Rupert but it was quite late when I finally arrived home. There's been a bit of a crisis here. I'll fill you in with all the details when I catch up with you. Hope your Tuscan trip is successful. 'Bye."

Tory stuck her tongue out at the machine and jabbed her finger hard on the erase button before walking over to the hall cupboard and pulling out her tote bag. She started to pack her belongings. Thank God her business was finished. The sooner she got out of here the better.

The phone rang just after six o'clock. She was tempted to ignore it, remembering that her father had promised to call when he arrived in Rome. But if she let it ring he'd guess she'd switched the machine off and, knowing him, would call every hour on the hour for the rest of the evening. She decided to get it over with and picked up the receiver.

"Is that you Tory?"

"Who else were you expecting?"

Rupert ignored the question. "Just thought I'd let you know I've arrived in Rome."

"Good." Tory was in no mood for pleasantries.

"Are you alright? Did you have a successful day?"

"Yes to both questions." A brief pause. "Thank you."

"Did you notice if there were any messages for me or haven't you cleared the machine?"

"I have and there weren't."

"Oh, fine! Well I won't keep you then. Are you staying in Venice tonight?"

"There's an Intercity train leaving just after ten. I thought I'd travel overnight; save some time."

"I see. Well could you switch the machine on again before you leave? Gianna sends her love by the way."

"Thanks. Is that it?"

"Yes I think so. I'll say goodbye then."

"*Ciao*." Tory said and slammed down the receiver.

"Everything is alright yes?" Gianna asked as Rupert returned to the sitting room. He looked preoccupied, almost as if he'd forgotten where he was. Rupert was aware that she had spoken but hadn't taken in what she said and remained lost in thought for several seconds. Finally he looked up, caught her eye and said; "Sorry Gianna, I was miles away. What was it you said?"

"I asked was everything alright?" Gianna waited patiently.

"I sincerely hope so," said Rupert. "Only with that daughter of mine you never know. I thought she sounded rather odd when I called just now. In a mood I expect. Perhaps I should have delayed my departure for a day and then I could have entertained her this evening." He shrugged his shoulders and held out his hands in a gesture of helplessness.

"What am I going to do about that young lady?"

Gianna jumped to her feet, came over to him and laid a hand on his arm. "Try not to worry Rupee. Remember she 'as no mother, she needs to know you love 'er."

"Is it really that simple?" Rupert asked wearily, "I would have thought that was obvious."

"To you perhaps, maybe not to'er." Gianna fluttered her fingers at him before suggesting, "I'll get us a drink, yes?"

"Fine, I'll have a large Scotch if that's alright with you?" He sat down heavily on the sofa, stretched out his legs, leaned back and closed his eyes. He was dog tired. He'd driven hard all day taking only two brief stops, giving himself just long enough to stretch his legs and have a quick snack on each occasion.

Gianna placed a glass in his hand. He opened his eyes and took a long drink, felt the spirit burn the back of his throat and tried to remember the last time he'd drunk neatScotch. "I think I'd better put some water in this," he said, smiling tiredly at Gianna and struggling to his feet. She pressed him back onto the sofa. "Let me get it. You look tired, an early night will be good, I think?"

Rupert could have climbed into bed quite happily then and there, clothes and all. Unusually for him he hadn't bothered to unpack his grip or even take his bags up to his room, simply dropped them in the hall when he arrived before phoning Tory. He'd phone Isobel after dinner, at the moment he couldn't summon up the energy to say anything remotely interesting.

The next thing he knew, Gianna was shaking him by the shoulder. "Wake up Rupee! Time for dinner!"

"Oh Gianna, I'm sorry, I must have dropped off. What time is it?"

"Eight o'clock, I'm being kind to you, I let you sleep."

Rupert rubbed the back of his neck trying to ease out the stiffness. "It's fatal to drink that stuff when you're feeling tired," he said, pointing to his empty glass.

"Tomorrow you know better perhaps?" Gianna smiled at him as she asked the question. "Now would you like to 'ave a quick wash before we eat?"

Rupert got stiffly to his feet and, telling Gianna that he'd only be a few minutes, he picked up his bags and walked slowly up the stairs. He closed the heavy oak door of the guest wing carefully behind him and went into the room that he and Isobel hadn't shared on his last visit. He unzipped his grip and took out a spare pair of slacks, his pyjamas and wash bag, leaving the rest undisturbed. He opened his brief case, pulled out his mobile and checked it for messages. Isobel's voice sounded faint and he cursed himself for not taking the instrument into the car, at least if he had they'd have been able to have a brief chat. He was relieved that she'd arrived home safely, wondered what the crisis was, no doubt he would find out after dinner when he called her. He longed to talk to her, hated the thought of spending a night without her, remembered with affection the brief time they'd spent here together. In the meantime Gianna was waiting.

Chapter Thirteen

Isobel's phone started ringing just after seven pm on Monday evening. Steven was the first with the news that James would be discharged from hospital sometime tomorrow, that Ian had told James of her kind offer which had been accepted. "Both gratefully and graciously," he added as an afterthought. These were two words that Isobel didn't normally associate with James but she acknowledged that Steven might be trying to make the situation easier for her.

"So what time shall I expect him?" she asked, without enthusiasm.

"Zelda hopes to collect him just after midday, after he's seen the surgeon. They'll probably stop on the way to have some lunch and should be with you sometime between three and four. Is that OK?"

"Zelda's bringing him down here?" Isobel asked in surprise.

"Well the rest of us are tied up and Zelda wants to pick up Samantha at the same time. She interviewed three *au pair* girls this morning and chose the one who could start next week, so things are slowly getting back to normal." Steven tried to sound as optimistic as possible, appreciating that his mother might find it difficult to come face-to-face with Zelda.

"Yes I see," Isobel said slowly. "If you put it like that it sounds like the most sensible solution."

Steven chatted on for a while, not wanting to leave her high and dry. After all she'd been home slightly more than twenty four hours and he, perhaps more than any other member of his family, realised that they were asking a great deal of her. Finally he ran out of steam, asked her to be sure to call him if she needed help and rang off.

She was just putting the finishing touches to her supper when Zelda telephoned. To begin with she was effusive, overwhelming Isobel with thanks for offering to look after James. Having fulfilled what she saw as her social obligation she launched into a long and complicated explanation of exactly what kind of care James would need. Did Isobel realise that he must get out and walk for at least half an hour every day? Not too briskly but he mustn't dawdle either. Perhaps if Isobel were to go with him she would be able to supervise him . . . ? Then there was the matter of his diet. Did Isobel know about the Mediterranean Diet. An absolute boon for heart attack victims, she explained, before going on to extol the merits of olive oil, plenty of fish, fruit and fresh vegetables. Did Isobel have muesli for his breakfast? The fibre was so essential for him. On no account should he be allowed to smoke and if he asked for a drink could Isobel please limit his intake to a glass of wine each evening? If he drank coffee at all it must be decaffeinated. Under no circumstances could he be allowed to do anything remotely strenuous, Did Isobel understand? Was she taking notes?

Isobel forced herself to listen until Zelda finally ran out of steam and then vented her feelings by letting out an exasperated scream after she finally said goodbye and replaced the receiver. Why, if Zelda was so concerned for James' welfare wasn't she making more of an effort to look after him herself? James hadn't arrived yet and already she felt as if her life was being taken over. What on earth would it be like once he was installed? She rang Joanna to cancel their lunch date on Wednesday, promising to rearrange it once James was settled into some kind of routine. Joanna made sympathetic noises as Isobel spilt out all the anger she'd been suppressing during her conversation with Zelda.

She'd already filled Joanna in with the details of her holiday when they'd talked earlier in the day and Joanna couldn't resist the temptation to ask for an update. "Have you heard from Rupert yet?" she asked. Isobel admitted she'd heard nothing since his brief message on the answer phone. "Call him right now!" Joanna said. "It sounds as if you could use a sympathetic ear and a bit of a cheer up."

Isobel explained that she'd already left two messages and didn't want to bombard him with phone calls, neither did she have a number for him in Rome where she now expected him to be. "I'm sure he'll be in touch when he can." she finished; more to console herself than to satisfy Joanna's need to see her old friend happy and contented.

"Well he can't call you if your line's permanently engaged can he?" Joanna asked, "I guess I'd better ring off."

Isobel managed to finish her supper before the phone rang again. She pushed her tray away and almost ran to the phone in her eagerness to answer it. Surely this time it must be Rupert? But it was Ian and, once again, she swallowed her disappointment. Had she heard from Steven or Zelda? Had they told her all about the arrangements for tomorrow or did he need to fill her in? He went on to thank her for what she was doing for the family and said he'd be along in a couple of days to pass on some work from the office; just some routine stuff which would take the pressure off the practice and at the same time provide James with some useful occupational therapy.

"Is that wise?" Isobel asked. "The work I mean."

"Oh yes, I've discussed it with his specialist who thinks it's important for James to feel useful and, providing there's no stress involved and he doesn't work for longer than two or three hours each day, there shouldn't be a problem."

"Well, if you're sure . . ." Isobel tried and failed to keep the concern out of her voice.

"It's important that James doesn't start to feel depressed, which could well happen if he has too much time on his hands." Ian reassured her. "I'm sure you'll be able to tell if he starts overdoing things."

It seemed to Isobel as if everyone in the family had suddenly become an expert on post-operative care for heart attack victims. Everyone that is except her, the one who'd be doing most of the caring. She glanced wearily at her watch as she said goodbye to Ian, nine thirty already, it would be half past ten in Rome. It was, she was sure, too late for Rupert to call, he was probably exhausted anyway after his long drive from Venice. Well she'd had a two week break from family responsibilities and during that time there were occasions when she'd felt positively spoiled. Now, a little over twenty four hours after coming home, she felt as if she'd never been away.

Rupert tried Isobel's number three times after dinner and came to the conclusion either that the international lines were exceptionally busy or that Isobel's friends and family were making the most of her now that she was back home. She'd hinted at a family crisis and he hoped it wasn't serious enough to jam her telephone with end-to-end calls that were keeping her line busy all the evening. His brain was already addled with Gianna's chatter and he wondered, not for the first time, how his brother managed to live so happily with it. Isobel on the other hand was so much more restful. God! He missed her. He must remember to tell her the next time he telephoned.

"Of course you do realise this is all your fault don't you?" Barbara snapped as she pushed past Isobel, almost knocking her over in the process. For Isobel, after only three hectic days of looking after James, Barbara's rudeness was the last straw. The phone never stopped ringing and she was constantly making coffee, tea or drinks for the old friends and golfing cronies who'd been pally with James when he lived in the area. How they'd discovered his whereabouts God only knew and she was fighting a losing battle trying to ration their numbers to save James from becoming too exhausted. Now to cap it all Barbara had arrived, unannounced, appearing at twelve thirty. "Expecting to be invited to lunch I suppose. Well you can think again Barbara," Isobel muttered to herself.

Before they reached the sitting room door she manoeuvred herself between Henry and Barbara. "Perhaps you'd like to go in and see James," she said to Henry. "Barbara, please come to the kitchen with me and I'll give you some coffee." She led the way and was careful to close the kitchen door behind them as they went in. She was determined to face up to Barbara once and for all and she didn't want anyone to overhear.

"Now Barbara," she began, filling the kettle and plugging it in. "Can you explain exactly what you meant by your remark just now?" She watched with grim satisfaction as the colour in Barbara's face slowly turned to puce.

Barbara, like most bullies, was unused to being challenged. She inflated her vast bosom and prepared to cut Isobel down to size. "It should be obvious, even to the most dim-witted, that a sensitive man like James would be distressed to hear that his ex-wife is openly carrying on with some louche Lothario." Her eyes, two hard grey marbles, rolled over Isobel from top to toe. She expected a quivering capitulation but, for once, had severely underestimated her opponent.

Barbara had dared to disparage Rupert which lit the blue touch paper and released in Isobel a flame of dislike which had been quietly glowing for many years. Now she was no longer married to James there was absolutely no need to be polite to his sister. The revelation cheered Isobel enormously and she continued her attack. "May I remind you Barbara," she said. "May I remind you that I wasn't the person to tell James a certain piece of gossip in the full knowledge that he might find it upsetting." She saw the puce darken a couple of shades.

"He had every right to know," Barbara replied defensively.

The bosom, Isobel noted with satisfaction, was now deflated. "James isn't part of my life anymore," she said. "He has a new wife and a new life and appears to be very happy with both."

Barbara snorted like an outraged stallion. "They've absolutely nothing in common except sex and we all know that isn't enough to keep a marriage going."

"How would *you* know?" Isobel said, and then, "I do believe you're jealous, jealous of your own brother's happiness." She turned away to make the coffee and put biscuits on a plate. Her hands were shaking and she couldn't bear to look at Barbara, who seemed suddenly to have lost all her stuffing and was leaning against the dresser as if to save herself from falling over. But Isobel wasn't finished yet. "I think James and Zelda should be left in peace to get on with their lives," she began; "and before I take you in to see James I would like an undertaking from you that you will do or say nothing that might distress him. Furthermore I must ask you to limit your stay to half an hour. Let's not forget that James has been seriously ill and still gets very tired." She picked up the tray, waited for Barbara to open the door and led the way back to the sitting room. Barbara didn't look at her once.

Her daily routine, usually so well ordered, had been turned on its head since James' arrival. She'd expected he and Zelda to arrive by four o'clock at the latest on Tuesday and it was close to four thirty when their car finally drew up. In the meantime Isobel had phoned the hospital to make certain James had left and then called Ian to find out if there'd been a last minute change of plan. When they finally arrived she discovered that Zelda, delighted to be reunited with James again, if only temporarily, had persuaded him to have lunch in some swish sushi restaurant and, "The time simply flew by," she'd trilled, clutching James' arm possessively and flashing a look at Isobel which said; 'You see, he really prefers to be with me.'

James had looked old, grey and exhausted. He'd lost weight in hospital and she guessed that the combination of Zelda's chatter and the journey to Hertfordshire had tired him out. Once Zelda was out of the way he'd pleaded exhaustion and gone straight to bed. Later that same evening he'd staggered to the bathroom and deposited his expensive lunch, entire and virtually undigested, down the lavatory. Isobel, hearing the commotion and fearing that he might be having another heart attack, raced upstairs and almost collided with him on the landing.

"Please Isobel," he gasped as she helped him back to bed, "no more fish this week, either raw or cooked!"

Isobel smiled in spite of her previous fears and James, always quick to capitalise, promptly asked for a glass of whisky and a sandwich. She'd provided both, ignoring Zelda's earlier instructions on both drink and diet for the sake of peace and quiet, knowing from past experience that if she refused he'd accuse her of not caring if he starved to death. She'd diluted the spirit liberally with Malvern water and although James complained bitterly that the whisky looked like gnat's piss, he drank it gratefully. Later when she returned to take his tray and give him his pills he'd squeezed her hand and thanked her for coming to his rescue.

Somehow she'd managed to persuade him to walk for half an hour every morning and to rest after lunch. She'd taken phone calls for him and given them to him in batches so that he shouldn't tire himself unnecessarily by making frequent trips to the telephone. Zelda rang every night after dinner and managed to bend his ear for at least an hour babbling on regardless of time. So far she hadn't visited, but was expected on Saturday. Isobel in an unguarded moment had invited her for dinner thinking that at least she might free up the telephone for one evening in case Rupert called.

This was the real reason for her short temper with Barbara she admitted to herself, wondering endlessly if she would ever hear from him again. She'd tried his mobile several times but couldn't make contact and concluded that either his battery had run down or he was so far out of range he couldn't get a signal. She consoled herself with the thought that he was most likely tied up with tedious negotiating or property hunting during the day and her own line was unusually busy during the evenings. Even so . . .

Her thoughts came to an abrupt end when Henry appeared suddenly in the kitchen.

"Our half hour's just about up I think." His tone was conciliatory. "I'm sorry Barbara was rude to you just now. She has of course been very worried about James."

"It's been an anxious time for all of us." Isobel's tone was crisp, thinking what a creep Henry could be at times. Why he always felt the need to apologise for Barbara God only knew. She poured soup into the food processor and started the motor, effectively killing any further conversation. The last thing she wanted was a heart-to-heart with Henry. He'd offered himself as a potential lover shortly after she'd divorced James and since then she'd tried hard to steer clear of him whenever they met at family functions.

"Well I guess we'll be on our way then." He shifted from one foot to the other, hesitated briefly in the doorway and, with a faint smile which showed his disappointment at Isobel's rejection of him, turned away reluctantly to collect Barbara.

Isobel waited until she heard Barbara making a noisy exit from the sitting room before leaving the kitchen to show them both out. "If you wish to come again it might be advisable to give me a ring first," she said to Barbara as she opened the front door for them. "I have to take James to see his consultant some time next week and Ian's coming down on Saturday morning to bring a little work from the office. So you see we do have to plan our days rather carefully Barbara."

"We shall probably wait until James returns home before visiting him again," Barbara said with a look of pure venom as she swept past Isobel towards the front door.

"Thank you for the coffee Isobel, it was delicious," Henry added and bent to kiss her cheek before they finally walked out to the car. He glanced sideways at his wife's stony face as he settled himself in the driving seat and quickly suggested they should find somewhere to have lunch thinking to divert the storm before it broke,

Rupert was forced to admit that navigational skills were not one of Gianna's strong points but then she wasn't a driver so he supposed he should make allowances. He brought the car to a halt as the road in front of them petered out into a rough track which was obviously unsuitable for road traffic. After three days of driving around the Tuscan countryside looking at a range of properties he was beginning to regret his offer of help. To make matters worse the weather had deteriorated sharply as they drove north from Rome. There had been a violent storm on the evening of their arrival and during the last three days they hadn't seen the sun at all. The wind was squally and what would normally be a beautiful landscape was blurred and greyed by frequent rain showers.

All this would have been bearable if only Rupert could have looked forward to returning each evening to an hotel that was half way comfortable, or at least warm. But Gianna had accepted a holiday villa belonging to an old friend and, from their first evening, he'd felt more cold, miserable and wretched than he could remember.

After the long drive from Rome they found the so-called villa with some difficulty at the end of a rutted track just outside the town of Barga. Gianna had warned him before they left Rome that the place wasn't completely renovated and she hadn't exaggerated. The light was already fading when they arrived and it took Rupert some time to locate the mains switch to allow them the use of the limited electricity supply.

The property consisted of two old barns which would one day be connected but which were, for the moment, separate. The living accommodation was in the larger of the two, a couple of bedrooms and a bathroom in the other. Both places were distinctly chilly and the owners had yet to install central heating. The furniture was both sparse and Spartan, there were neither rugs or curtains. None of the light bulbs had shades and their naked globes did nothing to soften the austerity of the surroundings. Rupert hated it on sight. When they'd unpacked he'd insisted on driving into Barga where, he hoped, they would be able to get warm and find a decent dinner.

Once in Barga they were forced to dash through driving rain in near-darkness but were rewarded by an excellent restaurant serving local specialities. Rupert ordered a wild boar casserole with chestnuts and porcini mushrooms and revived his flagging spirits with a glass of excellent Chianti before phoning Isobel. Like almost everything else at their villa the telephone wasn't connected. He was bitterly disappointed to find her line once again, engaged. He'd been looking forward to sharing with her the horrors of his temporary accommodation, knowing that she'd see the funny side of it and they could have had a good laugh together.

Thinking that there might be a fault on the line or that perhaps the receiver was off the hook, he got the operator to check the number. She confirmed that the line was busy and asked if he would like her to keep the call in hand. Just at that moment the waiter signalled that their food was ready and Rupert reluctantly abandoned the phone and walked thoughtfully back to his table. It was after eleven thirty by the time they finished and even taking the time difference into consideration, Rupert decided against trying to call again.

He'd offered the better of the two bedrooms to Gianna and his own provided scant comfort. The mattress had seen better days and the rain continued to lash against the uncurtained window for the remainder of the night. He tossed and turned continually, worrying about Isobel and wishing for the umpteenth time that he was anywhere but in the wilds of Tuscany. When finally he fell asleep in the small hours of the morning, he dreamed that Isobel was lost in the storm and wandering fruitlessly through the rain sodden landscape trying to find him.

He woke at eight in a cold sweat and climbed stiffly out of bed, recoiling as his feet touched the cold, uncarpeted floor. He searched in his briefcase for his mobile and tried to call Isobel but couldn't get a signal. Looking out of the window at the magnificence of the Apuan Alps he could see why. When Gianna came down to breakfast he was working like a maniac bringing in piles of firewood which he'd found stacked on one side of the barn. "I'll make this place warm if it kills me," he said by way of an early morning greeting. Gianna simply fluttered her fingers at him and went off to make coffee.

Now here they were miles from anywhere. Rupert stretched out a weary hand to take the map from his sister-in-law. He guessed, rightly as it happened, that they'd taken a wrong turning about ten kilometres back down the road. Patiently he turned the car and hoped that the property they were about to see would meet with Gianna's approval. So far the only place which was in any way suitable needed an access road and Rupert strongly advised Gianna against buying it.

In the past three days they'd seen several properties, including the initial object of Gianna's desire which turned out to be in a remote hamlet, Isola Santa, neither an island nor particularly sacred as it happened. The cottage was virtually derelict and the only other inhabitants of what had once been a very picturesque location were two or three old women and a few sheep which were living behind the altar in the remains of the church. They'd seen other splendid houses which had too much land, a water mill which turned out to be two buildings divided by a narrow lane and several places in Lucca which Gianna dismissed as either too small, too noisy or too dark. Now they were on route 12, following the Serchio river towards Borgo a Mozzano and Rupert prayed that this time they might be lucky.

He searched the landscape as they approached Borgo, looking for an avenue bordered with Tuscan cypress which, according to the owners, led up to the property. Thankfully they had a key so, once they found the place, they could let themselves in and look around in peace. Rupert steered the car round a sharp bend in the road and spotted, first the avenue, and then what must surely be the house, standing on top of a slight rise, slightly to the left of the approach road.

From the outside it looked promising. Built of mellow Tuscan brick it had once been a substantial farmhouse. They walked slowly round the outside first, Gianna exclaiming with pleasure at the breathtaking views in every direction. Rupert walking back several paces on each side of the house looking for missing roof tiles and, to his relief, finding none. A new roof would make a tidy hole in Gianna's budget.

When they'd completed their circuit Rupert fitted the large iron key into the solid chestnut front door, which alternating seasons of sun and rain had weathered to light grey, and went inside. They walked around in silence taking in the details, the beamed ceilings, flagged floors, the generous size of the eight rooms. Both electricity and water were connected and one look at Gianna's face told Rupert that their search was over. "Would you like to have lunch and think about it?" he asked, "or shall we go and see the lawyer and put in a bid straight away?"

Gianna looked at her watch. It was a few minutes after twelve and by the time they reached Lucca their solicitor would be ready to shut up shop. Now that she'd found the place she was in no hurry to rush ahead. "Today I shall buy lunch," she announced, "and we can talk. Perhaps Signor Lombardo will take a little less than his asking price?" Rupert was only too happy to oblige. At last they could start on the real action.

As he drove them back to Lucca he switched his mind into overdrive wondering how quickly the solicitor could draw up the *compromesso.* There were bound to be protracted dealings with the owner who might even decide to put the price up if he thought for one moment that Gianna was really keen. Once that hurdle had been overcome he would try to persuade Signor Lombardo to let him do a measured survey. He would need sections and elevations and details of Gianna's proposed alterations to incorporate into his final plan. They could then safely leave the solicitor to brief the notary who would check that the property was free from any outstanding financial charges. Tomorrow was Saturday so they might have to wait until Monday for a meeting with the owner. He would be extremely lucky to get away before Thursday or Friday. He prayed there'd be no distant cousin with a share in the property who would have to be consulted before the sale could go ahead. But he cheered up considerably at the thought of leaving. He decided to wait until Saturday morning before phoning Isobel. Surely her line wouldn't be busy if he called early?

Isobel was preoccupied and didn't notice Joanna until the two almost collided in Berkhamsted High Street. "You're up and about bright and early, how's the patient?" Joanna asked.

"The patient's fine but the hangers on are driving me crazy." Isobel laughed and tried mentally to check her shopping list at the same time. "In a moment of weakness or madness I'm not sure which, I invited Zelda for dinner and I'm just picking up a few last minute bits and pieces."

"Have you got time for a quick coffee?" Joanna was longing to hear all about Rupert.

"At any other time I'd love it but I'm expecting Ian at ten and it's almost that now. I've been out since half past eight and everything seems to have taken longer than I expected. I promise we'll have lunch just as soon as James has gone home."

"Well I'll hold you to that, there's a new place we might try. Don't leave it too long will you?" Joanna was about to ask if Isobel had heard from Rupert when another friend spotted her and Isobel made her escape and dashed for the car park.

She'd remembered to pick up her photographs earlier and they'd been burning a hole in her handbag ever since. She flicked through them quickly when she got back to the car, ignoring the views she'd taken, searching for pictures of Rupert. Her holiday seemed light years away and at least the pictures convinced her that it hadn't all been a dream. Rupert looked every bit as handsome as she remembered. Looking at pictures of him in the privacy of her car was almost as good as being with him again. She wondered again what their last Saturday night might have offered if Tory hadn't turned up. She fantasised about it as she started the engine, manoeuvred the car out of the parking slot and made for the exit.

The town had begun to fill up, the traffic was solid along the High Street and she had to wait for what seemed like an eternity before anyone stopped long enough to allow her to join the stream of cars. Once she was clear of the town she put her foot hard down and accelerated up the hill to Ashley Green. It wasn't until she turned into the drive she realised that, in her haste to get into Berkhamsted earlier, she'd completely forgotten to switch on the answer phone.

Chapter Fourteen

"Come on, come on," Rupert said, beating a tattoo with his fingers against the side of the telephone kiosk. He started to count the number of rings, his spirits lifting as the rings continued and he realised the answer phone wasn't going to cut in. Five, six, Isobel *must* be there, she *had* to be; eight, nine; perhaps she was in the garden? How long would he let the instrument ring before he gave up?

"Isobel, at last," he said, as the ringing stopped and the receiver was lifted. "Oh God, I can't tell you what a time I've had trying to get through. Your line seems to be busy all the time, I was beginning to think we'd never speak again . . ." His voice tailed off as the silence at the other end lengthened. "Isobel?" a brief pause and then more urgently, "Isobel."

"I'm afraid Mrs Campbell isn't here at the moment." The man's voice sounded cool, detached, almost as if he were a hotel receptionist or an answering service.

"She's alright I hope." Rupert clutched the receiver tightly as visions of Isobel lying injured or ill flashed across the part of his mind that still seemed to be functioning. "I assure you Mrs Campbell is perfectly well, or at least she was when I saw her earlier."

Rupert wondered if his imagination was working overtime or was there just the smallest hint of triumph in the disembodied voice? Who was it for God's sake and how had he managed to make himself so much at home in the space of a few days? Rupert cleared his throat. "Oh! Good! I'm glad to hear it. Would you pass on a message? I apologise for ringing so early in the morning but, as I said earlier, communications have been a little difficult. Would you tell Isobel that Rupert Northcote called? I'm sorry to miss her and I'll be in touch again as soon as possible."

The voice assured him that the message would be passed on and the receiver was replaced before Rupert could even say goodbye. He hung up and stood for a moment trying to pull himself together. His hands were shaking and he clenched his fists tightly before thrusting both hands into his jacket pockets. His brain was flying round his head in fragments and he found it impossible to make sense of the conversation he'd just finished. He needed time to think and, as if on automatic pilot, he walked towards the dining room where he and Gianna had shared dinner on their first evening in Tuscany. He ordered coffee and a grappa, although it was only nine thirty in the morning. He wished he still smoked, a cigarette would have helped to calm him down.

He tipped the grappa down his throat and choked on the raw spirit. He asked himself what the hell he thought he was doing knocking back alcohol this early in the morning, took a long pull from his coffee cup and tried to marshal his thoughts.

The voice had definitely belonged to an older man; that ruled out Isobel's sons. Whoever it was sounded cultured so it was unlikely that he'd been speaking to a handyman or gardener although he realised almost as he thought this that he was making a sweeping generalisation. But whoever it was had the run of the house or how could he be answering the phone? Was it perhaps a brother? Isobel hadn't mentioned a sibling of either sex during the time they'd spent together but that didn't mean she was an only child.

Suddenly he realised how much he cared. Was it possible that she'd been stringing him along? He wished he hadn't prevaricated when they'd been together in Venice. He should have told her before they parted how much he loved her but then he hadn't been sure. He hadn't wanted to hurt her feelings by making such a positive declaration until he was certain in his own mind that he could speak with sincerity. In fact if he were really honest he hadn't been sure until a few moments ago when that unidentified man answered the phone and he'd felt a sharp pang of jealousy for the first time in many years.

He finished his coffee, paid the bill, told himself to calm down and that everything would soon be sorted out. Looking back over the week his attempts to get in touch with Isobel had been a catalogue of minor mishaps which they would both laugh about when they finally made contact. All of a sudden he felt hungry and so stopped on the way back to the car to buy fresh rolls for himself and Gianna. He must finish the work on her property as soon as possible and then he could get back to England and Isobel. Now that he knew his own feelings he longed to tell her, needed to know that they were reciprocated and to put an end to all this uncertainty once and for all.

James struggled with his temper as he hung up on Rupert Northcote. Before he left the hospital his doctor had asked him to try and stay as calm as possible whatever the circumstances. He sat breathing deeply for several minutes before picking up the phone and dialling Zelda's number, hoping he would find her at home. He positively purred into the mouthpiece when she answered.

"Sorry to call you so early only we've been having a bit of trouble with our telephone out here and I want to be sure that it's working in case of an emergency. Do you think you could call me back just to be certain it's OK?" He replaced the receiver and when the phone rang again went through the motions of finalising details for this evening, checking that Zelda knew which way to come and that she knew that she was expected at around seven thirty, although he was sure that Isobel wouldn't mind if she came earlier. He listened patiently as Zelda ran through the list of things she simply had to do today and finished by saying that if it was at all possible she'd see him earlier but not to raise his hopes too much. In spite of her response James was smiling to himself as he hung up. "I'll teach you to chase after my ex-wife bloody Northcote," he muttered as he went in search of the morning paper, realising that he hadn't felt this good for a long time. His smile broadened as he opened the Telegraph. "I'd say there's a strong indication that you're definitely on the mend," he said to himself as he settled down with the financial section.

Isobel heard the murmur of voices coming from the sitting room as soon as she walked through the front door. Good. Ian must have arrived already and she could leave him to continue his chat with James until she'd unpacked her shopping. She dumped her bags on the kitchen table and, before even taking off her coat, went quietly into her study, picked up the telephone and dialled 1471. She jotted down the number which, according to the operator, had called at eight forty. An 0181 number she recognised as James' home. Her heart sank as she went back to the kitchen and began mechanically to unpack the food she'd bought for tonight's dinner.

There *had* to be a simple explanation she told herself as she stowed cheese and cream in the fridge. She'd always prided herself on being a good judge of character and was certain that Rupert was no philanderer. He'd seemed so sincere and at no time had he led her to believe that she was the love of his life. What had he said when she'd teased him about forgetting her? 'I need time Isobel.' An out-and-out rogue would have told her anything he felt she wanted to hear, wouldn't he? She hoped, not for the first time, that he hadn't been involved in some ghastly car accident. The way people drove in Italy terrified her. It was a good thing in a way that she was so busy looking after James, that, at the very least, kept her occupied most of the time. Which reminded her perhaps she'd better go and see if James and Ian would like some coffee.

Later the same day Ian changed gear, eased into the car park behind the *Moulin d'Eau* and thanked God for Kevin. He looked fondly at the picturesque building of weathered stone partially covered in creeper, where he knew he was about to be enfolded in discreet luxury and later, soothed to a peaceful, uninterrupted sleep by the fast flowing river that bordered the property. His mouth began to water in anticipation of the platter *des fruits de mer* to which he would treat himself later that evening and for which Kevin would pay.

Kevin was that phenomenon of the 1990's a Lottery Millionaire. What's more, Kevin, after his initial celebratory trip to the West Indies, during which he'd freely indulged in Rum Punch, romance and Reggae, had decided to follow in the footsteps of his all time hero Richard Branson and make himself into a multimillionaire.

Millionaire clients were scarce, even for London based firms like Ian's. Even rarer were those whose wealth outstripped their intelligence. The minute Kevin Palmer had walked into his office and started to talk about his plans to acquire a property in France, Ian's finely tuned nose smelled money.

Over the next few months he'd helped Kevin to buy a small, beautiful *château* in the Pas de Calais which had now been converted to incorporate several *gîtes* as well as substantial living accommodation for the new owner. Kevin had relied heavily on Ian's fluent French both in negotiating the purchase and during the subsequent conversion. The two of them had spent many pleasant evenings sampling the local cuisine and patting themselves on the back as the scheme progressed to their mutual satisfaction.

Kevin's early life in Dagenham hadn't really prepared him to become a French property owning entrepreneur and he was overawed by his new surroundings. He never tired of looking out over the extensive fields and woodland which stretched away to the sea. His favourite expression, which Ian had quoted at many subsequent dinner parties and which never failed to raise a laugh, was; "Marvellous innit squire, miles and miles of bloody nuthin!"

Strictly speaking this trip wasn't necessary. Kevin wanted his property to be listed in an upmarket holiday brochure, *Vacances en Europe*. The holding company insisted that all 'their' premises were furnished to the highest standard and certain key features, including the provision of a swimming pool on the larger properties, had to be incorporated before they would even consider including it in their glossy brochure. In return they promised a high occupancy rate and to shoulder responsibility for publicity and administration. For this service Kevin had to pay an initial registration fee and 20% of his letting income thereafter. Tomorrow Ian and Kevin were going to do a preliminary inspection and on Monday the representative from the property company was to visit to give the place the once over. If all went according to plan, Ian would then supervise the signing of the agreement with *Vacances en Europe*. Kevin could easily have carried out the exercise on his own but was keen to, 'Have the Law along to see fair play.' As he'd put it to Ian.

Ian had declined Kevin's offer of overnight hospitality using his backlog of work as an excuse. He'd stayed with Kevin on a previous visit and the cognac flowed so freely after dinner that he'd woken up with one of the worst hangovers of his life. Besides he'd had enough of Kevin's reminiscences about his previous life as a car body worker and his fantastic good luck in winning the Lottery.

It had been good to see his father in such high spirits. James had positively oozed bonhomie during their time together. Obviously his mother was proving to be a good influence. Dad appeared to be making such good progress that Ian wondered if he might be back at the office sooner than expected. There was the other hope of course that James might decide that divorcing his first wife had been a mistake and, when he was feeling stronger, would find the courage to divorce the second and they could all go back to being the same comfortable family again. It would be such a relief not to have old Grizzle around, constantly hovering over his father like a praying mantis.

His mother hadn't looked quite so relaxed now he came to think of it. Perhaps the strain of the unaccustomed visitors was proving too much? Funny, she'd never found it a problem in the past. Maybe she was just getting older or missing this Rupert bloke? Although Steve was convinced that, after what his mother had told him, it was just a holiday romance and there was no way the two of them were an item.

If only they could solve the on-going problem of Bruce; perhaps find a woman willing to take him on for however long he had left then things would really start to look up. Having him to stay certainly put the damper on their home life and it was terrific to be in France for a couple of days, even though it was a business trip. The food would be a treat in itself after their recent diet of microwave dinners.

It was a relief to offload some of the more mundane cases onto his father's capable shoulders and get away for a while. In the end he'd given James quite a stack to deal with. Most of it wasn't urgent and he'd asked his father to be sure to work at his own pace and not to tire himself. So James had some uncontested divorce cases, some conveyancing and sundry bits of executorial work which would involve him in nothing more stressful than making phone calls, filling in forms and checking that various procedures were in place to enable each case to progress as soon as possible. It would, at any rate, keep his father's mind active and make him feel that he was being useful to the practice.

"Well, isn't this cosy!" James said, rubbing his hands together and looking at the two women in turn. "Would you like me to carve?" he asked Isobel and, without waiting for a reply, picked up the knife and began to sharpen it with some relish. He failed to notice the two women wince at the sound of metal scraping against metal.

James carved the meat expertly as his father had taught him many years ago. Who'd have believed that a day which had begun so badly, with that annoying phone call, could get so much better as it progressed? Thanks to Ian he had a stack of work waiting for his attention and now here he was being entertained by both his wife and his ex-wife at the same time. His ego expanded as he sat at the head of the table. Candlelight fell on a few late roses which Isobel had picked and arranged in an old glass goblet. The scent drifted towards him, released by the warmth of the flames.

Zelda had taken full advantage of the new *au pair* and spent the afternoon being pampered. Now, after a massage, a facial and with a new hairstyle she looked as svelte as ever and, to his satisfaction, was doing her best to entertain him. Isobel had surpassed herself in the kitchen and he was enjoying a superb dinner. Isobel too was looking good he thought and wondered why she hadn't made the same effort when they'd been married to each other. It never for one moment occurred to him that each woman might be trying in some way to live up to the other but arrogantly assumed the reason they were both trying so hard was none other than himself. He thought briefly of Rupert Northcote and hoped he was pacing back and forth somewhere wondering why the object of his affection had failed to return his call. His self-satisfaction grew and his smile became broader as he settled himself more comfortably in his chair.

He glanced across the table at Isobel and wondered just how long she'd known this Rupert character. If he were to believe his sister the pair of them were old friends. Since his arrival in Ashley Green he'd been careful not to mention that never-to-be-forgotten conversation with Barbara and the only thing he knew for certain was that Isobel had lunched with Rupert in Venice. Now suddenly his curiosity was aroused and he began to speculate on the closeness or otherwise of their friendship. Had Isobel been to bed with him? If so, how had the bastard performed? Barbara had told him that he was half Italian. The Italians were reputedly good between the sheets. Had he lived up to the reputation of his fellow countrymen? James' expression clouded. He didn't want to think of Isobel being pawed by some foreign architect who fancied himself as Romeo. Was Isobel looking just a little bit tense under the social veneer? It couldn't be easy for her to be in such close proximity to a successor who was so much younger. Poor old Isobel. He would think of some way to repay her for looking after him so well and for being so nice to Zelda.

"That was a really delicious dinner." Zelda gushed as the meal drew to a close.

"I'm glad you enjoyed it. Do take James through to the sitting room and I'll make some coffee." Isobel's voice was crisp as she collected plates and the remnants of fruit and cheese and piled them onto a tray. Zelda didn't offer to help but took James' hand instead preparing to lead him towards the sitting room.

"I think I can manage to walk as far as the sitting room without assistance," he said, shaking the hand away and using the arms of his chair to lever himself to his feet. "I'm not in my bloody dotage yet," he grumbled as Zelda shrugged and left the room without waiting for him.

"Try not to spoil a pleasant evening if you can help it James," Isobel pleaded. "The last few weeks can't have been easy for her."

"They haven't exactly been a bed of roses for me either," James muttered. He picked up Zelda's half-drunk glass of wine and downed it in one gulp before placing it on the tray which Isobel was holding. His expression dared her to remonstrate with him and when she obligingly remained silent he picked up the nearly empty wine bottle, poured the dregs into his own glass and drank that as well. Isobel appeared not to notice but turned towards the kitchen then paused and asked: "Would you like Zelda to stay the night? It's quite late and a good hour's drive back."

James frowned and appeared to consider her question carefully. He'd thought that he might work in the morning and then perhaps take Isobel out to lunch. Besides it had been a long day and he could do without the sexual arousal that close proximity to Zelda would precipitate. "It's the *au pair's* day off tomorrow and as she's only just started to work for us I think it best if we don't ask any favours of her just yet. But thanks for the thought," he added, "and thank you for going to so much trouble this evening."

"Perhaps you should go and join Zelda," Isobel said quickly, "or she'll be wondering what's happened to you." She started to walk towards the kitchen thinking back to the days when she and James had still been married. She'd always trusted him least when he was going out of his way to be nice and she wondered what, if any, mischief he was cooking up.

It was nearly midnight when James closed his book, turned off the bedside light and prepared for sleep. After what seemed to him like hours of tossing and turning he admitted reluctantly that he'd drunk too much at dinner. Not by his usual standards of course, not with Zelda's hawk eye fixed on him. But the doctor had asked him to limit his daily intake and after he'd knocked back what was left on the table and with Zelda on her way home and Isobel tidying up the kitchen he'd sneaked a quick brandy. Perhaps he should have been more careful and listened to the advice of his doctor? No perhaps about it. What to do now? Good old Alka Seltzer that should fix it. Did Isobel have any? If so where did she keep it? The bathroom most likely. There was a medicine cabinet on the wall if he remembered correctly.

He switched on the light and looked at his watch. Half past midnight. It was a long time since he'd been up or awake so late. He padded to the bathroom, opened the cabinet, moved a few bottles about, was that a tube at the back? Damned silly place to put it. He reached into the cabinet and, in his haste to grab the tube, knocked several bottles over. A couple fell out of the cabinet and hit the floor, rolling in all directions and making a clatter on the smoothly polished wood. "Oh bugger!" he said, trying to rearrange the bottles in their original order whilst still hanging on to the tube of Alka Seltzer. Several more bottles went to join their companions on the floor. He put down the tablets and was just wondering if he dare risk getting down on his hands and knees when Isobel arrived at the bathroom door. "James, what on earth . . .?"

"I was looking for these." He waved the tube of Alka Seltzer. "Hope I didn't wake you," he said apologetically.

"I haven't been in bed very long. Thought I'd tidy the kitchen first. It always looks worse in the morning somehow. No don't bother to pick them up," she added as James bent slowly towards the floor.

James ran the cold tap, tipped toothbrushes out of the only glass and filled it up before tossing in a couple of tablets. He drank the fizzing liquid, watching Isobel as she swiftly retrieved the fallen bottles and put them on a small table next to the bath. Her hair was rumpled, she'd taken off her make-up and her silk pyjamas were clinging seductively to her body. She looked about fourteen he thought fondly and then swiftly amended her age to sixteen as he acknowledged just how he was feeling. He held out a hand to help her up as her fingers closed round the last of the bottles and was pleased and surprised when she took it. Perhaps there was a slim chance . . .?

"Thanks, I think I've got them all. I'll leave them on the table for now and sort through them tomorrow. Maybe there are some that are past their sell by."

James' mind was a long way from the shelf life of pills and potions. He grasped Isobel's hand more tightly guessing, quite rightly, that he had only seconds in which to act. He pulled her clumsily into his arms and held her against him. "Isobel! Isobel! It's been such a long time!" he murmured into her hair trying at the same time to ignore the sudden palpitations as his heart rate accelerated. He felt her body grow rigid against his own and then her hands against his chest gently pushing him away.

"James it's very late. We're both tired and don't forget you've been seriously ill. Finish your Alka Seltzer and let's both go back to bed." Her voice was coaxing as if she were talking to a small boy. She waited for him to empty the glass, watched him replace it, stood aside to let him pass then followed him into his bedroom.

James - never one to admit defeat - allowed his hopes to soar briefly; maybe she was going to join him? But, to his disappointment, Isobel merely plumped up his pillows, straightened the crumpled sheets and waited for him to climb into bed. She even tucked him in as he'd seen her tuck up Ian and Steve on the rare occasions when he'd been home in time for their bedtime. Finally she kissed his cheek swiftly. "Right then I'll leave you. I hope you'll be able to sleep now," she said and left him.

James pulled out the tucked-in sheets defiantly, switched off the light and resigned himself to counting sheep for however long it took.

Isobel's own heart was thumping as she reached her own bedroom. "My God! That was a close call Isobel," she said to herself as she got into bed. The sooner James went home to Zelda the better. If he carried on like this he could easily have another heart attack. Hadn't she read somewhere about some old boy breathing his last gasp *in flagrante*? Well not if she could help it!

She took her Venetian guidebook from her bedside table and found the picture of the *Scuola di San Rocco*. For several minutes she wallowed in the memory of that wonderful concert and the intoxicating mix of paintings, music and Rupert. Her thoughts went back to their first walk in Venice when he'd shown her the life of the young couple sculpted on the column in the *piazetta*. She pulled out the slip of paper which she now used as a child uses a comfort blanket and stared at Rupert's scribbled instructions. Her throat was tight with unshed tears. Wearily she turned off the light, thumped her pillow into some kind of submission and then cried silently into it.

Chapter Fifteen

When Isobel came down the next morning James was already working. He'd previously asked if he could use her study and called out to her as she passed the door. It was only eight thirty and he'd obviously been up for some time. In front of him was a legal pad already covered with his large, flamboyant handwriting and Isobel's desk was littered with papers. A large mug, now empty, stood at his elbow.

She felt a flash of irritation at the ease with which he'd made himself at home.

"Did you have a good night?" she asked, walking over to her desk and picking up the empty mug.

"No. Thanks all the same for asking." James replied.

"Well perhaps it would be a good idea to take things easy today and maybe have an early night?" Isobel suggested.

"Don't fuss for God's sake Isobel, all this enforced idleness is driving me mad."

"I promised the family I'd look after you. If you have a problem with that and want to leave that's fine by me, but while you're here . . .Have you had breakfast or shall I make you a tray?"

"I'd like some toast and coffee, you can forget the muesli. I thought I'd make an early start and then I wondered if you'd like to go out somewhere for lunch?"

Isobel looked at him in surprise. After last night she'd expected him to be in a bad mood. Until yesterday he'd been consistently brusque and off-hand and their conversations had been limited. She'd put his irritability down to the after effects of his illness and accepted it asking herself how she would feel in a similar situation. But there had been such a change in him during the last twenty four hours she wondered again what could have happened to bring it about. Perhaps now that he was picking up the threads of work again and begun to make a recovery his spirits had lifted in tandem? She gave up speculating for the moment and went off to make coffee.

When she reappeared a few moments later with his breakfast tray James pushed his chair away from the desk and turned round to face her. "You didn't answer my question," he said. "I asked if you might like to go out to lunch, somewhere good I thought." As the minutes ticked by and she didn't reply he reached for the telephone. "I'll say it once more. I fancy having lunch out. I don't care to eat alone. Would you like to come or shall I find someone else to keep me company?"

Isobel had always found it easier to respond to James when he was being stroppy and after all her frantic activity of the previous day she knew she'd enjoy a break from the kitchen. "If you put it like that," she managed a smile, "I'll be glad to keep you company."

Throughout the meal James was careful to keep the conversation on safe ground. He spoke warmly of Ian's valuable contribution to the practice and surprised Isobel by asking questions about her own business and if she missed it now that she'd retired. They exchanged information about mutual friends and their families. He wanted her to feel relaxed, to trust him, to be at ease with him in a way that she hadn't appeared to be in the few days they'd spent together; certainly not last night. He could still feel her body rigid against his own. He was unused to rejection and he was hurt by her lack of response. His approach might have been a touch clumsy he admitted but surely she realised that he was trying to bridge the gulf that had opened up between them? He played for time, waiting until the coffee arrived before moving to more personal matters. Finally, when the waiter had filled both their cups and left them alone, he leaned towards her slightly, put his elbows on the table and linked his fingers together making a bridge on which he could rest his chin. "Tell me Isobel," he began, "have you forgiven me?" He watched her carefully, intently, a predator and his prey.

"For last night you mean? Nothing to forgive."

More's the pity, James thought and then aloud, "No I mean for divorcing you and marrying a younger woman."

"I'm not the Almighty James, or a priest in the confessional."

Her tone was dismissive and she'd avoided answering very neatly, but then he was used to that when he interviewed clients and asked them awkward questions. He tried again. "Surely Isobel if you were still angry with me you wouldn't have asked me to come and stay?" He continued to watch. She looked at him across the table, her eyes were still the same shade of delphinium blue that he'd always remembered.

"Let's be quite clear about this James." Her voice, to his disappointment, was now matter-of-fact. "You're staying with me because all the other members of the family are unable for one reason or another to cope with you at the moment."

It wasn't the answer he wanted to hear and he did his best to look wounded. "Well I must say Isobel you don't pull your punches do you?" he said, allowing the waiter to refill their coffee cups and declining an offer of brandy or a liqueur without bothering to ask Isobel if she'd like one.

"Well what do you expect me to say?" Her voice sounded irritable. "You hurt my feelings deeply when you decided to leave. But to tell you the truth I haven't spent every night since then crying myself to sleep and longing for you to come back. Eventually I accepted that you'd found the happiness with someone else that you obviously didn't find with me and after that I just decided to get on with my life."

James made up his mind to stop pussyfooting around and went straight for the jugular. "So how long exactly have you known Rupert Northcote?" He leaned back in his chair and saw, to his satisfaction, that she was blushing. Was she about to confess that they'd been lovers for years? If so he could pile on the agony, tell her how upset he was to discover that she'd deceived him at the time of their divorce.

When finally she replied Isobel sounded defensive. "Frankly James I really don't think it's any of your business. After all you showed me quite brutally that you no longer wished to stay married to me so what difference does it make how long I've known him?"

"You were always such a goody goody, I was just surprised when I discovered that all the time you might have had your own lover but chose to keep it dark. That's all."

He saw the red deepen in her cheeks and watched her move around in her seat as if suddenly it had become uncomfortable. At last she met his eyes, her own were quite steady he noticed. "The truth is I met Rupert on the journey out to Venice, at Heathrow, quite accidentally. I'd never seen him before in my life but we got on extremely well. He was kind enough to show me round on the days when he wasn't working. We discovered that we had a lot in common, classical music and architecture for instance. You don't have to believe me but what I've just told you is the absolute truth. I'm only sorry that I deliberately misled your sister and she jumped to the obvious conclusion."

James was, if anything, disappointed by her frankness. She'd taken away his opportunity to twist the knife and he knew he should apologise for thinking the worst of her. But the thought that she was having an intimate relationship with another man still rankled and anyway he'd never enjoyed eating humble pie. "Are you going to see him again or was this just a *holiday* romance?" It was a cheap point but he couldn't resist making it, even allowing a note of sarcasm to creep into his voice. If he couldn't make her feel guilty then he might just succeed in making her feel foolish. It was one thing to have a fling on holiday when you were sixteen quite another when you were sixty. In fact if he were honest he would describe it as downright undignified. And if Rupert Northcote *had* picked her up at the airport whatever kind of man was he? He could just imagine him casting a lascivious eye around the departure lounge looking for a likely victim and choosing Isobel and for what? His heart beat a warning as visions of the two of them swam in and out of his mind. "You haven't answered my last question," he said, as the minutes dragged by and Isobel didn't respond.

"Why are you so interested suddenly?" Isobel asked. "We've scarcely spoken to each other for five years and suddenly you're behaving like Sherlock Holmes. I can only repeat what I said earlier that my private life is my own business."

James saw her eyes flash dangerously and knew that the time had come for conciliation. He reached across the table and took her hand. It felt cold. He continued to hold it as he played his trump card. "Isobel," he began in the soothing voice he'd used frequently and to such good effect with distressed divorcées. "Has it ever occurred to you that, although we're no longer married, I might still care for you? I should hate to see you hurt in any way. Can you understand that?"

He saw her eyes widen in disbelief and winced as she pulled her hand away abruptly. "Too bad you didn't think of that five years ago," she flashed at him. "I don't recall you telling me then how much you still cared. And all the years we were married, when I cried myself to sleep because you were out with some twenty years old amœba on legs, I wasn't aware of your caring then. I wouldn't mind betting that even though you don't want to live with me any longer you can't bear the thought of someone else moving into my life and perhaps taking your place."

James flinched as the truth came flying across the table. He'd forgotten how astute Isobel was at reading his mind. Damn the woman! Damn Rupert bloody Northcote and damn his sister for alerting him to what was obviously going on between the two of them. If Rupert Northcote had been a casual acquaintance Isobel would have said so. She was obviously expecting to see him again or she wouldn't have refused to answer his question. So what the hell was he going to do now?

What a relief it would be when the wretched man went home, Isobel thought as she made tea for them both on Sunday afternoon. She'd known ever since last night that he was up to something but nothing had prepared her either for his questions, his comments or his behaviour during lunch. Why hadn't she come right out in the open in the first placed and confessed to being in love with Rupert? He wouldn't have been able to argue with that. Her stupid pride had got in the way again. The fact was she daren't admit to anyone that she loved Rupert in case she never saw him again. She couldn't bear the thought that all the family would feel sorry for her and see her as a pathetic old woman who'd been unceremoniously ditched.

She shivered as she remembered James' clumsy behaviour in the bathroom last night and then smiled as she remembered the way she'd behaved in Rupert's bathroom and immediately awarded Rupert an Oscar for his performance! Then suddenly the intimacy of her present situation made her feel uncomfortable. She'd been mad to agree to have James to stay, should have known that he'd try to exploit the situation. She'd made it clear to Steve at the outset that she would look after James for two weeks and she must insist that he return home next weekend. How dare he pretend he still cared for her? What a joke that was! She knew from long and bitter experience that he'd stop at nothing to get what he wanted.

Rupert would still be in Tuscany so it was pointless to try and ring him in Venice. She wanted so much to speak to him, to hear his voice reassuring her as he'd done after that fateful meeting with Barbara. She told herself it wouldn't be long before they made contact and tried hard to believe it. Until then she must be patient, keep James at arms length and try to think positively about the future. She put the finishing touches to the tea tray and went reluctantly to join James in the sitting room.

Henry put down the paper in exasperation as he heard the unmistakeable sound of Barbara's voice lambasting the builder yet again. They were installing a conservatory and every morning Barbara went on a tour of inspection the moment the builder appeared. Henry was certain that, if she didn't ease off a bit, it would only be a matter of time before the poor man told her what she could do with her conservatory and pushed off to another customer on his long waiting list. He'd told Henry earlier that his order book was full for the next two years and for this reason was working on Sunday to try and prevent too great a backlog. Conservatories, it appeared, were the new must-have. Henry felt that the time had come to sort things out with Barbara once and for all.

Living with her had never been easy but since their visit to James he'd felt as if he were walking on eggshells. He'd tried in vain to discover the cause of her current bout of ill-humour, thinking that perhaps she was feeling guilty for spilling the beans about Isobel and undoubtedly, as far as he was concerned, helping to trigger James' heart attack. All he'd been able to discover so far was that Barbara and Isobel had had 'a few words' during the course of their visit. Barbara had refused to say any more.

"The man's an absolute imbecile." Barbara came panting into the kitchen and sat down heavily at the table - such a pity she could never do anything delicately or with grace, Henry thought.

He poured tea for her and pushed the cup across the table. She took it without thanks.

"You may call him an imbecile if you like," Henry began, "but you know as well as I that he comes highly recommended. If you carry on like this he's going to walk out sooner rather than later." He caught Barbara's look of surprise and pressed on. "You've been like a bear with a sore head since we went to visit James and I don't mind telling you I'm getting pretty fed up with it. You're not exactly the world's leading expert when it comes to building and I suggest you leave the poor man to get on with his job and stop manufacturing complaints."

Barbara's mouth fell open. Henry was normally so meek and mild. So what had brought this on? She'd been a bit short recently, so what? Whenever she thought of that brother of hers surrounded by doting women, two strapping sons to shoulder his worries, it made her want to spit. And it was all very well for Isobel to accuse her of being jealous. What did she know about anything? She had a glamorous lover making sheep's eyes at her for all the world to see and her father hadn't threatened to cut her out of his will if she went to university. Oh yes it was easy for her to talk.

Barbara had no illusions about her marriage. She'd inherited handsomely when her father died and since then had built up a profitable share portfolio. She studied the FT-SE assiduously, moving her money regularly, taking advantage of a fluctuating market. Recent dividends had paid for their stay at the Gritti Palace and were also being used to finance the conservatory so Henry knew which side his bread was buttered. If her portfolio crashed she was sure his devotion would disappear as quickly as the cash. But it would be stupid to antagonise him. There was after all no shortage of rich widows. She buttered her toast, noisily. "Alright you win," she said. "From tomorrow the builder is your responsibility."

Henry silently passed the financial section of the newspaper across the table. It wasn't much but it was the nearest thing to an apology he was going to get.

By Monday morning the mellow autumn weather and the ministrations of the *Moulin d'Eau* had worked their magic and Ian felt on top form as he drove towards Montreuil-sur-Mer and Kevin's chunk of real estate. They'd spent several hours the previous day going over the half dozen *gîtes*, checking every fixture to make certain they were in good working order. They switched on lights, tested taps, inspected furniture for dust. This morning Kevin's wife Michelle planned to put fresh flowers in every apartment and they were all quietly confident that *Vacances en Europe* would be including them in their brochure next season.

Ian drove through the impressive wrought iron gates at the entrance to the park which surrounded the property and immediately spotted Kevin. He was walking briskly across the grass, pausing every now and then to throw a ball for the golden retriever that kept him company. At least he looks the part, Ian thought as he sounded the horn and waved a greeting before parking on the stretch of gravel in front of the *château*. He waited for Kevin to join him. The sun slanted through the trees highlighting the pale rose brick and causing the dew to evaporate from the mauve-grey slates in an ethereal mist. Ian wondered if he should perhaps take his own advice and invest in a property over here as a *pied à terre.* With a few more people like Kevin on his books he should be able to afford it easily. He'd better not mention it to Susan though until Bruce had gone home. If his father-in-law got to know about it he'd renew his efforts to persuade them to sell their flat and go and live with him and convince them what a great favour he was doing them by enabling them to release their capital to invest overseas.

"Mornin' squire!" Kevin's voice cut across his thoughts and Ian returned reluctantly from his daydream.

"I take it I'm the first to arrive?" Ian bent to scratch the head of the retriever who promptly laid a well-chewed ball beside his left foot and looked up hopefully wagging his tail and waiting for Ian to throw the ball for him.

"Some posh babe from this European Vacations outfit phoned. Says she's stuck in traffic getting out of Paris. Should be with us eleven-ish."

"Good." Ian was in no hurry. He threw the ball and the retriever bounded away in pursuit. "Shall we walk for a while?" he asked Kevin, thinking that a walk through Kevin's hectares would be a novel way to begin a Monday morning.

"Sure," Kevin needed little persuading. Free at last from the pounding machinery of the car manufacturing industry he relished every moment spent in the open air.

They walked for a good half hour, taking it in turns to throw the ball, until they heard the sound of a car engine and spotted a Peugot being driven at furious speed along the drive. The pair winced as the car braked too sharply on the gravel causing fragments to fly in all directions and leaving skid marks on the surface that Kevin had previously raked smooth. They strolled in a leisurely fashion across the park, taking their time - after all *they* weren't late for the meeting. The two of them watched in detached amusement as their visitor unwound herself from the driving seat and ran round to the boot, presumably to collect her paperwork.

"Cor! She's tasty!" Kevin let out a low whistle at the sight of a pair of long, slender legs emerging from a skirt which was only just decent. Ian, who wholeheartedly concurred with Kevin's assessment but wasn't about to admit it, laid a restraining hand on his arm. "I should wait until we're definitely in the brochure if I were you." He paused and then added for good measure, "squire!"

"Tory Northcote," the woman said, holding out her hand as the two of them arrived. "Apologies for being late, I should have driven down last night and stayed in the area."

"No problem." Ian shook her hand - firmly, to show her who was in control, before introducing himself and Kevin. The latter lost no time in leading the way into the *château*. Tory Northcote was certainly a looker Ian thought as they waited in Kevin's office for Michelle to bring them some coffee. It was a long time since he'd seen a woman with such long, slim legs. Her chestnut hair reached exactly to her shoulders and was cut in a simple bob which swung every time she moved her head, which was frequently. Her eyes were dark blue, almost navy, the wide mouth looked as if it could pout deliciously, given the appropriate circumstances. She was just the right side of anorexic and could quite easily have been a model he reckoned.

As they drank their coffee she outlined the benefits for Kevin of being in business with *Vacances en Europe* before showing them the existing brochure and giving them the average annual occupancy figures. She explained that owners were allowed to reserve properties for their friends for a month each year, providing it was outside the main holiday period from March to October. Ian made a mental note of this last piece of information in case he decided to take an off-peak holiday at some time in the future. Tory then produced a folder from her briefcase and began to go through a check-list of the on-site facilities giving them no clues as to whether or not she was impressed by what they had to offer. Once the preliminary checking was over Ian suggested a tour and they began what turned out to be a detailed inspection of every *gîte.*

Nothing escaped Tory's eagle eye Ian noted as the inspection continued. Tory opened cooker doors, checked refrigerators, pressed mattresses, opened cupboards. Every time she spotted a feature which she thought might look well in the brochure she took a picture, using an up-to-the-minute digital camera. Kevin was trying his best to look cool but Ian saw him wipe the sweat from his upper lip at regular intervals as the morning wore on. At last they were finished and Ian was just about to lead the way back to the office when Tory said, "I just need to look at the swimming pool and if that's up to standard I see no reason why we shouldn't start to work together next year." They started to walk towards the back entrance, which led out to a terrace and the pool, when the telephone rang.

"I'll take Miss Northcote out to see the swimming pool," Ian said quickly. He'd been wondering all morning how he could wangle some time alone with her and this was the opportunity he'd been waiting for.

"Do you have plans for this afternoon?" he asked as they left the *château.* "More properties to visit perhaps? If so I hope they're not too close to us or we might have to negotiate a discount if there's local competition."

"Relax." Tory tossed back her hair and looked sideways at him. "It's a fabulous property, there's nothing to touch it for miles around, at least not on our books."

"Then if the swimming pool is up to scratch we're in business, is that right?" Ian asked, quickening his pace to keep up with her long strides.

"Got it exactly." Tory smiled at him for the first time since her late arrival.

She was so self-assured he hesitated before his next remark, fearing a brush-off. But then deciding he had nothing to lose and who-knows-what to gain he continued. " In that case why don't I take you out for lunch to celebrate?"

"I warn you my taste runs to expensive lunches." The hair was tossed yet again.

"I wouldn't have expected otherwise." The words came out easily enough but she looked as if she existed on a diet of lettuce leaves and mineral water.

"What about your friend?" she asked.

"What about him?" Ian told himself she didn't want Kevin along otherwise why bother to ask? "Leave Kevin to me, just follow my lead, OK?" He looked at her for a moment, his head slightly to one side and then before she could reply he said, "Shall we give the pool the once over and then we can get going?"

For a few seconds Ian felt guilty at refusing Kevin's offer of lunch, particularly as he would later be billing him for luncheon for two at the *Moulin d'Eau* under the nicely euphemistic heading, 'expenses'. He'd told Kevin he wanted to return to the UK as soon as possible. Tory, who'd also been included in the invitation, said she had other properties to inspect and that she'd skip lunch altogether to try and make up for time lost in the Paris traffic earlier.

Kevin had already put a bottle of bubbly in the fridge anticipating a celebration but, faced with two such busy people, he was impotent. He insisted on walking them out to their cars and Ian hoped that Tory would have the good sense to follow him as he drove away. He needn't have worried. Tory wasn't the kind of woman to pass up the opportunity of a free lunch.

Chapter Sixteen

A slow smile spread across Tory's face as Ian's car came to a halt outside the *Moulin d'Eau*. She looked up at the windows, which were partially covered in creeper so that some appeared as mere slits in the stone, and wondered if Ian was staying here. If he was this could become a *very* interesting lunch. She waited for him to walk over and open the car door before she slid out, ankles first, and watched with great satisfaction as Ian admired her legs. As she followed him into the hotel she had a bet with herself that he'd soon be panting to see the rest of her.

Their table overlooked the river. Tory looked down at the swirling water and felt her pulse begin to race in anticipation of whatever lay ahead. They were the only couple in the dining room so at least they shouldn't have to wait too long for their food. She'd overslept that morning, missed out on breakfast and, as a consequence, was absolutely starving. When the waiter brought over a basket of bread she helped herself the moment he set it down.

"Here's to a long and fruitful partnership." Ian raised his glass as the waiter poured Chablis for them.

"Santé!" Tory touched the rim of her glass against Ian's, giving him the benefit of the dark blue eyes at the same time. Ian was the first to look away and Tory continued to watch him as he picked up the menu.

"The sea food here is excellent," he volunteered without looking up. Tory had already made her selection when Ian was in the gents but decided to flatter his male ego and play along.

"In that case I'll start with the lobster medallion." The blue eyes dared Ian to deny her. After all she'd warned him in advance that he wouldn't get away cheaply.

"Do you work in France all the time?" she asked after Ian had ordered and they were waiting for their food.

"Unfortunately not, I'm based in London. My father and I have a practice in Southampton Row. I'm only just starting to build up the business on this side of the Channel. I suppose *you're* galloping all over Europe inspecting smart properties?"

"I was in Venice last week looking at some apartments. I expect to be in France for the rest of the week at least. I live in Paris which is fairly convenient as a base."

"Except perhaps when you're driving to the Pas de Callais?"

"Touché!" Tory laughed at the jibe realising at the same time that she was fencing with an equal.. She didn't however enjoy taunts from smarty pants lawyers even if she had been late for their appointment. So what?

Their food arrived. Tory was relieved to see that the medallion was generous, the lobster succulent. She speared a piece with her fork, dunked it in mayonnaise and felt her stomach leap at the prospect of food at last. She chewed, swallowed, licked a shred of lobster from her lower lip and brought her attention back to Ian once again.

"My mother's just come back from a holiday in Venice." Ian found the directness of the dark blue eyes just a tad disconcerting and said the first thing that came into his head. "She surprised the whole family by taking off completely on her own."

"Was your father too busy soliciting to keep her company?"

"Oh, they're divorced; I have a young and glamorous stepmother as well as a two year old half-sister.

"Lucky old you, I'm afraid I have to make do with my old pa." The wide mouth into which, a moment ago, she'd so eagerly been shovelling lobster, was now turned down at the corners. She watched as Ian carefully composed his features into a suitable expression of sympathy and decided to capitalise. "I'm afraid my poor old ma is no longer with us." She blinked her eyelids rapidly as if beating back tears.

"I'm sorry. We came close to losing my dad recently, an unexpected heart attack. Now that I've temporarily taken over the firm I realise just how much I should miss him if he weren't around anymore.

"How did it happen?" Tory wasn't really concerned about the health or otherwise of Ian's family but felt that some element of interest wouldn't go amiss.

"We're not altogether sure, most likely a combination of things I should think," Ian paused as the waiter brought their second course and Tory's attention was diverted towards a *filet de boeuf en croûte.*

"Funny how things happen isn't it?" Ian continued as the waiter disappeared and Tory began to attack her steak. "I mean there's my mother having a quiet *tête à tête* in Venice with a male friend when who should she run into but my aunt who jumps to all sorts of conclusions and promptly tells my father who, for some reason none of us can fathom is absolutely furious, even though Mum left her boyfriend, if that's the right expression for him, in Venice when she came home."

Tory's indifference to Ian's family was suddenly a thing of the past as she listened and, at the same time, recalled with vivid clarity the brief message she'd wiped from the tape on her father's answer phone. "Sorry Rupert but there's been a bit of a crisis, I'll fill you in with the details later." Could the heart attack of an ex-husband constitute a crisis? She waited for Ian to elaborate but he was bent on enjoying his venison casserole and she realised he'd said all he intended to say on the subject. She needed to help him and she would have to be clever about it.

"This boy friend is he somebody you know?" Again the deep blue eyes bored into Ian's own.

"No. Some character called Rupert, I don't remember his surname. It might be someone my mother met in her university days, although if he is it's strange that we've never heard of him. Quite glamorous by all accounts, an architect I think my aunt said. Has an apartment in Venice. Why do you ask?"

No reason. Your father wouldn't be the first man to flip his lid at the thought of his ex-wife seeing someone else would he?"

A plan was beginning to form in Tory's creative mind and if all went well she thought, after spending a week racking her brains wondering how she could put an end to her father's affair, she might just have stumbled on a solution.

"I think that's enough about my family." Ian brought the subject to a close. "You said earlier that you had to, 'make do with your old pa,' does that mean that you still live with him?"

"Not at the moment." Wild horses wouldn't persuade Tory to reveal her father's whereabouts in case Ian stumbled on the truth. "At the moment he's fully occupied with his own life but if, at some stage in the future, he needs to be cared for then I suppose yours truly will play the dutiful daughter."

The waiter brought the bill as they finished their coffee. Tory watched Ian study it carefully before scrawling his signature across the bottom. Good. Either he hadn't checked out yet or the hotel would be sending an account to his practice. She hoped it was the former. In any case if she wanted to make the most of the situation she must act quickly. She leaned towards Ian opening her eyes as wide as they would go and, once again, made Ian the focus of her fixed unblinking stare. "If you'd like to look at the pictures I took this morning my laptop is in the car. You could choose two or three shots to use in the brochure. Perhaps we could find a quiet corner somewhere?"

She could almost see Ian's brain moving into his trousers. "We can use my bedroom if you like," he said swiftly and Tory knew she was on her way. "I'll just go and get my briefcase," she said, pushing back her chair and almost running out to her car in her eagerness to move into phase two.

There was just enough light filtering through the ivy-bordered windows to show off the quiet luxury of Ian's room. He switched the light on as Tory took the disc from her camera and slipped it into her laptop and switched it off again at her request to enable the pictures to show up more clearly.

He stood behind her chair, looking over her shoulder trying hard to concentrate as image after image flashed onto the screen. He fancied her hair smelled of smoke but she hadn't smoked a cigarette whilst they were together so perhaps his imagination was playing tricks. He brought his attention back to the task with difficulty. "That would be a good one to use," he said as Tory flicked on a picture of the swimming pool with the *château* in the background.

"Right that's one taken care of now we need to find an interior shot." She scrolled back to the beginning. "How do you feel about this one?" She paused at a picture showing the sitting room in one of the *gîtes*. "The flowers are a nice touch," she added, pointing to one of the vases that Michelle had placed on the mantelpiece. "Shows the owner cares, don't you agree?"

Ian reminded himself that he was still working for Kevin and owed it to him to find the best shot. He longed to get the business over but asked Tory to scroll through the pictures again before finally selecting her first choice.

"Good. I'll send you all the details once I've finished the insert." She sounded frighteningly brisk Ian thought. Then, "May I borrow your bathroom?" she asked, snapping down the cover of her laptop.

"Sure, be my guest." Ian waved a hand towards the bathroom door and, as she disappeared, walked over to the window and looked out over the river to the dense woods beyond. His heart began to race and he wondered which of them would make the next move. He had the feeling she was several steps ahead of him already and found the admission just a tad disconcerting. He stood for several minutes waiting and looking out at the landscape.

Suddenly he lost the view. Tory had crept up behind him and her long slender fingers covered his eyes. "I think you'll find the view behind you is every bit as rewarding," she whispered in his ear. Ian swallowed hard and smiled to himself; she was going to make it easy for him. He removed first one hand and then the other and, pausing only long enough to plant a kiss on each palm, turned slowly round to face her. Her wide mouth smiled an invitation, her eyes looked darker than ever, the swinging hair was now completely still. She stood in front of him totally, unashamedly naked.

For what felt like an eternity Ian felt as if he were drowning. Whichever way he turned, twining limbs hampered his movements. His face was almost smothered in a tangle of hair and he found it almost impossible to breathe. Suddenly, miraculously he was soaring towards the surface of the ocean which, a few moments ago, he felt would claim him forever and he swam strongly towards the shore in an ecstasy of release. He lay on his back for several minutes in silence; for once in his life he could think of nothing to say.

When at last he opened his eyes he found to his surprise that the room was quite dark. He stretched out an arm, found the bedside light and looked at his watch. It was almost six o'clock. My God! Was it really two hours since he and Tory had fallen into bed? Or perhaps it was six o'clock in the morning? He'd totally lost track of time. He watched as Tory lifted her head, looked down at him and smiled a slow smile. He saw himself reflected in both her eyes which now appeared almost black.

"I'd like to use your shower if that's OK?"

Was she in a hurry to leave or did she simply want to freshen up for another session? "Help yourself," seemed to be the most appropriate response.

He still didn't move. The combined effects of the wine he'd drunk at lunch and the frenzied activity of the last two hours had taken their toll and he told himself that he was quite definitely out of shape. He must try and put some time in at the gym once he was on top of things at the office otherwise he'd be following in his father's footsteps before he was much older. He raised his head slightly as Tory came back into the room. She was dressed and her hair which had been a wild tangle a few moments ago was now restored to its original swinging bob. She'd re-applied her lipstick and if anything she looked more alert now than when they'd first met a few hours ago.

She sat on the side of the bed, crossed her legs and lit a cigarette before turning towards Ian and saying in a crisp voice; "Wake up Mr Campbell time to talk business."

"I'm sorry?" Ian struggled to clear his mind. "I thought we'd finished all that after lunch."

"So we did." Tory smiled again and flicked her cigarette into the ashtray on the bedside table; "This business is however rather more," she paused for a moment and then continued, "shall we say personal?"

Ian struggled into a sitting position. "You've lost me I'm afraid." What the hell was she on about? Was she about to offer him some dodgy deal in the holiday property market? In which case she could forget it. Surely she couldn't have forgotten his profession? She couldn't expect him to risk his reputation on the strength of two hours of steamy sex in which she'd been a willing partner. She knew the score didn't she? On the other hand she may be angling for him to introduce her to other property owners like Kevin in which case she might be in with a chance. He watched as she stubbed out her cigarette and made a mental note to wash his hair before he left for home or Susan would smell the smoke and wonder what he'd been up to. He saw Tory take a deep breath and braced himself mentally for whatever was coming.

"This may surprise you," she began, "but I have a strong suspicion that *your* mother is having an affair with *my* dear old dad." The silence stretched as Ian, who had been leaning back against the bed head, sat bolt upright. A few moments ago he'd been wallowing in post coital lethargy, now he was fully alert again his lawyers brain racing, his reflexes primed.

"You *must* be joking." His voice was dark, disbelieving.

Tory lit another cigarette, inhaled deeply, blew smoke towards the ceiling. "My father's name is Rupert Northcote, he's an architect, has an apartment in Venice where he works part of the time. I stayed with him only last week. My paternal grandmother was Italian. Does any of this sound familiar to you?" To Ian's dismay it sounded only too familiar. Why, why, why hadn't he remembered Rupert's surname? But then he knew so little about him, certainly not that he had a daughter or otherwise he might have put two and two . . . But she'd started the conversation by saying she wanted to talk business. What the hell did any business have to do with *his* mother and *her* father?

When he'd first joined the practice his father had given him some excellent advice. 'If ever you're uncertain about your next move, buy yourself some time by asking questions.' He'd used the tactic on many occasions since then and had always found it useful.

"Did you meet my mother when you were in Venice?" he asked. His eyes never left her face as he framed the question, he would know by her body language if she were to lie to him.

"Sadly I didn't have that pleasure. However if your mother's name happens to be Isobel then you'll know I'm not mistaken." He saw the look of satisfaction on her face and, sensing intrigue, decided to try to make light of the information.

"They're both of age and, if what you told me earlier is true, they're free agents. What they do with their spare time is scarcely any of our business."

But he didn't know that he was facing a woman who'd lost so many years of her father's company and now, having made contact again, was desperate to hang on to him. "My father," she began again, assuming an expression of deep concern. "My father is bad news as far as women are concerned. Perhaps it's just that he's more handsome than is good for him but women fall at his feet in droves. Even when my mother was alive he was always screwing around. You can imagine the anguish that knowledge caused her. Since her death relations between the two of us have been strained to say the least. Until last week I hadn't seen him for several months. I imagine you wouldn't want your mother to be hurt in the same way that mine was?"

Ian caught the concern in her voice. Was this why his father had been so angry in the aftermath of his aunt's phone call? Perhaps his mother had looked strained when he'd seen her a couple of days ago because she realised that Rupert was an ace philanderer? He wished he'd taken the time to talk to her to find out just what was bugging her. He was sure of one thing. The family wouldn't want Rupert Northcote to play fast and loose with their mother. This meeting with Tory could prove to be a lot more lucrative than he'd ever imagined. She'd still not mentioned business however and for the life of him he couldn't see . . .

"What do you think I should do?" He would bet his last tenner that she'd have a solution.

"I think you should warn your mother, tell her what a rogue she's dealing with."

"Suppose I decide just to let it ride for a while. After all Mother isn't exactly an *ingénue,* quite the reverse in fact. She drove a very hard bargain with my father when they divorced." He saw Tory swallow and guessed there might be more to come but was completely unprepared for what she said next.

"I think that would be a bad idea." Tory's voice now had a hard edge. The concern she'd showed earlier had completely disappeared. "If you go down that route I might just have to let your wife know exactly what kind of business her husband dabbles in on his little trips to France."

Ian watched helplessly as she pulled yet another cigarette from the packet and felt around the bed for her lighter. He retrieved it from the bedside table, activated the flame, held it towards her cigarette, noticed that his hand was shaking "Allow me," his voice was icy. The scheming little bitch! All that mock concern about his mother was a load of bullshit. She was obviously terrified that someone might make her father happy and displace her in what, by her own earlier admittance, was a fragile relationship anyway. He looked around for his dressing gown then remembered he'd left it in the bathroom and wished he'd taken the trouble to dress when she'd been in the shower.

"I think it's time for you to leave." His voice was devastatingly calm giving no indication of his real feelings. He pointed towards the door. It was a pity he couldn't get out of bed and fling it open with a suitably grandiose gesture but in his current state of undress it wouldn't have quite the required impact and then again one never knew who might be passing.

If Tory got the message she wasn't going to give him the satisfaction of having the last word. "I'll give you till Friday to make up your mind," she said as she put on her jacket and picked up her briefcase. Ian, feeling that he had nothing to gain by further argument at this stage, watched her in silence as she crossed to the door. She opened it and then paused and looked back at him. "Thanks for lunch." She smiled and left.

God Almighty what a mess he'd gotten into. But how could he possibly have known? Coincidences like this simply didn't happen in real life. Of one thing he was quite certain, Tory Northcote meant what she said and wouldn't hesitate for a moment to carry out her threat. Perhaps Steven had been right when he said that he thought his mother's affair had just been a holiday romance? What if Steve had been wrong and she was wildly in love? He didn't want to go there. What would Susan say if he admitted that he'd helped himself to a bit of nooky as a business perk. Did she love him enough to laugh it off, forgive him even? Christ what a mess.

He thought back over the last two hours and wondered from which of her parents Tory had inherited her skill between the sheets. If it was her father then his mother was in for a treat if she hadn't had it already! His heart beat faster at the memory of her silken skin; the twining limbs; the soft, full mouth exploring him; her total lack of inhibition; her cries as she climaxed. He had to hand it to her she was a woman made for pleasure.

Suddenly Ian could bear the inactivity no longer. He jumped out of bed, almost ran into the bathroom and stood under the shower turning the temperature to cold. At least he could wash the smell of her away if not the memory.

Chapter Seventeen

James had been watching Isobel like a hawk since their lunch on Sunday. She was becoming more tense as the days passed and he couldn't remember a time when he'd seen her so jumpy. Whenever the phone rang she dropped what she was doing and usually managed to pick up the receiver before the fourth ring. He'd always prided himself on being an astute observer of human behaviour - one of the many assets which made him such a good solicitor. Time and again he saw the disappointment on Isobel's face when the caller wasn't the one she wanted to hear.

Whenever he had a contentious divorce case on his hands he tried to find the Achilles heel of the recalcitrant husband. His years of experience had taught him that, sooner or later, he would succeed and then he could aim his arrow appropriately. After that it was just a matter of time before he was able to reach a settlement. Looking at Isobel it was obvious to anybody that she was unsure of Rupert Northcote's intentions or why would she keep on rushing to the phone like a lovesick teenager? He must play to that weakness.

If he were to say anything against Rupert, or try to cast doubts on his intentions, that would only make Isobel want him more. The way she'd blushed on Sunday when he'd tried to quiz her about their relationship told him all he needed to know. He was still smarting at the speed with which she'd pulled her hand away. He had, after all, only offered it in friendship.

So why did he mind so much that his ex-wife was having an affair, if that's what it was. He had a reasonable life with Zelda so he shouldn't be at all concerned about what Isobel may or may not do in the future. But during the last ten days he'd experienced a peace he hadn't known in the last five years and, although his conversations with Isobel could scarcely be described as intimate, at least they were conversations. More importantly their talks hadn't centred on the spending of money, the acquisition of new clothes or difficulties with the *au pair*. He'd had a holiday from Zelda and by God he'd enjoyed it!

The more he thought about his return to Wandsworth Common the more he racked his brain for legitimate reasons to extend his stay with Isobel. If he were absolutely honest it pleased his male ego to be seen out with a young and attractive woman but if there was no rapport when they were at home together then what the hell? If Zelda found it impossible to cope during a normal convalescence what would happen if he were to have another heart attack? Suppose he became incapable of keeping up with her energetic lifestyle? Would she replace him with a younger man and eventually sue him for divorce? If so she'd take him to the bloody cleaners and he'd end up in some piddling flat on the wrong side of Town. The mere thought of it appalled him.

He looked around Isobel's sitting room. It was a bit Colefax and Fowler for his taste but there were always flowers around and he enjoyed the wood fire that Isobel sometimes lit in the evenings, even if that blasted cat of hers did take up pole position. She seemed somehow to have a gift for creating a relaxed environment, although it didn't seem to have much effect on her own tension. The furniture she'd taken from their marital home had helped of course. Most of it they'd chosen together in the days when they browsed around antique shops looking for bargains. He had to admit he felt more at home here than in his own drawing room in spite of, or perhaps because of, the total lack of clutter.

He must persuade Isobel in some subtle way that if Rupert Northcote really cared for her he'd be making more of an effort to stay in touch. If he could do that maybe he needn't worry about having to move back to Wandsworth. He could sell it for a good profit, set Zelda up in a more modest property, which would still be an improvement on the ghastly place she'd been living in before he married her. And he'd still have enough left over to make his future life comfortable. Well now he had a positive plan. He would keep it at the forefront of his mind and sooner or later he would have a flash of inspiration and then he could shoot the fatal arrow.

"Where the hell have you been Jude? I've been trying to get you all morning."

"Sorry Sue, I've been with a client."

"That's what your secretary has been telling me for the last three hours but we all know what that means." Susan was distraught and the tears which she'd been trying to hold back welled up in her eyes making them sting. She brushed them away impatiently with the back of her hand. Tears in the office didn't sit easily with the upwardly mobile, successful PR image that she tried, and normally succeeded, in projecting.

"So what's the urgency then?" Judy was intrigued. Frantic phone calls weren't Sue's style and, according to her secretary, Mrs Campbell had called the office three times already. "Just for the record I really was with a client and we were conducting legitimate business. It's a bit early in the day for anything more exciting don't you think?"

"Oh! For God's sake Jude stop wittering on and listen. I've got to talk to someone or I'll die!" Susan's voice rose to a crescendo. For the last three hours she'd been staring at the small packet on her desk as if it were the most important exhibit in a murder trial and wondering at the same time if her life would ever be the same again.

"Sorry Sue, I'm all ears. I must say you sound a touch *distrait*. Has your dear old father driven you over the edge or what?" Judy had listened willingly to Susan's complaints about Bruce for the past three weeks and wouldn't have been at all surprised if the strain of having him around was at last beginning to tell.

"It's much worse than that." Susan's voice broke and the tears ran down her face taking streaks of mascara with them. Sod the image she'd just have to repair the damage later.

Judy must have heard the sobs from the other end of the telephone and the next time she spoke she sounded really concerned. "Tell me it's not one of the children," she pleaded with more understanding than Sue normally expected from a friend who had none of her own.

"The children are both fine." Susan said quickly. She groped in her bag for a tissue as the tears welled up again, absent mindedly removed half a sucked boiled sweet from one corner and scrubbed at her eyes vigorously.

"For pity's sake put me out of my misery," Judy begged.

"It's Ian," Susan wailed, "I think he's having an affair!"

"You have to be joking." Judy protested. "The last time we spoke he was working flat out at the office trying to cover for his dad. Or was he just pretending to be busy?"

Susan swallowed hard thinking how much worse it sounded when you said it aloud. Affairs were what other women's husbands had, her father-in-law for instance. She blew her nose and spilled out the whole story.

Ian had arrived home late last night from France. She was already in bed. He said he was absolutely knackered, had had a hell of a day and lost no time in joining her. This morning he'd left early for the office, said he had a lot to sort out. The clothes he'd worn in France were still on the chair where he'd flung them the night before. He'd asked her if she'd drop his suit in at the dry cleaner if she had a minute. Of course she'd checked the pockets first, just in case he'd left the odd tenner; instead she'd found a packet of condoms in his inside pocket. Not only that but they were French and only two remained in what had been a packet of three.

Susan paused for breath and Judy took the opportunity to try and calm her friend.

"Sue for God's sake Ian's not the only man in London to be walking around with French letters in his pocket!"

Susan choked on a sob, in no mood to appreciate Judy's attempt at humour. "But Jude, don't you remember, I'm on the Pill? What on earth am I going to do?"

Judy sat for a moment trying to take it all in. She couldn't believe that two of her dearest friends could be facing a marital crisis and wondered how she would feel if Mark ever played around. She racked her brains in an effort to come up with some words of comfort that wouldn't sound like too much of a cliché and failed. "I'm so sorry Sue," she began, "but let's face it you can't really accuse Ian of having a full blown affair on the strength of one used condom. Have you ever wondered before if he was up to something?"

"Never!" Susan was adamant. "But let's face it Jude he hasn't been going to France on business all that long."

"Exactly." Judy was quick to pick up on the slightest crumb of comfort. "So if Ian's seeing someone on the other side of the Channel she must have come into his life only recently. Take my advice and do nothing, see if Ian says anything or, more importantly, *does* anything to make you feel more suspicious."

"But I feel so impotent Jude, it's just not like me to sit back and let things ride."

"Well I suppose you could snip the ends off those French letters and hope that whoever she is gets pregnant if she fools around with Ian again!" Or if Ian fools around with her Judy thought but wisely kept *that* thought to herself.

It was a relief to hear Susan laugh. "I might just be tempted if I think Ian's seriously interested in someone else."

"I'm sure Ian's far too sensible to be looking at anyone else seriously. He's crazy about you and the children and I'm certain he's not about to put all that on the line for the sake of some scheming slag he met on a business trip." Judy paused for a moment and then added, "I tell you what you could do if you want another opinion. Why not ask Isobel? After all she's had years of practise dealing with James."

"But she's Ian's mother. Don't you think she'd automatically take his side?"

"I don't see why. After all she must have gone through a lot of what you're feeling at the moment. Don't you think that would make her more sympathetic towards you?"

"Well you may be right. I'll think about it. In the meantime thanks for listening; you're a real pal."

"I know you'd do the same for me," Judy said quickly, hoping that she would never find herself in the same situation. "Let's have lunch soon, but if there are any developments you'll let me know won't you?"

"Sure. I expect you're right and I'm worrying over nothing." Susan clutched the straw eagerly. "Give my love to Mark and thanks again."

Judy put the phone down and looked at her watch. It was too near lunchtime to do any work, besides the creative side of her brain wasn't functioning after the catastrophic news. What she needed now was a good old browse round Harvey Nicks to put her back on form again.

"The bastard! The cowardly little shit!" Tory choked on a piece of croissant which she'd dunked in her coffee and shoved into her mouth prior to opening the only letter in her pile of mail which looked remotely interesting. She pushed both coffee and croissant to one side and lit a cigarette before reading the letter again, more slowly this time, to make certain that she hadn't misunderstood the contents. When she reached the end she folded it carefully and replaced it in the envelope with shaking hands. She continued to sit at the kitchen table in her Paris apartment simply staring into space for several minutes. All the colour had drained from her cheeks; even her lips were pale and bloodless. She could feel her heart hammering and her normal cool poise had completely disappeared.

She sat for perhaps five minutes before the tears began to stream down her face. This, she told herself firmly, was the big one and she wouldn't be able to bluff her way out in a hurry. She squared her shoulders, blew her nose loudly, wiped her eyes and reached for the telephone.

The staff in James' office were longing for Friday to end and their weekend to begin. Ever since Ian had returned from France he'd been working like a demon. Even James' long suffering secretary wondered if she dare ask to work from home. Anything, she felt, would be better than staying in this madhouse. She had no way of knowing that Ian was in torment. After turning his problem this way and that he made up his mind that, if he were to persuade his mother that her new boyfriend was the kind of man who played around with the affections of not one, but several women, he would have to do it face-to-face. He'd invited her to have dinner with him on Wednesday evening. To his surprise she'd refused, saying that she daren't risk leaving James on his own in case he should be taken ill again. She'd promised to take Ian up on his offer once James returned to Wandsworth and Ian didn't like to think about how long that might be. At two o'clock on Friday he amazed all the staff by telling them that, as they'd all worked so hard during the week, they could leave early and take a well-deserved long weekend.

Once the office was empty he switched on the automatic answering service and by two thirty he was on his way to the gym. He smiled grimly to himself thinking that, for the moment anyway, he'd outwitted Tory Northcote. She only had his business card and his home number was ex-directory. He'd made sure that he was tied up with clients all morning and gave the staff strict instructions that he wasn't to be disturbed. If she called him on Monday he'd simply have to stall. Perhaps tell her his father had had a relapse? Anyway when the time came he would think of something.

Bruce was in an unusually good mood at dinner on Friday evening. He'd made every effort to look smart and was sporting a yellow silk choker and a pullover to match. He waited impatiently until they were all served before making his announcement. "I'm leaving in the morning," he said with an exaggerated calmness which he was far from feeling. He watched as Sue stopped eating. "So what's brought this on?" she asked. "Is Kathleen ready to come back to work?"

"Unfortunately not." Bruce, who felt that he'd been sidelined for the duration of his stay, was determined to enjoy being the focus of attention for as long as possible. "I'm going home to put the house on the market." He carried on eating, aware of the swift exchange of glances between Sue and Ian, and decided to let them sweat; that would teach them to shove him in a corner while trying to pretend that he didn't exist.

Finally, when he'd finished chewing, he washed the remnants of his lasagne down with a generous swig of Cabernet Sauvignon; "I'm moving into a hotel for retired executives," he announced triumphantly, for all the world as if he'd just been accepted as a member of an exclusive club.

"Sounds good to me." Susan said. "Don't keep us in suspense then, tell us more."

Bruce told. Aware that at last he had their undivided attention he spared no details. He told them of his conversation with a fellow lone luncher on one of his many forays into the restaurants around Wapping. Like Bruce he was a widower whose children were busy with their own lives. Bruce looked at them both in turn with his customary expression of mild reproach as he said this, as if the earning of ones' living was a personal affront to his well-being.

Bruce's new found companion Gerald lived in a wonderful hotel for retired executives and talked about it in such glowing terms that Bruce felt he had to go and see it for himself. The place was the last word in luxury and had a licensed restaurant, extensive leisure facilities and first class accommodation. In short, everything he could possibly want. Not only that but the residents, some of whom he'd already met, were all people with similar interests to his own. Bruce felt that this was too good an opportunity to miss and he'd lost no time in putting in an offer for an apartment which he expected to move into just before Christmas.

Susan offered up a silent prayer for the marketing guru whose creative mind had dreamed up the phrase, 'Hotel for Retired Executives,' to appeal to the likes of her father who would run a mile from 'sheltered housing' or 'homes for the elderly.' "Well I must say Dad you don't hang about once you see something you want," she began in an effort to share his excitement. "You're quite sure that it's right for you?" It would be terrible if he were to sell up and then discover he'd made an awful mistake. She could just see the soulful looks as well as hear the reproachful phone calls. He'd never been a man to suffer even the slightest discomfort in silence.

"I'm absolutely sure. In fact it could have been designed with me in mind." Bruce told them.

"Then let's drink to a very happy future for you." Ian raised his glass.

No sooner had Bruce left the flat on Saturday morning than Ian suggested they should go out for dinner to celebrate their freedom which was all the more heady for being unexpected. "Somewhere quiet and expensive," he suggested, thinking that he might as well try to ease his conscience at the same time. For some reason Sue hadn't responded with her usual enthusiasm and, for one awful moment he wondered if by any chance Tory had run out of patience and somehow managed to contact her. Just as quickly he dismissed the thought telling himself that there was no way Tory could have discovered their number and silently reproached himself for becoming paranoid.

Later that morning Susan was preparing lunch for the children when she wondered if perhaps she should ask Ian outright if he were seeing someone. She'd thought about little else since her conversation with Judy but Ian had behaved much as usual since his return from France. Try as she might she couldn't forget the slim packet which she'd hidden in a drawer underneath her underwear and she knew she wouldn't rest until she had a satisfactory explanation.

She'd thought about phoning Isobel but in the end decided against it feeling somehow that it would be telling tales about Ian. Besides, Isobel might be tempted to confide in James, who could tell Zelda and, before you knew it, the whole family would know.

She had a better idea as she put the finishing touches to the meal. She would suggest to Ian that he take the opportunity to bond with his children after lunch and take them out somewhere. That would leave her free to spend the whole afternoon making herself look glamorous and Ian would wonder how he could ever have been stupid enough to look at anyone else. After dinner she would pull him into bed and screw him senseless, just in case he'd failed to get the message.

Chapter Eighteen

It was eight o'clock on Saturday evening when Rupert drove into the garage in Venice. He turned off the ignition and sat for a couple of minutes resting his head on the steering wheel trying to summon up enough energy to collect his belongings and catch the *vaporetto* home.

His eyes were smarting from the effort of concentrating on the *autostrada* and every one of his muscles ached with fatigue. It was a small consolation but he'd had uninterrupted music during his long drive from Rome which made a welcome change from Gianna's prattle about her new home. Strange how you could enjoy someone's company enormously for a weekend when there were other people about to dilute their intensity; but spending the best part of two weeks virtually alone with them put a severe strain on the relationship. He'd heard how some married couples chose to take their holidays apart to avoid just this kind of stress and, for the first time, he understood why.

He climbed wearily out of the car, collected his grip and walked slowly across the square to the *vaporetto* stop. Once on board he inhaled the cool night air and the familiar smell of the canal and immediately began to feel better. Returning to Venice from anywhere was always therapeutic once you were away from the awfulness of the Piazzale Romà with its throbbing traffic. In a couple of weeks this same air would be damp and bone chilling but, for the moment, it was pleasantly refreshing and he felt the tension slip away as they drew closer to the Rialto Bridge.

His limbs began to loosen up during the short walk to the apartment and the after effects of his long journey gently slid away. His Italian home welcomed him with its usual aura of peace and order and he sighed with deep contentment to be back again. The light on the answer phone was blinking and there was a pile of mail next to it on the hall table. He put his grip in the bedroom and poured himself a glass of wine, realising that he was prolonging the moment of anticipation. Would there be a message? Verbal or written, he'd be relieved and pleased to see either.

He pressed the play button and listened, his face expressionless as he scribbled names and numbers. He riffled through the mail, separating the bills from the remainder. Nothing. Nothing from Isobel. He took his drink out onto the terrace and leaned on the balustrade remembering the first night Isobel came here and her delight at the view. He smiled ruefully into the darkness. If only he knew what was going on. There were two possibilities as far as he could see. Either the person answering Isobel's phone a week ago hadn't passed on his message or he had delivered it and, for some reason, Isobel had chosen not to respond. He could live with the former. The man who'd answered the phone didn't sound as if he were in the habit of delivering messages. But if Isobel was playing some devious game . . .? Oh God! He was far too tired to figure it out.

He was so fed up with the uncertainty he decided to call her right away and put an end to his misery. He walked back into the sitting room and glanced at his watch, it was almost nine o'clock, an hour earlier in the UK. She could still be having dinner, maybe entertaining friends or, worse still, her unknown companion could answer the phone again. No, he wasn't firing on all cylinders at the moment, he'd sleep on it.

On Sunday evening Isobel and James were watching the final instalment of Pride and Prejudice on BBC television. It was a first class production, superbly acted and James, indulging his current favourite pastime - watching Isobel, could see she found it totally absorbing. He was no fan of Jane Austen but had agreed to watch, seizing the opportunity to appear as amenable as possible.

It was a week now since they'd been out to lunch and, to his disappointment, she'd given him no indication that she might want to resume their old life together. On the contrary she'd been suggesting for the last couple of days that perhaps it was time for him to return to Zelda. So far he'd avoided setting a date for his departure but deep inside he knew that, unless he could find a way to dislodge Rupert Northcote from his prime position in Isobel's affections, his days in Ashley Green were numbered.

He continued to watch the screen thinking that no modern woman would put up with the kind of treatment that Elizabeth Bennet was receiving from FitzWilliam Darcey and suddenly he began to see pleasing parallels. He settled more comfortably in his chair with a self-satisfied sigh and began to plan his strategy.

The production came to an end and James saw Isobel wipe her eyes as the credits flashed onto the screen. He waited until the final notes of the sound track faded and Isobel picked up the remote control and switched off the set.

"Oh the suspense! I thought that wretched Darcey was never going to turn up for the wedding! I was on the edge of my seat for the last fifteen minutes!" Isobel laughed.

"I don't think that even the mighty BBC would dare to tamper with a Jane Austen work," James began. "It was an excellent production even if the behaviour does come across as a little bizarre for today's world."

"What do you mean exactly?" Isobel glanced across at him.

"Well I can't see the emancipated young women of today putting up with the likes of young Darcey, can you? They'd tell him to get lost, go and torment someone else. I mean keeping her in suspense like that! He's extremely lucky she didn't give him the elbow. After all with the Army around she had plenty of men to choose from! I don't think he deserved her."

There. That should show her he was able to see the woman's point of view even though literary criticism had never been his strong point. He could see Isobel was searching for words and mentally patted himself on the back for surprising her.

"But she loved him James, don't you see? And a woman in love will put up with a great deal if she feels there's the remotest chance of happiness at some time in the future."

James silently conceded the first round to Isobel and tried again. "Are you suggesting that, however badly a man behaves towards the woman who loves him, she'll continue to be there for him with her love undiminished?" He looked at her searchingly over the top of his spectacles.

"I think if he resorted to physical violence or habitually humiliated her she'd reach a point where she'd feel that enough was enough. But it's surprising what women are prepared to suffer." She paused briefly and he wondered if by any chance she was hinting at their own relationship. He was careful not to allow his expression to change. No flickering eyelid betrayed that her point just might have gone home. So he'd put himself about but most of his affairs had been short-lived and not really satisfactory and she'd been so absorbed with the children he reckoned that half the time she hadn't even noticed his absence. After a while it had become a habit, his way of adding some excitement to his life particularly when she became so involved in work and was often exhausted by the time he came home.

Isobel's voice cut across his thoughts. "James you're a divorce lawyer. You must have listened to dozens of cases of cruelty both physical and mental. Did you never wonder how much a woman was prepared to suffer?"

Oh bugger the woman! James reached for the Sunday paper in exasperation. He should have known better than to argue the toss with someone who had an English degree! Perhaps if he went back to Wandsworth she'd miss him, particularly if Rupert Northcote had given up trying to get in touch. Maybe he'd give it another couple of days. He had an appointment with the doctor on Wednesday anyway. He could either ask Zelda to come and collect him on Tuesday or, better still, give Isobel the opportunity to drive him up to Town on Wednesday.

At 8.55 am on Tuesday morning Rupert arrived at Marco Polo Airport with exactly an hour to spare before the Alitalia flight left for London. He'd spent the whole day on Sunday dealing with the mail, returning telephone calls and arranging with his cleaning lady to have the flat looked after while he was away. He'd met Giovanni early on Monday and they'd gone to Chioggia together for a final inspection of their development before discussing their next project over lunch, finally parting company a little after two o'clock.

He then got to work on his apartment which took him the rest of the afternoon. He cleaned out the fridge, threw away old newspapers and junk mail and finally sorted his clothes, leaving the dirty ones for Maria to launder or have dry cleaned. He kept a second wardrobe in London which meant that he could travel light as usual. His English cleaning lady already knew he would be arriving about lunchtime on Tuesday and would have the flat ready for him so that he could move effortlessly back into his London life.

Finally he settled down to feed data into his laptop. Gianna would give him no peace until she had the plans for her new house and the sooner he got down to it the better. It was nearly seven by the time he'd finished and, telling himself that he'd earned it, he went in search of a drink. He felt an unaccountable excitement at the thought of returning to London, even though he had absolutely no idea what lay ahead, apart from his work projects of course. On an impulse he dialled Isobel's number, he could arrange to meet her for dinner tomorrow if she was free. The line was engaged and, although he tried several times during the next hour, it remained so. "Nothing changes does it?" he said to himself and dialled Tory instead. In view of their recent conversation he felt he'd better let her know where he was likely to be for the next couple of months. Her recorded voice told him that she couldn't take his call but to leave a message. He complied before ringing her mobile. It was switched off. He gave up and went to have a shower.

As he sat waiting for the flight to take off he felt a surge of anticipation. At least he would soon be in the same country as Isobel and he could, he hoped, begin to unburden himself of all the things he'd been waiting to tell her for the last ten days.

I shall scream in a minute, Isobel told herself as James picked up the phone for the umpteenth time and tried to call Zelda. She was supposed to be collecting him and he'd been waiting, ready to leave, since eleven. It was now twelve thirty. The *au pair* had assured James several times that Mrs Campbell was on her way but so far there was no sign of her.

"Would you like me to make you a sandwich?" Isobel asked, thinking that if he were eating he might stop complaining about Zelda's unpunctuality.

"We're supposed to be eating on the way home if ever that bloody wife of mine arrives." James shook the pages of the Telegraph which he'd been trying to read for the past hour but, as time passed and Zelda failed to arrive, he'd found it increasingly difficult to concentrate.

Isobel looked through the window at the garden. She was itching to get her hands on it. She'd scarcely touched it for a month and the clumps of wilted herbaceous plants and dead roses reminded her there was a lot of tidying up to do before the days began to shorten and the ground became too hard to dig. She hoped the weather would stay fine for the afternoon and she could make a start at least. She couldn't wait to be free to organise her own life again. The garden was a priority - after she'd phoned Rupert.

He must be getting ready to come home by now she reckoned if he weren't here already. She made up her mind to phone his London number and leave a message for him there. She'd given up trying his mobile, realising that he must be out of range in the Tuscan hills and since she'd already left a message for him in Venice there seemed to be little point in leaving another.

She heard the sound of a car horn, and, glancing swiftly through the sitting room window saw James' grey Mercedes and realised that Zelda was announcing her presence. "About bloody time too," James grumbled as they heard the sound of hurrying footsteps followed by the ring of the bell. Isobel went to open the door and braced herself as Zelda slipped past her, scattering apologies like confetti. "Terribly sorry darling! Such a morning! You wouldn't believe the traffic!" She kissed James swiftly on the top of his head; for all the world as if he were a pet poodle, Isobel thought. James wasn't easily mollified. "We've been waiting for you for an hour and a half, where the hell have you been?" he demanded.

"An accident on the M25," Zelda explained. "There wasn't a great deal I could do about it was there?" It sounded tame but it was the best she could do faced with James' impatience. She wished for the umpteenth time since leaving home that she hadn't gone to the gym earlier but, faced with the prospect of caring for an invalid for goodness knows how long, she'd seen it as a last bid for freedom. She'd worked out for an hour, had a shower, changed and gone into the bar for some mineral water, when it happened.

"Well, well, we are looking classy this morning." She'd frozen to the spot at the sound of a familiar drawling voice which, she'd thought, had been consigned to her past forever when she married

James. He hadn't waited for her to turn round but strolled over to where she stood at the bar and kissed her full on the mouth. "How're ya' doin' darlin'? Long time no see."

"Nick," she said faintly, then, "What brings you to this neck of the woods?"

"Bought a flat, 'aven't I, just down the road. Use this place to work out."

Conversation had never been his strong point but he had other assets which had knocked her sideways until James came into her life. Her mouth still burned where he'd kissed it. He towered over her, six feet of tanned and toned male animal. He insisted on paying for her mineral water, watching her fumble for her purse, eyes half closed in detached amusement, which let her know, to her embarrassment, that he hadn't forgotten their time together.

"I mustn't stay long," she said, looking obviously at her watch. "I promised to pick up my husband and he'll worry if I'm late."

"Still married then? Same bloke you married five years ago? Must be a bit of a stayer then."

She'd ignored the remark, remembering how she'd unceremoniously ditched him after James proposed. "Business must be booming if you're buying property round here," she said. In spite of her shock at seeing him again she was curious to know what had happened to him since their last meeting. In those days he couldn't have afforded an end of terrace in Hackney.

"Can't grumble. Things looked up in a big way once we got over the recession. Never looked back. Good plumbers aren't that thick on the ground and there's a lot of clapped out central heating needs attention."

It was a long speech for him. "I'm glad things are going well for you," she said, not meeting his eyes, remembering the days when one look from him had her reaching for the zip on his jeans. She wasn't going to ask him if he'd married someone else, wouldn't give him the satisfaction. She knew he was watching her, enjoying her embarrassment and was aware of other voices, laughter from tables round the bar. She looked around quickly hoping to see a familiar face and, finding none, looked directly at him at last and knew that, if circumstances were different, she would want him again.

She'd downed her mineral water quickly, choked slightly, made some fatuous remark about exercise making you thirsty, looked desperately at her watch and told him she must leave. She saw him feel into the back pocket of his jeans, pull out his notecase and produce his business card. "In case you ever need a plumber," he said, smiling with lazy amusement as she thrust it into her sports bag without looking at it. "See you around sometime," he added as she backed away from him and almost ran out of the bar.

She looked across at James' glowering face, heard Isobel's voice offering her a drink or some coffee, thought ahead to weeks of celibacy, pushed all thoughts of Nick and his formidable physique to the back of her mind, heard herself say; "We've arranged to have lunch on the way home, I think it would be a good idea to get going, don't you agree darling?"

She looked at James, waiting for confirmation and watched him struggle to his feet. She immediately took his arm, led him out to the car and tucked a rug around his knees after he'd climbed into the front seat. Isobel brought out his luggage and helped stow it in the boot. James opened his window, reached for Isobel's hand and gave it a quick squeeze. "Thanks for everything, I'll be in touch," he said as Zelda got into the driving seat.

Isobel stood and watched Zelda reverse the car smoothly and swiftly down the drive and gave them a farewell wave as they disappeared. No sooner was she in the house than Digby appeared as if by magic and rubbed himself round her ankles. He'd maintained a low profile for the duration of James' visit, sneaking into the sitting room only in the evenings after the fire had been lit. "We're on our own again," Isobel said, bending down to tickle his chin and, "Thank God," she added as Digby looked up at her and purred.

Now, the sooner she sorted herself out the better. She would leave a message for Rupert first, have a quick sandwich and then begin to tackle the garden. She went into her study and dialled Rupert's London number. She was expecting a recorded message and when a voice said, "Rupert Northcote," it took a few seconds before she realised that it was Rupert in person and not his answer phone.

"Rupert?" She found her voice with difficulty.

"Speaking." His voice sounded cool, remote. Isobel was lost for words. She'd prepared a short message to leave on his machine but, faced with the man himself, she could think of nothing to say.

"It's Isobel." Had he really forgotten her voice after only two weeks?

"What an elusive lady you've become in the last couple of weeks. How are you?"

There was a pause. Isobel's heart began to race. She was aching to spill out the whole story of the last fortnight, tell him what a nightmare it had been. She needed his reassurance that everything between them would soon be as it was in Venice. But he couldn't have been home for very long she reasoned and it would be unfair to burden him with the whole story. She contented herself by saying; "At the moment I'm exhausted. The family crisis I mentioned when I left my message."

"Ah yes. I picked it up on the mobile. Since then nothing." Now he sounded reproachful.

"I left another message on your answer phone in Venice, the day after I returned." She was aware that she sounded defensive and disliked herself for being so.

"I played my tape very carefully when I got back from Rome on Saturday and I promise you there was no message from you."

He doesn't believe me Isobel thought in a panic as she listened to the calm, measured tones. She was beginning to wish she'd just got on with the gardening and waited for him to ring her.

"And did you receive *my* message?" This couldn't be Rupert talking. He sounded as if he were checking a meeting with a client and Isobel felt as if she were talking to a stranger. "There was a message waiting for me when I arrived home. Thank you. I'm glad you liked your present."

"I phoned about ten days ago, Saturday morning I think it was." There was a pause before he went on, "Someone took a message. I simply asked *him* to let you know I'd called."

There wasn't a degree of warmth in his voice and Isobel scrabbled back in her memory to the morning she'd left home in a hurry and forgotten to switch on her answer phone. James must have taken the message and deliberately withheld it. She would deal with him later. In the meantime Rupert was on the other end of the telephone waiting for an explanation. She could understand now the reason for his coolness. He must have thought . . .Well what had he thought? The worst obviously.

Suddenly she was angry. How could he have imagined anything remotely derogatory after all the wonderful time they'd spent together? He obviously doubted her integrity and that really hurt. What sort of woman did he think she was? Surely he couldn't think that she'd play around with someone else the minute his back was turned.

She broke the silence at last and this time it was her voice that was cool. "I think it must have been James who answered the phone. I'm sorry to say he didn't pass on your message but he's been rather ill recently and it may have slipped his mind." Why in God's name was she defending James? He certainly didn't deserve it if he'd failed to tell her about Rupert's call. Well that was another matter. She ploughed on. "I'm afraid he had a heart attack while I was away and came to me for a short convalescence. I won't bore you with the details but it's quite obvious that you thought the worst and frankly Rupert I'm surprised and disappointed. I thought we understood each other, that we'd both learned to be honest." The words came spilling out before she could check them and, having delivered her message, she slammed down the receiver and burst into tears.

"Well congratulations Rupe, you really fouled that one up," he said to himself as he slowly replaced the receiver. He'd never for one moment considered that James, of all people, could have been the man to whom he had spoken, half a lifetime ago it seemed now. How could he have been so obtuse? Put it down to overwork, pressure. No he couldn't use that excuse, not even to himself. If only one's personal life were as easily organised as the professional side how beautifully trouble-free and symmetrical it would be; exactly like a Palladian building. But what about the message that Isobel said she'd left on his machine in Venice? Mechanical failure perhaps? But his other messages were intact as far as he knew so what could have happened? Suddenly he remembered ringing his apartment from Rome and asking Tory if there were any messages. He tried to recall their conversation, remembering how abrupt Tory had been and she'd definitely said there were no messages. Surely . . . Even Tory wouldn't deliberately wipe a message from his tape? Or would she?

He thought she'd turned over a new leaf now that she had a job and was beginning to lead a responsible life. He'd been thrilled six months ago when she'd telephoned to tell him the news. He'd given her the down payment for her flat when she'd told him she was relocating to Paris; paid for her car, the laptop, the camera. He'd been so proud of her for taking the trouble to brush up on her French and wanted to do everything possible to help her make a good start. And was this her way of repaying him? Would he ever understand just exactly where he'd gone wrong with that young lady? His mouth was set in a grim line as he reached for the telephone.

Chapter Nineteen

Midway through Wednesday morning when the florist's van drew up, Isobel was balanced precariously on the top rung of a ladder pruning a wisteria. The pale purple flowers had framed a couple of upstairs windows throughout the summer, a picturesque reward for her careful training and she wanted a repeat performance next year. The van driver waited patiently for her as she came down the ladder.

"I should get my old man to do that if I were you," he said, thrusting a large bouquet towards her.

Isobel smiled at the thought of James climbing ladders or doing anything as mundane as pruning. "I'm better at it than he is," she offered as an explanation. It seemed much easier than telling the truth. Why was it still so difficult to admit she had no man, old or otherwise, to climb ladders for her?

"Well mind you don't fall and break anything" the van driver threw over his shoulder as he turned to leave.

"I'll be careful," she promised, beginning to feel sorry for herself all over again as she took the flowers into the kitchen.

Was this the apology she'd been waiting for since lunchtime yesterday? Her hands shook as she tried to remove the staple that held the envelope firmly to the cellophane wrapper. When it defeated her she pulled it away impatiently and tore it open to read the brief message. *Thank you again for taking such good care of me. Love, James.*

Tears of disappointment welled up in her eyes. She should have known that the bouquet - brassy yellow roses and overblown chrysanthemums - was a bit on the florid side for Rupert's taste. She was tempted to put them straight on the compost heap but as a gardener she realised the effort and nurture that had gone into their production and she just couldn't do it.

The deceit of the man, sending her flowers when he hadn't had the decency to tell her that Rupert called on Saturday. She was certain that it was a deliberate act of malice and so typical of him. She'd spent a sleepless night turning over the events of the last two weeks in her head. You couldn't live with someone for thirty years and not know how their mind worked. He was just a devious old sod who'd stop at nothing to get what he wanted. Why had he turned his attention on her suddenly? Was he just testing the water to see how she would react? Or was it simply that he was feeling better and decided to take advantage of the fact that they were under the same roof? Whatever, she congratulated herself for finding him resistible.

She filled a bucket with cold water and began to dismantle the bouquet, trimming the recommended two inches from the bottom of each stem and venting her spleen by bashing the ends of the roses with a hammer. She would let them have a long drink and arrange them sometime later.

Where was Rupert? What was he thinking? He'd said in Venice that he had a project in the UK. Was he perhaps in a meeting with a client; or inspecting a site; or checking on planning permission? And what had happened to the message she'd left for him in Venice?

She'd promised herself years ago that when she retired she would never sit back and allow herself to become pear shaped. She'd so looked forward to this holiday, seeing it as the beginning of a new phase in her life, promising herself that in the future she would be less conventional, more adventurous than in the past. She'd hoped to return home feeling a keen anticipation for the future, a woman free to follow whichever path she chose. Instead she'd just experienced an agonising, worrying night; her appetite not only for food but for everything else was non-existent and she was constantly listening out for the telephone. She felt exactly like a teenager after her first quarrel with a new boy friend. Once again she swallowed her disappointment and went back into the garden.

Rupert left the congested traffic of Hendon Way and sighed with relief as he joined the slip road for the M1. He put his foot down hard on the accelerator and relaxed as the car responded. It was great to be active again after the last twelve hours. He couldn't sit at home castigating himself any longer. His uncomfortable telephone conversation with Tory left him, as usual after any contact with her, feeling deeply guilty. Would he have been a better father to a son? How was it that nearly all their conversations ended up by him laying down the law, making a threat or, worst of all, totally losing his cool and shouting in a way which afterwards made him feel so ashamed?

Tory hadn't actually admitted to wiping Isobel's message from his answer phone but she hadn't denied it either and her off-hand replies to his questions fuelled his anger until he reached the stage where he could no longer control it. He'd given it to her straight that, if she hoped to remain a part of his life, he'd be looking for a distinct improvement in her attitude in the future. She'd responded in kind, telling him to, 'get stuffed,' before slamming down the receiver. That made two women in the space of an hour who'd hung up on him. Was he turning into some kind of inhuman monster he'd asked himself as he paced the floor in his flat wondering if he would ever salvage anything from the wreckage of his private life.

He slowed the car as he approached the High Street in Berkhamsted and turned left towards Ashley Green. What would he do if Isobel were out? Camp out in the car until she returned? Find the nearest pub and keep going to her cottage until he found it occupied? Leave a note and drive back to London? He couldn't decide in advance, he'd play it by ear. He might not be able to find the house. Briar Cottage, Ashley Green; it said on the card she'd given him, not a lot to go on. In the normal way he would have checked the precise location in advance but this was far from his usual behaviour. Perhaps he would find the place more easily if he were to park the car and walk? Maybe he would run into someone who could tell him where it was? On reflection that seemed like a good idea.

Reaching the sign that signalled the beginning of the village he pulled into the first convenient lay-by, stopped the car and climbed out. It felt good to be stretching his legs. He'd spent an inordinate amount of time behind the wheel of one car or another in the last two weeks and he missed his daily walks to and from the *vaporetto* and the harbour in Chioggia.

He scrutinised the names on the houses as he walked. Normally it would be the architecture that interested him but today he was acting completely out of character. He'd taken off from his flat on a sudden impulse when he'd reached the stage where he felt he must do something, anything, rather than stay there and continue to pace. He had absolutely no idea what kind of house he was looking for. Briar Cottage could mean anything from olde worlde thatch to a substantial country house or even a modern bungalow.

Ah! Here it was at last, Briar Cottage. He paused to admire the brick and flint walls and the twin pyracantha, one brilliant scarlet the other light orange, that had been carefully trained either side of the front door. There was an autumnal smell of burning and he saw a thin plume of smoke spiralling upwards at the back of the house. His pulse pounded in anticipation. She must be home. Isobel wasn't the kind of woman to leave a bonfire unattended. He rang the front door bell, waited a few seconds, there was no reply. He backed away and stood for a moment wondering what to do next. Suddenly he heard the sound of some kind of mechanical device, again coming from the back of the house. Perhaps she had a gardener who was at this moment using a strimmer or some such? He opened the side gate and walked towards the sound. Suddenly it stopped and he smiled as he heard the unmistakable sound of Isobel's voice: "Damn and blast the bloody thing!"

He turned left and saw her standing on the patio with an electric drill in her hand. It looked as if she'd been trying to drill a hole in the wall. "It sounds as if a little help might be welcome," he said, walking towards her, smiling and hoping she wasn't still angry with him. The drill, he felt, could become a terrifying weapon. He was relieved as he saw the look of surprise on her face turn to pleasure as she recognised him.

"Rupert! I love gardening but I'm absolutely no good at fixing things like this." She waved towards a winter jasmine that was hanging away from the wall. He decided not to waste any more time and immediately took off his jacket and laid it across the patio wall before holding out his hand for the drill.

Isobel handed him wall nails, hammer, wire and pliers in turn. She was wearing an old pair of corduroy trousers that had seen better days, a man's checked shirt and a thick, baggy sweater that concealed everything. She looked completely different from when he'd last seen her. He couldn't believe that he'd been lucky enough to find her at home. "I'm not surprised you found it difficult, those wall nails are absolute swine to get in. I'll leave the aesthetic bit for you," he said, stepping back onto the patio after he'd put the last wire in place.

"Would you mind very much if I finished it?" she asked. "The poor thing looks so bedraggled hanging away from the wall. I'll make you some tea when I've finished. It shouldn't take a minute now that you've done the hard bit."

He handed plastic ties to her one at a time. Was it really going to be this easy to bridge the gap that seemed to have opened up between them? There couldn't be any better test for a relationship surely than working harmoniously together even at such a mundane task?

"There that's fixed it, thanks for your help, I'd never have managed it on my own." Isobel stepped back and cast an approving eye over their joint effort, smiling up at him. It was the same smile that had delighted him on the first morning in Venice when he'd collected her from the hotel. He couldn't wait for what he was sure would be long explanations from both of them. He stretched out a hand and carefully removed a small piece of twig and a few stray leaves from her hair. "I don't think I've ever been so pleased to see anyone," he said, taking her in his arms.

He held her silently thinking how right she felt. Words seemed, not only unnecessary but out of place. He laid his cheek against her hair, inhaled the faint scent of wood smoke. He continued to hold her for several minutes until a sudden cool breeze reminded him that the afternoon was drawing to a close. He shivered slightly and held Isobel away from him; "You promised me tea." He smiled down at her.

"So I did, I'm sorry, I've become a little distracted."

"My fault. I needed to convince myself that you were real, that I wasn't in the middle of some dream. Your garden's lovely by the way, you obviously work hard in it, or do you have help?"

"There's an old boy in the village who does the lawns from time-to-time but I won't trust him with anything else. Anyway I find the whole process therapeutic. Once I come out here I forget any problems."

"Is that why you're out here today?" He bent to pick up his jacket, finding the air cold after Venice.

"Partly. But since I came home I've been so busy my poor garden's been completely neglected and as the days grow shorter I feel I should give it priority."

She led the way into the kitchen, lifted the bucket of flowers from the sink and filled the kettle. "James' thank you present," she explained, following the direction of his gaze. "They look rather flamboyant don't you think? Exactly like James! Are you hungry? I'm afraid I have no delicious cake but I could manage toast or a biscuit."

"Tea's just fine, thank you."

There was so much he wanted to say and here they were talking about tea and toast! But then he realised there was really no hurry, they had the rest of the evening in front of them. It was a good feeling.

"The main problem as you probably realise Mademoiselle Northcote is that the body is unable to respond to infection in the normal way. The research into possible treatment is on-going but every time science produces an effective vaccine the virus mutates and in so-doing becomes resistant to that very vaccine. There is no cure although there are drugs which can prolong life expectancy as the disease progresses. I'm afraid I cannot give you a happier outcome at the moment." The expression on the face of the specialist was sympathetic but Tory didn't want to hear any more. She just wanted to get her hands on that rat bag Pierre and strangle the living daylights out of him.

Vivid pictures of the night they met at a disco on the Left Bank flooded her mind. He was completely different from anyone she'd ever known before. He'd danced like a dream; introduced her to a variety of high octane cocktails and long before the evening was over they were both legless. When he took her home he hadn't waited for her to invite him in but had followed her through the front door and given her one of the wildest nights she'd ever spent. Even now, when she knew she would murder him if he were to cross her path tomorrow, the memory of his love making still excited her. But she couldn't waste time wallowing in memories. There was a lot she had to do.

The plan was already forming in her mind as she said goodbye to the specialist and walked down the endless corridor of the hospital that would lead her out into the autumn afternoon but which, in reality, led nowhere.

By Thursday Ian had begun to lighten up. As the days went by and there was no message from Tory he was at first puzzled and then relieved. He hadn't expected her to let him off the hook, she wasn't the type. And she'd been so bent on putting an end to her father's affair that he had the impression she'd allow nothing and nobody to stand in her way. Something must have happened to make her change her mind. Perhaps she'd been sent away somewhere by *Vacances en Europe* and was so busy inspecting properties; to say nothing of screwing their owners, that she'd totally forgotten her threat? Could she be ill perhaps or had her father told her that his affair with Isobel was over? Whatever the reason, for the moment he appeared to be safe.

He couldn't just leave it though, he'd have to do a little gentle probing, see if he could pick up a few clues. He dialled his mother's number, her voice on the answer phone invited him to leave a message. "Hi Mum, it's Ian. I was going to take you out to dinner, remember? Now that Dad's home, I imagine you have a bit more time on your hands. Perhaps you'll give me a call at the office later and we'll make a date. Cheers." For the moment he could do no more and although doing nothing was always frustrating he'd have to make the best of it.

It was strange that Isobel hadn't telephoned James thought as he spread Cooper's Oxford marmalade thickly on his breakfast toast. He ignored the look of silent reproach on Zelda's face and retreated behind the comparative safety of the Telegraph. His flowers should have arrived yesterday so why hadn't Isobel been in touch? She was normally so meticulous about the day-to-day niceties. He would give her until lunch time and if there was still no message he would ring her.

It was eleven o'clock on Thursday morning when Rupert finally left Ashley Green. He and Isobel had overslept but that was scarcely surprising considering the night they'd just spent. Yesterday they'd talked and talked, filling in the details since their parting. Rupert had taken the initiative this time. "The first time you came to my apartment you invited yourself to stay. At the risk of being unoriginal may I do the same?" he'd asked. That was shortly after they'd finished their tea and definitely before they started on the champagne. Rupert had brought a bottle with him and prudently left it in the car until he was certain that a celebration was in order. And what a celebration! They'd rustled up a meal together and washed it down with the best part of a bottle of claret. By this time neither of them was capable of pronouncing the word inhibition leave alone adjusting their behaviour to comply with its meaning.

They'd taken a long bath together. Isobel in a moment of inspiration lit a scented candle remarking as she did so that some of their wilder moments together seemed to have taken place in one bathroom or another! By the time they went to bed they were both relaxed and slightly drunk. Isobel hugged herself at the memory and went to clear away the remains of their breakfast.

James' flowers reproached her from their bucket. She must arrange them and then brace herself to ring him up and thank him and while she was about it ask him about Rupert's phone call. "Somehow James I don't think you're going to enjoy talking to me," she said as she loaded the dishwasher. She crossed the hall to her study and played back Ian's message from the answer phone. She'd completely forgotten his invitation but that was hardly surprising considering the events of the last few days. She decided to call him first; James could wait.

"Hi Mum, how are you?" His voice sounded crisp.

"I'm absolutely fine. Is it a good time to talk, you're not with a client are you?"

Ian assured her he wasn't and now was as good a time as any.

"I'm ringing about our dinner. Are you free tomorrow and do you think we could make it lunch instead? I'd like to fit in the hairdresser, maybe do some shopping."

Rupert was coming down for the weekend and, after looking such a fright yesterday, she was keen to improve things before their next meeting. She waited for Ian to consult his diary, humming tunelessly to herself, thinking back over last night and looking forward to the weekend.

"Can we make it one fifteen? I have a client at eleven thirty, should be through in plenty of time. Shall we say Luigi's, Covent Garden?"

"Perfect, see you then."

She replaced the receiver and lifted it again to ring James.

"Ah James! How are you? Not too tired after your journey home I hope?"

"Isobel? How nice!" James' smooth, dark brown voice came mellifluously down the wire. 'You won't think that when I've finished with you.' Isobel said silently to herself as she listened to his bulletin on the state of his health.

"Your flowers arrived yesterday, thank you. I apologise for taking so long to ring you but I've been rather busy since you left. You may be surprised to hear that I had a very interesting and illuminating talk with Rupert Northcote last night." She waited for him to respond but as there was complete silence from the other end Isobel pressed on. "I understand he telephoned, the same Saturday that Ian came down and Zelda had dinner with us. Was there some special reason why you didn't pass on his message?" She paused and heard James clear his throat. "I'm sorry Isobel it must have slipped my mind completely. Yes he did ring now you come to mention it but he didn't leave a message as such, just asked me to tell you he called."

Isobel wasn't going to let him off the hook so easily in spite of the flowers. "I'm deeply disappointed in your behaviour and to be honest James I think it's a shabby return for the care I've tried to show you over the past two weeks. If I didn't know you better I'd be inclined to believe you but ever since you first knew about Rupert and I you've been, well, overreacting to say the least. I'd just like you to know how distressed I am that you seem not to want me to be happy."

"There's nothing I'd like more than to see you happy Isobel," James purred, "but are you sure that Rupert Northcote is the right man for you?"

Isobel steeled herself against the note of concern in his voice which years of experience had taught her was entirely false. "James," she said at last, "listen very carefully to what I'm about to say to you. I've never been more certain of anything, ever; and I would be absolutely delighted if you would just leave me in peace to get on with my life. Do you understand me James?"

"I understand you perfectly Isobel."

James replaced the receiver slowly, feeling as if all the stuffing had been knocked out of him. Throughout his life, like most people he knew, he'd had his share of winning and losing. Like most he preferred the former. This time he knew with a sickening certainty that he'd lost and it felt bloody rough.

Chapter Twenty

"You're looking good Ma," Ian said as he bent to kiss Isobel before sitting down opposite her.

"I had my hair done this morning, it always helps, but thanks anyway."

Ian congratulated himself that he'd got their meeting off to a good start judging by the pleased expression on his mother's face.

"This is a treat for me," she said. "I can't remember the last time we went out for a meal together."

Ian stopped congratulating himself and began to feel guilty, knowing the real purpose of his invitation. But his compliment was genuine enough. She was looking good for a woman of her age; much better than when he'd last seen her. Then she'd been looking after James. Now the tension had disappeared from her face and there was a kind of glow about her that seemed to come from somewhere deep inside. He leaned forward, anxious to please her. "We're all grateful for what you've done for Dad over the last two weeks. It can't have been easy. I dropped in to see him yesterday and he looks so much better."

Isobel shrugged and waved a hand dismissively. "Well it's over now thank goodness and I've got the house to myself again. I spent most of yesterday in the garden. It's been so neglected while I've been away and I didn't have time to get to grips with it before your father arrived."

Ian ordered wine for them and as they studied menus wondered how he was going to broach the subject of Tory. Perhaps he'd better keep the conversation on safe territory for a while. As they waited for food he told her about Bruce's swift exit at the weekend and of the relief of being alone with Susan again and how pleased she was that her father wouldn't be living on his own for much longer.

His mother's sympathetic expression was encouraging and after a few more snippets of information about the children he felt he was safe to move from discussing his own life.

"We haven't talked about your holiday yet," he began at last, thinking to lead up to the subject of Rupert as gently as possible.

"I'm sure the family gossip has already put you in the picture. But, since you ask, I did have a wonderful time. Venice looked beautiful, quite the most fabulous city I've ever seen. Incidentally I managed to get to Murano and your glasses should be with you any time, if they haven't arrived already."

Her face looked so animated across the table. Was she still in touch with Rupert? He had to know. "Thank you for taking the trouble to get the glasses, Susan will be thrilled. Family gossip, as you put it, is notoriously unreliable. I heard that you didn't spend your holiday alone. Was that wise? We were all a bit worried." He wanted to add, is this the way to behave at *your* age, but felt that would be going a bit far. He saw his mother blush and knew he was on dodgy ground.

"Ian dear, I'm grown up remember? I don't think I have to tell the family all my movements or even who I'm spending my time with, do you? Since you all left home I've assumed you weren't that interested anyway. How come you're all snapping at my heels now that you think I might be having a bit of fun?"

Ian watched her take a long drink from her wine glass, waited for her to set it down and immediately topped it up. This was going to be harder than he'd imagined. He hadn't reckoned on his mother defending her corner so vehemently.

"This man you met. None of us know him. How do we know that he's entirely suitable? After all you were keen for Steve and I to marry women who would fit in with the family if I remember rightly?"

"There's a slight difference in our ages darling. I like to think I have just a little more wisdom now than when I was in my twenties. Anyway if you want to give Rupert the once over he's coming down for the weekend. Bring Susan and the children for lunch on Sunday and you can see for yourself just how suitable or otherwise he is."

So it was still on! Ian looked down at his plate to avoid showing her the shock on his face. He needed a head-to-head with Tory's father like a drowning man needed water! He'd have to pass on this one. "It's kind of you to ask us but I'll have to check with Susan first. She may have something booked," he said.

"Well you know I'll be pleased to see you all. It's a long time since you came down together. Give me a ring later and let me know."

It was Ian's turn to blush. He couldn't look at her but he had to try and find out what, if anything, was happening to Tory. "So

Rupert's back from Venice then?" he began, wondering if he would ever get around to passing on Tory's message.

"Yes he came back on Tuesday, I'm not sure how long he's staying. We didn't really discuss it when we met up on Wednesday."

Her eyes were sparkling as she talked about Rupert. My God they hadn't wasted much time! His father only left on Tuesday. Ian helped himself to vegetables. "Did he come back alone?" he asked, trying to make his voice sound casual. Looking at her from under half-lowered lids he saw a puzzled expression come over her face.

"I assume so, although we didn't really talk about that either. Why? Shouldn't he have?"

Ian ploughed on. "He has a daughter, did she come over with him?"

"I've really no idea. She didn't figure in our conversation. She's living and working in Paris at the moment I believe. Anyway how did you know about Tory?"

"Mum you're not going to believe this but I actually met Tory when I was over in France the weekend before last." The palms of his hands were sweating. He moved them from the table and wiped them surreptitiously on his trousers.

The puzzled look was replaced by one of astonishment. "Goodness me how that young lady gets about! The last time I heard about her she was in Venice."

His mother sounded decidedly waspish. "Did you meet her when you were in Venice?" he asked, wondering if that was the reason for her sharp reply.

"No, thank goodness. From what Rupert tells me she's been quite a problem."

Ian could well believe it. What the hell was he going to say next? If Tory was ill her father would surely have mentioned it, unless of course he didn't know.

"The thing is Ma, she sort of warned me." Ian swallowed hard and reached for his wine glass. God he was thirsty! He saw that the puzzled look had returned to his mother's face. He wished he were back at the office. Discussions with clients were a walk over compared with this.

"About what?" Isobel's voice sounded suspicious.

Ian cut himself a piece of cheese thinking that he'd have to put in some extra time at the gym to burn off all the calories he was consuming. "She warned me that her father has, shall we say, an eye for the ladies."

"Goodness Ian, what an old fashioned expression!" Isobel laughed. "From what I've heard that's exactly the kind of thing *she* would say. She turned up in Venice on my last evening. Didn't bother to phone her father until she was on the train from Paris and expected him to put her up at a moments notice. Damn all consideration for other people's lives from what I hear."

Ian knew only too well that his mother was speaking the truth. He began to draw patterns on the tablecloth with the handle of a spoon. This whole ridiculous situation was growing worse by the minute. It would be a long time before he was tempted to screw around again if it meant having to deal with this sort of aggro. But if his mother behaved like a normal woman of sixty and stayed at home knitting socks for her grandchildren or whatever grannies were supposed to do, he wouldn't be in this situation. If she chose to live in the fast lane she'd have to learn to take the knocks just like anyone else; although if he were honest he didn't really want a mother with grey hair and a curly perm who handed round toffees at family parties!

He glanced quickly at his watch. It was nearly half past two and he should be getting back to the office. He looked across the table, met her eyes and screwed up his courage. "The thing is Ma, she asked me to warn you off." Oh thank God he'd said it at last! He reached for the wine bottle and, finding it empty, poured himself a glass of water.

Isobel picked up her handbag and glanced round the restaurant looking for a cloakroom. "Thanks for your concern Ian," she said, "But I think I'll trust my own judgement if you don't mind. Thank you for lunch, I've really enjoyed seeing you again. The invitation for Sunday lunch still stands incidentally."

Ian's heart sank. He was going to have to confess. He felt as if he were ten years old again and admitting that he hadn't done his homework. "The thing is mother, I've been rather indiscreet."

Isobel held up her hand. "Before you go any further are you certain you really want to tell me?"

"I don't *want* to tell you but I *have* to. You see Tory made it clear that if I didn't stop your affair with her father she'd tell Susan . . ." He saw his mother's eyebrows rise alarmingly as his voice trailed away.

"Are you telling me Ian that you were unfaithful to Susan with Tory Northcote?"

"'Fraid so."

"Is everything alright between you and Susan?"

"Of course!" Ian was indignant. "We have our ups and downs, who doesn't? But everything's fine between us." Ian, remembering what they'd got up to after dinner on Saturday evening, fought hard to suppress a self-satisfied smile.

"Then this thing with Tory was just a one-off?"

"You bet your life it was! That young woman's dynamite on legs! I know it sounds like a feeble excuse but she made it very hard for me to resist." Ian's embarrassment was acute at having to confess a sexual indiscretion to his mother. Just like that ten years old boy he was afraid of what she might say but, more than anything else, he desperately wanted her to make everything alright again.

"I can imagine!" Isobel now sounded positively tart. "I'll have a word with Rupert this weekend. He'll soon sort her out."

The last thing Ian wanted was the two of them discussing him, maybe having a good giggle at his expense. "Do you really think that would be a good idea?" he asked. "I'd hate him to show up in Wapping with a shot gun!"

"I can promise you Ian that Rupert's sympathies will be entirely with you. I think perhaps we'd better forget about Sunday lunch though. I can't imagine it would be easy for either of you. Now I'm sorry but I really must go, I have some shopping to do before I catch the train and Rupert will be down this evening." She reached across the table and squeezed his hand. He knew she was trying to reassure him and smiled his gratitude. "You won't say anything to Sue about this will you?"

Isobel looked hurt. "Do give me credit for some finer feelings Ian. I may not be the most conventional mother but at least I know better than to interfere in your married life."

She'd made her point and he deserved it Ian thought ruefully as he kissed her goodbye.

As things turned out it wasn't until Saturday evening that Isobel found the opportunity to tell Rupert about her conversation with Ian. He hadn't arrived until nearly eight o'clock on Friday and although he was full of apologies for his lateness he was also excited by a meeting he'd just left with a consortium of architects who were discussing urban planning.

Over dinner he'd outlined their ideas for inner city regeneration. He'd compared cities in the UK unfavourably with their European counterparts and spoke of the need to create areas where young and old, single and married, rich and poor, could live harmoniously and safely together in places which, once reconstructed, would provide an attractive environment.

His enthusiasm was infectious and Isobel listened intently, asking questions whenever he paused for breath and occasionally challenging his views. She still believed that he was attempting to orchestrate people's lives, by creating a living space and then expecting the residents to live happily together and she had strong reservations about how possible this might be.

He'd defended himself by saying that at least he was trying to initiate a change from worse to better and Isobel, visualising some of the inner city squalor that she'd encountered over the years, could see that he had a point. By the time they'd finished talking it was almost eleven o'clock and Isobel hadn't the slightest intention of raising the subject of Tory just before they went to bed.

On Saturday morning her friend Joanna arrived unannounced. Isobel had mentioned over the phone that Rupert was coming for the weekend and Joanna, who'd never stopped asking questions about him since Isobel's return from holiday, could contain her curiosity no longer. An hour went by and, as Joanna showed no sign of leaving, Isobel suggested that she call her husband and they could all go to the local pub for lunch.

"He's really dishy!" Joanna confided later as she and Isobel were powdering their noses in the privacy of the ladies cloakroom. "Seeing you together makes me wish I were free again."

"I'm glad you approve." Isobel smiled into the mirror at her old friend. "It's always comforting to have a second opinion."

"Have you made any plans for the future?" Joanna was an incurable romantic and would love to see her friend settle down with a nice steady man. It wasn't every day that someone close to her began a new relationship. In fact as she grew older Joanna began to realise that excitement of any kind was becoming harder and harder to find.

"We really haven't had the time to discuss long term plans," Isobel hedged, "but I promise you'll be the first to know if there are any developments."

"Well mind you do." Joanna applied lipstick and then wiped most of it away. "I forgot we're off to see Tony's old mother this afternoon and she disapproves of lipstick. I'd better keep the old girl sweet or she might just go and leave her ill-gotten gains to somebody else."

Isobel was relieved that she and Rupert would have the afternoon to themselves. She was extremely fond of Joanna but she also felt starved of Rupert's company and, now that she'd found him again, resented every minute that they weren't alone.

"Shall we walk for a while?" Rupert said as they left Joanna and her husband. He tucked Isobel's arm under his own, took her hand and, finding it cold, pushed it into his pocket and held it closely. It was a perfect autumn day. There was a stiff breeze, the leaves were coming down and scrunched under their feet as they walked. Shafts of sunlight shone spasmodically through scudding clouds highlighting the rosehips in the hedgerows, making their brilliant orange shine even more brightly. Isobel needed all her energy to keep up with Rupert's long, easy stride and any attempt at conversation was out of the question.

Later as she was making tea he'd suggested lighting a fire in the sitting room although the pair of them and the house were as warm as toast. They sat with their legs stretched towards the blaze drinking tea and eating a delicious chocolate cake that Isobel had bought in Town. Digby's finely tuned feline intuition told him that there was a fire in the vicinity and his head appeared cautiously round the sitting room door.

"Hello! Who's this?" Rupert wanted to know. "I don't remember seeing him before."

"He normally takes off when visitors arrive. I haven't seen much of him at all since James came down, unless of course we lit a fire in the evening. Otherwise he waits until everyone's gone to bed and then he comes in for food and to reclaim his basket."

Rupert stretched out a hand and scratched the top of Digby's head and the cat, recognising a friend, wound himself around Rupert's ankles.

"It seems you're a hit." Isobel smiled indulgently across at the pair of them. Digby, having made his point, walked across to the fire and stretched luxuriously in front of the blaze.

"I can't remember the last time I sat down and had a proper tea." Rupert got up and put another log on the fire, stepping carefully round the cat, raked ash so that it fell gently from the dog grate to the hearth. Isobel watched him with affection thinking how effortlessly he'd made the transition from his own home to hers. She'd asked him to treat the place as his own when he'd arrived and was relieved that he'd taken her at her word.

A drift of CK wafted towards her as he finished stoking the fire and she basked briefly in the memories it rekindled. The light was fading and she felt it was time to clear away the tea things and get them both something stronger. She would soon have to think about dinner anyway. She stretched lazily. "Give me a minute to put the dinner in the oven and then I'll get us a drink. I have a brace of pheasant and they'll be happy to look after themselves."

"Pheasant! What a treat! I'll get the drinks if you like." He stretched out his hands and pulled her slowly to her feet then held her close for a moment.

Isobel's heart flipped over. She buried her face in the softness of his sweater, put her arms around his waist and felt she could stay like this for ever. Seconds passed. Rupert was the first to speak. "I think we need to talk don't you?" he said. Isobel pulled back a little and looked up at him. "Talk?"

"About us, the future, *our* future." He kissed her slowly and with his usual care; as delicately as if she might break. Isobel felt a moment of panic, remembering Ian's warning and then, just as quickly, dismissed it from her mind.

"Perhaps we should put the pheasant wherever it is they need to be put and I'll get us a drink and we can talk for as long as it takes. How does that sound?" Rupert was accustomed to acting swiftly once he'd reached a decision. It seemed to him that he'd been waiting forever to have a serious conversation about where they may or may not be going.

"Always the practical Rupert." Isobel teased him as she bent to retrieve the tray. After James' total disregard for any domestic task, however trivial, Rupert's offers of help were a godsend.

They sat either side of the kitchen table. Isobel took a sip from her gin and tonic and waited expectantly. Rupert reached across and took one of her hands, folding it into his own. "Since you left Venice," he began, "all I could think about was coming back to the UK and seeing you again. If I'm honest I never expected to miss you so much and not being able to get hold of you on the phone made things worse. When James answered the phone I thought I'd go crazy wondering what the hell was going on."

"As I said before I can't apologise enough." There was real regret in Isobel's voice. "If it's any consolation I've told James exactly what I think of him for being so mean."

Rupert shrugged. "These things happen. In an odd way I can understand his motives. Men hate the idea of anyone else getting close to their wives."

"Or ex-wives?" Isobel prompted him.

"Or ex-wives. Anyway lets not dwell on James. I haven't met anyone quite like you since Liz died, didn't think I ever would." The pressure of his hand tightened around her own. She watched as he twisted his glass nervously round and round with his free hand. "I keep asking myself," he continued, "what I'd do if you disappeared from my life and I simply don't want to think about a future without you."

Isobel daren't move, afraid that if she did she might spoil the moment for Rupert. Her hand lay still, supine, folded in Rupert's own. She held her breath.

"I don't think I'm doing this very well." Rupert squared his shoulders and looked directly at her at last. "I guess what I'm trying to say is that I'd like you to be a part of my life for as long as I've got left. We can marry or not, whatever you want, only please don't leave me again, I don't think I could bear it."

Isobel squeezed his hand reassuringly. He hadn't mentioned love once. Was this his way of saying he loved her or was love something he hadn't considered? Was he capable of loving anyone after losing Liz? She watched him drain the last of the wine from his glass as he waited for her answer. "Was that a proposal?" she asked, playing for time.

He looked surprised. "Wasn't that obvious? Sorry, I guess I'm out of practise. I don't like to think how many years it's been." He smiled apologetically.

"That's not what I heard." Her voice was light, bright. She hated herself for doing this to him but if they were to have any sort of future together it was important that their relationship should be based on trust. Even living alone would be better than an agonising relationship with another womaniser. She saw the smile slip from his face, waited for him to look guilty and was relieved when he didn't.

"Tell me more."

Isobel gave him the gist of her conversation with Ian. As her story unfolded she saw the look of polite interest on his face turn first to incredulity and then to anger. What was she going to do if he lost his temper? Would their weekend, which had been so perfect until now, be completely ruined? Might he storm off in a huff? Could this be the end that she'd feared so many times since her return from Venice?

When she'd finished he covered his face with his hands for a few seconds and then spoke wearily. "I simply can't believe it," he said at last. "Do you really see me as a modern Casanova?"
"Not for a minute!" Isobel jumped to her feet and went round to his side of the table, put her arms round his neck and laid her cheek

against the top of his head. "What I *do* think is that you have a daughter who loves you enough to want to keep you to herself."

"I have a daughter who, not contented with behaving like a slut, tries a bit of blackmail to add a bit more spice to her life." Rupert's voice was harsh, bitter.

"Let me get you a refill." Isobel picked up his empty glass, walked over to the bottle, refilled his glass and put it down in front of him before opening the oven door to baste the pheasant. "Don't be too hard on Tory," she said, returning to sit at the kitchen table. If she were to become a permanent part of Rupert's life she had no desire to be a buffer between father and daughter.

"You're asking too much Isobel." Rupert took a long pull from his glass. "I swear to you if she tries to make mischief again she's out of my life forever. And I really *mean* that," he added, seeing the look of disbelief on Isobel's face.

"She lost her mother. Remember? That must have been very traumatic for her." Isobel reached across the table. Now it was she who took Rupert's hand.

"You still haven't told me whether or not you think we might have some kind of future together." Rupert felt that they'd both taken their eyes off the ball with all the talk of Ian and Tory.

"Rupert there's nothing I'd like more than to be a part of your life but honestly the thought of marriage really scares me. I haven't told you before but Zelda wasn't the first woman in James' life, in fact there was quite a procession over the years. As you can imagine his unfaithfulness left a lot of deep scars and I couldn't face living with someone else if I thought I'd be spending night after night not only wondering where they were but with whom. You're a very attractive man and I'm sure there have been many women since

Liz who fancied the pants off you!" She saw Rupert smile and then without pausing for breath pitched in with her second concern. "Another thing that really worries me is that I'm five years older than you so, as you mentioned mortality, I feel I should warn you that I might just have less time left than you. Do you think you could face a second bereavement?" She smiled brightly at him wondering how she could talk about death in tandem with spending the rest of her life with him.

Rupert laughed. "If that's all you're worrying about, forget it. I've aged at least ten years in the last two weeks just worrying about what was happening to you. If you were to die tomorrow I might be tempted to blow my brains out, but I'd rather not think about that if you don't mind."

Isobel winced as a picture of Rupert holding a pistol to his head flashed into her mind. But she took comfort from the fact that he'd admitted to worrying about her. "Let's spend the next six months together," she suggested, "see how things go. If we're still speaking to each other and, perhaps more importantly, still alive, then we can talk about a more permanent arrangement, marriage even. After all we've spent so little time in each other's company and that's scarcely living together is it? I might drive you stark, raving mad once you see me every day!"

"Well, at least, that's something." Rupert sighed with relief as Isobel got to her feet and went back to the stove to put the vegetables on to cook. "I promise you I'll have a word with Tory, ask her to leave Ian in peace and persuade her that whatever she does isn't going to change the relationship between you and me."

"I'd be grateful if you would and I hope that Ian has the good sense to stay out of trouble in future. He has a charming wife and two beautiful children and I'd hate to think of him modelling his domestic, to say nothing of his love life, on James."

Tory took off from Paris on an Air France flight at eleven thirty five on Sunday morning. She'd worked non-stop after leaving the hospital on Friday putting her plan of action together. She brushed away angry tears as she looked out over Paris and tried instead to concentrate on what lay ahead. Even the thought of revenge wasn't much of a consolation. She should be feeling happier now that she'd made up her mind to inflict pain on those who'd caused her so much of it. Thanks to her, her father would soon be leaving England faster than he'd hoped. That would put paid to his sordid carry-on with Isobel Campbell. She ordered a vodka and tonic, opened a magazine and began to flick through the pages in a desperate attempt to blot out her thoughts.

Chapter Twenty ONE

It was so long since Rupert had known real peace and happiness that it took him some time to recognise the feeling. Thanks to Isobel his underlying sadness had disappeared and he was now back on an even keel. A few days ago he'd been creased, careworn and exhausted by the frenetic activity of the past two weeks and now he was all smoothed out and beginning to look forward again. Isobel had listened to, laughed with and loved him. The effect was miraculous. So often in the past he'd met women who demanded from him but Isobel gave unconditionally, although she'd made it quite clear of course that she expected him to be faithful otherwise there could be no question of a permanent relationship. He'd done his best to reassure her that during the past two years he'd really missed being faithful to anyone. Oh and he'd almost forgotten in his current mood of euphoria that he'd occasionally have to use the electric drill!

He smiled at the memory. Isobel had asked him to help her find the best place to hang the picture he'd given her as a parting gift when she'd left Venice. She'd asked his advice on light, height, even location; wanting to put the picture somewhere she would see it frequently, preferably when she had the time to appreciate it so that she could continue to enjoy the view of the Grand Canal. He'd laughingly suggested the loo but she'd begged him to be serious. She'd walked with him from room to room asking him to hold up the picture against various walls. She'd considered it with her head held slightly to one side, stepping first to right and back to left, insisting that he change places with her to see what he thought. He'd teased her saying that if he'd known it was going to be such a bother to hang he'd have thought twice about giving it, but he was secretly flattered by the care she was taking to find exactly the right place for it.

Finally they'd decided on the wall in her sitting room opposite and slightly to one side of the window so that the light fell obliquely, showing off the picture to advantage. She'd then produced the electric drill - apologetically. "You made such a good job of the wires for the winter jasmine do you think you could possibly do the same for your painting?" She'd smiled mischievously as she asked him. It was then that he'd taken her firmly in his arms, complete with electric drill, and finally plucked up the courage to tell her how much he loved her. He felt her melt against him, a gesture which told him more than words ever could, and they'd briefly abandoned the picture hanging . He'd begged her never to change; told her how precious she was to him and finally tasted her tears for the first time

He'd meant to return to London on Sunday night but, reluctant to tear himself away, waited until Monday morning, leaving at six thirty to try and beat the worst of the commuter traffic. "Your reputation in Ashley Green will be ruined," he said as she stood at the front door in her dressing gown to wave him goodbye. "Come back soon and ruin it again!" she invited. When you got to know her properly she was a lot of fun he thought as he turned the car into the mews and drew up again outside his own front door.

Maria let herself into Rupert's flat a little after ten am on Monday morning. She went immediately to his bedroom to put away the clean laundry, hanging his shirts carefully in the cupboard before putting pants and socks in their respective drawers. She hummed softly to herself as she worked, mainly to break the silence, which always seemed to be more intense when Rupert was away; partly because she considered herself fortunate to have a job where she was trusted and could work without supervision. During the two years that Rupert had employed her she'd grown to understand the way that he liked things done. Usually he left her a note to let her know if there was anything special that needed attention or sometimes just to say thank you for some service she'd performed. They rarely met but she still felt that he appreciated the high standard that she always tried to maintain.

She walked into the bathroom to put clean linen in the airing cupboard and frowned as she caught sight of a crumpled towel which had been thrown carelessly across a chair. Had *Signor* Northcote told her that *Signorina* Tory would be coming over? She was sure he hadn't. But there was only one person who threw towels about in this apartment and it wasn't the owner.

Maria went across to the kitchen. The mug of half drunk, now cold, coffee on the kitchen table confirmed her suspicions. The last time she'd stayed the *signorina* had slept in the sitting room, she'd better go and see what kind of a mess she'd left in there.

The door to the sitting room was shut. Maria knocked gently and listened for a few seconds. There was no sound; no invitation to come in. She knocked a second time, more loudly; again there was no response. She opened the door. The heavy curtains were closed and it was difficult to make out the state of the room. She crossed to the windows and opened the curtains, looping each one carefully back and repeating the process at each in turn. It was only when her task was completed that she turned to face the room and drew in her breath sharply, feeling her heart begin to thump as she saw Tory lying on one of the sofas. "*Signorina*! Is time to get up!" she called across the room. There was no movement. With a sudden feeling of deep foreboding she crossed the room and shook Tory gently by the shoulder. The skin beneath her fingers was ice cold. Maria stepped back quickly and crossed herself almost as a reflex action before turning and running from the room.

By the time she reached the kitchen she was shaking violently. Her brain had turned to jelly and she sat down heavily on the nearest chair, trying hard to regain control. She wrapped her arms around herself, rocking back and forth on the chair, repeating the same words over and over again. "Poor *Signor* Northcote, poor *Signor* Northcote."

Isobel glanced up as the first spots of rain began to fall. The sky was a dark and solid grey, promising a real downpour of autumnal rain rather than a quick shower. She collected her tools together reluctantly and replaced them in the garden shed. It was annoying when there was so much to be done but the rest of the work would have to wait until tomorrow. She walked into the kitchen and turned on the radio just in time to hear the weather forecast endorse what the sky had just promised. She crossed to the cloakroom and was just going to wash her hands when the phone rang. She ran across the hall to her study and scarcely had time to pick up the receiver when Rupert's voice came across the wire.

"Isobel? Thank God!" He sounded tense, urgent.

"Rupert! Are you alright?"

"Far from it. Something quite awful's happened."

Isobel sat down in front of her desk clutching the phone tightly, holding her breath, waiting; wondering what catastrophe could have struck in the few hours that they'd been apart. "Tell me the worst," she said at last, bracing herself for bad news.

"It's Tory," there was a pause. Images flashed across Isobel's mind. Tory in London, perhaps trying to contact Ian? Tory making who knows what threats to her father? Tory in some hospital, lying seriously injured? Rupert getting ready to leave for Paris?

"Are you still there?" she asked anxiously as the pause stretched.

"Yes I'm here," he cleared his throat. "There isn't an easy way to say this so I may as well come straight out with it. I'm afraid Tory's dead."

"Oh no! How terrible! Rupert I'm so sorry." What else could she say? Her brain had gone into spasm and she was unable to think of anything which wouldn't sound trite. "Tell me, what happened?" she asked, thinking, how would I feel if it were Ian or Steven? What would I want to hear from Rupert?

"It's difficult to say at a distance. I only have the barest details but, from what I've heard I'm afraid it looks like suicide. Maria found her this morning when she went in to clean the apartment."

"Maria?"

"Yes, didn't I say? Sorry but I'm not thinking clearly at the moment. I'm afraid that Tory is at this moment lying dead in my apartment in Venice."

"But Rupert, I don't understand. What? Why . . ." Her voice tailed off. She felt completely inadequate.

"Oh Isobel I don't know. Apparently there's a letter addressed to me which may throw some light. As you can imagine Maria's in one hell of a state. It was a ghastly shock for her to walk in and find the body."

Isobel heard his voice break, listened as he blew his nose hard. "I'm sorry Isobel, it's so difficult to take it all in at the moment."

She was instantly ready to help him. "Would you like me to come up? Or is there anything else that I can do for you?" She wanted to hold him, comfort him, try to ease his pain in some way. She smiled grimly to herself in spite of what she'd just heard. She hadn't expected the mothering instinct to feature in her relationship with Rupert. He'd always been so much in control. Organised, strong, self-sufficient.

"I've asked Giovanni to go to the apartment, call the doctor, police, look after the official red-tape until I can join him. There's a flight leaving this afternoon so I'll be out of here shortly. I'll phone you this evening if that's OK to let you know what's happening. Will you be home?" He was back to his usual crisp, business-like form.

"Would you like me to come with you?" Isobel asked, thinking how terrible to have to make that journey knowing the possible horrors that were waiting at the other end.

"It's kind of you but I can't imagine the next few hours are going to be either easy or pleasant. I've absolutely no idea what I'm going to find at the apartment. Maria was very emotional when she called and with good reason. In fact she was barely coherent. I feel in some way guilty that she was the one to discover Tory and even more so that I had to ask her to stay put to wait for Giovanni. I promise I'll call you this evening. I must go now but I couldn't leave without telling you. You do understand don't you?" His voice told her how grateful he was for her concern; that she was there to listen to him.

Ian put down the phone and sat at his desk tapping the front of his teeth with a pencil. Christ! What a drama this was turning into! Blackmail threats one minute and suspected suicide the next. His life was rapidly turning into a replica of a cheap paperback. His mother had mentioned a letter that was waiting in Rupert Northcote's flat. A bit disturbing that. Supposing Tory had named and blamed him? How the hell would he talk his way out of that? His mother had said possible suicide. What if it was murder? Might he be a suspect? At least his movements over the weekend could be corroborated thank God. Still it was creepy. Two weeks ago he'd made love to the woman. He felt a surge in his groin at the memory of that fabulous body and the blatant way she'd taken him then shuddered as he thought of her lying cold and alone in her father's flat with only time separating her from the post-mortem knife.

Isobel stared unseeingly at the television news wondering how Rupert was coping with who-knows-what horror in Venice. Her heart was aching for him and she knew intuitively that he would blame himself for what had happened to Tory. It seemed incredible now that just a few weeks ago she'd been complaining that life was routine and dull. She'd taken off for Venice hoping for excitement and she'd certainly found it! Retirement it seemed was going to be much more eventful than work had ever been and yet, at times like this, when she was waiting for the telephone to ring, there suddenly seemed to be absolutely nothing to do or perhaps more accurately nothing she felt like doing.

She thought of her parents and remembered the passionless patience with which they'd tolerated each other in the latter years of their lives. By the time the war ended they'd both changed. Her father's experience in the army had hardened him and when her mother raged about some glitch in her domestic arrangements he'd remained imperturbable. He'd confided that once you'd shot the enemy in cold blood and walked away from his corpse to look for the next victim, it was impossible to get excited because the window cleaner had forgotten to call. Gradually her mother conceded that it was useless to expect him to show any emotion about anything and simply gave up trying. Looking back and comparing their lives with what was happening so close to her own at the moment she almost envied them.

The weather forecast promised more heavy rain tomorrow and she pressed the remote control button impatiently, switching off the set. The sudden quiet was unbearable. She couldn't possibly concentrate on a book; she'd scanned the newspaper at lunchtime unable to take in even the simplest piece of information. Perhaps some music would be a good idea . . . ?

The sound of the telephone cut across her thoughts. She jumped quickly to her feet stumbling over a prone Digby in her haste to get to the instrument. "Sorry!" she called out to him stupidly as she ran towards the study.

"Hello! Rupert?" she said into the receiver.

"Right now I'd rather be anyone else but me." He sounded flat, weary, defeated.

"I've been thinking about you all the time since we last spoke. I *do* wish I could be more helpful." Isobel once again felt inadequate wishing she could think of something to say which would smooth the rough edge of the agony he must be feeling and realising with a dull certainty that there was nothing.

"You're at the end of the telephone; that's more than helpful. Everything out here has been so chaotic I don't know where to look next."

"You're not alone I hope?" Isobel had a sudden vision of him pacing up and down his beautiful sitting room trying to come to terms with Tory's death.

"No. Giovanni's still here. He's insisting I go home with him tonight. I must say it will be a relief to leave this place, it looks like a bear-garden at the moment."

"You must be exhausted. Try to get a good night's sleep if that's possible." She couldn't begin to imagine how Rupert's immaculate apartment could remotely resemble a bear-garden.

"I'd better fill you in with the details." Rupert's voice was businesslike again and Isobel wondered if he were trying to stop her worrying about him. "It looks as if my original diagnosis was correct and Tory took her own life." Isobel heard him clear his throat and sat clutching her own waiting for him to regain control.

"I'm afraid it gets worse the more I discover. According to her letter she'd discovered she was HIV positive and, although the illness was only diagnosed on Friday, the prognosis was so poor she decided she couldn't cope. There was a half drunk bottle of vodka and several empty paracetamol packets by the side of the sofa where she died. The illness was apparently a legacy from an ex-boyfriend. The letter from him to her was in the envelope she left for me."

"Oh Rupert I'm so sorry. What a terrible waste of a life." Isobel felt her eyes sting as her tears welled up, she had no handkerchief and tried to scrub them away with her knuckles.

"Are you still there Isobel?" Rupert's voice sounded anxious across the intervening miles. She managed a choking reply. "Yes Rupert I'm still here."

"Please try to be brave darling," his own voice was perilously close to tears. "Would you like me to tell Ian for you? You do see don't you? We can't leave him in the dark. He'll need to have a test."

Isobel's hand left her throat and clutched the side of her chair as she tried to take in Rupert's latest bombshell. Oh my God Ian! In her anxiety about Rupert she'd forgotten that Tory had been to bed with Ian. A series of pictures flashed in front of her each one more dreadful than the last. Ian confessing his indiscretion to her over lunch; Ian a victim of that unforgiving disease, slipping away from his family slowly and painfully as his immune system failed; two of her grandchildren soon to be fatherless.

"Isobel?" Rupert's voice was a gentle question in her ear.

"Sorry Rupert, I was just thinking."

"Wishing no doubt that you'd never heard of the Northcote family. I can't say I blame you."

"Don't say that! Please don't say that!" Her anger at what may or may not happen to Ian suddenly got the better of her and she heard herself shouting into the telephone. "I'm sorry Rupert," she whispered almost immediately, "I'm afraid it's just the shock."

"So shall I tell him?" Rupert persisted. "It might be easier man-to-man."

"No, no thank you. You've had a dreadful day and no doubt tomorrow will be just as bad. I already told him about Tory, that she was . . ." She didn't want to say the word dead but allowed her voice to die instead.

"Are you absolutely certain Isobel? It won't be an easy task." His concern for her at a time when his own suffering must be acute and the gentleness in his voice unleashed the last of her self-control and she cried openly into the telephone. She tried unsuccessfully to wipe her nose on the back of her hand, opened drawers in her desk, rummaged around for a tissue and, finding none, used her shirt sleeve instead. She swallowed hard, trying to regain control of her voice. She mustn't let Rupert shoulder any more of the burden than he was carrying already.

"I'll wait until tomorrow," she said at last. "After all even if I do tell him tonight he can't do anything practical until the morning and if Susan's around when he takes the call . . . I think on the whole it will be easier for him if I wait until he gets to the office."

She made a sudden decision. "Once I've told Ian I'll pack a few things and take the first available flight to Venice. I think we'll be able to face this crisis better if we're together don't you? I'll book into the San Antonio again; I shouldn't think Maria will want to cope with another visitor on top of everything else. I know it sounds trite but we will get through this - somehow."

"Will you really come all this way?" She heard his voice lighten with relief for a moment and then, just as quickly, his emotions surfaced and she heard the sound of his sobs, harsh and heart-rending across the wire. "Oh Isobel," he said at last, "I feel so guilty and so lost. I daren't think what it would be like if you weren't there to listen to me."

The sound of his agony scared her and she longed to be able to put her arms round him. Her own tears started to flow again and they cried together over the miles.

In a rare gesture of amity towards Samantha - a child to whom she'd never been attracted - Barbara held out one hand and patted her ample lap invitingly with the other. Samantha immediately ran to James, jumped on his knee and pressed her face against his chest. "It's just a phase she's going through," James explained, trying to spare his sister's feelings. Although it was more than thirty years ago now, he still hadn't forgotten the January morning when Henry had called to tell him the awful news that their first, and as it subsequently turned out, only child had died whilst asleep in his cot. It had been tough on Barbara who, after the birth had devoted herself tirelessly to caring for her new baby. He couldn't remember exactly when she'd turned to food as a consolation and he'd watched her grow larger as the years went by and her hopes of conceiving again slowly receded.

He knew it would be useless to try and persuade Samantha to sit on Barbara's lap. Once she'd made up her mind to do something there'd be tears and tantrums if anyone tried to change it. He stroked her back clumsily, hoping at least to keep her quiet and was relieved when Zelda appeared with the coffee tray.

"I think it's time this young lady went upstairs for a nap." James said, hoping to diffuse the tension which had been growing by the minute ever since they finished lunch.

"I'll find Sofia." Zelda said, picking up on the atmosphere as she put down the tray. She had enough to do looking after an invalid, acting as unpaid secretary and coping with a child who seemed to be growing more difficult every day, without the bother of entertaining Barbara as well. She wondered how long it would be before she could get rid of her. The damned woman always made her feel so inadequate. She scooped up Samantha, who set up a loud protest at being wrenched away from her father. Zelda carried her kicking and screaming from the room and silence descended once again as James and Barbara were left alone.

"Shall I pour?" Barbara asked and, without waiting for an answer, heaved herself out of her chair and crossed to the coffee table anxious to have first choice from the dish of chocolates which sat invitingly next to the sugar bowl.

"Black for me," James said. "I warn you that stuff's decaffeinated; doctor's orders I'm afraid."

"Have you thought that this might be a good time to retire?" Barbara asked as Zelda came back into the room.

"Good God no. Can't afford it for one thing," James replied with a meaningful look at Zelda. "However I have been thinking quite seriously that I might set up my office at home. I'd save time on commuting so in theory I should be able to cut back on my working day."

Zelda almost choked on her coffee. "I don't remember us discussing this darling."

"Nothing to discuss." James held out his cup for a refill.

"You're thinking of turning our home into a solicitor's office and you say there's nothing to discuss." Zelda's voice had a hard edge to it.

"Well it sounds like an excellent idea to me." Barbara smiled ingratiatingly at Zelda. "After all it will be much less stressful for James."

And bloody stressful for me, Zelda thought. The future suddenly seemed anything but rosy. The thought of ministering to James twenty four hours a day, seven days a week wasn't part of her future plan. She supposed there was always an outside chance that he'd miss the office after a while and resume his former routine but if not she would have to put her mind to the problem and negotiate some free time for herself.

Suddenly she had an idea. It popped into her mind, quite uninvited, and offered the first and only crumb of comfort she'd had in ages. The more she thought about it the more it appealed. She must act swiftly before it popped out again and her life resumed its recent, dreary monotony again. She jumped quickly to her feet, handing the dish of chocolates to Barbara in an attempt to convince James that she really cared about his awful relative. "I'll just go and see if Samantha's settled," she said and left the room.

She ran upstairs, scrabbled around in her sports bag and smiled with relief as she found what she was looking for. Was there a mobile number? Yes! Yes! Yes! She punched the buttons with fingers that quivered with excitement and couldn't believe her ears when he answered. "Hello Nick," she said, dropping her voice a couple of octaves. "You're not going to believe this but suddenly I'm in desperate need of a plumber!"

Chapter Twenty TWO

Ian couldn't remember a time when he'd felt such gut-wrenching fear. His years at public school and working with a father like James who focussed constantly on winning had taught him to consistently cover his back. Consequently it wasn't often that his days produced unpleasant surprises. The worst thing of all was not being able to confide in Sue. When he remembered what they'd got up to on their first evening alone after her father left he went hot and cold by turns. If he were HIV positive . . . No he wasn't going there. He'd taken precautions but he'd have to stay away from Sue until he knew for certain that he was in the clear.

His hands felt clammy and his fingers shook as he punched out the number of an old school friend, one of the few with whom he'd kept in touch. On one memorable occasion they'd played a scintillating partnership in the school cricket match, notching up an impressive score which had secured both the match and the trophy from their nearest rivals. Laurence was now working as a general practitioner in a busy partnership in Hampstead and Ian badly needed to talk to him.

Doctor Paige please," he said as the receptionist answered his call.

"I'm afraid Doctor Paige is tied up at the moment. Are you one of his regular patients?"

"No I'm a friend of his and I'm sure he'll speak to me," Ian replied wondering why these bloody receptionists always did their best to keep you from speaking to anyone but themselves.

"Ah! His patient's just leaving, I'll see if Doctor Paige can spare a moment. Who shall I say is calling?" The clear efficiency of her voice set Ian's teeth on edge.

"Ian Campbell."

"Hold the line a moment please."

Ian held. The seconds stretched as he waited. "It's only my life that's on the line here," he said to himself drumming his fingers impatiently on the desk and hoping against hope that his next client wouldn't be early. Another valuable lesson that James had passed on was that clients were always much more amenable if they weren't kept waiting and it had become part of their *modus operandi* to see them within five minutes of their arrival.

"Hi there you silver-tongued rascal, to what do I owe this unexpected pleasure?" At last Laurence was on the line.

"I needed all the smooth talking I could muster to get past that receptionist of yours," Ian flashed back. He heard Laurence chuckle at the other end.

"She's only doing her job and we've got a busy surgery this morning so if you don't mind could you make it snappy."

Ian had no choice but to jump in at the deep end. "Sorry to bother you in the middle of surgery. Fact is I've got a bit of a problem."

"Fire away."

Ian hesitated, finding it difficult to 'fire away' when confessing to something as delicate as a sexual indiscretion, even if the listener was an old school friend. "I had a one night stand in France," he began at last, "with someone who I thought at the time was a too-good-to-miss-opportunity." God this was difficult. He ran his finger round the inside of his collar and unfastened his top button in an attempt to breathe more easily. "I've just discovered that she was HIV positive."

He heard a low whistle from the other end of the telephone as Laurence took in the information. "You're absolutely certain about the diagnosis?" he asked.

"As sure as I can be. I had a message to say that she'd taken her own life. She left a note saying that she'd contracted HIV from an ex-boyfriend."

"Bloody hell!" Laurence exclaimed before asking, "Did you use a condom?"

"Of course I used a bloody condom!" Ian was indignant. "I may be susceptible to beautiful women but I've got more sense than to have unprotected sex with someone I hardly know."

"No need to lose your cool," Laurence warned, "I have to ask the questions before I can make the diagnosis."

"I'm sorry. It's just that . . ." His voice tailed away. He swallowed hard and loosened his tie. In the last few minutes his office seemed to have grown unbearably hot.

"You'll be relieved to hear that between heterosexuals male to female transmission is much more common than female to male and if you took adequate precautions the chances of infection are slight. However to set your mind at rest I can arrange for you to have a test."

I'd be very grateful," Ian said, meaning it. "I'd rather not consult the family doctor for obvious reasons."

"When was it exactly that you and she . . .?" Laurence paused.

"Two weeks ago exactly." Ian jumped in quickly in case Laurence was tempted to elaborate.

"Well normally I'd advise waiting for at least a month to give the virus a chance to replicate, that is if you are infected, which as I said before is unlikely. I can however refer you to a Harley Street clinic which specialises in Sexually Transmitted Diseases. They've only recently discovered that the HIV p24 antigen is detectable at approximately ten days post exposure. HIV p24 is a core HIV viral protein," he elaborated for Ian's benefit. Ian was in such turmoil he found it difficult to follow anything remotely technical. "Once they've done the test they'll send it off to the lab for analysis and with any luck you should have a result one way or another in a day. I take it you've got medical insurance."

Ian looked up as Gail put her head round the door to tell him his next client had arrived. He covered the mouthpiece. "Give him some coffee and tell him I'll be with him in five minutes," he said, before resuming his conversation with Laurence. "Yes I'm insured, thank God, so no need to worry about the cost. I take it the whole thing will be in strictest confidence ." He heard Laurence chuckle. "You're not the first married man to drop his trousers outside the marital bedroom. I think you can safely rely on complete discretion. How do you feel at the moment?"

"How do you think I feel?" Ian's exasperation spilled over. "How would you feel with a death sentence hanging over you?"

"As I said earlier you took precautions; I'm sure you have nothing to worry about. Infection usually only takes place after direct sexual contact or through infected blood."

"I kissed her quite a lot," Ian confessed before adding, "all over." He heard Laurence chuckle again and began to think that he was actually enjoying himself.

"You'll be relieved to hear that recent medical evidence indicates there's little chance of infection through kissing alone - wherever you kissed her," he added after a minute pause. "The belief is that the saliva has antiseptic qualities which prevent infection."

"Well that's something at least," Ian conceded, "but in the meantime you'll arrange the test?"

"No problem. And until then I'd advise you to keep your trousers zipped."

"Thanks a bunch," Ian said wiping the sweat from his face as he put down the phone and buzzed Gail to send in his client.

Isobel scanned the waiting faces anxiously as she came through customs and failed to spot Rupert until he raised his hand in a brief salute. She smiled with relief and walked swiftly towards him thinking how exhausted he looked. He hugged her briefly before taking her grip and leading the way out to the landing stage and a waiting *motoscafo*. "I'm using the taxi service as Giovanni needs the boat tomorrow," he explained, as he stowed her grip before settling on the seat beside her.

"I'm sorry I couldn't get an earlier flight," Isobel apologised. "I was really lucky to get a seat at such short notice."

"I'm lucky to have you here at all and I've been tied up for most of the day as you can imagine so if you'd come earlier I'd have had to leave you to your own devices."

Isobel took his hand. It was ice cold. He looked so different from the man she'd first bumped into at Heathrow. He was wearing a dark tartan shirt under a chunky sweater. He must have pulled the sweater on in a hurry and part of the shirt collar was caught inside. She longed to pull it out and straighten it for him but curbed the impulse. "Has it been absolutely awful?" she asked.

"I'm too numb from shock to really feel anything," he confessed. "At least when Liz died I was prepared for it, but this is such a bolt from the blue I scarcely know what to think."

He couldn't tell her about the horrors of the past twenty four hours; partly because he wanted to protect her from the reality of the tragedy, partly because it was too painful to put into words. His apartment had looked chaotic when he'd walked in on Monday evening. Although Tory's body had by then been taken to the mortuary to await a post mortem there was evidence of her short stay all over the place. The discarded bed clothes still lay on the sofa together with several items of her clothing. Her overnight case and handbag were in the hall. Someone, either Maria or Giovanni, had offered tea or coffee to the police and later he found the kitchen littered with empty mugs. The chaos was unimportant when measured against what had happened to Tory but somehow made it seem so much more squalid. He found himself thinking that when he died he hoped he would do so tidily.

Two police officers were waiting to see him. Their questions left him feeling embarrassed at the little he knew of his daughter's life. They'd asked him if he'd ever suspected that she might commit suicide; whether she was unhappy or worried about anything, money for instance; if there was a broken romance; if she had lost her job. Rupert was ashamed to admit there was little he could tell them as he and his daughter led completely separate lives, although he'd told them about her most recent visit and confided that he thought she'd been 'a touch temperamental.'

They'd listened sympathetically, on the surface anyway, before handing him the letter which was addressed to him in Tory's small, neat handwriting and which had been left on the table in front of the sofa. He'd asked to be allowed to go to his study to read it. He couldn't bear the idea of the pair of them watching him as he tried to take in the contents. He offered them a drink, needing an excuse to have one himself, before he dared open it.

His study was the only room which appeared untouched by the crisis and the order and normality of it soothed him slightly. He switched on the lamp by his desk and drank almost half of a generous measure of whisky before slitting the envelope.

Dear Pa,

Bad news I'm afraid. Had the result of a test on Friday. Would you believe I'm HIV positive? Some scumbag I threw out of my flat just a few weeks ago. No point in telling you who he is. He's already on death row anyway so no need to go after him with your shotgun.

There are drugs I could take and the consultant told me they're improving all the time but it's a slow and ugly death and to be honest I don't really feel up to it.

I resigned from my job before I left Paris. You'll find the keys to the flat in my handbag. Sorry I couldn't replace Mum.

Too bad we couldn't get it together.

Love, Tory

Enclosed in the envelope was a letter written to Tory and signed Pierre. It bore no address but confirmed that he too was HIV positive. Rupert couldn't remember how long he sat on in his study staring at both letters in turn thinking what a failure he'd been as a father. Had Tory really wanted to take Liz's place in his life? If she had how could he have been so stupid that he hadn't noticed? Was he really so self-absorbed that he was incapable of seeing her desire to please him? Was that what lay behind her wilful behaviour? When had their relationship begun to deteriorate? Oh if only she hadn't written 'Love, Tory,' his failure might have been marginally easier to bear. As it was . . . He couldn't remember the last time she'd signed anything 'Love, Tory'?

He wanted, needed to cry but the tears were locked inside him. When Giovanni tapped on the door he discovered that his whisky glass was empty although he couldn't for the life of him remember finishing it, or even drinking it. He'd left it to Giovanni to give the letter to the police who left shortly afterwards, arranging to meet Rupert again this morning.

Earlier today the police had taken him to the mortuary anxious that he should see Tory's body before they began the post mortem examination. She looked like an empty shell, her skin pale and smooth as a beautiful statue. There was no evidence of the essence that had once been Tory and after a few minutes he'd turned abruptly away from her cold corpse and left the room.

The police had asked more questions but they were mere formalities, establishing her date of birth, place of residence, occupation and confirming that she was a foreign national. They'd assured him that the post mortem would be completed in two or three days and that, if there was no reason to suspect foul play, that would be the end of the matter. They would then release her body for burial. They were courteous and considerate throughout but Rupert had the feeling that they were hoping that there would be no complications so that they could draw a line under their investigation sooner rather than later.

"I think we've arrived Rupert." Isobel's voice cut across his thoughts making him aware that the boat had stopped at the back entrance to the hotel San Antonio. They climbed out and Isobel waited for Rupert to pay off the driver. It had started to rain and he saw her shiver in the cool night air. "I booked myself in earlier," he explained as they walked round the side of the hotel and into the reception area where Signor Gallini was waiting to welcome them.

"*Buona sera Signora* Campbell. Welcome back to the San Antonio." He greeted Isobel like a long lost friend before handing her a pen to complete her registration card.

"No need to come up with us, I know the way." Rupert said when Isobel had finished registering and handed over her passport. "We have a room each," he explained as they walked up the stairs to the first floor and, seeing the quizzical look on her face, he smiled for the first time that evening; "I thought I'd preserve your reputation."

"Yesterday you were ready to ruin it if I remember correctly." She smiled up at him, hoping to lighten his mood a little.

"That was a million years ago." His shoulders slumped in defeat as he unlocked the door of her room.

"I only wish I could take the pain away." She touched his arm lightly.

"Thank you and thank you again for coming." He kissed her roughly; a totally different Rupert from the one she knew. When at last he released her she tentatively offered him a plastic airline bag. "I thought this might be welcome," she said with the trace of a smile.

He opened the bag and took out a bottle of Famous Grouse. "Now that's what I call an inspired choice," he said. "Thank you a third time."

A few days after his telephone conversation with Laurence Ian left the Harley Street consulting room which, to his great relief, didn't advertise their special area of medicine on the highly polished brass plate outside their premises. He couldn't resist punching the air as he walked towards the Underground, keen to get back to his office now that he knew he had a clean bill of health. His step was considerably more sprightly than it had been an hour earlier when he'd walked in the other direction. The consultant had advised him to go back in three months time for a further test, 'as an added precaution,' and although Ian thought privately that it was just an excuse to earn another fee he knew for certain that this was one request with which he would comply.

"My God old son that was a close call," he said to himself as he walked through the chilly afternoon air. Whatever had inspired him to buy those condoms when he'd popped into the gents before lunch at the *Moulin d'Eau* was one of those miracles which, strictly speaking, he didn't really deserve. There was no way he could have forecast whether or not Tory Northcote was up for it and supposed he must have thought that he had nothing to lose by being prepared. As he walked down the steps to the Underground he remembered suddenly that he hadn't seen those condoms since he arrived home and wondered idly what could have happened to them. He must have left them in his hotel room or perhaps Tory picked them up in anticipation of using them at a later date? Whatever. It didn't matter any more, he was sound in body and mind. He felt happier and more carefree than for several weeks.

He'd had to keep Sue at bay for the best part of a week and, after the performance he'd put in the day his father-in-law left, her appetite was well and truly whetted and he'd had to use all his ingenuity to keep her at arms length. He never thought he'd live to see the day when he'd actually pray for one of the children to wake up and so put paid to any thought of love making. Fat lot of good praying did; the pair of them slept the sleep of the just every night. He'd tried staying up late, pleading that he'd brought some work home to finish. On another occasion he'd feigned sleep when Sue turned unexpectedly towards him in bed a couple of times and he'd simply told her he was too tired. Thank God for private medicine so that he no longer had to keep up the pretence.

Perhaps it was his over-active imagination but in the last few days he'd thought Sue had started to look at him rather oddly. On a couple of occasions he'd glanced up from reading the paper or away from the television and caught her staring intently at him as if trying to fathom exactly what was going through his mind. Thank goodness that episode was now over and he wouldn't have to behave out of character any longer.

He felt a celebration coming on. He'd ring Sue once he got back to the office and suggest they go out somewhere. He'd tell her that the pressure was off now that his father was shouldering some of the work and take her somewhere trendy and expensive. After that he'd do his best to convince her that his tiredness and general lack of interest in sex was now firmly in the past.

Rupert leaned back on the sofa as he waited for Isobel to bring the coffee, stretched his legs towards the fire and closed his eyes. She'd been the rock to which he'd clung unashamedly for the last few weeks. Mercifully she'd stayed calm throughout, accepting whatever decisions he made without question. When he felt like talking she listened when he wanted to be quiet she left him in peace. She'd kept open house for Gianna and Miles, Caterina and Gino when they'd flown over to England for Tory's funeral. She was a healing presence at his side when they buried Tory next to Liz and, although desperately worried about Ian, she'd hidden her concern to everyone but himself. When, after the funeral, they'd gone to Paris to sort out Tory's flat, she'd insisted on cleaning it up and laughingly produced a pair of old trousers and what she called a working shirt. The speed with which she'd restored order and cleanliness from the chaos that Tory had left behind filled him with amazement as well as gratitude.

He jumped to his feet and took the tray from Isobel as she came into the sitting room, set it down carefully on the coffee table and watched as she poured for both of them.

"I've made up my mind to sell the apartment in Venice," he said when finally she joined him on the sofa.

"But Rupert you love it so much and it's such a beautiful property won't you miss it?" she said and he realised that this was the first time in the last few weeks that she'd questioned any of his decisions.

"I'll get Giovanni to find a better one, perhaps with a little more room. After all with only one bedroom it's little more than a bachelor pad."

"Won't it be difficult to find somewhere in such a marvellous position, particularly with that spectacular view?"

"I admit it might take some time to find a replacement but I couldn't bear to live there again after what happened. I hope you'll help me to choose somewhere halfway decent," he added, slipping an arm around her shoulders,. "Who knows, if all goes according to plan it could become one of your homes."

"Do you realise how grand that sounds?" Isobel asked. "Just how many homes do you think we're going to need?" It was a great comfort to Rupert to hear her talk of their relationship in the future tense. "I should think two will be enough don't you?" he said. "One over here and another in Venice. If you want to keep this place I'll be happy to sell the flat, that is of course if you're happy for me to move in. That way you can keep it as your personal bolt hole in the unlikely event that things don't turn out as we expect. I can easily commute from here. I don't want to stop working at the moment. There are some interesting projects coming up, including some from Giovanni. That's if you agree of course." He realised as he spoke that he sounded as if his future was all mapped out but what about hers? He scanned her face anxiously.

"It's your life Rupert." Isobel said quietly.

"But I hope that it might be yours too. I don't honestly know what I'd have done without you over the past three weeks."

"I only wish it could have been more. I keep asking myself how I would feel in the same situation and I can't imagine the horror of it. It's impossible for me to get inside your head so I can only imagine how you must feel."

"I'll tell you," he said, surprising himself. "I feel guilty more than anything. Guilty that I was over here when I could have been in

Venice. Guilty that I allowed Tory to get into one hopeless situation after another. When I wake up in the small hours I feel a dreadful despair and wonder what Liz would think of me. On other occasions I feel angry and want to go and seek out that man Pierre and beat him to a pulp. Then logic steps in and I accept that if it hadn't been him it could have been someone else. That's why I can't give up working just yet. When Liz died it was a very effective therapy. Do you understand what I'm trying to say?"

He got up from the sofa and went to put another log on the fire. Digby opened a lazy eye but didn't bother to shift from his position of sublime comfort, as close to the hearth as possible without actually cooking himself. Seeing no cause for immediate concern he closed the eye again and went back to sleep.

As Rupert resumed his place on the sofa he accidentally knocked the edge of the low table and sent his coffee cup flying. Digby immediately jumped up and fled the room.

"Fortunately it was empty," Rupert said, bending to pick it up. "You see what a clumsy, flawed human being you'll be stuck with if you do decide to take me on?"

"The most important word there is human." Isobel kicked off her shoes and curled up in the corner of the sofa. "I'd find it impossible to live with anyone who thought they were perfect; I'd be terrified of putting a foot wrong and just think," she leaned towards him and took his hand,"it was an accident that brought us together in the first place."

He kissed her fingers one at a time. "What makes you so certain that it was an accident?" he asked, smiling at her.

Printed in the United Kingdom
by Lightning Source UK Ltd.
125419UK00002B/43-108/A